SHEEP CAN'T FLY

SHEEP CAN'T FLY

WRITTEN BY
THE STUDENTS OF GARFIELD HIGH SCHOOL

WITH A FOREWORD BY
FATHER GREG BOYLE, SJ

IN CONJUNCTION WITH

826LA

Garfield High School Student Editorial Board:
Nataly Chavez, Jesus Enriquez, Eddie Flores,
Alexandra Jimenez, Jocelyn Marchan,
Jocelyn Mariscal, Gabriela Maldonado,
Ana Cristina Perez, and Gabriela Tiscareño

Published May 2009 by 826LA

© 2009 All rights reserved by the authors and 826LA

ISBN 978-1-934750-12-4

First Edition

826LA

826LA West
685 Venice Boulevard
Venice, CA 90291
310.305.8418

826LA East
1714 W. Sunset Boulevard
Los Angeles, CA 90026
213.413.3388

http://826la.org

Cover illustration and design: Amy Martin
Interior layout and design: Jessica Burkhart

Printed in Canada by Westcan P.G.

Distributed by PGW

*This book was made possible by a generous grant
from The Goldhirsh Foundation.*

CONTENTS

OVER THE RIVER...

OVERBOARD!

OVER THE RAINBOW

OVER AND OUT.

FOREWORD

Father Greg Boyle, SJ

Martin was having a bad day. A gang member in his midtwenties, he found himself, once again, sidelined by the crush of addiction, criminality, and gang-banging. I was trying to cut his meat up for him, break life into bite-sized pieces so that he could navigate his way around those old, tired obstacles. "Look, Martin," I tell him, "you have to crawl before you can walk, and walk before you can run." Martin steadies his gaze. "Yeah, but I know I can fly. I just need to catch a gust of wind."

What you will be privileged to read in the pages that follow is that "gust of wind." Though inspired by Joseph Campbell's *The Hero with a Thousand Faces*, this book is its own source of inspiration, lifting us all up from tired conformity to a discovery, personal and palpable, of the hero already present in each of us. As God clarifies through Deuteronomy, this hero's truth is not "mysterious and remote" but rather "...already in your mouths and in your hearts. We have only to carry it out."[1] These young writers have written pieces that have mined their own personal journeys and have discovered courage and truth and beauty *already* present in their lives.

I write this after having just buried my 165th young person killed in our streets of East Los Angeles because of the sadness of gang-banging. For over two decades, I have been the executive director of Homeboy Industries, the largest gang-intervention program in the country. I know lots of gang members so, consequently, I am asked to

---

1. Deuteronomy 30:11, 14 (New American Bible)

preside at many final *despedidas*. The visionary authors of *Sheep Can't Fly* offer a counterimage to the lethal absence of hope that undergirds the death and violence still so pervasive in our community. They have chosen to become what child psychologist Alice Miller calls "enlightened witnesses"—young people who, through their focused and attentive love, keen courage, and fidelity to personal truth, seek to return us all to ourselves. They have discovered in their own writing that the hero's journey has little to do with holding up a bar and then striving to measure up to it. You don't measure up—you show up. And so these gifted writers have come to know the truth of who they are: that they are exactly what God had in mind when God made them. They have become this truth. They have inhabited this truth. They call us all to return to ourselves and to embrace the same truth. Once you read the pages that follow, you wander into a power that is larger than any obstacle and *mas fuerte que la muerte*.

The poet Galway Kinnell writes that "sometimes it is necessary / to reteach a thing its loveliness."[2] Every hero's journey contains something of this reteaching. A little homey named Moreno just returned to the community after seven months of detention. He is a *chaparrito*, fifteen years old, who has been active in his gang from the age of thirteen. I am heartened to be among the first he visits upon his release. We sit in my office, and at one point, he retrieves an envelope from his pants pocket. He slaps it down in front of me and announces with great pride: "My grades...from probation camp."

I try to meet his delight. *"De veras,"* I say, pulling the transcript out of its holder.

"Straight A's," he says, nearly bouncing in his chair.

"Wow," I say, matching his glee, "Straight A's?"

"Serio pedo," he says, "Straight A's."

I unfurl the transcript. And there it is. Right in front of me. 2 C's. 2 B's. 1 A. Not the straightest A's I've ever seen. And I think to myself, "Close enough." So I decide not to tell him he's an unreliable reporter here.

---

2. Galway Kinnell, "Saint Francis and the Sow." In *A New Selected Poems* (New York: Mariner Books, 2001), 94.

"*Mijito*, on everything I love," I say, putting the transcript back in its envelope, "if you were my son, I'd be the proudest man alive."

Moreno rushes his fingers to his eye sockets, hoping to stem the seemingly inevitable tide of tears.

I look at this kid, and I think he has now been returned to a situation that is largely unchanged. His father is in prison for the rest of his life. His mother, a heroin addict, is missing in action. His grandmother, whose charge it now is to raise this kid, is not up to the challenge. And I know that thirty days before this moment, I had buried Moreno's very best friend, killed in our streets for no reason at all.

So I lead with my gut.

"I bet you're afraid to be out, aren't you?"

This pushes the play button on Moreno's tear ducts. He wails and sobs and rests his head on his folded arms on my desk. I let him cry. Finally, I reach over and touch him on the arm. "You're gonna be okay."

Moreno sits up, almost with defiance; he wipes his tears and declares deliberately, "I...just...want...to have a life."

"Well, who told ya you wouldn't have one?" I ask him. "Remember all the letters you wrote me from camp—telling me of all the gifts and talents you discovered in yourself. I know you think you're in a deep, dark hole. But you're really in a tunnel, and it's in the nature of tunnels that if you just keep walking, the light will appear. I can see it. I'm taller than you are."

We stare at each other for a moment, a sense of kinship sinking in for the both of us.

"You're gonna be fine. After all," I tell him, handing back his grades, "straight A's."

The hero's journey began as all of us discovered we've only always been the very shape of God's heart. Loveliness.

The students who have contributed to this effort have been faithful to their own truth and call us to our own courageous fidelity. I especially want to commend the fine work of the editorial board: Nataly Chavez, Jesus Enriquez, Eddie Flores, Alex Jimenez, Jocelyn Marchan, Jocelyn Mariscal, Gaby Maldonado, Ana Perez, and Gabby Tiscareño. All the students would acknowledge the gracious and beneficial presence of their "enlightened witnesses": Arlette Crosland, their teacher; Kevin Stack, their GEAR UP adviser, and everyone at 826LA: all the tutors, executive director Joel Arquillos, and director of education Julius Diaz Panoriñgan.

I have felt deeply honored to be connected, so momentarily, to the young people whose fearlessness fills the pages upon which you are about to embark. Sheep flying. Who would have thought? All we needed was that gust of wind.

INTRODUCTION
Garfield High School Student Editorial Board

Sheep can't fly, can't they? You hear the word sheep, and your first instinct tells you that the sheep is a follower, a timid and unintelligent creature. Sheep tend to follow each other, and they naturally become stressed when they are separated from their flock. When people act like sheep, they lose themselves among the crowd. They lose the drive and enthusiasm to do what they want. They lose their ability to decide what is right and what is wrong, and—most importantly—they lose their will to detach themselves from the flock.

Living in East Los Angeles, the heart of Latino pride and culture, for the majority of our lives has defined our perception of home. Many of us have come to realize that there is a greater and somewhat frightening world outside of East LA. We understand that in order to grow and learn, we must venture out of our comfort zone like sheep that leave their flock. That journey has and will continue to demand courage, self-reliance, and individuality, all of which are necessary to become the heroes of our own lives.

We have realized our own personal journeys with the help of Joseph Campbell's *The Hero with a Thousand Faces*, which argues that all heroes follow one journey: the monomyth. The monomyth, or hero's journey, is a fundamental pattern that almost all stories follow. The monomyth can vary from story to story: some may have all the steps of the hero's journey (Campbell counts seventeen), while others may just focus on a particular stage. Three phases—the departure, the initiation, and the return—form the core units that comprise the seventeen smaller stages of the hero's journey. All heroes must accept a call to adventure and depart for a foreign world; there they must confront challenges, which serve as a rite of initiation; and they must return to their original, ordinary world to share the knowledge they have learned. As Joseph Campbell sums it up:

> A hero ventures forth from the world of common day into a region of supernatural wonder: fabulous forces are there encountered and a decisive victory is won: the hero comes back from this mysterious adventure with the power to bestow boons on his fellow man.[1]

Although the steps are alike in some stories, the form that the steps take differs in every individual story. All heroes walk the same path, and each hero must persevere in order to develop and obtain self-knowledge. Courage, self-reliance, and individuality are the qualities that enable our heroes to accept the call to adventure, to face their trials, and to ultimately return to their lives enlightened. That is the goal we all seek as we face a whirlwind of changes in our lives.

A year ago, when we heard about our chance to write for this book, it was something out of this world. We never would have imagined being called to embark upon this journey. Some of our fellow students deemed themselves incapable of this demanding opportunity; they feared they could never meet the challenge. Not only did we accept our call, but we showed other students what is possible. We are strong, determined individuals, and we saw a great chance to learn more about ourselves and our potential. We wanted to succeed, to be able to look back on this one day and say, "I wrote this book."

Did we doubt ourselves during the writing process? Yes. Creating characters with human-like desires and fears, who are motivated to search for the truth they are entitled to, was an absolute challenge. But with the help of the 826LA tutors, family, and teachers, we found stories hidden in our minds and hearts, sometimes even taken from our own lives. Our characters project who we are, and our

1. Joseph Campbell, *The Hero with a Thousand Faces* (Novato, CA: New World Library, 2008), 23.

short stories ultimately allowed us to see our lives in a more enlightened way. They needed to be told in order to prove that everyone has a journey.

All individuals encounter journeys they are hesitant to embark upon. We all attain a fear of the unknown and an attachment to the consistency of our lives. Society is the flock, and we are the sheep following others. Our fear is just like that of the sheep that is too fearful to live away from the crowd. This fear is a hook dragging us back to society, back to the crowd, and ultimately back to the fenced pastures of our own mental uncertainty. This is the obstacle that keeps people from flying.

The variety of people we have in our class has made one thing certain: age, gender, race, religion, and sexuality don't matter. What matters is our own will and drive to make what people say is impossible, possible. It's all about understanding who you are and how capable you are of fighting for what you want. It is the black sheep that receives the impulse to leave the flock and live its own life. To fly is to liberate oneself from the chains of the past and present, and to look beyond, into the future. When you have realized who you are, and when you surmount the obstacles on your own journey away from the flock, you begin to fly. You must be the creator and the controller of your own universe and of yourself. But when you live your life believing in others rather than yourself, you will never fly. Just like the black sheep, we have learned not to approach new opportunities in trepidation, but to find the courage within ourselves to wander into these new worlds. We will return with our souls enlightened, our fears vanquished, and the spirit and will to fly.

OVER OUR HEADS–

Rafael Cruz
SHEEP CAN'T FLY

Heading in the right direction
Following my admiration

Something evil draws me away
And my knowledge starts to decay

I dig myself in really deep
I start to become a sheep

I get to the edge of the cliff
And stay there, really stiff

A quick glance at the big blue sky
Makes me realize that sheep can't fly.

Gabriela Maldonado
WHAT DOES IT TAKE?

What is a hero? What does it take to be one? I don't really think it takes much. Heroes are everyday people, from the person who helps a stray dog to the one who saves a human life. There are so many people out there considered heroes, and they are greatly revered and admired by those around them. In our stories, however, heroes come in many shapes and sizes. Heroes are your family members who stand by you, your parents who work to support you, and even your friends who are there when you need them. I would describe a hero as someone who speaks greatly and takes action, and my personal hero is my mom. My whole life, I grew up without a father, so my mother kept on working and persevered to support me and my siblings. That is a hero.

Why do we need heroes in our culture? Well, that is obvious to a person who lives in East Los Angeles. This town is ugly and dangerous at times. But even when we have the luxury of having our Mexican or Latino/Hispanic families and people we can ethnically relate to nearby, danger lurks so close, and gang-related deaths are very near. And that's why we need heroes, people who are willing to help the ones who can't help themselves, hardworking people who will do the right thing, people who will give to the community and make it better.

My experience contributing written work to this book has taught me that I can do things if I make the effort. I'm not primarily a writer, but this story and a series of others have encouraged me to try. I really like literature, and this book has given me the chance to show my skills as a writer and as an aspiring artist. I'm very sure that contributing to this book has helped other students realize their real talents and the sources of their inspiration—poetry, life experiences, and literature. And, of course, art. I know it took a lot for the other students and me to edit and rewrite. I know it was long, frustrating work to do all of that, but in the end, it all paid off and paved the way for us to keep on going.

One of the most important things we've accomplished while putting this book together is learning about ourselves—it's very surprising to see how the unique mind of each student truly shows on paper. Everyone learned something new: some learned to better their writing skills, and others found personal epiphanies. As for me, I have learned to create original writing from my ideas, much as I do with drawing and painting. I've learned to appreciate writing in a more concise and thorough manner: it's very similar to drawing. In my case, drawing takes immense patience. Every little detail is necessary to make the whole piece a lot more interesting. Once I found out that descriptions in a story make the reader truly see what's going on, I was much more encouraged to continue writing my story. I saw how much easier it became when every small detail made a big difference.

We're more the same than we are different. Just because I wear heavy boots and black clothes every day doesn't make me different from the girl sitting next to me. I can relate to my fellow students about similar shared hardships. We have all written different stories about heroes, but what I've noticed is that we are all pretty much the same. It's something I can't completely describe with words; it just makes us all feel like a whole. We all knew this was a difficult task to endure, and we all bore it. I know that deep down, we are all very grateful for this opportunity, and everyone persevered with great effort.

Gabriela Tiscareño
EARNESTLY GRUMPY

The atmosphere on the planet was heavy with the hustle and bustle generated by the concerns of its citizens, who ran to and fro between things they sought to delve deeper into—their latest discoveries, newest theories, and sudden epiphanies. Space cars hummed above like worker bees trying to find the biggest hive with the most honey. On the streets walked the younger generation, resentful for being restricted from the air for their competitive and reckless behavior.

Amid the crowd of walking youth ran an especially peculiar little alien who believed he had come upon a theory twenty billion times more fantastic than the leading scientist of their time. The alien dodged power-walking teens and jumped over benches, growing ever eager to reach the laboratory. He hoped it would be open so he could test his latest experiment. With growing anticipation, he came upon the sight of Martianstein, a slightly smaller alien, entering the building like a puppy running to get fed. Earnest paid the bike rental man, picked up an asteroid bike, and took off at impressive speed. Jumping off at the lab entrance, Earnest ran in after Martianstein and managed to catch a glimpse of the back of Martianstein's head just as the elevator doors closed after him.

Eagerly, Earnest waited for the next one. As he entered a crowded elevator, Earnest saw the fresh new faces he assumed were the new apprentices to the prestigious League of Scientists. He saw the anxiety on the young faces, and he entertained the idea of tormenting them for just a little while.

"Are you the new elite team? Wow! Congratulations! Good luck discovering new galaxies!"

They looked at each other in surprise, looking for a sign of confirmation from their fellow apprentices, who were also evidently unaware of this requisite.

Earnest turned to look at a martian whose eyes were opened wide in terror, scared by Earnest's lie. The martian farthest from Earnest just looked straight ahead, although Earnest noticed his fingers shaking slightly and a bead of sweat trickling down his forehead. Amused, Earnest said, "Oh, don't worry too much now! Rumor has it it's not so hard!" As the elevator came to a stop, Earnest said good-bye, stepped out, and, with a quick glance over his shoulder, waved goodbye to the panic-stricken faces. He walked back around in the direction he was originally headed with a wide smirk.

Oh, those naive scientists, they'll believe anything! Shows how little they know! Surely I would never have been fooled, thought Earnest with a chuckle.

Turning right, he saw little Martianstein running down a corridor. Earnest sped up, knocking over the dazed Martianstein. "Hey Marty! Where are ya headin' in such a hurry?"

Martianstein got up, rubbing his head and looking very annoyed. He picked up his glasses and looked up at Earnest. "Greetings, Earnest. To what do I owe this... *pleasant* surprise?"

"Well, I noticed you were in a hurry, so I just wanted to know what the big deal is."

Martianstein, while cleaning his glasses, raised his head slightly and looked at Earnest dubiously. "Well, what a fine observation. I'm sure that's not the only reason why you saw the need for such a *formal* greeting. Anyway, I don't have much time to explain."

"Are we feeling too important this morning? Ha!" laughed Earnest. "You've gotta tell me, Marty. Don't think I'll let you leave until you do."

Martianstein looked down at his watch, clearly not sharing Earnest's sense of humor. "If you must know, I received a rather important call from the...Planet Agency...and they are seeking my help in determining whether a certain...

uh...*portal*...is functional. OKAY! I'll be on my way now!"

"Aw, come on Marty! Don't be short with me; tell me... what portal? Where is it? What for?"

Martianstein looked around as if he had quite little interest in their conversation. "Earth."

"HA! Are you serious? I would've never expected such a brainiac like you to ever believe that myth! Earth does not exist! I'da thought you knew better!" said Earnest, shaking his head in disbelief.

Martianstein looked down at Earnest's seven-year-old medal and realized the possible reason for Earnest's enthusiastic interest in his affairs. *Oh, that Participation Medal,* Martianstein thought to himself. *Perhaps one day he'll figure it out.* Martianstein rolled his eyes and heaved a deep sigh. Looking up at Earnest, he shook his head in defeat.

"Yes, well, silly me. If you don't have any further inquiries, I'll be on my way now. Have a nice day, Earnest."

Earnest was completely bewildered by Martianstein's terse reply. "That Marty is a funny fellow. He must be hiding something from me...doesn't he know I am not easily fooled? Like I'd actually believe that Earth nonsense! But why would he lie to me?"

Suddenly something occurred to him, and he gasped. "What if it *is* true? What if Marty wasn't lying? Earth! Why, that would be fascinating to see, and if I were the first to arrive, I could return with my discoveries and become world-renowned!" Earnest looked at the medal around his neck and was filled with pride. This medal was his most prized possession. He had won it at the Young Scientist Convention when he was just eight years old. He could still remember the day he received it. He was so proud of his accomplishment, yet memories of his mother's reaction the morning he set off to the convention disappointed him. He remembered it as if it were yesterday.

Earnest, in his excitement, had jumped off the last three steps of the staircase in a hurry, scuttling past his mother, who stood in the doorway. The green walls were a blur as he headed out the door toward the gate.

"Wait a minute! And just where do you think you're going?"

Earnest came to a sudden stop, his wide smile reversing into a frown. He slowly turned around to face his mother, disappointed by the delay. He tried to sound respectful.

"Yes, Mother?"

"You heard me. Where are you going?"

There was that look again, the one she always gave him. His mother wore it when he left the house, suspicious of mischief from her only son. It was the look she gave him after he had shattered the glass in the fish exhibit, when he had lost his great grandfather's relic, and when he had damaged a fellow classmate's "genius" invention two years prior. To Earnest, she seemed almost incapable of any other facial expression. Before, when her face displayed such a warning, Earnest would leave home, fearful of having upset her. But now, since this was the only face he ever saw on his mother, it implanted only a sense of aggravation...or, on rare occasions, amusement.

Earnest looked up at his mother modestly, trying to contain his frustration. Today was not a day to be amused by her assumptions. It was a special day.

"To the Science Fair!" he said quite innocently, and he threw his arms up into the air with a hint of frustration. He had told his mom about the Science Fair at least ten times the week before, and now there she was, questioning him in a scolding tone.

His mother released her arms, which were folded across her chest, and softened her angry expression.

"Oh...that's right. Well...good luck then..."

She attempted an encouraging smile and remained standing, her eyes conveying a sudden wish for him to not respond and be on his way. Earnest was taken back by her response. He had half expected her to apologize for her attitude and then ask about how his invention functioned. Looking at her suspiciously, he slowly turned around toward his initial direction.

As he walked away, he pondered his mother's reaction. *Just like that? No "Oh, great! Good luck! I know you'll do well!"? No sincere words of encouragement? I worked so hard on my project. Doesn't she think it has the potential to win first place? I have to win! I bet no one comes close to my invention! I mean, I would expect it from Director Folley, but my mom? Director Folley has always been so skeptical of my inventions. This is the year to prove him wrong! Apparently, now I have to prove myself to two people. I have to leave with a medal. I just have to.*

And he did. He had to admit, he was confused when the judges failed to distribute first-, second-, and third-place medals, but he felt gratified receiving a medal. Since winning the medal at the Science Fair, Earnest was most anxious for another opportunity to show the planet his potential to lead the way into a more advanced future. Apparently, he still yearned to be recognized for the potential no one but him seemed to acknowledge.

Earnest decided to follow Marty. From a distance he saw Martianstein turn a corner into another corridor. He ascended four flights of stairs, made a left turn into a hallway, and entered an elevator on the fifth floor. Turning right into a tunnel, he disappeared into the darkness.

Walking through the tunnel with trepidation, Earnest suddenly doubted whether following Martianstein was a good idea. He proceeded carefully, anxious to discover Martianstein's secret.

At the end of the tunnel was a large, round, white door, and through that door was a hallway with several doors lining both sides. The hallway seemed to extend hundreds of feet. He knew the doors would be locked, unlike the entrance. Reaching into his pocket, he took out his cousin's genius invention, the one Earnest called "The Unlocker." He was so grateful that his cousin left it unattended at their last family demonstration. Earnest felt it was not unlawful to steal his cousin's invention when his cousin had stolen his idea, after all.

Looking at each door carefully, Earnest found a door numbered "51." He heard small footsteps approaching and concluded it was Martianstein. Earnest skidded back out the white door and stood behind it. Seconds later, Martianstein ran out in a hurry, clueless as to Earnest's presence.

Assuming it was safe, Earnest sped back into the hallway, placing the Unlocker against the door. Allowing it some time to identify the code, he waited for the door to open.

Stepping inside the laboratory, he immediately saw where Martianstein had previously been. It was a large cylindrical object that was capable of fitting four average-sized martians inside it. The door was slightly ajar, and papers were spread across the table sitting parallel to the oddly shaped object. Observing that the code had already been inserted, Earnest concluded that Martianstein had left in such a hurry that he did not bother to erase the code or close the door. With mounting curiosity, Earnest stepped inside the cylinder, closed the door, and pressed the biggest button.

Feeling a sudden lurch in his stomach, Earnest felt his feet touch new ground and felt the strange air of an unfamiliar place smoothly whip his face. Fearfully, Earnest mustered up the courage to open his eyes. Blinking repeatedly, with his head held upward, he saw a murky gray sky. Against it were ugly, distastefully-designed pillars overlooking the region like a monster menacingly protecting his territory, pronouncing his control over all that roamed the area. He smelled something foul, very much unlike anything he had ever smelled. He surveyed his surroundings and realized that he was in some sort of dingy, gray alley. There were odd-shaped drawings that curved in and around each other, creating a labyrinth of symbols that, presumably, were in place to advise inhabitants of the structure's purpose. Earnest could not determine any other reason for its existence. In his opinion, it could hardly be considered art.

He heard a loud, obnoxious noise that prompted a woman somewhere to yell, "It's an alien!"

Looking down, Earnest saw a furry creature wagging its tentacle pathetically. It appeared eager to serve him. Earnest looked around for the old female creature and saw her running down the alley, her heavy white bags strewn on the floor in disarray.

Attempting to make the smell more tolerable, Earnest raised his finger toward the sky, commanding his powers to filter the air. Oddly, his powers were ineffective. At that moment, Earnest realized that he should not be there.

That's odd! My powers don't seem to work... Maybe

they'll work where the atmosphere is cleaner. I must leave this human dwelling. This has to be a mistake! There seems to be no life here. No, I cannot make an assumption from what I've just seen. I need to go to the nearest place with a concentrated population. I do hope that's possible. I almost don't know what to expect. Creatures on Earth are so peculiar.

Earnest beckoned to the little creature, apparently named Alien. "Come on, Alien. Let's go."

Turning around the corner, big buildings came into view. Earnest was not impressed. *Ha! I'm sure they're proud of these. Is this all they have to show? For their sake, I hope not.*

Attempting a second time to use his powers, he punched in the coordinates for his desired destination on the command system wrapped around his wrist and waited for the latitude and longitude to appear. When they did, Earnest wrapped his hands around the underside of the little creature and pressed the bright red letters reading "enter" on his wrist.

Earnest and Alien landed in what seemed to be another deserted location. Earnest was about to yell in frustration. It seemed nothing was going according to plan.

"Well, I didn't plan this trip, but it is upsetting that my brilliant ideas keep failing. This sight is so disappointing, wouldn't you say so Alien? ...Alien?"

Looking around for Alien, he saw the furry creature crouched behind a gray cylinder, shaking with fright and with what Earnest finally decided was a tail tucked between its legs.

"Oh, how could I forget? You're human...or...some sort of sub-human or something! You wouldn't know anything about the wonders of transporting. Aw come on, shake it off! We need to get going."

Alien stood trembling and remained staring at Earnest.

"I said LET'S GO!"

The creature bolted from its position and took off at amazing speed.

Earnest rolled his eyes. "Eh, go ahead. You're useless anyways."

Turning a corner, Earnest saw humans of all sizes walking in large groups. The majority of their skin was covered, and to make it worse, they wore annoyingly brightly-colored clothing and hats. Some of the humans were holding miniature humans in their arms or holding onto their hands. Some large-sized humans were embracing each other. The sight of all of this was sickening.

One couple in particular passed right in front of him. The male spoke to him directly: "Hey kiddo, nice costume."

He smiled down at Earnest. Earnest was outraged.

Why, they're acting as if I were an inhabitant of their planet. How dare he associate me with an inferior race! How dare he even speak to me! What is a kid doe? And why is he patronizing me? Humans are despicable!

"Cute costume. I take it you're lost too?"

Earnest turned around, startled. "Huh? Are you speaking to me?"

"No silly, I was talking to the wall behind you. Of course you!"

The creature speaking to him was small and female. She had light brown hair, piercing green eyes, and small pink lips. She had a big, bright, round, colorful object in her hands. Earnest stepped a few feet away from her, but when he realized she would not cause him any harm, he got closer and looked into her eyes. "Who are you? And what is it that you possibly think I can do for you?"

The little girl grinned. "You talk funny. How old are you?"

"That is no business of yours. Now walk away, human; do not disturb me."

"Aw, I know you're scared. Disneyland is a safe place though. No one here will hurt you. Just come with me to the lost-and-found. I know where it is. This happened last time, and the time before."

"What did you say this place was called?"

"Disneyland?"

"Disneyland...is this the home of Disney people?"

"No, I wouldn't call it that. The Disney characters aren't real. Didn't your mommy tell you?"

"Who are these people you keep referring to?"

"I don't know what game you're playing, but I don't feel like playing. So just come with me, and you'll be all right."

Earnest was bewildered. *Why does this creature insist on remaining by my side? Why does she think I need her help? What does she want from me, and why does she not fear me? She looks so powerless. If only my powers worked I could send her away. Far away.*

"Have you seen *Monsters, Inc.*?"

"What? What are you babbling about now, and why are you still here?"

"*Monsters, Inc.* Have you seen it?"

"I have not seen a monster's ink! I do see several monsters, though," Earnest said in hushed tones.

"What did you say?"

"I said monsters stink. Listen! Uh...creature?"

"Lily."

"What?"

"My name is Lily."

Earnest stared at the creature, bewildered as to why she thought he would care for how she was regarded on this planet. He had no interest in familiarizing himself with any individual. His main goal was quite simple: figure out the nature of these odd beings, return home with his findings, and begin a campaign for the destruction of an incompetent society and the remodeling of a dual society.

"Okay, creature. How about you wander off now?"

"Oh look!" Lily interrupted. "It's Princess Belle!"

"Yes, run off to your...Princess?" Looking at this Princess Belle creature, Earnest stood transfixed. This creature was truly beautiful. She was wearing possibly the oddest clothing and the brightest shade of yellow he had ever seen. Despite her peculiarity, her beauty still emanated.

"Come on!" Lily said, pulling his arm and stopping in front of Princess Belle. "Umm...Belle? Can I have your autograph?"

"Well hello! My, what a cute dress you have on! Who is your friend?"

"He won't tell me his name. Just call him Grumpy."

"Like the Seven Dwarves?"

"Oh no, he's worse."

"Well Grumpy, I love your costume. I think my friends at Toy Story would love it!"

"Uh...toy...uh...wait, what?"

"Oh, children! Where are your parents?"

"Mommy is waiting in front of the restroom. She knows I'm here."

"Why won't she come?"

"She's waiting for my little brother to come out of the restroom, and Grumpy here hasn't seen much of Disneyland."

The two females continued conversing, and after the smaller one used her evil ways of insisting, the creature Belle stopped waiting for "Mommy" to appear and allowed them to go on their way.

After getting Belle's autograph, Lily tugged Earnest, shaking him into consciousness.

"What's up with you, Grumpy?"

Earnest could not explain what he was feeling. He had never been so captivated by anything other than inventions at science fairs. All he knew was that he wouldn't mind having Princess Belle live on his planet. Although she served no purpose, she was certainly something he'd like to take back home.

As Earnest continued walking with Lily, he continued thinking. He was wondering what had compelled him so about the beautiful creature. He was afraid of succumbing to humanlike temptations. More determined than ever to abandon this annoying child who took it upon herself to torture him, Earnest looked around and around as if in a daze, staring at all the brightly-colored hats and smiling faces. Looking at the high, white mountain and the large contraptions moving the earthlings who were squealing in delight, Earnest was disgusted by the sight of them.

These beings are a disgrace to the universal race! Could there possibly be a better example of their low intelligence? Is this any way to live? Don't they fear for their future? These humans don't seem to be taking the necessary precautions to ensure a stable future for the next generation. Their lives are so unfulfilling. Yes, clearly. Clearly they are unintelligent. Now, the question is, how have they managed to be in existence for so long?

He began contemplating how he could destroy this planet and return home. *It would give me so much pleasure*, thought Earnest, *to wipe those ignorant smiles off their faces and to muffle that loud, irritable laughter. There is no space for this species in this universe. I can already imagine all the glory I'll receive when my beloved planet discovers that I have found an inhabitable region where more technology can thrive. After all...Earth is just an insignificant speck in this entire universe, and these humans are worth far less.*

Awakening from his blissful daydream into this horrid reality, his thoughts filled with mischief. Looking at Lily, Earnest realized he needed to find a way to distract her if he was going to put his ideas into action.

Just then he found his answer. Suddenly he heard a loud groan from dozens of people standing near each other in a long line. They were pointing up at the object stuck on a mountainous edge. He smiled wide and thought, *I can fool this deficient child.*

Suddenly Earnest pulled on her arm, like she had done to him earlier.

"Oh, looook Earthling!"

"Huh? What? Look at what?"

"Humans. Up there! What's happening?"

"Oh no! They're stuck!"

"Stuck? As in permanently? Yes...too bad...what a tragedy...do you think I can get up there?"

"You? But you're little! Maybe someone else can help them. I don't think *you* can."

"He—help?" *Now why would I want to do that,* Earnest thought. "Well...maybe I can. Just sit here."

Lily was surprised to see Earnest act so deliberately determined. She couldn't help but trust his word. Her curiosity prompted her to do as he had suggested, so she sat on a bench and continued to lick her lollipop.

Earnest strode over to the line that was hundreds of feet below the stuck humans. He held his head high, wearing a wide grin. His brisk step amazed the people standing in line. They had never seen a child behave in such a manner, especially when lost in a place like Disneyland. Some adults stared down at Earnest in amusement; others, in concern. Children broke into bits of giggles. As Earnest approached the fence, he attempted to hop over it with a boost from his powers. He jumped up but came straight back down, and the crowd began to laugh.

"Need a hand there, son?" said a man as he turned to his wife with a chuckle. She frowned, her husband's smile faded, and she said, "Are your parents stuck up there?"

Earnest reflected on her question. *Ah, you pathetic creatures! Don't you realize I am going to release the greatest terror your planet has ever seen?*

He balled his fists and pushed the swinging gate open. He raised his hands and waved them swiftly, attempting to demonstrate his powers by lifting the contraption and sending it flying.

Children broke out laughing at his public display.

"Mommy, he thinks his costume gives him powers!"

The adults thought it was adorable.

"Oh honey, look, he wants to summon down his parents!"

Humiliated, Earnest was perplexed as to why he was powerless on this planet. Panicked, he tried again, but again he failed. The children broke out into laughter once more, and the adults were embarrassed for the little child.

As Earnest stood in concentration, he felt a hand on his shoulder. Turning around, Earnest lifted his head and gazed into the face of an older man. The older man wore a kind smile. He was the only person not laughing, and his smile did not seem to contain ridicule. It seemed to suggest that he sympathized with Earnest. He extended his hand to Earnest, who, grateful for an escape, held onto the man's hand and followed him into a cave. He was disappointed in himself for having accepted refuge from a human and was eager to redeem his dignity.

Once inside the cave, Earnest finally lifted his head and saw the tracks to his right. He noticed they were climbing up steps into an unknown area, which he assumed led to the tracks where the humans were stuck. The man looked behind him to see if Earnest was still following him.

"Come on son, we'll get your mommy and daddy down from there. Just follow me. Watch your step there."

Leading him into a room with several control systems, he sat Earnest down in a chair.

"Just sit tight. Lisa will watch after you. You can see on this surveillance video that everyone is still okay and that we will get them down real soon. You'll see."

The man closed the door behind him. The Lisa woman was sitting in her own chair with an object, similar to a book with several pictures, held up to her face. She quickly glanced at Earnest and went back to the article she was reading. From behind the magazine she said, "Cute costume, kid, you're the first I've seen with it." Earnest stayed silent and walked closer to the object that projected an image of the occurrences outside. He wanted to reach the humans, but he wasn't sure how he would do it. He turned his attention to his miniature command system, calculated the altitude levels where the humans were located, and punched in new coordinates. Pressing "enter," he braced himself for the transporting.

Once again, he felt his feet touch solid ground. He was at the edge of the cave, many feet higher than he was before. He climbed the few more steps that led out of the cave and walked onto the tracks where the stuck object was situated. He heard a loud gasp from a woman inside. The male sitting beside her quickly spoke. "Hey buddy, what're you doing up here on the tracks? It's dangerous!"

The woman sitting next to him said, "Oh, someone should get him down from here! Or at least into the roller coaster car!"

"Relax." The man looked around, as if carefully choosing his words. "Hey bud, that's a nice medal you got there. What's it for?"

The man's question caught Earnest off guard.

"Huh? Oh...I won it at a science fair."

"What? No way! That's awesome! What did you invent?"

"Spotless. It cleans up after messes."

"Wow, that's great! I never won anything in all the science fairs I've been in."

"You've been in science fairs?"

"Yup. Plenty. I always wanted to be a scientist. I always thought it would be amazing to invent something that others could really use and admire me for, but boy, pleasing people is hard. Especially in that field. You always need to be better than the next guy. Man, it's tough."

"So what did you do instead?"

"Art. I just found the beauty in simple things. I wanted to share that with others. It doesn't make their lives easier or anything, but people need distractions. That's why I came to Disneyland today."

"You mean this isn't what you do every day?"

"No! Wow, I wish! The last time I came was like six years ago."

"Why would you waste a day of your life?"

"Waste? I don't consider this a waste of time."

"So you take breaks from improving your life?"

"No, of course not. It's not like that. Listen. I kind of thought the same way you do, but then I realized if I live every day in preparation for the next, my work is never-ending. Until my death, of course. I don't want to prepare for my death. I want to enjoy the life I've been given. There are a lot of things worth living for in the world, not just advancement. If I spend all my time focused on how I will fix the next day, I won't enjoy the present day. If you really think about it, you'll never enjoy *any* day. You need to take breaks and start living your life."

"So...you never bothered to work on that project from your science fair."

"Nah. It took me a while to realize I'm not meant for that kind of stuff, and I'm glad I eventually learned that and, well, accepted it too. Otherwise, I would've truly wasted my time. You know what else is a waste of time?"

"What?"

"Being stuck up here."

Earnest grinned. Earnest was not offended by this man. He surprised Earnest by proving to him that he did indeed use the brain nature had given him, and put it to some use as well. Earnest looked down at all the people on the ground staring up at him in horror.

So these people attempt to enjoy every day of their lives? They're all so different. It doesn't bother them? They have time to choose to spend a whole day to dedicate to laughter and amusement? Earnest thought about the way earthlings interacted with each other. They were neither competitive nor judgmental. They accepted him the minute they saw him. Granted, they didn't know he was a martian from another planet, but despite how foreign he was to their lifestyle, they accepted him. All they had to offer him were smiles. The kind old man, the worried woman, the furry creature, and even Lily.

Earnest looked down at his wrist and saw a little light signaling the temporary return of his powers. He wiggled his fingers and felt strength in them. He placed his hands against the cart and mustered up all his power to push the cart down the tracks.

The cart started with a jolt, and the passengers sat up in surprise and relief to see that the ride was fixed. They turned back to look at Earnest, still worried about his well-being.

He smiled and waved at them, making his descent down the stairs and back into the cave.

When he finally reached the ground, Earnest dodged the humans who rushed to check whether he had been hurt. He scuttled past the crowd to a remote area where he hoped not to be seen. He still needed to collect his thoughts and determine what he was going to do next.

"Grumpy!"

Earnest turned around, looking for that voice he had heard all day. It was Lily.

"That was amazing!"

"What was?"

"How you tried to help them! I didn't believe you at first, but wow!"

Earnest smiled at Lily. She kept grinning, apparently astonished that he was capable of showing delight after having been bitter for so long. Then Earnest heard another familiar voice.

"EARNEST! Wh—what are you doing here?"

"Martianstein?"

"You can NOT be here!"

"Why not?"

"The portal! It's defective! Our powers don't work here. It's dangerous to come ill-equipped!"

"Who's he? Is he your little brother?" asked Lily. Earnest and Marty ignored her.

"No, I'm sorry Marty, I can't leave. There are a couple of things I need to do."

"No, you must come back. The committee has found out,

and they ordered me to bring you back immediately! Let's go! You have no idea what's in store for you if you stay any longer. Or us, I should say!

"Uh—Marty, not to change the subject, but uh—how'd you get here?"

"No time for that now. I'll explain later. You're in major trouble right now, and we need to plead your case at home."

"You don't need to do that for me, Marty, honestly."

"Huh? Why not?"

"Listen, I take full responsibility for my actions. I'm sorry for breaking into your experiment site. I'll plead my own case, but I'm not too worried about what they say, or of what punishment they'll find suitable."

"You do realize you'll probably be banned from all laboratories and from scientific research, right?"

Earnest smiled. "Yeah, I figured. But that doesn't worry me too much. What's more important is that they learn about Earth. Before they decide to do something drastic, that is."

Martianstein, staring at Earnest in disbelief, half expected him to take off a mask and reveal someone else. He could not believe that Earnest was sincerely indifferent to being banned from science. Science was the reason that Earnest considered Martianstein his rival for so long. He eyed Lily, who was listening intently to their conversation.

Earnest also looked at Lily and grinned. "Oh, Marty. We have a lot to talk about. And do me a favor: don't worry too much about it."

Martianstein walked him to the space car and opened up the doors. They both got inside, put on their glasses, and prepared for flight.

"Bye, Grumpy!" yelled Lily, waving enthusiastically.

"Earnest," said Earnest.

"What?" asked Lily.

"My name is Earnest."

Ana Cristina Perez
SAVING MYSELF

We will always come back to our roots, peeking back at the people we once were to discover how we have changed, and how our changes have made us who we are.

I love East Los, the place where I was raised, the place where I ran down Cesar Chavez Avenue blabbing "ta-ta-mama" in corky Spanish. Coloring books fascinated me as a child, but now what intrigues me is learning about myself, and my mental and physical capacity. As a small child, I thought a hero was Prince Charming saving the princess from the wicked spell, rescuing her, and taking her far away to live happily ever after. But now, after being introduced to Joseph Campbell's definition of a hero, I have concluded that being a hero means something more than just having the courage to save a person.

When I first heard Mr. Campbell's definition, I asked myself, "Why is this man trying to teach us about heroes? It doesn't take a genius to figure out what a hero is." But, surely enough, I was wrong. A hero isn't just a hero; I had failed to realize that there is first an intriguing journey. I was even more perplexed when Campbell mentioned the "monomyth," explaining how all heroes—even we—follow the same path, take the same series of steps. The journey's patterns are all the same, even if the forms it takes are different.

I started analyzing my own life. I started wondering if I had yet heard my call to adventure. That was when I started getting paranoid. Would I end up lost, without any purpose in life? To me, heroes then became people who are willing to surpass their pasts and journey into the future. Heroes are people who become the judges of their own happiness and their own lives, and never let the voices from outside try to disparage their capabilities. People don't need to help others to become heroes, but rather need the courage to help themselves. When you save yourself from society, you become a superhero. You see yourself change little by little, and you just don't disregard that change, but learn from it just like I have.

I was in Dance class with Ms. Martinez (my tenth-grade World History instructor, who was now my junior-year dance teacher) early as usual. She was eating her Nature Valley peanut butter bar and drinking from the magenta milk cartons they gave at school for lunch. She asked me, "How are you doing, Ms. Perez?" She always addressed everyone by last name as a form of respect. Of course I was tired, very exhausted from finals, and scared of final grades. I hadn't slept much that week, and the circles under my eyes had become more prominent than ever. I lied to her with a smile, saying, "I'm doing fine, just trying to survive school." She looked at me and nodded her head in approval, and I sensed she knew what I was talking about. She stood up, put her hand on my shoulder, and said, "I know you're going to make it, Ana. I can see you wearing the white robe and people calling out to you, 'Dr. Perez.'" At that instant, I couldn't contain my smile, and all I told her was that I would. I knew I never told her what I wanted to become, but by the way she looked at me, she made me realize that I had proven myself just by knowing that people would recognize that I had the potential to be someone great.

Ms. Martinez never failed to see my potential for success. My parents, on the other hand, have been skeptical about the extent of that success, and my brother is uninterested in my aspirations. He tries to fight for our parents' attention and thinks that success is a big competition between him and me. Only I have hope for myself. When the words flew out of Ms. Martinez's mouth that day, it made my finals, fatigue, and lack of sleep all worthwhile. I was sure that my efforts were evident. I just needed someone to remind me of what I had achieved. Ms. Martinez saw through me. Sometimes the look in a person's eyes assures you that you possess something special and that only a few can see that. Her look demonstrated that she saw my efforts and knew how hard I was working to graduate, go to college, and one day attend medical school. It was then that I understood that it was enough to know that I wanted to succeed. If I understood that, it was bound to show one way or another. If I saw it, it was enough. If I knew and I felt it, it was enough.

That day made me understand that my family will not fully understand what I am going through because they live a different lifestyle and have a different way of thinking. What my parents taught me now seems so illogical and strange. Harsh as it might sound, I will never live up to their expectations, and they will never understand who I am becoming. Only now, as a senior, have I begun to put the pieces together and discover that my education has exposed me to a very different lifestyle and a very different mindset. I've adapted to rigorous course work and grown to desire education. I know and feel there is so much out there for me to learn and experience. I need to find my own faults and learn from them to become a better person. They must now adjust to the new reality that I'm no longer a child. My parents cannot tell me what life is like; only I can experience what it is to live. I have to venture into my own journey. I used to look at people and judge them by the image they projected. Now I've grown interested in what they have to say and what they have to offer to the world. Now I look at my classmates who are a part of this book, and I just think how magnificent it is for us all to understand a little more about what it feels like to journey on our own; to realize that it's inevitable; to pass this on to future generations, looking back and saying, "Hey, we learned that in Ms. Crosland's class."

But many other kids my age may go on living without finding their purpose in life, and some never get the chance to understand who they really are. But I've learned that we cannot change, we cannot transcend if we don't understand ourselves. There is a saying that "Childhood is what we spend most of our adult life trying to get over," but do we really? I think it's not our childhood, but our insecurity and our fear of being inconsistent that we try to get over.

Childhood is something I'm scared of going back to, but it's really that I'm scared of living and accepting others' rules and ideas. I would rather do the exploring myself. Just me. I don't want to wait for the moment. I used to live my life conscious of what others would think of me, but now all I want to do is make myself happy. I want to know that I'm living the moment right now. I want to share a piece of it with you.

Gabriela Maldonado
DAREDEVIL DELIVERY

Loud noises from cars and people along busy Sunset Boulevard flood the morning air. Everyone is in a hurry to get somewhere; streets are crowded with men and women going directly to work. Everyone is moving, yet sleep is so deeply present in their expressions, it's almost tangible. What really wakes them up is my tall blue mohawk...like they've never seen someone like me in these streets before. Tour buses, for the daily exploration of Hollywood, are parked, waiting for eager foreign tourists. The smell of an early start is here, and by the looks of it, that'll turn rank later in the day when people start sweating under the burning rays of the scorching summer sun. I can almost feel the sting in my nose ring, like the smell is pretty close. Pedaling through the car-infested streets is tough, and with my first delivery of the morning already checked in and completed, I decide I deserve a little break.

I head off to the local Dutch bar, De Hems. Lovely. I remember now that I lost a package or two. Man, the manager is gonna yell his face off at me again when I get to the station. I don't see how I'll find those boxes now, and I'm so stupid for always forgetting everything. Why they even hired me for this job is beyond me. Anyway, I get to the bar, lock my steed on a pole in front, and walk in with my enormous messenger bag still intact against my sweaty back. Adriaan van Buren, or Adri, the owner of this fine establishment, is first to greet me. He tells me with that thick Dutch accent of his, "I ain'ts gonna keep your tab open today, Sid; you're vorking."

I give him a look that says, "Aw, come on," but he just

shakes his head with a mocking smile. I may be only twenty-two, but I've been coming here almost every day since the day I turned twenty-one. Adri has been one of those uninfluential father figures to me, in a funny way. So I take a seat on one of the bar stools, waiting to catch a glimpse of my girl, Darby. She's the only person in the world who can make my life worth living.

I sit like a patient, obedient dog until she finally shows up with a bottle of Jack Daniels in one hand and a shot glass in the other. She's coming toward me, and if I had a tail, I'd be wagging it. She stops in front of me on the other side of the counter with a smile on her face. The left side of her long, black hair is pulled behind her ear, and her big, brown eyes have a conniving twinkle in them. She puts the bottle and shot glass in front of me. Thinking she's offering me some, I reach out to pour myself a drink, but she quickly takes them out of my reach. I know I have a stupid look on my face when she finally says, "I came to a decision today, Sid."

She doesn't sound so serious, so with ease, I ask, "What's that?"

"Quit binging on alcohol, or I won't put up with you any longer." Just like that, she says it.

"I'll do anything for you, baby, but you're asking too much! I can't function without it. You know me! I'll be like a car without gasoline!" I almost sound like I'm whining, and for good reason, too: it catches me off guard.

"I don't want you getting drunk all the time, and I worry too much when you're out on the streets with a beer bottle in your hand. You're a sweet guy, and you really don't need that junk in your life, okay." So with that, she moves on to serve the customers, leaving me bewildered. Without saying goodbye, I leave with a screaming phrase in my head: *must get clean now!*

But how? All my life I've had to deal with this stupid alcohol thing. This mess goes a long way back...and it's not so pretty. See, me and my parents never really got along. My folks would always fight for reasons I can't remember right now, and I don't want to say I was neglected, just left alone to fend for myself. I was an only child, so the pressure to be their pride and joy was all on me and me alone. They'd complain about me not going to school while I secretly hung around the dirty back alleys of Hollywood. I would hang around with the stinky, old bums because they had liquor and they never gave me a hard time about how I was throwing my life away. I didn't think I would slip into alcohol so quickly, but after my parents got fed up with me, I just ignored everything and went on drinking. It was a way to forget, I guess. I learned over time that their problems were not worth my time. Their arguments were almost never about me, so there you go.

I'm standing outside the bar, and people are walking past me. Cars are going faster, and to me, nothing seems to stop. Everything is going a lot quicker before my eyes, like my head can't get that message across to the other side. I can't believe she would just blurt it out. She's seen me stupid as heck before and...oh, now I remember. She went straight home from the bar that night. Adri kept telling me to shut up after my drunk shrieks started annoying the other people who were staring at me. I don't really feel like doing this, but what else can I do? I should go to another bar where she won't see me drown my misery. I find one about a mile away from De Hems and go in like a regular customer. I ask for a beer this time, not feeling like drinking heavy right now. One beer turns into four, but I can take it. I've done worse. Darby has really got me thinking. I really do want her to be happy, and this alcohol thing isn't going so smoothly for her. I guess she has a point; maybe it is a little too much. Dang, I forgot I'm still en route. Good, I'm not even buzzed, so I can finish this thing. After I finish delivering these packages, I think I'll go visit Andy the Super Woman. She's been my partner in crime since childhood. I need to hear some words of wisdom and sense.

Andy is the best. The best there will ever be. She was just like me, except her drug of choice was, well, drugs. She would do anything! Then she went to a magical place in New York, she says. She met people who helped her out in one of those twelve-step AA programs, got clean over time, and came back amazing me with the sober results. Not only did she get clean, she looks clean, too. She became a sponsor in order to help others like me. She's not as punk as she was before, but she's still as insane. She's been telling me to join her cause and go straight edge, too, but I'd never listen. Maybe I'll take up her offer, for Darby's sake.

I don't know if you've ever done this, but it's mighty tiring pedaling a pretty tall bike past a bunch of jerks in cars yelling at you for getting in their way. And I'm a very skinny guy. I don't think these legs were made for this. The beer is reaching my system by now; I can feel it. So now, I can't blame the jerks for almost hitting me because of my crooked steering. Relief is all I feel when I get to Andy's apartment building near Cherokee Street. It's small, but it keeps her content. I lock up my bike against the front gate with a whole mess of chains I have stashed in my bag. Now I have to struggle up these stairs to get to the third floor. Lovely. It feels like I'm climbing a long flight of stairs in the middle of a desert. I'm ready to collapse, because that's how unbearably hot it is, when I notice I'm already at her door. It only takes two knocks for her to open, and she's dressed to kill for the baseball field. See, she goes to Van Nuys Sherman Oaks Park to play in a league with mostly guys. Yeah, she's tough.

"I need your help. See, this morning, Darby told me to stop my drinking, and I was wondering—"

She starts laughing and says, "I knew you'd come crawling to me sooner or later. So, she's finally had it. It's about time too, Sid. You're going nowhere with that messenger gig you keep messing up, and, as your caring friend who's told you many, many times in the past, you should lay off the booze. Well, tell you what. Let's go to New York and help you out with your problem. I'm not so sure how long it's gonna take you to sober up, but I'm willing to stay long enough to help you out, all right?"

She's a goddess worth worshipping.

In a matter of days, we're at her apartment bright and early, packing our essentials for the trip. Can't say what to expect, but I hope it's all for the better. Her van is stuffed and ready to go. I look out from the balcony overlooking Cherokee Street and wave goodbye to a place that ignores me completely. Oh well. I'm going to the big Empire State, anyway.

We're already on the road and still in California. I lay my head against the window and think about—what else—Darby. I honestly don't think there'll be much of a difference, but if she sees it, then my hard work will surely have paid off. We're listening to Tribe 8, the Devotchkas, Die Toten Hosen, and so on, but I'm growing incredibly bored. Andy's still driving, and it's clearly visible by her red eyes that she's getting tired. I offer to drive for a while, but she won't let me. "I got it," she says. All right then. I keep offering her my services, but she's still being stubborn. When I try to help but people refuse, I don't feel right. So, to settle down, I search for some booze in the back but can't find any. I ask her where it's stashed, and all she does is laugh at me. "You really thought I'd have alcohol in here?" She's still laughing, and I guess I shouldn't have kept my hopes up. See, I'm real stupid sometimes.

Days and days and days go by. Truck stop after truck stop; it seems endless. There is literally nothing to do but stare out the window and wait to puke. Over these past days, I've been feeling like throwing up, and I almost can't wait for the moment to come. Have to relieve myself from all this water. And this heat! It's laughing at me! Even the nights don't get any better. I smell like all the booze I've ever drunk in my life is becoming the sweat coming out of my pores. It's gross, and I want Andy to turn back and at least let me die in a cooler place. Man, going across the stupid country was a bad and horrible idea from the beginning. Andy is getting pretty sick of my complaining, but man! Every turn makes me dizzy as I move from side to side. After every turn, I let my head drop so that I won't have to look at the road while it's moving before my eyes. Every bump we run over makes my innards heave upward—all the more reason to stick my head out the window and puke all over the road.

Boredom is eating me away, and for some reason, maybe because I can't stand it any longer, I want to punch myself in the face and pull at my hair. I'm delirious, and the heat ain't helping a bit. Why people like the idea of summer fun is beyond me, and I'd like to see them spend it in a tight little van where you can't even cross your legs. I start singing Patti Smith's "Pissing in a River." I'll have to admit that I'm not the best singer out there, but who wouldn't want to sing such a beautiful song out loud? Andy is still going strong though; apparently my singing makes her laugh.

"Why don't you write to the babe so you won't get so bored?"

Hey, that's not a bad idea. "Hey, do you have some paper around he—oh, here it is. Let's see, what should I write about?"

"How 'bout writing how awesome your best friend is and how you couldn't do a thing without her." Ha, you gotta love her.

Throughout this whole time, I write. I write about how there's no beer, it's still hot, Andy and I sing horribly, and I miss Darby tremendously. And I really mean it.

After five torturous, horrible, and smelly days of crossing the country, we get to a dump called the South Bronx. It's a rush. Some places are nice; others, not so nice. I look at Andy with a "what the heck" kind of look, and she says, "Hey, don't give me that."

There's an innumerable amount of homeless people on the street, and here I was thinking the ugly part of Downtown LA was bad. Since leaving home, I haven't touched a single drop of that intoxicating medicine. And I feel very awkward about it. See, it's almost every day that I drink, and five days really makes you feel that difference. I still feel like puking, too. I wonder how proud she would be of me if she knew. Better be worth it in the end. I thought I wasn't gonna make it in the first place. Andy tells me that time away from home can be helpful to enjoy things other than my failing job as a bike messenger. I see lots of people looking busy with, I imagine, heavy burdens on their shoulders like work, family, and all that other important stuff.

"First, we gotta get you a job, boy," she says, breaking into my daydreams of big NY.

"Yeah, but there's nothing really I can do but ride a bike," I complain. At the same time, I'm excited about where this will lead. Hopefully, into lessons of responsibility. That's how much I want to change for Darby.

"That's right, but you can't be messing around with all these cars here, and you're reckless. Can't really trust you, buddy."

"I knew you'd say that." Not even my own friend trusts me, but that's all right.

Already on the streets of Morris Heights, we're strolling down and keeping our eyes peeled for "Help Wanted" signs, but no luck so far. After a good two-hour-long search, we finally give up and agree to continue this tomorrow.

We head off to a place called Jackie Robinson Park, and lots of children are playing and running all around. It's a really big piece of yard, but I'd say not as nice as Sherman Oaks Park. We find an empty bench and collapse on the hard seats. I listen to the birds singing from atop a nearby tree and notice that more start coming. They look so happy together, and that makes me think of my folks, along with Darby. That's something I would love to see someday soon: me and Darby enjoying a beautiful day at the park, playing like kids on the swings. The birds continue singing, and for once in my drunk, bum life, I feel like I'm at peace and no one is able to take that away from me.

Early the next morning, after leaving the Jerome Motel, Andy and I go off job-hunting again. Walking down the streets of the South Bronx brings in the smell of freshly baked bread from a nearby bakery. Suddenly, I realize that we haven't eaten anything for a while! I point to a small restaurant sitting at the corner, and Andy nods in agreement. We walk in, and I'm practically drooling all over myself. The smell of breakfast blows my mind. We sit down and wait for a waitress to take our order.

Andy asks, "Hey, how are ya holding up so far? We'll get you a job, no worries."

I have one hand under my furry chin and my elbow on the table, and I just wanna go back home and see Darby. "I feel homesick," I whine.

"Hey, don't worry. Getting a job will distract you, and

you won't have to deal with getting stupid now and then. Trust me. If you want, we can have a little fun tonight."

Andy knows how to have fun, so I get cheery inside. Food comes in, we eat quickly, and off we go again.

We're strolling by East Burnside Avenue and pass a restaurant called Jimbo's Hamburger. Then we glue our eyes on the "Help Wanted" sign taped on the front window. We walk in, and I'm almost offering myself when the lady cashier with a name tag on her shirt that says "Becky" hands me an application. She gives us a friendly smile and says with a very soft voice that she hopes to see me soon. I thank her, not stopping my signs of obvious appreciation for the application, and tell her I hope to see her soon, too. "You have no idea how much I really need this, so thanks a lot again!" I tell her. She chuckles at my way of thanking her, and I can't help but join her in weird yet buddy-like laughter. I'm thinking, man, people are cool here. She didn't even make an ugly face at me.

Already dark outside, we go back to the motel and drop off the application to fill out later. Andy's promise of fun goes along with a little celebration, so at about ten at night, she takes me to a flashing arcade when, down the street, I spot my heaven on earth—a bar! I wanna go there instead; I need a drink! She's already entering the arcade, and I start to run toward the bar lightly so that she doesn't hear me sneaking off. I walk in and yell at the bartender, "Hey, bring me some Jack, will ya?"

I have no idea what just happened because for some reason, I wake up lying on my back on a cold, paved street. I'm aching all over. The left side of my face hurts, but I know I don't have a broken jaw because it feels like it's still in place. Everything is spinning round and round, and I just can't keep my focus on a single thing. Andy is looking down at me, or at least I think it's her. It's too blurry to tell.

"Hey stupid, you're finally awake. You owe me big for pulling you out of that fight. Get up. It's late."

Huh? What fight? Oh—I must've gotten so drunk that I got in a fight. Man, I really am stupid! I sit up with difficulty, and my brain feels swollen in my cracking skull. At least that's what it feels like. I put every bit of effort into standing on my own, but my head is beating and throbbing immensely! I grab my knees as I get up so that I don't fall right on my face. I'm swinging all around the street until Andy catches me and puts one of my wiggly arms over her tough shoulders. I tell her under my breath that I'm really sorry, and she sighs with obvious disappointment. Now I want to whimper like a lonely, pathetic dog.

Ever since Andy took me in, it's been all for the better, although I'll have to admit that it hasn't been exactly perfect. I got the job at the burger place, and it's nice how, after doing this, people are starting to really look at me and take me seriously. I actually thought that my torn-up clothes would have people thinking that I was homeless. I haven't gotten my neat uniform yet, but when I'm sweeping, mopping, and wiping tables, people don't give me so much guff. I'm not doing a bad job, either, just in case you're wondering. Responsibility is an immense job as it is, but I guess being devoted to changing can really pay off.

I've been writing letters to Darby about how awesome it has been out here and how much I miss her. I write about how I got a job I'm actually good at. She writes back, saying that she really is proud, that not only will it all work out, but it'll also help me become a better person. My heart feels as heavy as a boulder thinking of what her reaction might be when she reads my letters. I mention that I got her name carved and added to the collection of tattoos on the side of my scrawny neck by Andy the other day. She writes, "That's so sweet, you freak."

God, I can't wait to see her again. I'm in a little boy's fantasy of growing up and being the great man that Darby would like, but I gots a long way to go, Andy says.

Starting a brand new life after a long run with alcohol is actually happening. Everything is going a lot smoother now. Live while we have life, die when we're dead, I guess. I'm not saying that I wouldn't like a drink once in a while, though. It's tougher than I expected.

We're still in the South Bronx, and Andy has been an enormous help. As a sponsor, she's been guiding me into a new life little by little. What a sponsor actually does is stick with the victim and be there like a best friend. It works lovely because I've known Andy my whole life, and I trust her. With her around, nothing can really go wrong.

I still write to Darby, but I haven't gotten anything back. Maybe I'm sending it to the wrong address, or maybe the mailing is really bad from here. Or maybe she's been too busy; I don't know, But I hope I get some letters soon. I'm desperate for any answer, I know. In my letters to her, I've written how I'm actually doing it. I'm getting sober little by little, and each passing day is working wonders. Becky from Jimbo's Hamburger and I are becoming good friends. She's been teaching me a lot about New York. There are so many new things to learn about this notorious state.

It's been months, and Andy and I are still staying in the cheap motel. I'm feeling at home already, and I'm growing to like this ugly city. You meet interesting people each day, and work isn't much of a pain. Andy has been keeping me on track. She's really helpful, and it still gets me how she knows so much. It's the experience, I guess.

We're sitting on the only mattress in the room, way in the back, watching the telly. Andy is flipping through the channels, and it's a bunch of news and special programs. "Hey, I think it's almost over, buddy," she says.

"What?"

"Well, how are ya feeling so far?"

"Pretty cool, pretty cool. Wait—you're talking about the sober thing? Oh yeah, I don't feel like drinking at all."

"I'll be! I knew bringing you out here would help. You feel like going home yet? I think you're ready to go show off the new you."

She sounds enthusiastic, and I feel really proud of myself. I get to go home now! Man, a bum like me made it through. To be entirely honest, I've been craving a drink, but I won't dare go near one. With the cash I've made at the burger place, I bought myself a new bike. I missed the acceleration speed, and it's been keeping me out of trouble. I also realize my balance is a lot better. Man, that alcohol was really messing me up.

"Yeah, I wanna go home already! I wanna fix myself back on the bike messenger job, see the people. I even miss the stars on the sidewalk! But most of all, I wanna see my girl."

I'm such a romantic, even for a guy who wears tattered clothes. Hey, anybody can find love, right?

A couple of days later, I've left Jimbo's place. I've said my goodbyes to Becky and the manager. They've been good to me, really great people. I will miss them a lot. Andy and I are packing our stuff into the small, rickety van, and I'm loading my bike onto the back. I feel the need to say goodbye to the neighborhood. I don't know why. Maybe I'll miss this junk hole of a city. The few neighbors outside who see me wave goodbye actually wave back. Man. New York will miss me. Now I feel like crying.

We finish the last bits of packing up and go off. Andy and I decide to put on some music, and we don't say a word. It feels really peaceful, no noise on account of the music. Everything seems to drift into quiet sleep.

In matter of days, we're back in Hollywood. Man, I feel so strange being here again, even though I've lived here my whole life. It's weird, but the very first thing I want to do is go to the hills overlooking LA. It'll complete me, but I really should go see Darby first.

Andy drops me off in front of De Hems. After she drives away, I'm still standing there. I'm not so sure what to expect, and I'm so nervous. I feel my heart beating against my chest. The palms of my hands are sweaty, and when I wipe them off on my shorts, they're still sweaty. Well, here I go.

I step in and notice the bar still has its regular Joes. This place hasn't changed a bit. Adri is still looking pretty big, and when he turns his big head toward me, this wide smile grows across his face. See, I was always his favorite customer even when I couldn't pay for the alcohol.

"Sid! Vhere have you been?"

"Oh, you know, here and there. How's it been?"

"Business is still good. How 'bout a drink? On me."

"Nah. See, I was sobering up while I was away. By the way, where's Darby? She still around?"

"That's great! Darby, though, left about two months ago, I think."

"What? Where is she?"

"To tell you the truth, I'm not sure. But I've seen her around vith a boy. He vould come and chat vith her all the time."

"What boy?" My heart literally falls into the pit of my guts. I have a hard lump in my throat, and I'm trying to say something, but nothing comes out. My eyes are wide open, and I try to move until I'm finally able to make the effort to walk outside. I think Adri is telling me something, but I can't hear anything. I just want to be alone.

I don't know where to go, so I just sit on the hard pavement outside of the bar. And I start to cry. I don't remember the last time I cried. I can feel the stares of people passing by, but I just don't care. It's up to the point where I think the blood in my heart will begin to drip out of my eyes. I get up because I can't stand being near this bar anymore.

I don't remember what I spent the rest of the day doing after I left the bar. Now, I find myself at the bar I went to a long time ago after Darby told me to get clean. Now, for sure I'm drowning my misery in alcohol. I want to get this over with, so I keep ordering shots of Jack. I'm not sure how many I've drunk so far, but I feel sublime right now. Can't seem to sit still on my stool. Some jerk next to me shoves me and yells, "Watch it!"

"What I do?"

"You spilled your drink on my suit, punk!"

"Wah, wah, wah! 'You spilled your drink all over my nice suit!' Listen buddy. Uh...where'd you go? ...There you are. I'm having a bad day so...leave me alone."

"You're out of it, man. Just watch yourself."

"What are you talking about?" Yeah, I'm not even sure where I am right now.

Jerk next to me is getting mad. I can tell.

"Hey listen, buddy," I tell him, "this is a Patti Smith song dedicated to...I don't even know, but here I go. Ahem!"

Then I start singing "Pissing in a River":

What about it, you're gonna leave me,
What about it, you don't need me,
What about it, I can't live without you,
What about it, I never doubted you!

Next thing I know, jerk is trying to shut me up by swinging a fist at me. What's his problem? Can't think of anything else to do, so I try to hit him back. Of course, I miss. Everyone's got doubles. I feel a hard glass smash against my face. Didn't hurt though, but I'm seeing stars. It'll burn after a while. The back of my head hits the counter, and I realize I'm falling straight to the floor. Jerk is strong; I'll give him that.

Lovely. My face burns so bad. I try to touch it, but at the same time, it feels like little bits of glass are burrowing into my face. I sit up, and I'm not lying on the pavement this time. It's grass, and the cool night breeze makes me feel like I'm on top of the mountains. But I'm on a hill. I haven't gotten full vision yet, but I can make out the city lights ahead of me. I must be in the Hollywood Hills, but how'd I get all the way up here?

Oh. It hurts...a lot. I can't help but mope. I feel so lonely, but then again, these lights are watching me. They're guiding me and looking out for me. I start to cry again. I'm such a wimp, I know, but I can't help it.

A couple of days later, I'm on the streets again. I'm still riding for money, and I'm not drinking. Not since that night. And about Darby, well, I'm still heartbroken, but as long as she's happy, I'm happy for her. Her happiness has always mattered to me from the very beginning, and it was probably what I wanted for her.

Alcohol is definitely not something I'm going back to. Life is just as good without it. Besides, I'm a lot better at delivering packages, and I'm not bumping into cars or running reds as much as I used to.

Now I go to Sherman Oaks Park every weekend to watch Andy play. It's windy today, but it feels nice anyway. I'm sitting way on the top of the bleachers behind the field so I can get the whole view of the game. Andy cracks me up. She's sliding all over the place, and she's got dirt all over her. I look up and see a bunch of clouds forming into all kinds of shapes. This is nice. Maybe me and Andy'll go back to the hills tonight. I just want to lie down and doze off.

Jesus Enriquez
OH MY DEAR XBOX

Oh, my dear Xbox,
I remember when I first saw you.
Perfection to mankind.
You were water nourishing my survival.
The answer to my longing desire.
The gaming experience of a lifetime.
Choosing you was the doorway to my paradise.
When I was sad you were there.
Your graphics put me into a trance-like state.
You never failed to amuse or impress me.
When I was ten feet under homework,
you were there to pull me out.
You always helped me when I needed you most.
Always gave me what I needed.
Rechargeable battery packs to keep me going day and
    night.
Wireless headset mic so we could hear each other's voices.
Xbox Live membership so we could keep in touch with all
    our friends.
Microsoft gamer points to buy whatever we needed.
Unfortunately, times began to change.
I was never able to give you that HDTV of your dreams.
I began to notice:
everything you gave me was already mine.
You cheated me out of my time.
Everything you called a present
was bought with my money.
I loved you so much I just had to forgive you.
Sure, there were others.

But I still gave
our relationship a shot.
I thought that everything would eventually
fall into place,
But of course it never did.
The day that changed it all came along.
The day that took my joy and love
and even your short-lived life.
The red ring of death.
Fried circuits and a failed system.
Oh, my dear Xbox, how I miss you.
Your passing hit me hard,
but you know as well as I do
there is always another console.

Jeanette Perez
A SEED IS PLANTED

A seed is planted,
As it waits to
Sprout from its rich
Soil, when it prepares itself to live and
Survive this world,
The first days of its bloom
Are its innocence
Something priceless, but as
Its days of life
Come, they are bound, to end
That one pure part of itself
Is torn apart by
this cruel
World then and only then
Does that sweet
And innocent being
Perish, hoping to
One day be what
It once was and
Make a change for
The better

Rafael Cruz
SHADOWS OF AN ASSASSIN

Stepping on a rock, I climb a tree. Soaked and muggy, my body is calling out for a stop, but the adrenaline pumping in my body helps lift me to the high branches until I can see over the entire mountain. I push myself to the limits because I must be fit for anything that comes my way.

While I rest in my room, my master walks in. "Angelous, today you will prove yourself. You've been here since you were a child. You have learned the ways õf the assassin, and my boy, I think you are ready for your first mission."

Time freezes, and the blood in my veins heats. My insides feel like they are ready to burst. My eyes take a slight turn toward him. I tell myself, *I'm not ready.*

Julius orders, "Pull yourself together! You knew this day would come. It is something that all of those in the brotherhood must experience."

He speaks of the person I must kill. He tells me that he is within the city of Serene; that it won't take one night to kill him, but many; that I must gain information from those around him about his ways and customs. He says that the man is the emperor, Caesar.

I put on my long, white toga. The robe helps us hide and blend in with the people if we are ever discovered. I grab a few silver coins from my table and put them in my pouch. I go downstairs and into the garden. Taking a few minutes, I start to meditate before I head to Serene, a place where I have no experience.

When I was two, my parents were killed, and I was left in this place, the hideout of a brotherhood of assassins. We don't call ourselves anything else but brothers. Our master, Julius, trains us in fighting and fills our minds with learning. We believe that poverty and corruption come from those who have power over people, and to fix it, we must end the lives of those who are in power.

With grit between my toes and sweat running down my neck, I feel like a dog without an owner. The sandals I am wearing don't keep the heat from burning my feet. I am following no road, and there are few trees that can give me shade, but occasional old wells keep me hydrated.

Two suns and two moons pass in this way, and I am exhausted. I come to a small river and stop to splash my face. I must be close to Serene by now. I turn my head and see a man coming my way. Is it Marcus? My old friend? Marcus had been an assassin but left the brotherhood a few weeks ago. He once told me of the pain he felt when he ended his victims. The wrinkles in his face show years of seeing too many deaths. The light no longer shines in his eyes. White as snow, his hair tells me it is he I see.

"Angelous, is that you?"

"Yes, Marcus, it is I."

"I can't believe it! I thought I would never see you again."

"Yes, my friend, I did as well."

"So, Angelous, what brings you here to the middle of nowhere?"

We talk for a long time. He gives me a few words: "Follow what your conscience tells you, and Angelous, before you go on your way, I have something for you." He hands me a long and beautiful sword. The golden grip makes me feel like an important man. The sun reflects off the silver blade as I turn it around. I slowly run my fingers over the blade and hang it on my back.

Walking under the burning sun, something in me says that what I am to do is wrong, but why? Odd memories haunt me.

"*Angelous, you are worthless! You can't even prepare a delicious dish for me, and you expect to learn how to handle a sword!*"

"*Master Julius, I took the whole day preparing this food for you.*"

"*It's disgusting. Now go to your room; I will deal with you later.*"

Darkness falls and there it is, Serene. I get to the city gates, and my heart pounds inside my chest as I approach two guards. A small fire dances for them, keeping them warm in the absence of the sun. I hear them talk about women as if they were merely objects. I walk past them, and one of the guards shouts, "Who are you, and what is your purpose here?"

I look back, and he falls to the ground. The other guard laughs at him. Looking closer, I see they are drunk. This is why I have come to Serene, to end things like that before me. The emperor has the power to stop this, but he doesn't. He is just like them, careless and corrupted. The cold winds make me shiver. Houses nearly crumble to the ground, and the homeless wander the streets.

Something pulls on my robe; it is a young boy.

"Sir, please, I am hungry...can you spare me some change?"

"Sorry, kid, I don't have any. Shouldn't you be home? It's late for a boy your age to be in the street."

"Sir, I do not have a home. My mother and I live in the streets."

"Where is she now?"

"She is probably doing the same as I, asking for change."

"Sorry, I don't have any coins."

The boy looks down and walks away. I remember the silver coins in my pouch. I shout to the boy and tell him to stop. Grabbing the coins from my pouch, I hand them to him.

His frown turns into a grin, and he thanks me. Before leaving, he tells me, "The gods will repay you."

Are there gods? And if there are, why do they let this happen?

I start my work by getting to know the city. I have to know every place in Serene—every street, every corner, and every single hole into which a rat can crawl. I find a small abandoned hut in the heart of the city, next to the palace where my victim resides. From the hut I can climb onto other rooftops where I can see into the inner city walls where the emperor lives. A small pile of hay in the corner is a perfect place for me to rest. Mud covers the cracks in the walls, but at night the icy wind finds its way inside. The night becomes darker, and the rain starts to pour fiercely. I toss and turn, trying to fall asleep, but I can't. Once again I tell myself that if this is what it takes to complete my quest, then let it be.

The sun greets me as the light hits my face. It is time to pursue my victim. Not long after leaving the hut, I see him. He is surrounded by many laughing women and guards, seemingly careless of what is around him. A pregnant woman follows him. Who is she? Is she a servant? She doesn't dress as if an empress.

I see the boy sneak past the guards and approach the emperor. It is the same boy who asked me for money the day before. He asks the emperor for money, saying his mother is sick. Arrogantly, the emperor says, "Get away from me, you filthy kid! You are not worthy of talking to me."

Those around him start to laugh with no sense of the kind of society they are living in. The guards turn and push the boy away from the emperor.

These people—these people live in a cave, a cave where they cannot free themselves from the chains that are holding them back. I see why my master sent me here, to free the people from those chains.

Days turn into nights, nights turn into days, and those days into weeks. I examine Caesar's ways of life and his habits, and always I see the same pregnant woman close behind him.

The day is finally here, and I wait until nightfall. The bricks that form the wall of the palace make a perfect ladder for me to climb. I jump onto a small balcony and look around, cautiously creeping toward the building's door. It's locked. I hear footsteps coming my way. Quickly, I hide in a dark corner under the door's arch. The guards walk past me. I step deeper into the shadows, and the sword on my back clangs against the wall.

The guards turn, and one asks, "Did you hear that?"

"Yes. Is that a man?"

"Hey! What are you doing here?"

I turn cold as ice. They come closer and draw their swords from their waists. I draw my own. I tell them, "Back away: I don't want to hurt you."

They rush at me and swing, but I block their attacks. I kick one in the stomach, making him fall. The other one swings his sword, but I duck. I strike one of them, and he shrieks in pain, dropping to the ground like a sack of grain.

The other cries, "Please! I have a family to take care of! I beg you!"

"I don't care." Without further words, I end his life.

I make my way upstairs, following the lit torches on the walls. I get to a large hallway leading into darkness. I keep walking, and once again I hear footsteps, this time with screeching wheels following. I have nowhere to hide, so I grab my sword and get ready. I see the guards pulling a wagon, and I charge at them with all my might. They have no time to pull their weapons out, and I leave them on the ground motionless. A white sheet in the wagon covers something. I move the cart, and a hanging hand startles me. I take off the sheets, and it is the pregnant woman lying there, pale and dead. I see more stairs leading up. They must head into Caesar's room.

I take my sword as I enter the room.

Just then, Caesar turns around. He opens his eyes

and shouts, "Who are you, and what are you doing here? Guards! Guards!"

"Your guards will not come."

"Who are you? I demand to know!"

"My name is Angelous, and I am your condemner."

"You fool! You are talking to your emperor! Kneel and kiss my feet."

"Clearly you do not understand. You are the one who is going to kiss not my feet, but the tip of my sword, for what you have done to those who are your people, your city."

A candle flies at me, but I move out of the way. It hits a wine bottle on a shelf behind me, knocking it over and breaking it. In a second, the flame from the candle spreads up the drapes, starting a fire. I jump at Caesar like a wild animal and bring him to the floor. He struggles and tries to push me away. My thoughts go blank, and in an instant the struggle is over.

The blaze behind me grows. His room has turned into his grave. I turn to the door, and my hand reaches for the handle. A cry breaks out. I turn once again and see a golden crib I hadn't noticed. I walk to the crib.

A baby boy is there.

What have I done? A baby? It can't be—during the time I was following this man learning about his ways, I never noticed a baby. The man I had just killed never held a true relationship with any woman—but that pregnant woman, the one dead on the cart, could it be? Looking at this young and innocent soul makes memories of my lonely and loveless childhood flash across my eyes. I can't let that happen to this baby.

The flames reach the roof, and it starts to crumble. My eyes water, and my nose is filled with smoke. I must save this baby, or the fire will take him. This baby is blameless; he is innocent of anything anyone else might have done. I gently pick him up and hold him in my arms, leaving my sword in the crib. I have never held a baby in my arms; I am scared. I don't know how to be a father or how to care for a baby.

I climb down the stairs as flames devour the palace. I hear horses racing toward me and people shouting, "Water! We need water!" Men and women, some quiet, some crying, surround the burning palace. I step back and join the crowd. I must get away from here. Turning around, I head into a small alleyway. I look at the baby, and he smiles in his sleep. I keep walking and run into the same boy who asked for coins a few weeks ago.

"It was you, wasn't it?"

"What are you talking about?"

"The fire, it was you who started it."

Surprised, words won't come out of my mouth.

"Don't worry; I won't tell anyone." He smiles and walks away.

What will come next? My master will certainly not be happy with my decision. As soon as I saw this baby, my conscience spoke to me, telling me that I must care for him. But I have to return to the brotherhood.

I step outside the walls of Serene and take one last look at the city. I walk down the same path I came on. I steal some milk from a cow to feed the baby. Again, two suns and two moons pass.

I see Marcus once again, this time sitting on a rock. This time it seems as if he is waiting for me.

"Is that a baby I see in your arms?"

"Yes, yes it is. He is my baby."

We have a long talk as I explain how I came into possession of the child.

"Angelous, I am going with you. If you are going to do as you told me, Julius will not let you leave the brotherhood. You will need my help."

"Why do you wish to help?"

"Angelous, he whom you call master is more than what meets the eye."

"Yes, Marcus, I know."

"Julius is my brother."

"Your brother?"

"Yes. A time came when he changed. He abused the power he had over those who followed him. I saw things that broke my heart, until one day I couldn't handle it anymore. So, I left."

"That is the reason he didn't kill you."

"Correct, but now you must put an end to his disgrace."

As we get closer to the hideout, my feet slow down. I take a look at the baby, my baby. His eyelids close, and his small nostrils flare as he takes short breaths, not having any problems in the world. If only I were like that: free of care. I return to reality and make my way to the top of the mountain where our hideout is located. We finally come to the outer doors of the burrow. I look at Marcus, and he does the same. We have arrived. We enter the doors, and Julius is there waiting for me.

"Welcome back, Angelous; I see you have brought goods from Serene."

I look at the baby and remain silent.

"Marcus, is that you?" Julius asks.

"Yes, Julius, it is I."

"Let the gods bless this special moment. Angelous, Marcus, please...come inside and tell me about your adventures."

I step inside. I shouldn't have returned. Something is wrong.

As the door closes behind me, something cold touches my neck. I try to turn back.

"Do not dare turn if you value your friend's life. I know what you plan to do, you ungrateful little rat! After all those years I cared for you? This is how you want to repay me?"

Impossible! How did he find out?

"I know of your plans to leave the brotherhood."

"What are you talking about?"

I turn around to see Marcus unconscious on the floor.

"Marcus! What have you done, Julius?"

"Don't worry, Angelous; he is only taking a nap."

"What are you doing?"

"What we assassins do...kill those who are an obstacle to our plans. Oh, Angelous, you are just like your parents, weak at heart. I should have killed you that night I killed them! Their compassion to others always got in the way.

One day they came to me and told me they wanted out, just like you. I told them of my plans to take over Serene and how their service helped me, but still they wanted out. They were no longer useful to me."

A tear falls down my face. "Now I understand why you sent me to Serene. You wanted me to get rid of the king so you could barge in and take over the land."

"Yes, Angelous, you are very smart. It is such a shame that I have to kill you."

"But how did you find out that I wanted to leave the brotherhood?"

"As you grew, conflicts between us arose. When I scolded you, I saw the fire in your eyes, but yet you were loyal to me. I knew the day would come when you would turn against me."

The baby starts to cry. Julius pulls out his sword.

"That baby you have in your arms must die. Kill him! Or I will kill you."

"I will not!"

"Very well, then I will do it myself."

"I will not let you!"

"Ha, what are you going to do? Kill me?"

"I will not fight you. I have put down my sword. I renounce killing. But you will not harm the baby."

Julius swings his sword at me. With the baby in my arms I run outside.

"Brothers! Come and join me!" Julius calls for the others to stop me.

I stop and look around. Men surround me, not letting me pass. *This is it, I am dead.* I kneel down. One of the older men raises his sword. I close my eyes, but suddenly I hear something drop to the floor. I open my eyes and see the sword on the floor. The man is also kneeling with his head down. I look around, and every other assassin does the same. *What is going on?*

"You fools! Kill him! I, your master, command you to!"

The men stand and form a line like soldiers.

"Why won't you attack? Once I am through with him, you will all pay!"

Julius charges toward me and swings his sword again. This time I don't run; I just step aside. He misses and swings once again.

"Fight like a man, Angelous!"

He raises his sword, and the sun reflects off his blade, blinding him for a moment. He continues toward me, rubbing his eyes. Just then a strong wind causes him to lose balance. He stumbles and trips on his robe. In front of him, a cliff awaits. Unable to see, he rolls down the side of the rocky mountain, not letting go of his sword. He lies at the bottom of the cliff, wincing in pain. I make my way down to Julius with the baby still in my arms.

He looks at me, managing to laugh. "So the student has beaten the master?"

"No, Julius, you did this to yourself."

"Get away from me. Leave me alone!"

He turns his head but doesn't let his sword go. Shaking, he laughs once more. I turn around and go back to where I left Marcus. I look at the baby as he opens his eyes and smiles.

Four years have passed since the death of Julius. Things have changed. There is less poverty in the streets. That which was once an empire rests only in people's memories. No one controls anyone. People live in a free society. The brotherhood I once knew is now gone, and I live within the city of Serene as a normal and proud father.

"Papa, Papa, Grandpa Marcus said that he is going to teach me how to use a sword so that when I grow up I can help people."

"Joshua, I told you not to bother your grandpa."

"He doesn't bother me, Angelous. Besides, someone has to take over our duty of protecting the people when we are gone."

"Yes, Marcus, you are right. Okay, Joshua, your first lesson is today."

"But Papa, I am not ready."

"My boy, pull yourself together. You are going to be just fine."

Rafael Cruz
LIGHT IN A SHADOW

Hidden within the shadows
Deep within him is sorrow

Tonight a life will be taken
His soul will be awakened

Burning fire
Just like his desire

A single cry
As he asks, "Why?"

He becomes a father
What was his past, doesn't matter.

Nataly Chavez
FADED

Two sisters and one fading path on grass.

A path from long ago from early evening trips to the
    playground.

A time of no homework, but of Cardcaptors and Digimon.

A little girl skips playfully here and there, smiling back at
    her sister.
Her eyes fall upon the swings and anticipation grows.
A distant voice tells her, "I'll race you!"
She takes off struggling with sandals that are too heavy.

They hurl themselves to the swings, laughing, pushing
    their bodies to reach the sky.
Hot beads of sweat run down her neck but fade with the
cool breeze, making her body tingle.

Her body rocks back and forth like a newborn baby.
The sun sets, the years pass

She still passes along the same path, but now
It fades as fresh grass hides the dirt that used to be
Kicked by two girls.

Now only one crosses it.

Where's the other?
Long gone, married off

Her voice more distant than ever.

Jocelyn Mariscal
ALONE IN THE DARK

I always loved the backyard when I was alive. Now, I love it more than ever. I spend most of my time here when I'm not people-watching or scaring the bejesus out of them (we can use our ghostly energy to become solid, move objects, and enter people's dreams). There's the fresh smell in the morning, the birds chirping, and the bees buzzing. As I lay on the green grass, the dew wets my nightgown, and the flowers tickle me. My body may be gone, but my soul still remembers the sense of touch.

When people die, they become ghosts. Some look at their surroundings for a few seconds and disappear, going to wherever the dead go—heaven, hell, reincarnation, or someplace else. My parents must have gone to one of those places since they're dead and I haven't seen their ghosts lingering around. Once, though, I did see an angel hovering over a person. I swear. I mean, what else could it be? What other human-looking being has large, white wings? He was very cautious, trying not to be seen by ghosts. He was the handsomest thing I had ever laid my eyes on, and he was watching over an old lady. Lucky old lady.

Anyway, those ghosts who don't disappear are stuck here on earth with unfinished business or something. Some have grudges they can't let go of. Others are too scared to leave earth. They stay behind figuring out their problems and don't move on. Some stay stuck on earth for so long that they forget themselves and go crazy. I'm one of the ghosts stuck here on earth, and hopefully that won't happen to me. I stayed because I just couldn't leave my sister Daisy. She is the only living family member that I know of.

I have bigger things to worry about than crazy ghosts. There are other creatures to be on guard against. Dark, gremlin-like creatures, as tall as five-year-olds, with dark brown reptile skin and large, beady red eyes, hunt ghosts down. I call them the death hounds because death is present everywhere they go. When I had just died, another ghost had saved me from them. He warned me about what those creatures do to ghosts: they feed on ghosts' auras, our source of "life," which gives us our ghostly powers. They also feed off the fear and sorrow of humans; that intensifies those emotions even more and keeps the death hounds alive. For all of my ghosthood, I have been avoiding these encounters.

In the backyard, the flowers' sweet fragrance lingers in the air, attracting colorful butterflies like magnets. A huge tree looms before me with a tree house in the middle of its thick branches. It has a broken window from which I can see the Victorian house my sister and I lived in for four years. We moved there when we were adopted from the orphanage where we'd stayed a year after our parents' death. Peeling, yellow wallpaper, decorated with daisies, covers the walls, and a small, blue sofa with rag and porcelain dolls sits in a corner of the tree house. There's a little table with chairs upon a red rug in the middle. On top of the table is a vase with withered daisies surrounded by an antique china tea set. Other than the layer of dust, the musty smell, and the cobwebs that clutter the corners, nothing has changed. Everything in the tree house has remained untouched since I died of tuberculosis three years ago.

I dangle my legs off the edge of the tree house's balcony. The golden sun hits my pale skin as I take it all in. Heading toward the front yard, I see children riding their bikes in the street; my sister is among them. Parents chat with their neighbors. It's just another lovely summer afternoon in suburbia.

Out of nowhere, a white truck swerves down the street at high speed. My sister Daisy is in its path and doesn't even have time to flinch. With a crash, her little body goes flying in the air and lands on the hard pavement, covered with shards of glass. I freeze.

"No!" I scream.

With a squeal of tires, the white truck speeds off—and crashes into a lamppost at the end of the street. There's an explosion as the top part of the lamppost falls on the truck and goes through the windshield, instantly killing the driver. Appearing out of thin air, with a confused look on his face, the ghost of the driver stands next to the destroyed truck. Within seconds he disappears, like sand blown by the wind. *I hope he goes to hell.*

Parents are running and yelling for their kids; the children scream and cry. Some run toward the truck as others circle the dead body of my sister. Silently, I head in that direction while people pass through me. In the middle of the circle, I see our adoptive mother Sydney crying, holding Daisy's lifeless body in her arms.

"Somebody, help! Call the ambulance! Oh my God, no! No!" She's hysterical, crying and rocking back and forth with Daisy's body.

Through all the chaos I hear a little voice scream my name. "Luna!" I see my sister, standing next to her lifeless body. I blink twice. *She...she can see me?* She's smiling and floating toward me, giggling along the way, trying not to get swept away by the breeze as she isn't used to being weightless. I stare, dumbfounded. *We can be together again.*

Frozen in place, I see a most horrible sight: the gremlin-like death hounds have arrived. They're everywhere: on top of cars, on top of roofs, at both ends of the street. Growling, they pounce, clinging to people, feeding off their fear and sorrow. I spin around, making sure none come close to me. I see my neighbor Michael running inside his house.

"Daisy, hurry!" I yell. She looks around and screams as one of the creatures attaches itself to Sydney, who cries even harder. Hearing her screams, a bunch of the monsters come and rush up to Daisy. They encircle my sister, as hunters stalk their prey. Their dirty yellow claws grab my screaming sister, and they fly away on their bat-like wings. *Whee-oo! Whee-oo!* The rest of the death hounds are all flying away as the ambulance arrives.

"Daisy! No!" I scream.

Staring dumbfounded at the blue sky I had been admiring before, I collapse to the ground. The sun causes my surroundings to look like mirages. At first, I'm too shocked to do anything, but soon my whole body is shaking. In the distance I hear an ice cream truck go by, playing the familiar "Pop Goes the Weasel" as if nothing has happened. Close by, a siren wails, and I'm so numb that I don't notice anything else.

Floating over the sidewalk, I watch my surroundings. Looking at the crowded street full of onlookers, I notice a small child crying, screaming for his mother. His tear-stained face looks so helpless, so lost that it almost breaks my heart. Finally, a panicked lady sighs and takes the child in her arms, comforting him. I try to blink my sadness away. *Daisy doesn't even have anyone to comfort her. My poor Daisy.* Sighing, I remember the time Daisy had gotten lost at the mall.

Sydney was taking us to a sale. It was the first time Daisy had been to the mall, and she was completely mesmerized by all the shops. Sydney and I kept telling her to keep up because she kept stopping to look inside the windows. Inside stores, Daisy would hide between clothing racks, and my heart would stop for a second before she jumped out with a "Boo!" I'd chase after her, yelling, "Stop that!" She wouldn't listen. Fed up, I wandered off to the toy section, keeping an eye on Sydney so I wouldn't get lost. After a while, as I was examining a Barbie doll, Sydney came up to me with a worried look on her face.

"Have you seen Daisy?" she asked.

"I thought she was with you." We both looked at each other. "Maybe she's hiding between the clothes again," I said, trying to convince myself. "She's probably doing this on purpose." Thinking this was true, my anger rose.

"Maybe." Sydney didn't sound convinced. My heart started beating faster. We started calling out Daisy's name and looking between the clothing racks.

"Daisy! I'm not playing anymore. Come out, and I'll share my candy with you," I yelled. There was no response. The sound of my heart pumped in my ears. *Daisy would never refuse candy—oh, God.* "Daisy! Where are you?" Desperate, I started throwing clothes aside. "Daisy!"

"Look, hee hee," a girl giggled. Turning, I saw a little girl's strawberry-blond head. *Daisy.* I went and pulled her hair for making me worry. "Daisy, how could you—oh I'm sorry, I thought you were someone else," I apologized.

"Mommy!" the little girl wailed.

"Look, it was an accident! Oh, come on!" The little girl pointed in my direction, and I ducked as her mother looked my way.

Sydney came up to me, and her hopeful expression fell as she saw I was without Daisy. "We should go to the front desk to make an announcement," she said, on the verge of tears. With my head down I followed, fighting back my tears. *Daisy, how could you do this? We're supposed to stick together. It's supposed to be us against the world.*

"So anyways, my family got lost," said a familiar little voice.

"Really?" said a woman.

My head snapped up. There was Daisy, standing next to the front desk, talking with one of the store employees. My eyes bulged out, and my mouth hung open in surprise.

"Daisy!" Sydney and I both exclaimed.

"Oh look, there they are. Thank you for finding my family. Hi!" Daisy waved at us.

Running, I embraced her, and Sydney hugged us both. I started to cry with relief. "Don't you ever do that again! You scared me," I managed to say between teary gasps.

"But *you're* the one that got lost. I was hiding, but you didn't come to find me, and when I looked, you and Sydney weren't there. I was scared for you. What if you got lost and I never found you again?"

"Oh, Daisy," I sniffled.

Laughing with relief, Sydney said, "Let's promise not to get lost, okay?"

"Okay," Daisy and I said.

"I promise to never lose you, Daisy. That was a horrible feeling. I don't want to feel it ever again," I vowed.

"Yay!" Daisy cheered.

Too bad I didn't keep my promise.

The coroner comes and takes away Daisy's remains, as well as those of the truck driver. Cops are questioning people, taping off the scene, and taking pictures. News vans crowd the street, with reporters asking questions and videotaping in front of the tragic scene. It's all surreal to me, like something out of *CSI*. I hear the shuffling of feet and some barking, and turn to see a skinny eight-year-old boy standing in front of me with a white, skinny lit candle in his hands, looking directly at me, with a bloodhound slobbering next to him.

"Are you just going to float there for all eternity, or what?" he asks, carefully crossing his brown arms because of the candle.

"Maybe. I'm not in the mood, Michael," I sigh. "Did you see what happened?"

"Yeah, I'm so sorry."

Michael is the shy dark-haired boy who lives next door to Daisy. He's the only person I know who can see me; a ghost-whisperer, some might call him. All animals, on the other hand, can see me, including Michael's dog, Clark. I remember the first time I met Michael, when he first moved next door.

"Hi! I'm Daisy. What's your name?" asked my sister.

"I'm Michael," said the little boy, softly.

"Cool name. Where are you from?"

"The big city."

"So, are you an only child?" Floating out of the tree house, I saw Daisy. She was sitting on the brick wall that separates the house from the neighbor's. I shook my head: one day she is going to get herself killed climbing that wall.

"Yeah," he responded.

"Really? I'm an only child now. I used to have a sister, you know," she sighed. If only she knew I was still around.

"Um...what happened, if that's all right?"

"Yeah, it's okay. My sister Luna, she was fourteen, she died last year because she was sick. She was the coolest sister in the world. She wouldn't share sometimes, but she was always there for me. She was like my mom, too. Our parents died when Luna was eight and when I was one. We were always together."

"Oh...I'm so sorry."

"Thank you. But that's okay. My adopted mommy tells

me that Luna wouldn't want me to be crying all the time. I do miss her, though. A lot," she sighed, hugging her teddy bear. Changing the subject, Daisy asked, "Do you want to be my friend? We're both an only child."

"Oh. Um...sure." He sounded surprised. Curious, I moved over to where Daisy was sitting so that I could take a look at whom she was talking to. There was a little dark-haired boy staring up at my sister. I floated above the wall to listen better. Suddenly, he turned stiff and slowly moved his head in my direction. Our eyes met. *He can see me! But oh my God, why couldn't it have been Daisy?*

"Luna," he says, interrupting my flashback. His eyes are serious, and I frown. "You have to do something. You can't just abandon your sister." Lowering my face, I twirl locks of my hair. He's right. "I think I know where you need to go." I look up and our eyes interlock. *Oh no.*

"The caves," I whisper.

"Yeah," he sighs.

Both Michael and I had stumbled upon the limestone caves at the edge of town. We had sensed a dark energy that felt horrible, as if we'd been rolling in filth. The energy came from the caves. We were too scared to enter, but we saw enough to keep us away. A pack of the death hounds had encircled a lonely ghost in front of the cave, and the ghost had no choice but to flee inside. Afterward, all we heard were screams.

"I have to go to the caves. They must have taken her there. Oh my God. Why do you have to always be right?"

Michael brings out a picture of Daisy and places both the picture and the candle on the sidewalk to make his own little altar. "Look at her," he says, and I do. "She needs you. Don't leave her behind. You know where to go."

His eyes are filled with hope, giving me courage. The caves. She has to be there, at the edge of town in the cluster of limestone caves, where the dark energy radiates from. The death hounds living there are dangerous, but to save my sister I would even go to hell for her. *Follow the bread crumbs, Luna. You have to go to those caves.*

The swirling fog clings to my eternal nightgown. I gulp. Torches line the cave walls, marking a path and lighting the way. Their eerie glow pierces through the suffocating darkness, making shadows. My imagination runs wild, seeing creatures everywhere. Placing my arms in front of me, I hover a few inches off the ground, letting a breeze lift up my weightless being. Slowly, my eyes adjust to the dim light, and I look around the cave. Pointy rocks hang from the ceiling like icicles, with water dripping from the tips every few seconds.

Spiky rocks rise from the floor like swords. I nervously twirl a lock of my hair around my finger. My paranoia rises: I feel like I'm being watched. I look back to where I think I came from, but the surrounding fog makes it hard to know. *Maybe I'm too late—no. I'm not a coward. Daisy wouldn't leave me behind, and I can't leave her.* Breaking the silence and interrupting my thoughts, a bone-chilling cackle that could freeze hell over bounces off the walls. It's them. I remember their dry-looking skin, claws, bat-like wings, and most of all their cold, red eyes that make me quiver in fear. Without thinking, I start floating back to the entrance. Frantically trying to find a way out, I start flying through walls. *Oh my God, oh my God, I can't do this, I just can't.* Practically sobbing, I stop and listen. Silence. I sigh. I imagine those monsters torturing and draining Daisy of her ghostly energy. I remember my sister's terrified face as the death hounds took her away, right after she had turned into a ghost and could finally see me. I promised to always be with her and to never lose her. I failed to protect her. I have to keep my promise this time...no matter how scary the creatures may be. Raising my chin, I head in the direction of the cackle.

As the passing breeze blows me closer to the cackle, I hear the most horrible screeches. Covering my ears, I stop in my tracks. From the glow of the torches I see the creatures' horrible shadows. Their claws are in the air, and their wings are flapping; they seem to be dancing. The song "Jeepers Creepers" comes to mind.

Jeepers, creepers, where'd ya get those peepers?
Oh, those weepers, how they hypnotize!
Where'd ya get those eyes?

That song always gives me the goosebumps, and seeing the shadows of the death hounds dancing makes me feel the same way. My hands close into fists; I hover behind a large rock, peeking over to the other side.

There is a sea of the winged death hounds, all dancing in different circles around clusters of crystals that reflect rainbows along the walls. They are chanting and dancing to the beat of drums balanced on top of a huge, flat, rock, which serves as a little stage. On the stage, there is a throne of rock and crystal, and sitting there is one of the ghastly creatures; it appears to be the king. Its long claws tap the side of its throne in tune with the rhythm, *ba bump, ba bump.* Holy— I nearly stumble through the rock. I stop myself in time, making myself solid and leaning on the rock. *Phew! I almost gave myself away.* I'd better be careful they don't see me. The closest monsters raise their heads and sniff the air. One of them snaps its head in my direction, piercing me with its cold, red eyes. *Oh, no.* I stare. My eyes are glued to its eyes, and my mouth hangs open in surprise.

In unison, the death hounds turn in my direction. The king on the throne stands up and points a claw at me; it shrieks, sounding like the squeal of tires. I go deaf for a few seconds. One of the creatures jumps on the rock I am leaning on. "Ah!" I stumble back, and just right when it is about to pounce, I grab one of the torches and throw it at the creature. It howls in pain. I grab more torches and throw them in front of me, creating a barrier of fire between the monsters and me. Thank God for fire. The creatures scream loud enough to shatter glass. I hear the fluttering of wings: bats. Not knowing where to go, I follow a breeze, letting it carry my weightless body after the bats. Oh well, they know I'm here. All I have to do is float and hide now. Hold on Daisy, I'm coming.

"Daisy? Are you here, Daisy?" I whisper. Floating above the stalagmites, I try to be as quiet as I can to avoid the death hounds. I hear a whimper around the corner. "Daisy?" Swallowing, I move closer to the sound. My nerves are on end and about to explode like dynamite.

Slowly rounding the corner, I hear hurried breathing, then *boom!* I flinch back and scream, "Ah!" In a flurry I try to get out of the death hound's reach. It starts screaming, calling the rest of its pack. I gulp, but before I have time to escape, I'm surrounded. Oh, no. I feel like crying, and my throat is clogged up. I close my eyes tightly. This is it. *I'm so sorry, Daisy, that I couldn't save you. Please forgive me.* I can sense the death hounds leaning closer, then pausing. Two things happen at once.

Like a human, I experience a rush of adrenaline. I let myself fall, right through the ground. The death hounds, not expecting that, end up plunging at each other, landing in a pile, with surprised looks on their ugly, ragged faces. Not feeling scared anymore, I become mischievous. A few moments later, I appear above them, but this time, I am prepared.

In my arms I have a couple of flaming torches, which I quickly throw at the monsters below. "Take that, ugly!" I shout, giggling. Howls rise up and greet me. The death hounds scatter, some climbing the walls to try to reach me, and others ducking the flaming torches I throw down at them. I taunt them: "Climb, climb, as fast as you can; you can't catch me—I'm a ghost!" Focusing my energy on a stalactite, I tear it from the ceiling and let it drop on the monsters below. "Bye bye, bad guys." I leave quickly.

"Hee hee hee!" Laughter echoes along the cave walls. I hear the scraping of claws, like those of a desperate cat scratching the door. After there are no more sounds, I am on the move again. Shifting from behind a boulder, I turn my head left and right, making sure there are no more death hounds. Sighing, I slowly hover up to the ceiling, hoping to get a better look of the cave in the dim light of the torches. *Oh, Daisy, where are you?* Looking below, I see nothing other than the pointy, jagged rocks and their shadows cast on the walls. Closing my eyes for a moment, I hear the faint sound of someone singing and playing guitar. I follow the melody, and as I get closer, the voice gets louder. *It's like an angel is singing.* I sigh, recognizing the song; it's "What About Now" by Chris Daughtry.

> *This broken heart can still survive*
> *With a touch of your grace*
> *Shadows fade into the light*

I am by your side
Where love will find you.

Ahead, I see a small tunnel. A bright light glows from it, like a lighthouse. Still accustomed to human actions, I turn my wispy body solid and crawl into the light instead of going through the wall.

The tunnel ends, but I'm so blinded by the brilliant light that it takes a while for me to stand up. The voice has stopped singing. "Hey, are you okay?" It's a comforting voice: deep, gentle, and masculine. Slowly, I open my eyes to a most glorious sight. The light I saw emerging from the tunnel is that of hundreds of candles, perched all around a small alcove. A guy, about the age of eighteen, is sitting on a rock with a guitar in hand. His curly hair is dark brown, and he has dark green eyes and olive skin. He's dressed in black jeans and a blue shirt, but wears no shoes. *He is too good for those clothes. Oh my God, he is so cute.* All my thoughts rest on him and him only. He flashes a smile in my direction. *Ahhhhh! He smiled at me!* "Are you lost?" he kindly asks. *Oh no, I'm perfectly where I want to be.* He pats the rock next to him, and I float over to the rock, admiring him. He continues singing the song from before and plays his guitar, captivating me.

Just hold on
There is nothing to fear
For I am right beside you
For all my life
I am yours

Smiling at him, I think of nothing else.

One second I'm staring at the most beautiful creature in the world, and the next thing I know, I'm sitting on the swing in my backyard. I look around the sunny, green backyard. How in the world did I get back here? Looking around the backyard again, I search for the divine creature I'd been admiring. "Luna," calls a familiar voice. Out of nowhere, there's a tall man with light brown hair and warm, green eyes so much like my own, walking in my direction. I stare and blink. Stopping in front of me, he says, "Hi, honey." My voice breaks and my eyes widen. "Daddy?"

"Yeah, it's me," he chuckles.

"But you're dead! You and mom both died in that car accident back when I was eight!" I blurt out.

"So are you, pumpkin," he retorts, sadly.

"I'm sorry. It's just that you're supposed to be in heaven or reincarnated or whatever. You're not like me, still wandering around."

He caresses my cheek. I look at his hand surprisingly, as if he had grown an extra finger: his hand didn't go through me. How is he able to touch me?

Seeing my puzzled expression, he tells me, "Anything is possible here. Besides, we're both the same."

"So...where are we?"

"Let's call it a dream."

"Ha ha ha ha, ghosts can't dream. We can't even sleep."

"You may not be able to sleep, but that doesn't stop you from daydreaming. Right now, you're in a dream-like state where anything is possible and I can communicate with you, even though I don't like the circumstances," he says. *Circumstances?*

"Wait, you mean to say that you're doing what we earthbound ghosts do? The whole entering people's dreams business?"

"Yes, but listen, there isn't much time. Have you forgotten all about Daisy?" *Oh...my...God—Daisy!* "Don't forget your mission, Luna," he says sternly.

"I'm so sorry. It's just that—"

"You don't have to explain. Just don't give up, you hear?" He touches my cheek again. "That's the family motto, remember? Never give up. Promise me you'll do that. Protect your sister," he pleads.

"Yeah, well, look how I did last time. She died, became a ghost, and was kidnapped."

"Luna. Don't be so hard on yourself. Everything happens for a reason."

"But, Dad—"

"No *buts*. Understood?" His face is hard.

I stare at him. What if I fail? What happens then?

Biting my bottom lip, he sees my pained expression and sighs. "I believe in you. I know you can do it. Just never give up. Okay?"

"Yes, sir." I salute him like a soldier. I'll never know unless I try.

"That's my girl." Holding me tight, he whispers into my hair, "Be safe...and kick some butt."

"Wait, why can't you help me?"

"I already did. Besides, I already crossed over, sweetie. I can't go back to earth. I can only watch and help when I enter dreams."

"Why? That's not fair."

"I've already lived my life. I have to keep the balance between the living and the dead, and going back isn't keeping the balance. It would just cause more trouble for the living. I moved on, and you should too."

The next thing I know, I have left my father's warm embrace. Confused, I look around. I'm back in the candlelit alcove, and the guy is no longer next to me. In his place is one of the ugly death hounds. "Are you okay?" it mockingly asks, baring its yellow, pointed teeth. Ugh, it had all been fake. Snickering, the creature wraps its claws around the guitar and raises it high above him. *Oh no you don't.* The guitar comes down and splinters with a loud crash on the rock I am hovering over.

"Uh, hello? I am a ghost, if you haven't noticed," I say.

In disgust, the creature flings the guitar remains behind him, and I laugh. It stares at me, cocking its head to the side. I stare back, its red eyes boring into mine. His eyes change color—red, orange, brown, light brown, yellow, green. Blinking, I again see the handsome guy.

"Do you want me to sing you another song?" he sweetly asks. He is spinning a web like a spider, and I am caught. My mouth hangs open. *Of course I'd love another song.* Practically drooling, I stare at him and then shake my head. *Dude! What's wrong with me, drooling over a guy like that? I'm forgetting Daisy. Snap out of it!* The heavenly-looking guy smiles at me, causing me to stagger backward. Maybe if I play along, I can get something out of it. Noticing my hesitance, he stops smiling and turns back into the evil creature, lunging at me with his open mouth.

I drop to the floor, and my hands struggle to close the mouth of the creature on top of me. Its breath is rancid like rotten meat, and its skin is rough like sandpaper. Claws slash at my arms and face. It can touch me? I try to grab the nearest candle, but my hand goes through it. I wasn't solid; I guess I'm rock-solid to these creatures no matter what. A pain strikes my chest. Silvery light emerges from me and is sucked in by the monster. He's draining me! Weakness takes over. In desperation, I turn solid and grab a lit candle. Hot wax drips onto my hands, and with the flame still burning I stab at the creature. As it howls in pain, I slide under it and escape the alcove via a small tunnel.

Emerging from the tunnel, I stop short, looking at my surroundings. *Whoa.* All around there are clusters of crystals, surrounded by people of different shapes and sizes. They all look weak and exhausted. They are all ghosts, but they are blurry and slowly fading. I move from cluster to cluster, looking for Daisy. As I pass by, they look up at me, pleading like homeless people begging for food. Finally, I see a familiar face with strawberry-blond hair. "Daisy!" I scream. "Luna?" She looks at me, and we both cry.

"We have to get out of here," I say. I move to embrace her, but my hand goes through hers. She's so weak that even ghosts can go through her. "Oh, Daisy, please, let's leave this place."

She doesn't move. "We can't leave them behind," she says, pointing at the other ghosts, who all stare at me. Guiltily, I lower my head.

"I'm sorry, but there's nothing we can do for them. Let's go." I motion for her to follow, but Daisy doesn't budge.

"You would never leave me behind, so why them?"

"There are too many of them. They're all weak! I won't be able to deal with them and the creatures at the same time." Daisy shakes her short, straight hair and looks like she's about to cry. "Please, Daisy, don't do that…"

Why am I not immune to adorable faces? I pull my hair. Daisy smiles once she realizes she has won. But what can I do? I look around and spot light shining from a crack in the ceiling. I float up there and brush off loose pieces of rock. "Look out below!" I warn. The ghosts slowly move away as chunks of rock start raining down. I break through the ceiling, and an explosion of light bustles through. A way out! I try to pull some ghosts up, but it's no use: most are so weak my hand goes through them. Those with enough energy float through the exit by themselves, and with the help of a passing breeze, the remaining ghosts desperately float up to the opening.

"Ohhh..." Groans come from the tunnel. Out comes the angelic guy who had been singing songs to me earlier, rubbing his eye. Like before, I am hypnotized and move toward him.

"Luna, come back!" I stop in my tracks and look at my panicking sister.

"Come to me..." hisses the beautiful creature. I obey, leaving my sister behind, not wanting to wake up from this beautiful dream, not wanting to go back to reality.

"Luna!" she cries. Once more I stop. What am I doing? Shaking my light brown locks, I break away and turn back to her, ready to leave this horrible place.

The next thing I know, there's the sound of scraping claws and hissing. More death hounds are entering the room, and slowly they encircle my sister and me. We are the last ghosts left. The handsome guy has changed back into its ugly monster self. I rush to my sister to protect her. Whoosh! Some of the death hounds jump to the opening, preventing escape. It's not like I can pull Daisy up: she's still too weak. I quickly analyze the room, looking for another escape.

Suddenly, there is silence. In front of me, the death hounds part. Entering the room is their king, the death hound I had seen earlier sitting on the throne. He is bigger than the rest, with longer claws. Daisy and I step back, away from him, but the death hounds around us move closer. There are no torches to help me this time. Hmm... I look back at the king and my surroundings. I turn to Daisy, checking to see if she understands what I want to do. She nods. As the death hounds pounce, Daisy and I dive beneath them, past the king and the tunnel. We both stand in the candlelit alcove and float through the wall to the other side. Angry screams come from the tunnel, and I can't calm my nerves.

"Let's go!" I whisper to Daisy, and gladly, there's a small enough breeze to help her move with me throughout the cave.

The rocky walls surround me, suffocating me. I raise my head high, trying to look brave for Daisy, but it is beginning to get hard. Time passes slowly, and there's still no exit. I try to swallow the lump in my throat as my claustrophobia grows. How far underground are we? Where are we? Where's the way out?

"Awooooo!" There's howling nearby. Daisy and I look at each other, not daring to make a sound.

After the howling diminishes, Daisy whispers, "What's that on your arm?" I notice a whitish-yellowish spot. As I move, the spot moves as well. What the—oh! It hits me and I look up. There's a small hole in the ceiling.

Following my gaze, Daisy, unable to control herself, yells, "Light!"

"Shhhh! You'll give us away." But it's too late. *Clink, clink, clink.* There are scratches on the walls; the death hounds are on their way. "Oh, no," I groan. Dirt begins falling on my shoulders. *Huh?* Putting my hand over my eyes, I notice that the small hole is getting bigger.

"Look out below," says a familiar voice. I move away as rocks crash on the ground, but Daisy remains in place. The rocks go through her, and the whole time, she looks up.

"Uh, hello up there?" I say, waving dust away from my face.

"Hey!" Michael says, grinning.

"Michael?" Daisy and I ask in unison. My mouth drops open. Next to him is Clark, his bloodhound, who apparently did all the digging.

"Yeah. You didn't think I was going to let you be all alone?"

"Wait, Michael can see ghosts?" asks Daisy.

"Yeah, he's a ghost whisperer. I'll explain things later," I say to Daisy. I turn back to Michael. "This is not a game. You can seriously get hurt; you're still human, for God's sake." *Clink, clank, clink!* The sound of claws and hissing gets louder.

"I know this is serious. Now hurry up; we don't have all day."

"Daisy, you first," I say.

"How?" she asks.

I try to grab her arm, but she is still too weak. My hand

doesn't have a full grip on her hands; they're still going through. "Can you float up there?"

She tries but goes only halfway. The ground starts shaking, as if a stampede is near. I float up to the opening next to Michael and Clark. "Come on, Daisy; I know you can do it." She floats up again, and I try to grab her hands, but they pass through.

"Try again; you're almost here," Michael says encouragingly. Daisy looks up at us as if she is about to give up.

"Oh no you don't. Do not dare give up on me. I will not leave you behind."

"Ahhhhh!" Screeches are heard, and now the death hounds are entering. Pausing to regain some strength, she smiles and tries one more time. This time, Daisy has enough strength, so I grab her hands and pull her out. Clark quickly starts filling in the hole, trapping all the death hounds, burying them completely so that no sound comes out from the cave.

Daisy and I collapse on the ground. The sun is shining brightly, as it was the day before, when this all started. Beyond the limestone caves and the green forest, I see the edge of town. Everything looks the same, yet everything has completely changed. *I am no longer alone. Daisy and I are finally together again.* Breaking the silence, I burst out in laughter, relief flooding through me. Daisy and Michael join in; Clark howls.

Going back to our old Victorian home, Daisy and I sit on the front porch, looking at the crime scene from the day before. "What now?" Daisy asks.

I think for a while, enjoying the happy warmth going through me. "We do what not many ghosts do: help. Instead of pestering people, we help. We'll protect humans and fight the death hounds. Besides, it's better than doing nothing." I smile and shrug.

"I agree." Daisy smiles and snuggles next to me.

"Take that, you evil monster," I yell as Daisy and I throw rocks at the death hound from high above, where it can't reach us. Growling, it runs away, leaving alone a very puzzled-looking human in the damaged car. *If you only knew.* Making sure the death hound doesn't return, we watch a bystander call the ambulance and help the person out of the wreckage. A year has gone by, and I feel better than ever.

Every day is a new adventure, and I don't get tired of helping people and ghosts alike, even if they don't say thank you, even if they have no clue they're being helped.

Interrupting my thoughts, Daisy says, "Hey, look. What's that?"

Looking up at the sky, I notice a bright light. Squinting, I see two figures emerging from it. No, it can't be.

Excited, Daisy yells, "Look! Look, Luna, do you see what I see?"

"Yeah, I see." But is it real? The bright light dims, and it's impossible not to recognize the figures with the outstretched arms. There's a tall man, with light brown hair and friendly, green eyes, who looks so much like me, and a petite woman, with familiar straight, strawberry-blond hair, who resembles Daisy: our parents.

"Come here; we can be all together again," my mother says. "And from where we're going, you'll still be able to help people. In fact, you'll be able to come and go between this world and that of the dead who have moved on."

"Really?" Daisy innocently asks.

"Yes, sweetie, why don't you come and find out?" my mother slyly responds.

"How about it, kiddos. You would make great guardian angels," chuckles my dad.

Guardian angels?

"You'd get to have wings," he adds.

In a daze, I smile. Holding hands, Daisy and I enter our parents' embrace, never hesitating as the four of us step into the light. *Bring it. I'm ready for anything.*

Susana Flores
BLITZ

"Farewell, Richard."

Planting a kiss on her rose-red lips, I say, "Goodbye, Lily."

Watching her tears run down her face hurts, so I hug her one last time and walk away.

The mist in the air makes my teeth chatter. At the army recruitment center, I notice all kinds of men, some from my own neighborhood. Mr. Robinson and Mr. Dickinson are here as well, their faces overloaded with distress. I feel some of it wash over me. Our bus arrives. As I wait to board, an abnormally large man jumps out of it and shouts out names so loudly that his spit becomes part of the mist in the air. I'm number 60.

After we board, it's a bumpy ride, like a busted carousel. I become sick to my stomach. I feel my breakfast hiking up my esophagus. We come to a sudden stop. "Get off in the order of your numbers!" they yell.

We all get off, trying to stay calm despite our ominous fear. I shake like a loose twig on a tree. They start to pass out white slips, and as we each get one, we are told where to go. I obediently follow the directions and find the barracks.

The doorknob is very shiny, but the door looks like it's about to break at any moment. As I push it open, I see rows of assigned bunk beds. The others give me angry looks, except for one fellow who's much older.

"My name is Lucian," he says. "What's yours?"

Surprised, I say, "Richard Blitzkrieg—call me Blitz!"

Lucian smiles and asks, "Who did you have to leave

behind?"

"My pregnant wife. Who did you have to leave?"

"My wife and four children. Looks like I found someone to relate to," he says in a raspy voice. His five o'clock shadow needs to be shaved, and he looks like he hasn't had any rest in days. But I feel comfortable around him. He cleans his shoes and folds his clothes while we talk. He's old, but energetic and talkative—just the person I need while I'm here. Everyone else talks about how they want to be here, and by the looks of it, they all signed up for the war except Lucian and myself. They all chat about tomorrow's haircut. I stroke my hair and think that it's time for a change.

As I step through the door to the "barbershop," a bright, blinding light hits me in the face. I notice all the men lined up against the wall.

"It's time," Lucian says.

He gets called first. He sits down, panicked, with paranoia all over his face. The barber is enormous, and his hands are huge—bigger than my face. I'm nervous as I watch him manhandle the others in front of me, and I realize I need to toughen up in order to survive this.

"Richard Blitzkrieg!"

I sit on the rubbery chair. The barber almost strangles me with a sky-blue robe, then begins. He grasps my hair; I groan and ache. Loud noises and vibrations hit my head by surprise. The haircut only takes a minute, but it feels like the longest hour of my life. A heavy blow on the back of my head is the sign to leave. I turn toward a mirror, and I don't see Richard anymore: I see a soldier. I'll never see myself the same way again.

A terrible month has passed; we've already been flown in to France. My muscles, sore from brutal boot camp, convince me to sleep a second more, but dreaming of battle wakes me up. Lucian is also having a nightmare; I wonder if it's because of yesterday's news. We're getting gear tomorrow, and we're going straight to the battlefield. I wake him and ask if he's fine; he doesn't answer me. I worry.

"Lucian!" I whisper anxiously.

"What, Blitz? Can't you see I'm trying to sleep? Tomorrow

is the day! This could be my last good night's rest! You should get some, too. Now go to sleep!"

I try to take his advice. But before I can even close my eyes, they wake us with a loud scream and tell us to get dressed. We don't get enough time to do anything. As soon as we are all dressed they ship us to these large buses, just like the ones at the town recruitment center. I can't find Lucian on the bus. What am I going to do without him on the Western Front?

A jolt suddenly startles me.

The doors snap open, and all around me is the smell of gunpowder and loud explosions: gunshot after gunshot after gunshot. I begin to shoot in a panic and try my best not to shoot at my own troops. As I try to take cover, I hear someone scream—someone who sounds a lot like Lucian.

The Germans have him pinned down; Lucian's poor face is full of distress. I shoot at the Germans but miss. They forget about Lucian and return fire. Then comes one of the loudest explosions I've heard all day. The noise stops, and suddenly I'm staring up at the sky, lying on the ground just like all the others. Excruciating pain pierces my chest. I hear another gunshot...and Lucian's voice, promising to help me.

I think of Lily and what my child might grow up to be. All I can do now is imagine.

Gloria Rosales
DREAMERS

Going my own way
I face my worries and troubles
Fending for not only myself
But my dreams
My aspirations that shine like the reflecting water
My dreams that will last as long as the air I breathe
Even though I fight against other lifeless beings
My own dreams spread like the splashing waves
We are fighting...

Jeanette Perez
THROUGH THE CAVE

Nothing can keep me from that special place that has kept me alive through everything. That place is my sanctuary. My parents say I am not their child. I would agree with them, for I love to read and write fiction. Fiction delivers a world of imagination where anything can happen. Fiction can offer the perfect world of adventure, which can bring great joy and great sadness. Even more than that, fiction helps you be you, and reminds you who you are and what you live for.

My parents do not understand these things and say things every day that are hurtful to me. They bring me food and textbooks since I am no longer allowed to attend school. *You are not to have any fun or enjoy any literature. No books. Do you hear us? They are strictly forbidden. You are one of those who are possessed by It.* My father's voice booms throughout the little room where I am locked up. Of course It, as my father says, refers to people like me: people who enjoy literature, who create something from nothing and let our imaginations bring books to life. My parents, who are against all of that, say It is a bad, dangerous thing. I tell my dad, "I want to read! Please don't take my books from me!" But he always says the same thing: *You are strictly forbidden!* And then, wham! He smacks me across the face, and I feel my face redden and my eyes water. Although this is my daily routine, it never hurts less.

I love my parents and my family. I may be different, but that does not mean I am bad. That does not make me the alien they treat me as everywhere I go. When I am sent on an errand, people stare and whisper. It makes me uneasy, but I just smile and greet them while in return they make disgusted faces and leave as fast as they can. I don't know if I can last any longer.

It all started the day I was born. I found out later how different I was, how unusual it was to be aware of my surroundings from the beginning.

The hospital room was filled with people: my father James, my older sister Auburn, the twins Jake and Damien, and of course, my mother Marie. On a small table in the corner was a blue-green vase with a fresh bunch of lilacs inside, purple and full of rich, sweet scents. The vase was the only thing that was full of life. The walls were a plain white, the chair was a creamy color, the phone's color matched the chair, and the window was shut. There was no sunshine; the sky was dark and gloomy.

Auburn said in surprise, "What is that, Mother? There on her face? It's gross! Did the doctors stretch her face out?"

"Yeah, looks like... I don't even know what to make of it," Jake said in disgust.

"Darling, what's that on her eye," my father asked in shock.

"I don't know! Is—is it some sort of disease? I mean, look at her face!"

My mother couldn't stand looking at me any longer so she covered my face with a blanket.

"If there's something horribly wrong with her, the doctor will know, but the twins and Auburn must leave the room." My father left to fetch the doctor.

"Oh my sweet, why are you so, so different? Why must you be ill?" When Mother uncovered my face, I smiled; she rocked me back and forth while everyone else was in a distant place outside of the room.

My father returned with the doctor. He was serious, his expression filled with worry.

"Let me see the child please, Mrs. Parker. May I?"

My mother gently handed me to the doctor. His hands were icy cold.

"From what I can see, it's a strange and peculiar case."

He seemed lost in his own little world until my father's voice boomed throughout the room: "DOCTOR! Tell us what is wrong with our child!"

"I'm terribly sorry, Mr. Parker. I seem to have gotten lost in my own thoughts. Now as for your daughter, listen carefully to what I have to say to you."

"Yes, whatever it is, please tell us! Tell us what is wrong with our child!" My mother cried, tears running down her face. I didn't understand why she was so upset. I tried to cheer her up by smiling.

"There, right there on her face. According to my studies, it's called a *smile*, and then there, you see that in her eye? That is a *twinkle* or a *spark of joy*."

"Is there anything we can do? Is it a disease? Please, doctor, you must help us!"

"I'm afraid the only thing you can do is wait, wait and hope that as the years go by, it fades away and never comes back. I'm afraid there is nothing I can do for your daughter."

"Thank you, we shall do as you instruct. If it does not go away then we shall just have to deal with it in a different way, won't we?" Father said while looking at my mother.

"What other way can there be?"

"Patience, Mrs. Parker. You are free to leave today. I wish you good luck and hope that your daughter gets well." With that, the doctor left the room.

My father took the twins home and came back later for my sister, my mother, and me. The car was red and wasn't much to look at, but it fit everyone. I looked out the window trying to make out the world that I had just entered. It interested me so much that I couldn't help but imagine so many things. But then my stomach began to rumble, and I wondered how I could catch their attention. I could just wait until my mom decided to feed me, but my stomach was rumbling again, a bit louder this time. I could no longer hold it in. They needed to know my situation.

"Waaaahh! Waaaahh! Waaaahh!"

Ugh! What was that horrible sound? Wait! Was that me?

"Mom, shut her up! What's wrong with her?" Auburn

seemed to have noticed whatever it was I was doing.

"Honey, she must be hungry. Give her her bottle," my mother said.

Auburn forced it into my mouth. It was disgusting! Eww! They couldn't expect me to drink this! I spit the liquid out.

"Ugh, you brat! Mother, look at what she's done! Eww! I am so not feeding her anymore." With that, the bottle disappeared, and I was left with nothing.

When the car stopped, my mother made her way to my side to pick me up. Her grip on me felt like she was afraid to even touch me. I could see that our house was small, with windows covered in spiderwebs. The garden was full of weeds, and it looked almost as if no one had lived there for years. My father was opening the front door of the house but had trouble getting the right key in the lock. We waited, but he just couldn't get it right. His hands were shaking, and his expression was blank as if he was trying hard not to show any emotion. I wondered what was wrong with him.

Finally, Auburn just took the keys from him and opened the door.

"Mother, what did the doctor say?" Damien asked.

Mother looked down at the floor and started to cry.

Jake embraced her. "Don't worry, Ma. It's going to be all right. She'll get better; you'll see."

"Yeah, right! Can't you see she's a freak and she'll never be like any of us? Why bother? Why don't we just abandon her somewhere? She won't ever get better," Auburn said with a smirk.

Mother cried harder. She handed me to Damien and left the room.

"Now look what you've done! Auburn, can't you be considerate of Mother just for once?" With that, Damien took me with him to his room and, over the days to follow, became more of a parent than my father or my mother.

He was the kindest one of all to me. He really understood me, though he never did show it much around my parents. He took care of me when everyone else was gone, and played with me as no one else would. Auburn and Jake would go to school early while my dad and mom got ready for work. Damien was the only one who would feed me, change my clothes, and do everything I needed. When it was time to go to school, Damien would take me to our next-door neighbor's home. That was how I moved through life, year by year. Before I knew it, I was beginning kindergarten.

Nothing changed when I started school. My mom never attended parent conferences, and I began to wonder whether Damien was my real dad. My parents were getting complaints from school, something about me showing too much interest in reading. One teacher actually told my parents that I was coloring and talking to myself, as if someone was really there.

My parents got really upset. They took away my books, and then they took me to a room where there was only a chair and a desk. I spent one hour in there for every letter I wrote. I didn't like it, but there was nothing I could do—until the day when I realized my mind could fill this place. After that, images began to swirl around the room in different colors.

Before I knew it, I was in second then third grade. No one would really talk to me at school, and when they did, they called me a freak. One day at lunch, I was sitting by myself at a table, and an idea came into my head. I took out a pencil and paper, and wrote without stopping. By the end of lunch, I had four pages of a story. I thought it was nothing special, but apparently it was worse than talking to myself while coloring. My parents' faces went white as chalk when they read the letter from school. This was all it took to get me homeschooled, and, after study time was over, I now had to do chores around the house so that my mind was too occupied to think "horrible thoughts."

I struggle out of the store with four bags full of rice and tomatoes. I'm only in sixth grade, and it feels as if my hands are about to fall off. I try to keep everything balanced so I don't drop anything. As I cross the street, I have a feeling someone is watching me.

Out of nowhere, something falls on my face.

"Ahhh!"

I drop the bags and reach toward whatever it is. It's furry.

"Will you stop the racket? I'm only trying to get a ride. What in the world do you think you're doing, young lady? Dust yourself off and pick up those groceries. They should not be on the ground. You have to be more careful. People will think you've completely lost it."

The thing is talking. The thing is talking! Oddly, I find myself doing as it instructed.

"Allow me to introduce myself. I am Steven. I—"

I reach up to pull him off my head. He is red and brown, and looks *weird*. Carefully, I look around. People are staring at me, people who know my parents! I quickly grab the bags along with my attacker. He looks like a ferret, one with awful colors. I wonder where he came from.

"Hey, quit the yakkin' in your head, will you? I don't have all day, young lady! You need to make a very important decision now."

Huh? A ferret is *talking* to me? "Who are you? Wait! What are you talking about?"

"Well, are you, or are you not, going to go forth with your mission?"

"What mission?"

"If you want to make things right, follow me."

"I'm sorry. I can't. For all I know, this a trap set up by my brother. I don't know you." I set him on the concrete curb.

"Kira! What on earth are you doing?"

That sounds like my father! No sooner do I turn than Steven is flying, crashing into a wall.

"Nooo!" I run toward Steven. He is bleeding.

Something catches my arm. It's my father. Struggling to get free, I pull my hand as hard as I can, but it's no use. Steven is out of sight now. It seems to take forever for my father to drag me home.

"What did you think you were doing? People were staring at you like you were a lunatic! Don't you know how to act when you're out on the streets? Talking! Talking to a ferret! Dear Lord!" Pacing in the kitchen, he looks as if *he* were the crazy one.

My mom comes into the room.

"James? What's going on here? Kira, where are those groceries I asked you for?"

My dad gesticulated wildly. "Our daughter was talking to a ferret in front of everyone!"

"You did what? How could you? Why? What were you thinking!" My mom comes toward me and grabs me by the shoulders. "Honey, you can't be doing this! You know perfectly well that we are trying to cure you! What you are doing is not normal, can't you see?" She is shaking me softly, and I feel my head wobble like a bird's head when it walks.

"Enough!" screams my father. "Kira, go to the punishment room!" He leaves without another word, and I have no choice but to go to the room yet again.

I have been in here for hours, and my eyes are growing tired. They are almost completely closed when something jumps on my lap. Steven!

"What on earth are you doing here? If my father sees you...well, the consequences will be severe."

"We don't have much time! We need to leave right now before your father comes back."

"Where are we going?"

"Never mind that right now! Get your things ready!"

"All right, but it's not going to be easy."

I rush to my room and quietly begin packing a small bag with only what is necessary. No one is in sight when I make my way back to the punishment room.

"Okay, Steven, I'm ready, but how far are we going?"

"The trip is not what you think. Be prepared and follow me."

He leads me to my backyard, scurries up a tree, and comes down again just as fast with a couple of leaves. He then throws the leaves over our heads, and suddenly we are standing in front of a cave.

"Wow. How did you do that?" I ask. I never thought something like that was possible.

"Never mind how. You need to go inside that cave. It's the only way," Steven says, standing on his two front legs right next to the entrance.

"But where does this lead to?"

"I already told you, you need to go in there if you want to find your true sanctuary. But if you don't believe me, so be it."

"No, I believe you. I just don't know if I should be leaving. I've always wanted to, but now I'm not so sure."

"*You're not sure?* By any chance did you get hit on the head in the last twenty-four hours? You have wanted to leave this place for the last three years, and now you say you're not sure? Kira, you need to do this! I know you're afraid, but use that as your motivation!"

"Steven! I'm weak, no stronger than a weed growing in a dark place! Can't you understand that?"

"Fine, have it your way! Be what your father is, what your entire world is! Be a failure! Live in a world where everything is as lifeless as a dead rose! Is this what you have become? Someone who has lost all faith in herself? I cannot stand such idiocy!"

Nothing more need be said. I realize Steven is right, and I cannot allow myself to become something I have been fighting not to become. Now my time has come. The air suddenly changes from a blazing hell to a sweet, calming sea breeze, then a rich smell of earth—the unmistakable scent of life when the morning sun rises and brings with it the feel of leaves and trees and all living things—flowing around me in a way that makes me feel like I'm floating and dancing.

"All right, Steven. I'm ready. I—well, I now understand what I have to do." As I say this I feel my body resisting. I'm immobilized, like I've been trapped in quicksand, a deadly trap that I cannot escape from.

"Kira, pay close attention. Inside is the key to your mission. No matter what happens, you must not give in to temptation and back down. Fear will try and overcome you, but do not allow that to stop you. No matter what, always remember what you're there for, and keep a firm stand. You will find others and be reunited with the one that first came."

I have no idea what he means by that.

"Right. Thanks, Steven." I gave him a hug and head toward the cave. I have an ominous feeling as I approach, and once I'm inside it's so dark I can hardly see. On the path I hear what sounds like growling. It becomes louder and louder, as if whatever is making the sound is getting closer. I turn around and see that the cave is collapsing. Immediately, I start to run, going deeper into the cave. Looking for shelter, I find a corner where I can bury my face between my knees and place my hands over my ears. I wait for the impact to be over.

Then there is nothing; the sound of emptiness fills what's left of the cave. I decide that it's safe to get up, but soon I feel panic: what if I don't get out? What if I don't find the way I'm supposed to go? Slowly, I move toward where the entrance was and reach for the rocks that are blocking my way out. No use—they're too heavy to move.

"Steven! I'm trapped!" I wait for a few minutes, but there is no answer. I am all alone, and there is no one to help me. I'm scared. My feet can no longer carry me. My body has been drained of all its energy. I decide to rest for the night. Tomorrow will be another day, and maybe I'll find a way out of here. I curl up against the wall, which is nice and warm, and I immediately fall asleep.

I wake up a couple of hours later. I get up and pick up my bag. There's only one path. I have no choice but to follow it. After some time, I find myself in a very well-lit chamber in the cave, standing next to the biggest book I have ever seen. I feel like an ant staring up at something as large as a human. There can be no such thing as a book this big. Carefully, I walk toward it, thinking it might be a trap. I reach toward the book, and my whole body begins to tremble. With great care, I try to turn a page, but because every page weighs as much as a sack of rice, it's not easy.

After what seems like hours, I am able to turn the pages. My eyes must be deceiving me. This can't be! I'm filled with horror. The pictures on the page can't be true! There are images of burning buildings with people lying on the ground, all of them dead. I recognize one of the buildings even though there is nearly nothing left of it. There are other images of houses, all of them deserted. It is the most horrifying thing I have seen in my life. Under the pictures, a caption reads:

*Here are the remains of the Pharmacy of the East,
one of the best pharmacies of its time—until it was
destroyed by those possessed by It. They have destroyed this world and everything that once lived.
They were the beginning of the end.*

Everything my parents thought, everything they said
about people like me can't be true! We never caused anyone any problems. *Your kind doesn't deserve to live! Your
love for books and imagination will ruin us! There's more to
life than just reading! Mark my words: the day this world
ceases to exist, it will all be your fault!* My father's words
shoot through my head like a bullet though my stomach.
My hands are shaking; my eyes remain fixed on the page,
looking at the images.

Then the images change. It is the same scenery, except
everything is perfect. Everything is how it's supposed to
be. Nothing is ruined, and everyone is living in harmony. I
feel as confused as someone who doesn't know the answer
to $2 + 2$. The caption under these images reads:

*The Pharmacy of the East is one of the best of its
kind. It delivers the best customer service and refuses service to no one. Everyone lives in peace.
Those with special needs (with It) have made such a
positive change in our community. Now everything
is balanced, and no one is discriminated against
for what they like or who they are. Children are
allowed to enjoy themselves and do as they wish—
play, read books, color—as long as they are safe
from harm.*

As soon as I finish reading, the book shrinks to pocket
size. I pick it up and examine it. When I look up, I find
myself in front of a door. I put the book in my pocket and
open the door slowly. It is pitch black, but there is no other
way out of the cave. I have no choice but to walk into the
darkness. Soon I am in a room filled with piles of books,
and I feel as if I am being watched.

A strange voice booms: "Are you going to stand there
forever? On the move! I need those books now!"

"Where am I?" I turn around, but no one's there.
Everywhere I turn, all I can see are books, books, and more
books.

Then I see my parents. "Mom! Dad!" I want to go home, though I know if I go back, all of these books, everything, will go up in smoke. Then my parents disappear.

"Didn't you hear me? I said move! I need those books," a woman yells.

I run as fast as I can, but my feet slip. I lose my balance, falling through a hole in the floor. I end up out in the open, stuck in a pit of mud.

"Ow! Aw, you have got to be kidding me! Mud? Anyone out there! Please! I need help!"

A pair of eyes, completely white, appears from out of nowhere. Whatever it is, it just stares at me.

"Please help me—I'm stuck!" I yell as loud as I can.

"How did you get there?" The pair of eyes comes closer to me until I see a girl around my age.

"I was running and wasn't looking, and I kind of fell into the pit," I explain.

Her figure starts to change, and she becomes a giant bird that looks ready to eat its prey.

"Hold on to my beak so I can pull you out. Hold on really tight." She moves closer, and I take hold. With one swift move she pulls me out of the pit.

"Thank you so much! You're—"

"A freak, that's what I am. I don't even know why you're standing there now. You should have run away. Don't you think I'm going to eat you?" She returns to her normal self.

"Why would I ever say such a thing? You're no freak. You're very special—a shape-shifter, am I right? I've always wished beings like you existed."

"You mean it? Wow! Thanks! I'm Phoebe. Nice to meet you." She smiles, extending her hand.

"Nice to meet you too. I'm Kira...and thank you for helping me out." I smile back and shake her hand.

She suddenly bursts out laughing.

"Um, are you okay? What's so funny?" I must have made a funny face, because she only laughed harder. "What? Did I do something wrong?" Her face is as blue as a blueberry.

"No! I'm sorry! I can't help it! You have no shoes, and you look like you're covered in chocolate! Well, except your head. That's the only thing that looks normal." She starts to calm down a bit.

"Nice to know I amuse you. I'll be on my way now."

"No! Please, I'm really sorry. I just couldn't help myself. Please forgive me. Where are you going? Can I come with you?"

"I have no clue where I'm going, but you can come with me. I guess I'll be wandering around until I find the answer."

We start walking in a random direction, and along the way we encounter the weirdest things I have ever seen. We walk for a couple of hours until we reach a clearing with what seems like every kind of fruit tree. My mouth melts like cotton candy in water as I walk up to a tree that has really nice, juicy-looking apples. But something jumps in front of us, knocking us both to the ground. I look up and see big, white, sharp teeth and the eyes of a creature that growls so loud that I jump to my feet and back away.

"This place is forbidden to all outsiders!" I can now see it is a wolf, a white female with lavender eyes.

"I'm sorry. We didn't know, but can you please just let us get something to eat? We're really hungry, and we have no food."

"What did you not understand about outsiders?" She growls, stepping forward but limping. I notice a knife in her right leg. I slowly move toward her.

"Kira, lets go! We'll find food elsewhere. Please don't go anywhere near her."

I can't do what Phoebe is telling me. I have to help this creature.

"Get back! If you come any closer, I'll rip you to shreds!" She steps back slowly, pain flashing in her face, and she falls to the ground next to the apple tree. I rush to her and slowly pull the knife out. She whimpers a little. I rip off a bit of my shorts and tie it around the wound.

"Thank you. In return you may have some fruit, but you only have five minutes." She looks away, saying nothing more.

"Really? Thank you very much!"

Phoebe and I run to the nearest tree and begin eating. When we are finally satisfied, Phoebe takes some fruit for the trip ahead.

"Thank you so much for the food. I hope you feel better soon," I say.

"Yeah, yeah," the wolf practically whispers.

"Do you want to join us? We're trying to find whatever it is that can help me help my world." I really hope she'll come. She seems so lonely.

"Thanks, but no thanks. I'll stay here." She looks up at the sky.

"If you're sure. Well, goodbye, and thanks for the food."

After we leave the pasture and cross a bridge, Phoebe says, "I think she has anger management issues."

"Don't say that! It's not nice."

"But it's true! I mean, didn't you see how she was acting?"

"That's still not a nice thing to say, you know..."

"KIRA!" Phoebe screams as the wolf comes from nowhere and tackles her.

I rush over to them. "Please let her go! Please don't hurt her!"

"I'm not going to. I just wanted to scare her for saying those things about me." The wolf climbs off Phoebe.

"So, care to join us?" I'm quite happy she followed us.

"Yes, but only because I can tell you're the type that gets into a lot of trouble and needs help. I'm Shikha."

With that, we continue on our way.

The next day we are still walking after five hours and thirty minutes on the road. My feet ache really badly, and my pace is starting to slow down. Shikha and Phoebe are far ahead of me.

"Yo, Kira! Come on! Don't be such a slowpoke," Shikha yells.

Phoebe, now in her bird form, is getting a ride from Shikha. She sings, "Aw, come on Kira, only a little bit left!"

"I'm coming! You guys have it easy! Shikha, you're obviously used to long walks, and Phoebe, you only have to transform into something light enough and you can ride on Shikha's back."

My feet drag across the earth's muddy surface. I feel like

I'm not walking straight anymore. My feet begin to wander off the path. Soon, no one is in front of me, neither Phoebe nor Shikha. I am alone. My head spins. Suddenly, I no longer feel the earth's soft soil. I'm flying. Something catches me. I don't know where I am or what's going on, and I give in to exhaustion.

What in the world! What is she trying to do? Kill herself? Lousy, good-for-nothing girl! She's quite light. Doesn't she ever eat? I wonder where she came from. No one comes by this place anymore. I'll take her with me, just to make sure she's okay. Hey you, wake up! Well, let's see if some nice cold water will do.

"Ah! Cold! Cold! Cold!" I jump up, wiping the cold water off me.

"Hey, Sleeping Beauty. That water helped a bit. You're finally awake," a male's voice says.

"What?" I turn around to face him. He has purple-black hair and gray, clay-like eyes. My body freezes.

"Somebody in there? Hello!"

"Huh? Oh, um, I'm sorry. Where am I?" I ask while looking around.

"You are in the Myst Library, built in ancient days by an extinct race that was advanced beyond our knowledge. Now it's all ruins. It's pretty safe, so you have nothing to worry about," he says while sitting on a sofa chair.

"How exactly did I get here, and where are Shikha and Phoebe?"

"I don't know who you're talking about, but you fell from the edge of the cliff, and I happened to catch you. I brought you here because I thought you were alone. I'm Koko," he says, while cracking his wrist.

"Thank you for saving my life. It's nice to meet you. I'm Kira. I'm sorry, but I must be going. I have to find my friends." I start to leave, but he pulls me back.

"You can't leave. I won't let you. Your friends should be fine, but you have everything anyone ever dreamed of here. Let me show you around." He grabs my hand and takes me deeper into the Myst Library.

"No, please, I really must be off. They need me, and I

need them." I try to free myself from his grip. He reminds me of the grip my dad had on me when I was trying to go back to Steven. I shudder at the thought.

"Not until you see this awesome collection I have. It was falling apart, and I put it back together myself."

We go up a flight of stairs and enter a room I will never forget. A thousand shelves reveal true beauty—rows of books in different colors calling out to me. Never in my whole life did I think I would be in a true library. I search through the shelves, and a book called *Pearl's Earth* catches my attention. I begin to read it, and in a matter of minutes, I forget about everything else in this world. Hours later, when my stomach starts to rumble, I realize I need a break.

As I get up, I see figures in the distance in front of me, much like my dad's and my own when I was younger.

I told you! No reading! No books allowed! Why have you disobeyed me?

But, Daddy! I want to read it! Please, Daddy!

I wince as he hits me on the left side of my face followed by harsh whippings with a belt.

You thought you could disobey me and I wouldn't find out!

I shiver in fear.

You're really going to get it this time!

Tears roll down my face as I witness what my father did to me that day. I remember that by the time he was done, I thought someone had poured boiling water down my back.

"Hey Kira, I brought you something to eat. Are you okay?" Koko asks as he puts down a plate.

"Yeah, I'm okay. How long have I been here?" I slip the book in my bag.

"I would say about four days, yeah, around that." He sits down across from me while eating a bit of toast.

"Say what? You're lying. Wasn't I here for just a couple of minutes? I have to go find Shikha and Phoebe!" I get up and run downstairs.

"Kira, come back! Here you have what you want. No one will ever tell you what to do. Books! All yours! You can have them! I'll give you anything you want. Don't leave!"

I hear Koko's screams thoughout the library. I can't stay. I need to find my friends. I have wasted too much time here. I don't even know if they're all right.

"You'll regret leaving this place, Kira! No one gets away from the mighty Myst and goes unpunished!"

I don't stay around to find out what he means. I run as fast as I can and find a road ahead, and I don't stop until I'm out of breath. I fall to the ground from exhaustion and feel something poking my side. I rise just enough to feel around and find that it's the book about the Pharmacy of the East. At first, the images are blurry, but then they become clear. It is unbelievable. Everything is almost as it was in the last scene, the one with the smiling children, but there is something different about it.

It's balanced. I don't quite understand. There is the world of books, but also the world where my parents live, and nothing is destroyed. That means both worlds can exist without wiping out each other. The answer I have been seeking is inside this book! Now I have to find my friends and show them.

It takes me a couple of hours, but I finally find Phoebe and Shikha.

"Shikha! Phoebe! There you are! Where have you been?"

"Kira! We've missed you so much! We've been looking all over for you! We were worried sick! Even Shikha was busting her butt looking for you. Now she's exhausted and taking a nap."

"I'm really sorry, Phoebe! I was walking behind you when I started to drift off. A guy named Koko said I fell off a cliff, but then he wouldn't let me leave, and he took me to the Myst Library, and I started reading this book. I'm so sorry. The Myst was too much for me to snap out of."

"No biggie. The only thing that matters is that you're all right." Phoebe gives me a big warm hug. I can't believe how lucky I am to have found both of them.

As I let go of Phoebe, I can't help but remember what Koko said when I ran away from the Myst, and all the happiness drains from my body. I don't want to get my friends in trouble, nor risk their lives. I have to keep watch over them. "How long has Shikha been sleeping?"

"Two hours. I'm going to go wake her up so she can eat something. She hasn't really been eating." She walks over to Shikha and pokes her side. "Hey Shikha, wake up, time to eat," says Phoebe.

"I don't want to! Leave me alone!" Shikha throws a paw at her and then rolls back to sleep.

"Shikha, it's me, Kira. You need to eat something, and if you don't get up Phoebe and I are going to jump on you and poke you." I reach toward Shikha and poke her very gently.

The next thing I know Shikha is right in front of me, looking like she's going to kill me. "Kira! Where have you been? We've been looking for you all over the place! Do you know how many days you've been missing?"

"I didn't leave because I wanted to. I'm sorry I caused you guys so much trouble, but now is not the time to be mad at each other. We have to leave as soon as possible."

"What do you mean by that? Kira, what's going on?" There is a hint of panic in Phoebe's voice.

"I finally figured out what I've been looking for—what I have to do. But that's not why I want us to leave. Koko gave me a warning when I was running away from Myst. He said I would regret leaving and that no one ever gets away from the mighty Myst unpunished.

"I don't want to put your lives in danger. You guys should go your own way. I would never forgive myself if something happened to you." I turn away, not wanting to see the looks on their faces, hoping that they will leave and not risk their lives.

"You are out of your mind if you think I'm going to let you go on by yourself. We're in this together," Phoebe says while stroking Shikha's head.

"You got that right," Shikha growls. "Same goes for me, Kira! Get ready! There's going to be a war." Shikha's into all kinds of fighting.

"Thank you. Now come on. We all need to eat."

After we each have our share, Shikha and Phoebe go to sleep, but I'm not really tired. Instead, I stare at the stars that never stop shining and guiding us through our journey. A couple of minutes later, I hear a loud rattling in the bushes.

"Who's there?" I begin to panic. What if it's Koko? I have to get away from here; I will not allow my friends to get hurt. I quietly slip away from Phoebe and Shikha. I run through the trees, and something jumps onto my shoulder.

"Ah! Get off me!" I struggle to push my attacker away, but I find nothing but air.

"Stop all that fidgeting, Kira! Is this how you greet me after all this time? Sheesh! Sometimes I ask myself why I even bother."

Steven?

"How on earth did you find me? Where have you been?"

"That doesn't matter! We must hurry. I'm afraid Koko will find your friends soon enough. We need to get them to safety."

"How do you know all of this?"

"No time for explanations! Now run back to the campsite! We have to reach Phoebe and Shikha now if you want them to live!" Steven runs up to the top of my head, sending a shiver down my spine.

I run as fast as my feet will carry me, and within a couple of minutes, we are back at the campsite.

"Shikha! Phoebe! Wake up! We have to go now!" I begin to panic when they don't move. I run to Phoebe's side and try to wake her, but it's no use. She's in a deep sleep. I move on to Shikha, but again, no use. "Steven, they won't get up! What do I do?"

"Anything! We can't waste even a minute! Get water and pour it on their faces!" Steven jumps off my head and down to the ground. I find a water bottle inside my bag and pour half of it on Phoebe, half on Shikha.

"Hey! What did you do that for!" yells Phoebe.

"Hey, what's the big deal?" growls Shikha, while shaking off the water.

"We have to leave now. Koko is getting close. Come on! Steven will guide us! Phoebe, can you change into something that can carry Steven and me?"

"You want to go by sky or land?" She starts to change into an enormous bald eagle.

"Land would be best since Shikha can't fly."

"Right, on it." Phoebe changes into a towering wolf, bigger than Shikha, with grayish fur and ocean-blue eyes.

"Come on, Steven! Shikha, follow us, okay?" Phoebe bows down so that Steven and I can get on her back. As soon as everyone is set, Phoebe and Shikha begin the race of their lives.

"There they are! On the move! If you bloody creatures don't capture them, it will be the end of you!"

My body freezes as Koko's words run right through me. I turn to see griffins, panthers, and rhinos.

"Come on, Phoebe! We have to lose them! Shikha, can you last a bit longer?"

"Just keep going!" Shikha growls as a griffin takes hold of her back.

"Shikha! No! Phoebe, stop! We need to go back! They got Shikha!"

Phoebe stops suddenly, and she sends me flying into a tree. The impact is harsh, but I quickly climb down and run toward Shikha.

The griffin releases her, but her back is bleeding.

"Kira, get out of here now!" She struggles to get up.

Within a few seconds, we are surrounded by Koko's creatures.

"I warned you, Kira! No one goes unpunished when they leave the Myst." He smirks.

"Kira!" Phoebe's voice booms as she attacks our pursuers and sends a large number of them flying. She is back to her normal shape and has a sword in her hands. Shikha starts attacking whatever comes in front of her. Steven is nowhere in sight. We are outnumbered. There is no way we will make it out alive.

Steven is back and signaling to me. "Kira, this way out!"

I signal to Shikha and Phoebe. They start to retreat slowly, still fighting so that we won't be overrun. Up ahead, purple rays of light are shining so bright that I think it's the sun. As we get closer, it starts to fade away. It is some sort of portal inside a tree. My heart sinks. I knew this moment would come, but I didn't think it would come so fast.

"Kira, you know what you have to do! Now go! We'll keep them busy," Phoebe yells as she battles a griffin.

"She's right, Kira! Go while we can still hold them

back!" Shikha's back and legs are badly injured, and she stands on two legs while trying to battle a rhino.

"Shikha! I don't want to go back!" I fall to my knees by the path that leads home. Everything seems to have gone by too quickly. My heart betrays what I feel; it will always belong here.

Shikha says, "Kira, listen to me! You have to go back. You are no longer merely a weak child. Nothing is going to be the same ever again, and you must go back. Remember why you came here in the first place."

As much as I wish she were just plain wrong, I know nothing more can be said. I have to go back.

"Now get out of here," Shikha yells, pushing me through the tree trunk. The last thing I see are my friends battling against those fearsome creatures.

Somehow I'm back in my room. Quickly, I reach into my pocket and find the book still there. I run to my brother's room.

"Damien! Where are Mom and Dad?" I am out of breath, and my legs feel like jelly.

"Kira, where have you been? Mom and Dad have been looking all over for you! They're at the police department right now! Why are you such a mess?" His face is full of worry. I missed my brother, but now isn't the time for a reunion. I have to find my parents.

I run out of the house without another word and head to the police station. After what seems like hours, I reach the parking lot, and there are my parents. They stare at me for a couple of seconds, and I freeze, afraid. I reach toward my pocket, grab the book, and walk over to my parents.

"Kira, where have you been? You've been missing for two weeks!" My mother raises her hands to hit me, but for once, I'm not scared. I wait for the impact, but nothing happens. Instead, I feel arms embracing me. My eyes open and grow wide when I realize my father is hugging me.

"Marie, don't you hit her! She's back! Our daughter, she's back." Tears fall from my father's eyes. Something in him has changed, and in my mother as well; it is as if they have switched places. I never thought my father would one day be my protector. I return his hug and then break away.

"Please, hear me out." I take out the book and show them the images I first saw—everything destroyed, nothing left of our home or the others that met the same fate.

"Dad, this is what you and Mother think will happen at the hands of people like me, but that's not true."

Lurching toward me, my mother knocks the book out of my hands. "You see! Our world will be nothing but a memory because of people like you!" My dad grabs her by the hands.

I immediately reach for the book, ignoring her violent wails. With a shaky voice, I try to explain everything to them. "Here are more images, but look: it's my world, the one I want to live in. The two worlds can coexist as one, in peace and harmony."

My dad looks at the book. "Kira...is this really possible?" His fingers trace through the book. "All right then. We'll make it work."

My mother is still unsure, but I see something peculiar in her face. I don't know what she sees, but whatever it is, her expression softens; she now understands.

"Kira, come on. We have to show everyone and prove to them that people like you aren't bad." She gives me a tight hug. "Don't you ever leave us like that again, understand?"

All I can do is nod.

It's been a couple of months since I got back and tried to convince everyone. It wasn't an easy job, but the book seemed to change hearts and minds. Soon enough, there were children running around, coloring the sidewalk with chalk, and reading, but also doing their homework. Everything is perfect.

"Kira! Can you please come in the house?" my mom calls.

As I walk over to the front door, I see a little girl hopping on one leg. Inside the house, I find my parents in the kitchen.

"Kira, Damien is waiting for you at the park. Oh, and here. Take this." She hands me a picnic basket, and my dad tosses me a soccer ball. I look at the ball and can't help but smile; this is no longer a dream. My family, as well as the community, accepts everyone for who they are, and my parents are spending more time with my siblings and me. I am allowed to go back to school. Everything is balanced.

"See you later, Mom. Bye, Dad!" I wave and run to the park.

In the distance, I hear my name being called. I turn and see Jake and Auburn next to Damien. They have finally accepted me for who I am. My body feels as if it is a bubble flying freely in the air. They call out to me, waving and smiling. I drop the basket and soccer ball, and run toward them. Within moments, I'm tackled by Auburn, then Damien, and yes, Jake as well. They tickle me so hard that my sides ache and tears roll down my face. Once they stop, we just stay there, lying on the grass. My head tilts to the side, and I spot a little girl hiding behind a tree because she isn't allowed to read. She is who I once was, which is now nothing but a memory. She drifts away with the leaves and the refreshing summer air, never to return.

Rafael Cruz
CROWDED LEAVES

In a crowd, people feel comfortable:
As one they can't be hurt.
A bunch of leaves forms a gorgeous tree.
A time comes when a single person decides to leave the
    crowd.
Like a leaf breaking away from the tree.
Through challenges they will go.
A disintegrating leaf will travel with the wind.
A person will have changed,
Independent unlike the rest

Maria G. Mena
LILY BY THE SUNSET

Lying in bed, Georgiana recounts precious memories.

Life-shattering occurrences.
Hardly anyone would be able to relate.
A letter with an arranged betrothal.
Broken dreams.
The only condolence was her dear sister, Harriet.

On a boring trip to the bridal store
A boy she met, Charles his name was—
Oh, how different he was.
They went to the Huntington Gardens that day
He took that pink lily from the garden
and placed it in her hand
and held another with good intentions.
They fell in love,
so deeply,
nothing could be done to escape.

Months passed.
Behind her parents' backs
even Harriet's
they secretly met.
He proposed with that pink lily.
It couldn't be helped any longer.
She ended the arranged engagement,
only to be trapped in her room by her parents.

Such an unforgivable act of greed:
They only cared about money.

She gave Harriet Charles's information
and they plotted.

On Georgiana's wedding day,
Charles and Harriet broke through the cathedral door.
With a pink lily bouquet in hand, he knelt and asked
    Georgiana to be with him.
She accepted, with tears streaming down her face,
in front of hundreds of bewildered eyes

In bed, Georgiana remembers those days.

Tomorrow they're to be married; what a splendid day that
    will be.
Two destined souls are soon to make their vows.
Tomorrow at the Huntington,
they will marry,
in that lily garden,
by the sunset.

OVER THE RIVER...

Mirian Martinez
THE ROAD OF TRIALS

Heroes surround every one of us. They could be your friends, family, or people you don't even know. From my perspective, a hero's journey starts when struggles occur, and those struggles develop your inner hero. A true hero is someone who doesn't think only about himself or herself, but also about others. A true hero is capable of understanding the world and its misfortunes.

Life is a roller coaster. It has its ups and downs, and a true hero goes on the ride and learns from each rise and fall. Ultimately the hero will triumph over his fears and obstacles to become a better person. One hero's journey that I have personally witnessed was when my mother decided to come to Los Angeles and look for my father. She had to make a huge decision: stay in Mexico or come to Los Angeles. Her call to adventure was when she realized that she wanted a better life for my brother and me. She took the risk of coming to LA and crossed the first threshold when she crossed the border, moving between a world she was familiar with and one she was not. Starting a new life in the United States was her belly of the whale. Her road of trials was adapting to this new life and once again living with my father.

But life got tougher, not only for me and my brother, but also for my mother, who was challenged to survive a series of obstacles. She wasn't getting along with my father; they constantly argued for no reason. She knew something was wrong with my father but didn't know what it was. He would constantly leave the house during the evening and wouldn't come back until late at night. My mother didn't like this at all. Soon she decided to follow him and realized that he was cheating on her. She could not believe it, and neither could my brother and I. We had no idea what was happening or why we were leaving our father once again. We moved to an uncle's house, and he helped us when we needed him the most. To this day we still thank him for everything he did for us.

It was really hard to survive without the help of my father, but my mother never gave up. She looked for a job to give my brother and me the life she had planned for us. During those struggles, she found someone who really cared about her. This was rescue from without, her rescue by forces from the ordinary realm. For us, my stepfather is our real father because he is there for us when we need him. He is always there to give us advice, listen to our problems, and to give us his love. He is there like a real father should be. Now, I see my mother as the master of the two worlds because she survived her road of trials. To me, she's a true hero.

Studying the hero's journey helped me learn much more about myself. Before, I didn't care about heroes; the only ones on my mind were the ones on television like Spider-Man, Batman, and the Power Rangers. I didn't pay much attention to the real heroes, the heroes that surrounded me. I just looked at them as ordinary people. But as I learned more about the hero's journey, I realized that I was wrong. I am surrounded by heroes. My friends are heroes because they are always there when I need them. My teachers are also my heroes because they prepare me for the future, and that's what a true hero should do, help others in the best way possible.

I also learned that I am capable of doing the things that I set my mind to. You can achieve anything by working hard. Writing my hero's journey was very difficult and stressful, but when I finish writing, I feel relieved, surprised, and proud—relieved because I get time to relax and think back on how much time I spent, surprised because at first I can't believe I actually did it, and proud because I get the chance to say, "I wrote that." And that is an amazing feeling.

Eddie Flores
HOMECOMING

"*Hola*, Juan, *¿cómo estás?*" asked Mario. His voice was crackling.

"*Bien*—just here in Los Angeles, living day by day. *¿Y tu?*" answered Juan. He was happy to hear his brother's voice; they had not heard from each other since Juan left Honduras.

"Juan, are you seeing anyone?"

"No, not since what Tania did to me. What about you and Olga?"

"You know, she left us," said Mario.

"Oh, yeah, I remember," Juan said sarcastically.

"Well, what I'm trying to get at is, will you give me a hand while I'm in Los Angeles?"

"How can I help you?"

"I just need a place to stay for a little while."

"Sure," said Juan, "you can stay at my house."

"We won't be too much of a problem. You know it's only going to be Everr and me."

"Hey! Everr should be big by now."

"Yeah, and cute like his father," said Mario.

"Then I definitely want to meet him."

"Everything is set, then, for next week. We'll see you at the airport in Los Angeles."

We have just gotten off a flight from Honduras, and my uncle Juan is driving us to his house. Before we left for the U.S., my dad had just told me, "La vida allá tiene muchas oportunidades." (Life over there has many opportunities.) To me this is a big joke. Can you imagine a drunk mechanic and his son living in a city of hope? How will I have any opportunities?

My uncle parks in the backyard, and we get out of the car. There's a woman standing near the house. "I have a surprise for you," he tells us. "This is my good friend. Her name is Olga."

"Nice to meet you," my dad says, surprised.

Olga answers with a weird confidence and joy. "No, the pleasure is mine. And what is the young man's name?"

"This is Everr," my uncle says.

"Hello, pleasure to meet you. How do you know my uncle?" I ask.

My father and my uncle have a brief conversation off to the side, and then my father goes into the house.

"Oh, he's been a friend of mine ever since college in Honduras," Olga replies. "We went to the same bilingual school."

"Oh, I went to an elementary school that was bilingual. I'm sure you can still notice my heavy accent, though."

Olga laughs. "*Ay dios mío*, I remember when I started to speak English. Don't worry—my accent was worse."

"Excuse me for a moment; I need to talk to my uncle."

Uncle Juan is standing next to the grill, holding tongs and a knife, and wearing a "Kiss the Cook" apron. This is the first time I've seen him do anything other than ride a horse. I have fond memories of him in Honduras at the *carrera de cinta*, where most people knew my uncle as Juan "*Caballo*." "Where is my dad?" I ask.

"Your dad is taking too long."

"What is he doing?"

"Don't worry; your dad is in the restroom. Go tell him that the meat is cooked."

I step into the house, which is very well-decorated. The living room is magnificent, with love seats that match the curtains and pictures of the family in nice frames. Nice lamps, too. In my mind, the single life is worth everything. My uncle cooks, cleans, and has adapted to life without a wife. I remember my dad telling me, "El día que te cases, búscate una buena mujer. Que cocine, limpie, y todo lo de la casa." (The day that you get married, find a good wife. She should cook, clean, and do all the housework.) To me that was the worst advice ever. My grandma, on the other hand, told me, "Nunca es malo aprender." (It is never bad to learn.) I think my grandma is right.

After admiring my uncle's living room, I make a right and see two doors. I knock on the left door and say, "Dad, the food is ready!" Nothing happens. The door on the right side must be the bathroom, so I try again. "Dad, the food is ready!"

"I'll be right there."

I leave and go back to the small barbecue. My dad comes out a minute later, looking rushed. My uncle yells at him: "Go with Everr and move the table so we can eat!"

"Okay!"

The tables are like the ones they have in the parks, only this one is heavy and made out of wood.

"Everr, you get one side, and I'll get the other," says my dad.

"Okay—ah, ¡espérate!" (Wait!) I yell with dread.

My dad quickly runs to my side. "Son, what happened?" he asks.

"I think I have a splinter in my thumb."

Relieved, my dad says, "Oh, don't worry. Let's keep moving the table."

"Okay."

I grab my side of the table, my dad gets the other, and we lift the table up. Wow, it's heavy. We work hard to move the table to the middle of the yard, which is only a couple of feet away.

My dad and I sit down next to each other, and my uncle and Olga bring plates, cups, napkins, and maybe six bowls of food covered with aluminum foil. "We have a little bit of everything," says my uncle.

"Oh really, Uncle? What do you have?"

"*Tajadas verdes, chismol, baliadas*" (green plantain, Honduran salsa, tortillas with refried beans), says Uncle Juan, "and carne asada, tacos, hamburgers, and rice and beans."

"*Qué rico*, just like eating at home. Right, Dad?"

"Yes, almost like in Honduras," he agrees. My dad's forehead is wrinkled, and it seems like steam is going to come out of his ears. "Are we going to eat or what?"

"Of course!" says my uncle. We start to eat. "How are the *tajadas verdes*?" he asks.

"They are just like our mom's," my dad says.

"Who do you think taught me how to cook like this?" says my uncle. "Olga, you can see he has always been the spoiled one in the family."

"Yeah, I remember when he used to tell me—" Olga says.

"I thought you were only friends with Uncle Juan," I interrupt.

"No, I also met your father before."

"Pa, is this true?" I ask. I look at my dad and give him a wink.

He fills his mouth with a *tajada* and some *chismol*. "Uh, um, uh," he mumbles.

"Slow down, Mario. The food is delicious, but you had this privilege almost every day."

My dad looks angrily at my uncle. The wrinkles in his forehead appear again. He keeps eating.

Olga asks, "Mario, what kind of work do you do?"

"I was a mechanic."

"And how did you pay for Everr's bilingual school?"

My dad takes another bite, and his mouth is full again.

"Dad, really, how did you pay? I've never seen you work on a car."

My dad starts to cough incredibly hard. I start patting his back. "Dad, are you okay? Drink some water!"

He keeps on coughing, and his face turns red. "Déjame... ir...al...baño..." (Let me go to the bathroom...)

"Run, Dad!"

My dad goes running. After he goes inside, my uncle keeps the conversation going. "Everr, where do you think all the money for your education came from?"

"I don't know. If you know, why don't you tell me?"

"Let's make sure to ask your dad when he comes back."

My dad arrives three minutes later. "Ah, I should eat more slowly."

"Pa, where did the money for my education come from? You never told me."

Everyone looks at my dad anxiously. It feels like he is testifying and everyone wants to hear what he's going to say. "Well, I had some money saved up."

"I don't mean to be nosy, but where did the money come from?" Olga asks.

"From my work as a mechanic."

"Juan always told me that you never did anything. You were like Snoopy, always relaxing on top of the house."

"It's true. From the day he got married, Mario never did anything; he never had any responsibility," Juan adds.

I knew some of this was true. My father was always at home. He never spoke about his relationship with my mother. "Pa, how did your relationship with my mother end?"

"Everr, would you really like to know?" asks my father.

"Yes."

"Well...um..."

"Mario, what's wrong with you? Either you tell him, or I'll tell him," says my uncle.

"What do I have to tell him?"

Suddenly, Olga throws *chismol* at my dad's face, and he falls back, away from the table. She walks to him and says, "Coward, you won't tell him, but I will."

"What is there to tell him?"

"Tell him who I am."

"Olga, I barely know you."

"Don't be a liar!"

"Me, a liar? Never!" my father insists.

"First, you're a moocher—" Olga starts.

"I never needed anyone's support! Everything I have, I worked for."

"Yeah, right, then why did I send 4,722 lempiras to you every two weeks?"

"You, send me money? Don't make me laugh."

"I have all the receipts from MoneyGram," says Olga. "You didn't need the money for hospital services for Everr!"

"I've never gone to the hospital," I say. "What's going on?"

Olga keeps going. "You said I couldn't speak to Everr because he was sick—"

"But the money was for Everr's education!" says my father.

"And why didn't you explain to Everr that I was here in Los Angeles?"

"Why would I need to know that?" I say.

"Everr, I am your mother!"

"What…how is this even possible? Dad, is it true, is Olga my mother?"

"Everr, why do you think your imbecile of a father was nervous?" asks Uncle Juan.

"Me, nervous? About what? There's nothing. It was just a fling."

Olga angrily spits at my dad's face. "You are garbage. You didn't even tell Everr anything. Maybe it was just a fling, but at least I'm not a man who doesn't take responsibility."

She turns to me.

"Everr, I never abandoned you."

"What is going on? All of you are liars."

My uncle steps in. "Let me explain. Your dad is garbage. He and Olga met when they were eighteen. They had a relationship, but they made some mistakes. The first was Olga believing in your snake of a father and his love. And then you were born. At least Olga worked to support you."

"Juan, I am your brother," says my dad. "You're supposed to be on my side."

"No, Mario, some things are unjust and unforgivable."

"But it was our mother!"

"Don't blame Mom."

"But it was her fault! She was the one who told me that the love between Olga and me wasn't going to last."

My uncle punched my dad in the face. "This is what Olga should give you, some of your own medicine."

"I *am* responsible! I cared for Everr!" insists my father.

"And what about what you did to Olga? You think all of this was a small thing?" yells Uncle Juan.

"I don't care. What's done is done. Everr, who do you

believe, your dad or them? Take into account who you have lived with most of your life. I raised you."

"I don't even want to look at you," I say. "You hid things that were really important from me."

"Everr, how did you want me to tell you? These things are not easy to understand. Look at how you're reacting."

"There is no excuse, Dad. You failed me."

"Please understand—"

"No, there is no forgiveness for what you have done. Olga deserves respect, even more now after you played with her emotions."

"Everr, please tell me you will try to understand."

"Only time will tell."

I walk off with Olga and Uncle Juan.

"Everr, can I have a hug?" Olga asks.

"No, not yet. I can give you a chance, though."

"Sure, if you let me," she says. "And Juan, thank you for helping me catch Mario in his own lie."

"You are nobody to judge. Let God judge him," I say.

"But he deserves it," Olga says.

"Yes, he deserves all this and more. But don't let your heart do the judging."

Eddie Flores
THE PHOENIX

I see it in your glass-like eyes,
The sum of all your lies.
Your soul speaks,
Like the New York winter's breeze.

And it will never be the same,
The way I mention your name.
The image is there and will never leave
My mind but still I know

The gaze in your eyes
Where there lies an emptiness not even space has

But will I ever know,
From here where to go?

The future is a place all unknown,
Where the sun can illuminate

Ana Cristina Perez
THE LIVING PROPHECY

Amber, my assistant, comes in clacking her heels. "Would you like me to order your coffee?"

"Must you ask me what I want when you already know?" I roll my eyes in annoyance.

"Patrick has just called to confirm he will meet Jacqueline and Robert for the magazine layout."

"Well, did he expect I was going to take flowers to his door in congrats? Why doesn't anybody focus? FOCUS PEOPLE! Where is my agenda? Jesus! Doesn't anything get done when I'm not around?"

Hectic phone ringing, magazine photo shoots, clothing imported from France, designer appointments, the clacking of endless heels, the yelling, the paperwork, the balance sheets, new interns, my headache, but I escape the chaos of *Posh*'s office for some time alone.

Darkness settles out on the horizon as the sun shoots shadows of orange and red flames across Central Park. The breeze softly caresses my skin, and the memory comes back as if waking from the dead.

Hesitating, my grandmother said, "Chloe, honey...um... Mommy and Daddy have gone on a trip."

"And they didn't take me? Why wouldn't they take me? I bet they didn't want me to bother them, or maybe they were afraid I was going to ask for another dollhouse. But it isn't fair! It's not like I have so many," I say in a whining childish voice.

"No, no, they won't be back again. They are in heaven. You have to be strong; we have to be strong. There was a car accident, Chloe. Sometimes things are meant to be. We don't always have control of what happens, and we don't have control of time." And then, just like that, my mind shifts to a mossy aroma with memories of fresh-baked bread and sweet honey that remind me of my childhood. The birds would chirp from afar as my mother would spread the plaid picnic cloth onto the grass. She would always let me be the first to take a bite of her tropical fruitcake. The sun lit her smile, and the dark shades of her brunette hair reflected light into my eyes.

The sun kisses my cheeks...I take a deep breath...exhale...and look across the pond. My body starts to sway in the cold breeze. It's late. I follow the crescent moon's fluorescent shine as it illuminates my path over the pond's bridge back home.

Ring...ring...

My cell phone wakes me up with a sudden start. I drag my hand to the lamp stand and with small yawns answer, "Hello."

"Good morning, Chloe. You have a scheduled appointment this evening at Nobu at 7:30 p.m."

Meeting? Nobu. 7:30. Scheduled appointment. I don't have a meeting. What is this nonsense?

I look at my alarm clock: 5:30 a.m.

I can't fall back to sleep. In the kitchen, the coffee maker begins to brew. Coffee is always my morning smell of comfort. Clumsily crawling out of bed, I walk to the window and look below to 57th Street and the rushing taxicabs driving like madmen. It's crazy how time works. We go on and do what we have to do, but at the end of the day, time is just time. It's just another day, but that morning call monopolizes my thoughts. Is it the layout designer or the fashion stylist? I'll just find out when I get to work. It irritates me when assistants call so early. Have they no consideration that I might actually be *sleeping*?

✧✧✧

7:00 p.m.

Golden runners hang from the walls of the Japanese restaurant, and the wooden floor reflects the stone-covered walls. The vapors of sizzling grills and tempura blur together as the maître d' smiles and says, "Hello, Miss, right this way please."

How does he know I'm supposed to meet someone here?

He leads me to table at the far end of the dining room where a young man in a black tuxedo sits, swirling a glass of red wine. He stares at me with sultry brown eyes. He stands as I approach the table and pulls out the chair like a true gentleman. His physique resembles one of those muscle-toned actors only found in action films.

"Hello, I'm Ethan," he says.

"Chloe," I say, shaking his hand.

"Would you like a drink?" asks Ethan.

"No, thank you." Looking around the restaurant I ask, "I'm sorry, but what is this meeting about?"

"Do you like New York?" he asks.

Did he not hear me, or did he completely ignore my question? How dare he!

"Oh, of course I love New York. It's the city that never sleeps. There is always something *important* for me to do. And you?"

"I just arrived yesterday, and I find it too big for me."

"What brings you to New York?"

"You and business." He laughs, and the small white fencing of his teeth spans across his thin lips to the tip of his two prominent dimples. Just like the innocent smile of a child.

He said *you*. What does he mean?

"What about you? What brought you to New York?" he asks.

"Me...well, it was fashion."

He seems to be hypnotized by my white pearl earrings and asks, "Those are very unique earrings. Vintage?"

"Not exactly, my grandmother gave them to me. She passed away when I was very small. She was like a mother to me," I say.

"I understand. It's always hard when you lose somebody you love, but you're a successful woman despite your circumstances. You're very strong. That is truly impressive. Listen, I know this is not the time to hear about your life, but if I were you, I'd be careful."

Silence.

"I'm sorry. What...what did you say?" I ask, nervously looking at his face.

"You are in danger."

"What...what do you mean?"

His eyes drift downward to my red pencil skirt, and I immediately stand up from my chair and retreat from the table in fear. Before I know it, he grasps my hand and with a warm soothing touch pulls me close. I'm about to yell for help when he whispers, "I want to protect you." I look into his eyes and see the outline of my silhouette on his retinas.

"I'm sorry. I have to go," I tell him.

I move my hand away from his and retreat from the table without saying another word. Outside the restaurant, my hands shake, and my forehead begins to sweat in terror.

A cold breeze hits me, and I jump in fright. My coat flutters in the wind as I fight my way through the fog obscuring my sight. The stenches from the alleys overpower my nostrils, and the dirty streets are splashed with human spit and garbage. I feel like a black blotch of dried gum remaining in the streets. The neighborhood dogs howl in desperate cries of loneliness. Couples argue outside the restaurant. Why would I be in danger? Who would want to hurt me? The person who confirmed the appointment was not Amber; it was somebody else. How could I have missed it this morning? How could I have been fooled? But who called me? How did she get my number?

I've had insomnia for the past few days. The mere sight of food makes me nauseous, and I'd rather not eat. I look in the mirror, and my face becomes paler and paler by the hour as if death embodies me, like the appearance that haunted me after my parents' death. I was so lonely then, when I would get home after school to find nobody waiting for me. The house was empty, cold, and silent at night. There were no longer the good-night kisses or the wake-up calls of "Good morning." No night and day went by without me thinking of them. Grandma always said it was meant to be. I never understood why until my grandmother died from a heart attack. Perhaps I wasn't meant to have anybody. Maybe it was meant to be. Why would Ethan tell me that, tell me that I was in danger?

But at work, I can't stand Amber's sluggishness. "What are you waiting for?" I yell. "For the love of Christ! Get the mailing orders into my office! It's complete chaos having you around." I turn and stumble, hitting my head on the corner of a wooden desk. I get dizzy, and my vision blurs. My hands begin to tremble, and I lose my balance. The back of my head throbs. I can't breathe.

NO! STOP! It's too late; my mother and father's bodies lie lifeless on the floor. I approach them and see the dark little circles in their chests. I hold them, sobbing in silence as the tears run down my face; their eyes stare into infinite space. I close their eyes and yell for help, but no one is there. I'm alone in the cold.

"Dial an ambulance!" someone yells.

The sirens wail and flickering red-and-yellow lights flash all the way to the emergency room. The yellow metal paddles of the defibrillator touch my chilled skin. My body shakes as electrical waves run through my chest.

"One...two...three...she's back! She's back!

Tick...tick...tick...tick...

9:30 a.m.

The rapid snapshots of the vision of my parents swoosh in my memory. My body aches, and my hands feel as if they are swollen. I rub my eyes, which burn from the bright fluorescent lighting, and touch my hair, but I feel thin wires attached to my forehead and temples. I realize I'm in a hospital room, and I rip the wires off and begin to yell for help.

"Chloe, calm down. Everything is fine. I'm Dr. Glynn, a neurologist," says the doctor.

"If everything is fine, why do I have wires attached to my head?" I look at him skeptically.

"We just want to do some analysis. When you arrived at the hospital, you were gone for five minutes."

"Gone?"

"How do you feel?" asks Dr. Glynn, while his voice is overpowered by a racket of yelling through the empty hospital halls.

"Where is she? Where is Chloe? I need to see her," yells Roseanne.

"I'm sorry, ma'am; she's in intensive care. She isn't in any condition to be disturbed."

"Ha ha ha. Look at me, lady. FYI, I am her best friend. How do you like that?"

If there is anything that Roseanne Brindle can do, it's fight to get her way around things. She wouldn't have left the hospital without seeing me first.

"Ma'am, you can't—"

"I'm going in. Oh, and I'm not *old*, so stop calling me *ma'am*."

"Roseanne, I'm so happy you're here. Was that you yelling?"

"Chloe! Are you all right? I heard what happened. Right when I was coming in, I heard yelling, and I could have sworn it was you, darling. That ridiculously unfashionable lady wouldn't let me in, can you just believe it?" says Roseanne with a little girl's voice, half scared to death. Her rosy cheeks are lightly dusted with pale pink blush over the precise freckles that sprinkle her cheeks. The black satin color of her nail polish reflects the crocodile print of her purple Prada clutch.

"Don't worry; I got a little paranoid because I woke up and found wires all over my head." I had to lie; Roseanne wouldn't understand. I had seen the death of my parents; a faceless man in a mauve cloak killed them. My grandmother told me my parents died in a car crash, but what I saw felt so truthful, so realistic. The trip...what if they died a different way? What if they went on a different trip? Why wasn't she ever direct with me? I had a right to know!

Roseanne looks around in disgust at the depressing white hospital walls and asks, "When are they letting you out of this place?"

"I don't know."

"Oh gracious God, they better let you out. This place is not good for you. It will only make you feel worse, honey. I'm going to take you with me right now. I'll be back. I'm going to look for that doctor."

"No, Roseanne...come back!"

She ignores me.

Her clacking returns a few minutes later. "They said I could take you. Am I not brilliant?"

"That is why I love you." I smile.

"Call me if you need anything. I might work late tonight. Take care," she says, giving me a kiss on the forehead, then closing the door behind her.

I can't do anything, and I feel utterly weak. In moments like these, I love Amber even if she is always clumsy. I trust she will take care of my agenda and my calls for the moment.

Stop thinking about it, Chloe. Don't torment yourself. I know my grandmother would never lie to me; she would never do anything to hurt me. I just know she wouldn't. She was the only one I had when my parents died. Maybe it was just an illusion; maybe I'm just tired. But what if what I saw was true? Who could have killed my parents?

In my sleep, I twist and turn. A frosty wind whips the pine trees with an icy touch, and the white stained marble statue of an angel kneels over a grave. Eyelids closed in deep sorrow, her hands are clasped to her heart in longing for someone. The wind bends the pine trees into each other as the ocean sky slowly begins to cast a gloomy darkness into the necropolis.

Someone grabs my hand and swings me into the air; I land on the edge of a chapel's steps. I can feel the brittle ice on my back. Before entering the chapel, a floating light penetrates my bosom with extreme pressure. I awaken from my sleep in a cold sweat. I trace the floral tiles around the room, trying to ignore my nightmare, but I jump in fright from my ringing cell, which displays a phone number I don't recognize. It stops before I have a chance to answer it.

(020) 8002-9002

I can't resist. My hands twitch, and I bite my lip in desperation before I call the number. I dial (020) 800, but the second line rings, and it's Roseanne.

"Hello," I answer.

Roseanne says, "Oh good heavens, Chloe! I've been trying to reach you for ages; it seemed like the earth sucked you in."

"What do you mean?"

"It's just that it worries me that you haven't responded to any of my calls or text messages. Is everything okay?"

"Roseanne...I really need to speak to you. Can you come by for coffee?"

"Anything for you, sweetheart. I'll be there as soon as I can."

"Thank you so much. I'll see you then."

I tap my shaking fingertips on the wooden table, up and down. Tick...tick...tick...I observe the asymmetrical gold print of my watch. 10:26 p.m. Ding... *Jesus!*

"Come in, come in, Roseanne." I welcome her with a big hug.

"Chloe, come on! I know you better than this! What's going on?" she asks.

"Did you by any chance call me on Tuesday morning to remind me of an appointment?"

"Chloe, how can you think I would call you in the morning?" she asks.

I know she would never do that. Roseanne says it's not good to call a person in the morning: it can only mean bad news. She doesn't want to spoil anyone's day by disturbing them that early, but I had to know. A woman did call me, and Amber always identifies herself before telling me anything. I only thought that maybe Roseanne might have called me since Amber is my only assistant. I don't have male assistants; I don't like them. I prefer working with someone like me, though even working with Amber isn't perfect.

"No reason, just curious. Roseanne, I think dreadful things are happening. I don't know if they are products of my imagination, but I'm having nightmares about my childhood, and I don't know what they mean. I wake up in terrible sweats, always realizing that I have my hands clasped to my heart as if my breath was being sucked away...I'm so, so scared! I can't tell anybody except you because I trust you, and I know you won't think I'm crazy."

Roseanne's eyes tear. "Chloe, don't scare me."

I tell her, "You know, I wish my grandmother was by my side. Every time I feel scared, I just wish she were here to console me."

"Is there something that happened to you when you were a kid?" asks Roseanne. "You never talk about your childhood."

"I can't recall my childhood clearly. But there was this man, Ethan, who I met a few days ago, he...he warned me... he said he wanted to protect me from danger, and since then I haven't been feeling like myself."

"Have you tried getting in contact with him?"

"No, I'm scared, but before you called me, I missed a call. Look."

Roseanne's expression changes.

"He just arrived in New York from who-knows-where."

"I think this is a UK phone number. I mean, I could be wrong..."

Roseanne and I look at each other in disbelief. Could that man, Ethan, have traveled across the ocean just to warn me?

8:36 p.m.

Stopping to think if I should redial the UK number or

just go to bed, I am suddenly overwhelmed with curiosity. I dial, and a man picks up.

"I knew you would call," says Ethan.

How did he know it was me? Who is this maniac?

"Why did you call me a while ago?" I ask.

"It would be best if we met in person. You can't trust phones. You never know when someone is listening."

"Where do you want to meet?" I ask.

"London."

"London? But I'm in New York," I say, appalled.

"A jet will be on the way to pick you up; we can converse in the air. It would be refreshing, don't you think?"

"How can I trust you?"

"That's the reason why we are meeting, so you can get to know me."

"I'm not going. I have a photo shoot tomorrow morning. Sorry, but I have an incoming call—I have to go. Good night," I lie and hang up.

Going to another country with a stranger is totally out of the question. I don't even know if I can trust him. What does he think of me, huh? That I'm just going to hop on a plane with him and go to London? What the heck am I going to do there? Honestly, who would agree to go to another continent just like that? I don't know anything about him or what he does. Is this worth risking my job and putting *Posh* magazine at risk? Ha ha ha! It's like one of those fairy tales that little girls picture in their heads: they wish that someday they will go far far away and live happily ever after. But I can't do that. I have a job, a company to lead.

But he must know something very important if he'd rather not speak of it over the phone. I pace slowly, step by step, up and down the tile floor.

But what will happen to my company? *Posh* will end in complete chaos without me. If I do leave, who will take my place? Who could be a better editor in chief than *me*? I know the business; I know the game. Oh my God, what am I going to do? My temples are pulsing. I need some painkillers.

Why even try looking for painkillers? I'm going to get another headache anyway. What if this meeting is something that was meant to be? But what if he wants to kill me or something? What if he wants money and uses me to extort money from *Posh*? Just picture it in the news headlines. It would be ridiculous, nosy reporters sitting at a TV anchor desk saying in a conceited tone, "At the height of her career, *Posh* magazine's editor in chief Chloe Winsly was kidnapped, and the perpetrators are demanding a ransom from the *Posh* board of directors." But what if they don't want to help me and turn their backs on me? Then I'd really be in trouble. And my job is important. I love my job. I get to boss people around, and I'm in control. That is me.

Anybody who takes my spot will ruin our company. I just want to cry. I think I'm going to be sick...nausea. I lie hopeless and helpless on a white satin sofa, unable to make the right choice. I don't want to regret this decision. Roseanne will kill me when she finds out what Ethan has just asked me to do. Maybe I should call her to see what she thinks. No, she'll freak out. She will probably throw her heels in the air and have an attack of hysterics. Just imagine what I'm going to tell her: "Hey, Roseanne, I'm going to London with a man I don't know. What do you think?" That would be insane. It doesn't even sound logical or realistic.

Roseanne! Yes! I'm going to ask her to take my place while I go to London. If I'm trapped or something, I'll call her, and I'm sure she'll find a way to save me. I trust you, Roseanne. Sorry, your days at *Prime* magazine are over. You will hate me and love me for it. I have no choice. I have to decide, or the thoughts of my unknown past will haunt me forever. I have to go with Prince Charming, who will fly me off to Whateverland.

We sit opposite each other, while two glasses of wine sit on a black table between us.

"Do you know who you are?"

"Yes. I'm Chloe Winsly, editor in chief of *Posh* magazine, thank you very much."

"Do you know how your parents died?"

"Where are you going with this?"

"Don't you remember what I told you? I want to protect you. People have lied to you enough. Don't you understand?

I'm going to talk, and you'd better listen to me before you say anything."

He's coming on too harsh. I haven't even said anything.

"Your mother and father where born into a secret cult called the Order. They believe that if a person dies, it leaves way for a new and cleaner soul that will wash away human desire, the ultimate sin for them. By having you, your mother and father committed that sin, and everybody knew there would have to be a sacrifice for the cleansing. But during childbirth, your mother suffered internal bleeding. According to the Order, that occurrence was holy, divine. But there were consequences to the holy birth. By the Order's law, your parents had to surrender you to them, and then you would become the sole leader of the Order on your twelfth birthday.

"Your mother refused to give you up. She protected you. She took you into hiding when you were ten because she knew they would take you away. The Order killed your parents after they refused to tell them where you were. What the Order didn't know was that my father was your father's best man. They made a pact that my father would protect you. A few years later, after your father's death, the Order discovered that my father was looking out for you. For my protection, my father then sent me away to boarding school in England.

"Weekly letters were sent to me from my mother, saying that if my father died, I was to protect you. She said you were in hiding with your grandmother, but my mother failed to tell me where exactly. I found out that my father was killed by the Order a few months after I had received my last letter. From my mother's letters, I knew your importance to the Order, but I also had to know what you looked like. Who was this mysterious girl I was supposed to protect? I think that was the other reason why I escaped to find you."

"This cannot be true. My parents…they weren't killed. They died in a car crash. My grandmother told me."

"She wanted to protect you. You were young back then; I was, too. You would have gone insane if she told you the truth."

"What about you? Is that why the Order killed your father? To find you?"

"The Order never knew my father had a son. My father wasn't even part of the Order. To them, he was just your father's best friend. So I was under their radar, and I could leave boarding school to find you. I've been searching you ever since. It's taken years."

"So now what? You found me."

"I'm supposed to protect you, but I've realized that the charm of a child always leaves prints of beauty behind. There was something special about you when I first saw you at Nobu. There was a grace in your walk when you approached the table, and your perfume hung in the air when you left the room. Skepticism never left your face. You left that night, and I ran after you, but you disappeared. The Order is probably still looking for you, so you need to be careful," Ethan says at a frantic pace.

Is Ethan interested in more than just protecting me? His compliments…I thought he was going to hurt me that night. Do I really have a good walk?

"Why do they still want me? I'm no longer twelve."

"They want something you have. I don't know what it is, but the one who ruled while your parents were still alive gave your mother something right after you were born, something called the sacred syllable. She was supposed to give it to you. They want that."

"But I don't have anything."

"That's why you have to be careful. They don't know that. They think you have it."

If there has ever been a moment in my life when I've felt scared, confused, attracted, and angered all at the same time, it's now. I am utterly unable to speak because it's all just so overwhelming. Ethan knew all of this before we even met for the first time. He had the courage and the persistence to keep going after so many years, just to find me. I feel so bad about having judged him.

He walks to the front of the plane, and I'm suddenly aware that I'm attracted to him. I must have felt it before at Nobu, seeing his slick dark brown hair; but now I also notice the aroma of his cologne, the movement of his hands, the sound of his voice, and the way his lips move when he speaks. Tingling inside, I want him to come back and sit with me. I want him to look at me the way he just did. Ethan comes back to his seat with a tiny scarlet box.

"Open it. It's for you. It's a bracelet; it's supposed to repel bad karma."

I ask, "Where are we landing?"

"On the outskirts of the city," he responds.

"Is that where you live?"

"Yes, since after I left boarding school."

Rusty, cracked wooden fences sequester the cottage, and oak trees mingle around it. A gray cement bridge arches over the river, and patches of daisies outline the tip of the bridge. In the distance, fields of tall grass wave back and forth to the song of the wind. Inside, freshly baked yams with specks of brown cinnamon are waiting on the table, and lavender-scented oil permeates the cottage. The golden sun radiates through the red veils over the windows.

The small cottage has been my home for some time while I'm figuring out what I'm supposed to do. I've been so fortunate to live with Ethan, and our relationship has become more intimate since the airplane ride. He refuses to tell me why he lives so far away from the city. But I sense he is just afraid of being in danger and leaving me alone. His smile is the first thing I see every morning when I wake up next to him. Just waking, looking into each other's eyes makes me realize how sincere Ethan is. It feels like the first morning after your wedding night when, after the stress and commotion, it's just the two of you.

"When I was looking for you, it never occurred to me that I would find you in such a public career. Fashion is very out there. People are seen in the newspapers, going out of the country for business or out to fancy dinners with important people," he says, as the palms of our hands meet and he begins to run his fingertips across mine.

"It was just a different lifestyle. In fact, sometimes I don't care anymore who I was. I mean, I was growing up in a cave. I was living a fairy tale. My life has always been about designer bags and clothes, and now I look back and I think I desired all of that because I was empty inside.

Material possessions overpowered my better judgment. I had lost my parents and my grandmother. The pain of losing them made me forget how much they meant to me. Fashion, popularity, and money filled my fuel tank. Business, socialites, and dinner parties were my love."

He says, "I brought you here because the big city wouldn't have given you the tranquility you would need for reflection. You need time to sort out the missing pieces of your life."

"You've given me enough to know that I have you. I know what you must be thinking. 'She doesn't know how much of a threat the cult is,'" I respond.

"I never thought that. I'm just scared that the Order might hurt you, and I'll be failing both our fathers."

"You shouldn't be afraid. I'm safe with you. I like being with you!"

He is the star of my sky and the wind of my boat. I can hear the brittle, crisp leaves falling from the white birch tree. His hands caress mine; our eyes lock, looking into the end of life, living a static moment as we lie outside the cottage. The silver leaves cushion the grass, and we lie there looking at the clouds blooming at the end of a soft dying day. I won't go; I look ahead to a world that robs this ecstasy away, and destiny laughs. "You complete me, Ethan," I whisper softly in his ear. The warmth of his embrace traps my perfume between our chests. In front of our eyes, time shuffles and passes under our noses while we remain lost in each other.

I stand in front of Ethan near the wishing well as the birds twitter and butterflies flutter in the wind.

"Make a wish," Ethan says softly.

I close my eyes, and in the blackness of my sight I throw a penny into the well, wishing...I want to wish, but I can't stop thinking about my parents. The Order killed *my* parents. They killed what was most important to me. My parents protected me for a reason: they wanted me to live. I'm not going to let the Order destroy my life now. The Order will never be powerful again if I'm supposed to rule. They will be nothing without me. I have to find a way to finish them before they find a way to finish me. My mother's sacrifice to protect me will be avenged. I take a deep breath.

"Where is the Order now?" I ask.

"Highgate," he replies.

Highgate is inscribed in bold rusty letters over the gate's arch. Ethan told me a myth: every spring night, figures in black walking robes and masks take men and women into the dark depths of the forest where they are sworn to secrecy about the world they will encounter. Before me stands a tomb, a stone crypt staring at me—right at me— as if it wants to know me. The wind smashes the black gates against each other, and they squeak like fingernails violently scratching a chalkboard. I open the gate, and a sudden burst of electricity rushes through my hand. It burns, forcing my hand away from it. How am I going to get through this gate? What if it starts to rain, and I get electrocuted and die?

I squeeze my lean body through the metal bars of the outer edge of the fence. Inside, the passageway is humid, and the dew of twilight obscures my vision. I turn the corner of the never-ending corridor, and I see men being forced to kneel and kiss a skull at the feet of the initiators. The initiators are similar to the man I saw in my vision when I was taken to the hospital. Replicas of grim reapers roam around the room. Their feeble skinny bodies, hiding beneath mauve cloaks and faceless white masks, bow and dance barefoot. Their pale hands and feet are as white as snow.

What is this place? I've seen the outside of this place in visions, terrifying visions that wake me up in a cold sweat. Now to see it, live it, the thought of being here makes my heart race faster and faster. I close my mouth before my heart can leap out of my throat. I gulp, and instantly somebody grabs my hand from below.

"Young child, is it really you? It's her. It's the child," cracks the voice of a woman, old, raggedy, and hunchbacked, her shriveled mouth outlining a smile that shows the empty gap of her missing front teeth.

"Leave me alone, woman." The touch of her hand leaves the outline of her grip imprinted around my wrist, which begins to slowly turn a faint blue. Two men come running toward me as if the devil were chasing after them. Their thick hands grab me, and they carry me off. I scream at the top of my lungs, wiggling my way out of their arms, but they wrap their hands around my neck, and I slowly begin to lose consciousness. I can't... I can't breathe... I...

The candlelight flickers in the dark room. Down the hallway, I hear footsteps. A herd of men appears at the door. A feeble man in his mid-sixties crosses the threshold. The other men whisper, "Svair, it's the child. She looks like her mother."

"Tie her up!" yells Svair to his men. Then he asks me, "Chloe, where is Ethan?"

How does he know about Ethan? In a whisper, swallowing the tears, I say, "You've never cared about anybody. All you wanted to do is destroy the hearts of those who were loyal to the Order."

"I have a right to know where he is. I am his father."

I lift my head to see Svair's silhouette beside the flickering candle. *It can't be possible. Eth—Ethan told me his father died. He said the Order had murdered him. It just can't be possible.*

"His father is dead." I'm too weak to lift my eyes away from the floor. The rope around my wrists keeps my blood from circulating.

Svair approaches me and whispers in my ear, "Ethan killed your parents."

"No! He didn't!"

Svair's wrinkles appear as deep as desert cracks of dry dirt. Dry lines stretch from the corners of his eyes. White electric waves sprout from the black hole of his pupil, and his iris mirrors the image of my weak body. The vein in his forehead pops and outlines the root of his vicious temper. As he yells, another green blood vein pops out on the left side of his neck.

"Yes. I made him do it. And you know what? It gave me great pleasure to know that he was the one to finally destroy them. You see, the Order never needed your parents. Abelard, the head of the Order, made a terrible decision in bestowing the power to them after he died. They thought they could rule and hide you because they had power to do so. They promised to give you up, but they violated their promise. I should have been the chosen one. I had to get rid of them to assume the power that has belonged to me all along. It's your useless father's actions that have damned us."

No...it just can't be. Svair is not Ethan's father. Ethan couldn't have made up the whole story on the plane; his eyes were telling the truth. He would never kill his own father's best friend. Svair is lying; he wants something from me. He's playing with my head.

"Your father was a pathetic coward to have kept you protected; no matter his rank, he betrayed the Order. Abelard thought your parents were worthy for having created you, but no one is worthy when they betray our brotherhood. Your father was the iron gate that prevented us from reaching you, but you know where the sacred syllable is. Why else would your parents have sacrificed their lives for you, child?"

Looking up with a cold stare, my voice echoes through the room: "Shut up! You have no right to disrespect the name of my father."

"Did Ethan ever tell you I was alive? He set you up, Chloe. Can't you see it, you foolish child? All the love, all the passion he had for you was a lie. A plan that he and I created to destroy you! Ethan knew where you were all along. He turned you in. Look at you! You are nothing! You have nothing! You never did, and you never will. You are no prophecy, and you don't have the sacred syllable. You are only a reflection of what your parents were. Foolish child. Poor foolish child."

"Tell the truth, Svair. Your lies are over. Your words mean nothing to me. You destroyed my parents; you are in debt to me. There is nothing holding me back, not even you. You are a worthless, spiritless soul. Mark my words, Svair. You degrade me, and you are only laughing at yourself, laughing at what you will become. Your words speak your own fate, and your actions condemn you. You have nothing to do with me. If you had, I would have been dead by now. I am alive because you desire something I possess, something I will die for before giving it to you."

"Lock her up," commands Svair to one of his men.

Escape, Chloe. You have to escape before they lock you in. Ducking down, I crawl between the man's legs and run out of the room, through the corridor, and out the metal bars that I entered through. Where am I going to go? I don't want to see Ethan. He's only going to ask where I've been. I need some rest. I need Roseanne. I need to find a pay phone. I need her help. She needs to get me out of here.

I run out of the dark forest and into the London streets in a frantic search for a pay phone. A red fenced, crystal telephone booth stands right across the street.

The other line rings and rings, and Roseanne isn't picking up. Please, Roseanne, answer.

"Hello," she answers.

What time is it? My watch says 11:23 p.m.

"Roseanne, it's Chloe," I say in tears.

"Christ, Chloe. What's wrong? Are you still in London? Where are you?"

"I need you to get me out of here."

"What happened? Where are you?" Roseanne begins to scream across the phone line.

"That's not important. I need you to book a plane for me. Call right now, and then tell me where I should go."

"I'll do it right now. I'm going to use another phone. Don't hang up."

Silence.

"Chloe? ...I got you a plane."

"Where? What time?"

"Heathrow. Flight 36. In three hours."

The wind feels colder than last month. I walk down the staircase and into the Archway tube station in London. The tunnel runs endlessly, and the silver chrome benches glisten in the lights. The tunnel is empty, and only the train's

shrieking ringing can be heard from afar. I stand in shivers when, in a matter of seconds, slow shakes begin to resound against the tunnel's walls. The light bulbs begin to vibrate, and the lighting begins to fade away. The train screeches to a halt. The shakes get louder and louder. The ceiling begins to crack slowly, and then it falls down, smashing the top of the train. I hear my heart pound in my chest. Now I know I'm going to die. I touch my ear and feel warm blood.

Ahhh! I awake, sit up in bed, and hear the panting sounds of my breathing. Droplets of sweat run down my forehead, and goose bumps make my hair stand on end. My hands are clasped at my chest, and touching my ear, I feel the same warm blood. Frightened, I run to the restroom, almost breaking my neck by tripping on a chair leg. The piercing around my earring is swollen; it aches. The metallic hook of the earring is irritating my ear. My grandmother gave them to me on my twelfth birthday. They bring so many happy memories of the times we spent together. Back in San Francisco, the ocean would shine through the glass windows, reflecting the light onto the mirrors. I remember the satin lace dresses she would sew for me. I would sit on the burgundy piano bench and just run my finger tips over the piano keys, not caring about the time. There was always something on top of that old piano. Grandma had endless sketchbooks and stacks of floral and solid fabrics scattered across the room. She said that color and patterns inspired her. She had over ten huge dress forms, all of them always standing against the wall with ball gowns hanging on them. I remember she had given me a form as tall as I was. I used to love sticking crazy colored patterns onto it. "Chloe, be careful; less is more," she would call across the room. I can still smell the aroma of coffee and chocolate coming from her mouth when she spoke to me. The gold chocolate box was my favorite; it was always positioned in the middle of our coffee table. Now that I think about it I haven't had chocolate since she died. There isn't anybody to offer me chocolate from the golden box any longer. To this day, it remains empty, standing perfectly in its glass case.

That is what my nightmare made me remember. My thoughts run unspoken, and my childhood memories hit the ground. Heading to the glass case, I observe up close the silver art carved around the golden box. Miniature women under peach trees sit on the edge of the river, refreshing their feet. A round silver pearl sits atop the lid as a handle. But when I open it, a small folded piece of paper sits inside the box. Unfolding the paper, I see the black ink bleed through the yellow parchment. It reads:

Dear Chloe,

I am sure that by the time you receive this letter you will be old enough to know your father and I wanted the best for you. Our destiny had been sealed from the instant you were born. You were special; you were meant to take over the Order. I was more than just a mother. I lived a tortured life, not knowing when you would be safe. I wanted you to have a normal childhood where you could run freely in the garden.

I destroyed your childhood by taking you away from enjoying adventure. I want you to know that I did it out of motherly protection. How would I have felt if the Order got their hands on you? I would have died. I couldn't give you up because I loved you the instant you were in my arms. From infancy, your little bare feet would splash in the water. How you would run to your father in hopes that he would bring home a new book on foreign adventures to you. You were a child amused by exploration, and your father feared you would be an easy target. I would have given anything, including my life, to at least know that you would finally be safe. Your grandmother always told me to tell you the truth, but I just didn't want to see you hate me or be afraid that I would leave. Ethan contains a piece of us and our close friendships. I'm sure that you must have heard of Ethan by now. Your grandmother should have told you. You can trust him. He is a very genuine boy. I'm sure that by now he has become a full-grown man; he was only seven when I met him.

The Order has been on the hunt for the sacred syllable to reopen the vault and drink the forbidden potion. But they will never succeed. You have what they want, sweetie. Chloe, you must not give it to them. You will be safe as long as you don't surrender it.

I have the sacred syllable? But I don't have anything. Neither my mom nor my grandmother ever gave me anything. What is she referring to? I can't take it anymore. All this confusion and mystery is blurring my mind. I can't think straight. My life has become a mystery game. I've just heard so much information about my past that it's all scrambled and thrown up in the air. And my ear still hurts. Where did I leave my earrings?

I pick up the pearl earrings, and, under the strong fluorescent lighting, something unexpected appears among the antiquity and detail. Lettering around the top part of the pearl earring reads:

MORI RESURGERE EST ATQUE PRAEDICTUM SUM

This cannot be true...this cannot be happening...is this the key? It's the sacred syllable. It's what the Order is searching for. Why didn't I notice before? I could have kept on living; I would have died without knowing the earrings were what they were searching for. Of course, Svair doesn't know. Ethan told me it was given secretly to my mother by the leader of the Order. Svair doesn't know I've had them all along, right in front of his face. He was blind; he was completely blind, and so was I. I put on my earrings and head to the living room.

Ring...ring...ring...

"Hello?"

"It's Ethan. Get ready—I'm picking you up," he says in a rush.

Click.

"Hello! Ethan!" I yell. *What is going on?*

Ding...

"Chloe, let's go," he proclaims, grabbing my wrist, pulling me out the door.

"Where are you taking me? Let go of me! You're hurting me!" I plea as I pull myself away from him.

"We're going back to London," he says.

"For what?"

"I should have known that you were going to see the Order. Now they know you're alive, and they will use you to get to the sacred syllable. Even if you don't know it, they will kill you. I don't want you dead. There has been so much blood shed in the past, and I don't want you to be a part of that. Why did you run away?"

"Why are you doing this to me, Ethan? I'm doing this for us. The Order has done enough already. Why can't you see that? They killed your parents and mine, and now they want to kill me. Do you expect that I'm going to stand here and see my own life slip out of my hands? I will not give up my freedom to live. I still have a lot of things I want to do with my life, and a part of that is having you by my side. I need your support and not your questioning. I need to fight on my own. This is my fight," I say, sternly angry at his protective behavior.

"Did you kill my parents?" I ask, looking at him.

"What are you talking about? How could you say that? Our fathers were best friends! You don't actually believe that, do you?"

"No, I knew you would never be capable of doing that."

"Did the Order tell you that? Don't believe anything they say. Do you hear me, Chloe? Promise me you will never believe anything they say. They only want to weaken your mind so they can get to you. They want to see your pain. I don't want you to lose yourself in their false pretenses. Promise me."

"I promise."

His attention switches from my eyes to my ears.

"Why is your ear bleeding?"

"It's nothing. Leave, Ethan."

Ethan must never know that I'll be leaving New York again tonight. I have to go alone. I don't want him to intervene. I have to show him that I'm not weak, that I'm not capable of confronting my own duties. I have to finish what has been started, or who will?

The entrance to Highgate is unwelcoming once more, and so is the weather. The rain begins to pour harder and heavier on my head. From afar, I see Svair coming toward me. I know it will not be a nice welcome.

Svair, with infuriated redness in his face, says, "You worthless creature! Where is the prophecy? We know you have it!"

"I'd rather die than see you triumph over my dead mother and father. Besides, don't you remember Ethan's parents? You murderer! You killed everyone we cared most about," I say angrily, as my tears blend with the pouring rain. "You above all people betrayed the Order! You betrayed one of your own, and you have betrayed the Order's brotherhood. Yes, my father. You heartlessly killed him, and now you wish to be hailed as a god! You talk about loyalty and truth, yet you fail to realize that you are the only stain on the Order."

"How dare you insult us all! Those who speak the words of death and judgment must die. Your filthy mother gave birth to you, yelling and pleading to be killed instead of you, and guess what? She got what she asked for."

"The only filth and stench here is you and all that you represent! Maybe my mother knew I would one day hate the Order. Maybe she knew that I would one day destroy it. Maybe you should have thanked her for taking me away. I know you'll regret killing my parents and Ethan's parents. You want the sacred syllable and the prophecy? You want it? Well, you're looking at it, and you're going to have to stop me from stepping on it."

I unclip my pearl earrings, throw them on the ground, and crush them with my foot until the pearls pulverize into a million pieces of dust.

"*Mori resurgere est atque praedictum sum*. Death is rebirth, and I am the prophecy," I say.

"Never," he claims with devil-red eyes.

Svair grabs me by the throat. I scratch him and pull at his hands, but I slowly begin to lose consciousness. I can no longer breathe; the light fades, and only the shadow of Svair's face is visible through the rain. All I feel is my body suddenly being soaked in water.

Ethan approaches, panting, and he screams, "Let her

go! You're killing her! Chloeee!"

Ethan runs toward my body. I am breathless and cold. "Murderer," Ethan shouts at Svair. Ethan runs toward him, grabs his collar, and throws him onto a rock. Red blood streaks down the rock. Ethan pleads to my lifeless body, saying, "Chloe...Chloe, please come back. I need you...you must live. You aren't supposed to die. Not today, not now." I slowly open my eyelids, as if waking up from long winter hibernation. Small specks of pearl lie on top of the thick mud. Ethan suddenly grabs his chest and begins coughing. He stands stagnantly as blinding champagne-colored lights rip out of his chest. Trapped in my physical body, motionless and speechless, I cannot yell *no*, but I can hear it echo in the void of my heart. The champagne light roams through the air and into my hand. An extreme force grips the palm of my hand, and tears run down my pale cheeks.

A shadow covers me as wings burst from my shoulder blades and a halo crystallizes over the crown of my head. I look down at my body. What is happening to me? Am I dead?

Weightless, transparent, and cold, I begin to drift away from earth. I exhale a fluorescent bud of light. Our spirits have detached from our bodies. I can't see or feel myself; only a faint echo of my mother's voice whispers in my ear. "Let him go; let the light in. It's not your time." I release the spirit, and the sun shines closer. Reaching to touch the sunbeams, my thin pale hand is branded with a scar. A gray human shadow stares over me, and my shoulders hunch in sore pain as my chest shakes. I kneel next to Ethan as his lifeless body lies in a cushion of dead leaves. My chest to his...buh-bump...silence...buh-bump...silence...our heartbeats no longer chant to the same melody. The touch of my warm red lips to his cold white lips is the line where our destiny parts. I gaze at his lifeless shell and softly close my eyes as a single tear streams from my eye into his. He is no longer a part of life. The only thing that remains is one mark, a burn mark on the palm of my hand.

Tick...tick...tick... 10:45 a.m.

Roseanne and I sit on the red cushions as we wait for our lattes at the coffee shop.

"I'm so sorry about what happened to Ethan and your parents," says Roseanne, her voice soft and filled with pain after I finish telling her my story.

"He saved my life, but I failed to save his."

"I never knew you had a secret lover all along. Why didn't you tell me, Chloe?"

"Because I didn't know that I loved him," I respond, looking at the table as she takes my hands. I look up at her.

"Are you going back to *Posh* magazine?"

"No. I've resigned."

"What? What are you going to do now?"

"I've saved enough money to live on my own for the next four years. I need time for myself. I'm going back to my birth home. I belong in London. My parents are buried at Highgate; I saw their tombstones while I was there. I'm going to stay in Ethan's cottage."

"Why are you going back to that place?"

"Because I'm the living prophecy," I say, looking out the window of the coffee shop at the sight of a little girl skipping down the street. My mother was right. I was meant to live.

Nataly Chavez
CYCLE OF WINTER

It was the end of autumn. The night was still except for the distant howls of the mountain wolves and the stream's calm current. In the darkness, a beautiful and delicate girl lay at the trunk of an old willow tree. The moon cast a silver glow on her hair, stars twinkled in her blue eyes, and her silk wings fluttered softly in the wind. Dawn was approaching, and the sun's rays slowly began to spread among the trees, announcing the beginning of a new day. The dried scarlet leaves rustled as the wind swept through the forest. She closed her eyes, and a smile spread across Samara's rosy mouth as she heard a soft humming approaching the willow. She opened her eyes to a lively face looking down at her. Her cousin and best friend, Sandra, handed her a dark blue cloak.

"Happy birthday! Promise me you'll cover yourself with this. You always seem to be cold, even when the sun is out. It worries me. And who knows, maybe it'll protect you on a crazy adventure."

"Well, you don't have to worry about that," Samara said. "I won't be going anywhere anytime soon."

They spent their day running through the trees chasing butterflies and making flower crowns in celebration of her day. All she cared about was spending time with Sandra. They could spend hours together, never getting bored. They had no secrets from each other, but Samara felt something was coming, and for once she would not be able to share it with Sandra.

As a red sun set, the night was blurred with fuzzy light radiating from hung lanterns. The entire village of Dirus began coming together under the Party Tree's massive cover. Its thick trunk rose higher than any tree in the village, and the branches extended upward, forming the shape of a giant mushroom. Men and women carried gifts wrapped in bright neon colors—turquoise, magenta, and pink—while their children lost no time in formalities and began chasing their friends. A crowd danced to the upbeat music of violins, pulling Samara along with them. An elegant couple stood side by side away from the crowd, holding hands and smiling brightly. Catching sight of them, the girls skipped playfully toward them. The woman had dark curly hair that reached her hips, and wore a low-cut burgundy dress and lace ribbon at her neck. Her husband wore a lavish black vest with a silver chain at his vest pocket, and slick dress pants.

"Happy birthday, Samara. Are you enjoying the feast?" said the woman.

"It's beautiful, Aunt Lily. Thank you both," Samara said with a joyful smile.

"Well, it's not every day that the village's most wonderful person turns seventeen," her uncle said while putting an arm around Sandra and kissing her forehead.

Samara felt a twinge of jealousy but tried to put it aside with an insincere smile.

"Mom, I've just met the most charming boy! I think he's from the next village; his name is Matthew." Sandra said excitedly, with a gleam in her eyes.

Her father's eyes widened with such panic that he let her go.

"*Which* boy?" he asked, as he extended his neck to look around the crowd. "It's that boy with that ridiculous smirk on his face, isn't it? Oh, God, I knew this day would happen, but not so soon!"

"Saul, would you grab a hold of yourself?" whispered Lily.

"Oh, my little girl's life is flashing before my eyes!" he said, as he took a deep breath and tried to compose himself. "Well, I'll just go meet this boy. Come on, Sandra." He took her by the arm.

"Ugh, fine, just promise me you won't *embarrass* me!" hissed Sandra.

"*When* have I embarrassed you?"

Their voices trailed off, and Samara was left alone with her aunt.

"Samara, it's about time I gave you this," said Lily, holding out a silver moon necklace in the palm of her hand.

"But it's yours, Aunt Lily."

"It's your mother's, and she wanted you to have it on your seventeenth birthday."

"My mother?" Samara couldn't believe her ears.

Suddenly, something in the shadows caught Lily's eyes— a tall man covered in a gray cloak, smoking a pipe.

"I'm sorry, honey. I have to attend to someone. We'll talk about this later. Promise." Lily's voice was hurried, but firm. Samara knew she would have to wait.

She watched after her aunt and noticed her uncle walking toward the cloaked man as well, with a serious expression on his face.

"It was a disaster!" said Sandra, startling Samara.

"Do you know who that is?" asked Samara.

"No, I bet it's an old friend. Who cares? Come on, the fireworks are about to begin!" She tugged Samara by the arm.

As loud bangs began and colorful lights exploded into the sky, Samara kept glancing back at her aunt and uncle. The night dragged on, and a rich smell of cinnamon filled the air, dazing Samara into a bottomless sleep.

Samara found herself at the boundary of a great wood. Dark trees towered, casting shadows over a curved path. Suddenly, she heard a man's voice close to her ear. It was a tall elderly man, with long gray hair. His bright blue eyes seemed to pierce through her, and a majestic confidence radiated from his face. "A path has been laid out for you," he said. "It is time you fulfill your destiny as the Goddess of Winter. The season cycles have been broken by Tatiana, the Mistress of Darkness, who seeks to stop the winter season from beginning. You must prepare for the sacrifices ahead, but you won't be alone. Remember, what you see isn't always what it seems."

"Who are you?" said Samara. One blink and he was

gone. A gasp escaped her mouth as her fingers entwined themselves around a long, blue staff.

Awakening in cold sweat, Samara's lungs prevented her from catching her breath. A scream was caught in the back of her throat. The celebration was over; it was near twilight. Sandra was sitting beside her, her eyes filled with fear and worry.

"You were having a bad dream," she said. The minutes skulked on into the lifeless night. Not even the owl's hoot or the rustle of the leaves were heard in the stagnant darkness.

"Something's wrong," she said. "Winter should have begun by now. I can feel the weariness of the animals. They are waiting for something that will not come." Samara remembered the sparrow she had seen days ago—up in a tree, flapping its wings desperately, as if unsure whether to fly off or remain, twittering like a dying grasshopper. Samara began to piece everything together. *Could the man in my dream be telling the truth? How could he know my destiny? What sacrifices was he talking about?*

Over the next week, Samara isolated herself from everyone. Her mind was racing with doubt. One day, after walking for hours, she found herself standing in the middle of a green meadow. On the horizon, she saw the edge of a cliff and heard an angry tide. *If the man in my dream was right, that I am to become the Winter Goddess...how do I transform?* As she looked over the brink, her hair swept into the air, whipping at her face, and the fresh breeze sent shivers through her body. Childhood memories with Sandra crept into Samara's mind, causing a stab of guilt to prick at her stomach.

Tears swelled in her eyes and poured like a heavy storm. *Water is ever flowing*, she thought. *It changes and takes many forms.* Then, a voice in the wind whispered to her gently, "Focus your mind on the water, and you will find your answer. It is the key to your transformation." Her eyes took one last glance to her home in the east. She spread her arms, took one last breath, and plunged into the raging waters below. A thunderous splash echoed in her ears as she was absorbed by the dark tide. Even as shadows devoured her and pulled her deeper to the bottom, dazzling white sprites appeared, sucking Samara into another world. Iciness surrounded her, sucking away her last warm breath. No longer did she feel the need for warmth or the bright colors of flowers. Gradually, her body's numbness faded, the river was gone, and Samara lay under the willow tree.

As the hours dragged on, Samara's blue eyes finally opened. Taking a breath, she choked on the salty water in her throat. Propping herself up on her elbows, a sharp pain vibrated throughout her body. She couldn't move, and the bright sun burned her eyes and skin. Looking up, Samara recognized the willow tree. *Nothing happened,* she thought. *It was only a nightmare.* Blurred images of sea creatures and white lights were still flashing in her mind. Panic began to grasp Samara as she realized she was wet, and a salty smell lingered in the air. As the wind blew harder, she felt a nauseating feeling at the bottom of her stomach. She no longer felt she was in her own body. This body was icy and bitter. A whisper flowed through the trees, and a twig snapped in the bushes. A cloaked man stepped out and removed his hood, revealing a mane of long gray hair.

"You can no longer stay here," he said. His voice was wise and caring; it was impossible to doubt him. "You won't survive."

Samara's heart stopped as she saw his face clearly. A very familiar set of blue eyes were fixed upon hers.

"Wait!" She took two steps back. "You were in my dream! And...you were the man my aunt and uncle were talking to at the feast."

"Yes, I'm a *family friend.*"

Samara gasped.

"I'm here to help you. You don't need to fear me. All you need to know is that I am Zanzabar, the wizard of this land. Somebody asked me to look after you, and that's what I'll do. And now that you have gone through the metamorphosis, you—"

"Are you speaking of Sandra?"

"She is not the only one who looks after you."

"And this metamorphosis? What does that...mean?"

Frustration began to rise in Zanzabar.

"Didn't Lily tell you *anything*?" He spotted Samara's watery eyes and tried to keep control. "There's something you should see."

He led her to a nearby river. Kneeling before the water, Samara couldn't find the courage to look at herself. Very slowly, she leaned forward. Her once brown hair had turned into a hue of blue, marked with silver streaks. The Goddess of Winter had now taken her place.

"Is that me?" she shrieked.

"Yes, you are now the Carrier of Winter. But every carrier must follow the Decree of the Four Seasons. Most importantly, you cannot be involved with mortals. You have a duty, and associating yourself with their kind can jeopardize everything. Don't allow yourself to feel for them: neither sympathy nor mercy."

"They have never harmed me."

"They will if you let your guard down."

"I understand, but why me?"

"It is your birthright." His eyes darted side to side, then toward the darkness of the trees. "We must hurry and head north before the sun reaches its peak."

"For what?"

"To begin the season of winter. Surely you have noticed that winter hasn't arrived yet. It is upsetting the balance of nature. Everything needs to die at some point to leave a place for new life to grow again. Each season has its purpose; therefore, nothing can be disturbed. Now, do you trust me?" he said, extending his hand.

She hesitated. *If Aunt Lily and Uncle Saul trust this man, then so should I,* she thought, reaching for his hand. Samara extended her wings and rose in the air, higher and higher. At her side the wizard rode on a wooden broom. His eyes focused north. They flew for hours, crossing mountains, deserts, and plains. Finally, as the sun began to set, they made their way down until they could feel the smooth emerald grass under their feet. A great murky wood lay before them. They stood side by side in silence. Zanzabar extended his hand, and a misty gas oozed from his fingers. A blue staff hovered in front of Samara's bedazzled face. A silver crescent moon rested at the top of the staff, and strings of purple beads dangled from it.

"You will need this along the way," Zanzabar said. Seeing how oblivious she was to the staff, he sighed. He had no choice but to teach her how to protect herself in the wild. "Look Samara, I know you were not raised knowing about enchantments. Your aunt did that to protect you, but now you're vulnerable. Magic has always been part of your ancestors and yourself. You can do anything if you set your mind to it. Of course, you know that, since you can speak to animals."

"How did you know that?" she asked, inhaling sharply. *What else could he know?*

"I know more than you think. Now, take your staff and try to bind me. Pretend I'm a real danger to you. Build up your fear into anger and aggression, concentrate it, and release it toward your enemy. The realm you're going into is known for the wild animals and dark creatures that inhabit it. They feast on fear. Now try it. Just focus."

"What if I hurt you?" she asked, with a worried expression on her face.

"You won't. At least, not yet. If you do, then it would be a marvel." He gave a small warm chuckle.

Samara felt a prickle of annoyance. She took a deep breath and thought of how perfect Sandra was and how *everyone* just loved everything about her. If Samara did something great, Sandra did something even better. She started to feel hot tears in her eyes. *No, don't cry. That doesn't solve anything; it just makes you look pathetic and weak.* A strong sensation ran through her body, like thunder rubbing against metal. She lifted her hand, directing it at Zanzabar, her eyes no longer blue but a bright white, like a star in the middle of the forest. An intense energy erupted from Samara's palm, forming a magnetic ball. Finally, she released it straight at Zanzabar, who was ready with his staff at hand. He attacked Samara's hex. She came out of her trance only to see Zanzabar's face full of pride.

"It seems I was wrong about you," he said with a hearty laugh.

And so it went for weeks—learning with Zanzabar, preparing for the danger ahead—until a cold bitter afternoon when Zanzabar led Samara to the boundaries of Varau, the Mortal Realm. "There's good here, but also evil and deceit. Be careful, and remember I will guide you through anything." Zanzabar glanced at Samara one last time, then flew into the endless sky.

Samara stepped forward into the realm. Nothing could come between Samara and her destiny. Winter would soon come.

Dark clouds began to cover the red glow of the evening sky. *A good sign,* thought Samara. Raindrops splashed the ground, marking it with dark shades. As she walked among the bare trees, she lifted her face toward the night sky, and heavy drops hammered Samara like blades. A loud crack erupted from the black sky. Her blue eyes glowed like torches in the middle of the fog. She extended her wings and flew over the forest. An icy wind escaped her mouth and dispersed over the trees. At the touch of her breath, the rain changed into white snow and covered everything in a white sheet. Flowers shriveled and died, and animals ran to their homes to find shelter in dim corners.

Samara landed and walked in darkness, with only the light of the moon to guide her. Out of the corner of her eye, she noticed a faint light coming toward her through the trees. The light trapped her in a trance, reminding her of home. Then she slammed her foot against something small.

"Ouuuch! Watch where you're going, will you?" said the wheezy voice.

"I'm so sorry! I was following a light in the trees," she said. She raised her hand to point, but it was gone. A pointy finger poked at her knee. She jumped.

"Excuse me, young lady, what light?"

"A light, as if someone were holding a lantern," she answered.

Samara looked down. An old gnome was looking up at her with a puzzled expression. His white beard was soaking wet, his skin was creased, and his protruding nose was red as a berry.

"Are you lost, my dear? Sorry if I frightened you. Where are my manners? I'm Oswald."

"I'm Samara."

"It's a pleasure to meet you. It's good to know that there is still beauty in the world, for it has certainly abandoned this place."

Samara smiled kindly. "Did I hurt you?" A look of concern came over her face.

"Not at all. Just...a little...dizzy," he said, bringing his immense hand to his forehead. "Would you mind helping me back to my home? It's not far from here."

He grabbed hold of her and led her to a small wooden shack. There, he invited her in for a cup of tea, which she refused; just the thought of something hot made her twinge. The room was filled with old baskets, rotting meat, and animal fur. Samara spotted a tattered sack with a stained shirt sticking out next to a bloody ax.

"You're leaving?" she asked.

"This forest isn't what it used to be. Years ago, the forest was bright and homey. Now everyone, not that there are many of us, has decided to leave for a better place. Evil now resides in this forest. Tatiana, the Mistress of Darkness, has captured control of the gargoyles of the Lost Temple. She seeks to cover the wood in shadows forever. And now that winter is finally coming, she will be able to carry out her malicious plan." His voice quivered in fear.

"Does your wood have a queen?" she asked.

"Yes, but she cannot defeat the powerful forces of the Mistress of Darkness!"

"Where can I find her?"

"Her castle rests on a hill. It's a three-day journey from here. But...but you don't intend on going there, do you?" His voice trembled even more.

"Why not? If she's the queen, she has to do something about it!"

"But it's too dangerous. The road there is full of evil creatures who will hurt you!"

"Thank you for your concern, Oswald, but I'll be fine. Honest."

"I just don't want to see harm come to such a beautiful girl such as yourself."

"I'm ready for anything that comes my way, Oswald."

"Well, in that case, here," he said, pulling out a small silver whistle from his pocket and handing it to her.

"Whenever you're in grave danger, blow this whistle and help will come, wherever you are."

"Thank you, Oswald," she said, looking admiringly at it. "I hope to see you someday. Goodbye."

"Goodbye, my pretty."

Samara walked deep in thought, wondering what the queen was like. She stopped abruptly and listened intently. Absolutely nothing. She felt someone was watching her, lurking somewhere in the shadows. Her grip on her staff tightened as she continued walking.

It wasn't long before she came across an arena built of large stones. There were no roofs or solid walls, but instead rock arches and a high solid platform in the middle of the area. Shadows were everywhere, and Samara could hear a malicious cackle echoing. Slowly, a large pack of winged goblins began to climb down from the stones. Evil smirks spread across their faces, revealing teeth that looked to be covered in yellow and black slime. Their entire body was covered in a red skin, like a bloody scab, with small spikes and bumps all over. They limped and hunched awkwardly toward her, encircling her from all directions. She prepared to attack, but there were too many for her.

"Well, well, well, what do we have here? You're not lost, are you?" asked a lanky goblin. Even from a distance, Samara smelled the reeking odor of sweat, blood, and dirt.

"I must have gotten off the path," she said, trying to keep calm. "I didn't mean to intrude. I'll just be on my—"

"You weren't intruding, beautiful. We were just about to start dinner. Stay." His snarl made her freeze in fear.

"I really shouldn't," she said. She took a step back, abruptly bumping into a massive goblin coming up behind her. She could hear his heavy breathing and smelled the stench of raw meat and dirt. Just as she raised her staff, the goblin grabbed a hold of her arm, jabbing his sharp claws into her skin. She shrieked in pain, fighting against his grip, but it only made the pain spread, making her knees shake uncontrollably.

"Do you know what we do to lost folks?" continued the goblin. "Once they've crossed into our territory, we can do whatever we want with them. You can shout all you want. No one will save you now," he said, erupting into a malicious laugh as all the surrounding goblins joined in.

Anger began to make her blood boil, and with great effort she lunged her foot backward into the goblin's groin, making him loosen his grip and fall hard on the ground, groaning in pain.

"Get her!" screamed the lanky goblin, reaching for the wooden club hanging from his belt.

Samara tried focusing her energy. With her staff, she shot rays of lightning at three of them, who flew back and landed hard on the ground, unconscious. More came at her. She dodged and fought back, hitting them with her staff, but not before receiving several blows to the stomach. It was no use; there were too many of them.

She remembered the whistle Oswald had given her. She escaped the goblins' clubs and flew to the top of a tall stone. As soon as she blew the whistle, the serene sound of a wolf's howl was heard all over the forest. The exquisite sound surprised Samara; she lingered, listening to the vibrating echo of the howl, oblivious to the menacing goblins growling around her. Everything became a blur as the howls washed through the arena. When everything quieted, Samara found herself alone.

The snow continued to fall, trees croaked, and strange rustles echoed throughout the forest. It was morning when Samara came upon a circular clearing with an oval stone in the center. Stepping toward the stone, she was startled by an auburn fox that jumped from an uprooted tree trunk on the other side of the clearing. The fox looked calm and held a thin branch with red berries in its mouth. Catching sight of Samara, it stopped dead in its tracks. Their eyes met, and time stood still. The fox seemed ready to attack; a growl burst from its throat while it kept its gray eyes on Samara. While the fox prepared to pounce, the sun escaped the cover of the clouds, blinding Samara. The fox began to take another form, until a man with dark wavy hair, green eyes, and a slim figure stood before her. Her heart began to beat faster and louder; she feared the whole forest would hear it.

"Hello. Pardon my intrusion, but I haven't seen you in this wood before. My name is Rook," said a gentle voice. He held out a firm hand.

Samara's mind was high as the clouds, but her hand extended to meet his. At his touch, a magnetic rush tingled from her fingers to her toes.

"My name is Samara. I'm searching for the queen of this wood."

"She is my mother; I can take you to her if you like."

Rook led her back to a pearl castle with numerous high glass windows and thick ivy spread over the walls. Approaching the doors, Samara noticed a gorgeous woman with wavy blond hair in a blood-red dress sitting on a bench overlooking a beautiful garden. Her cheeks had a ruby flush, and her green eyes glistened with the rays of the sun. She was an untouchable beauty.

"Welcome, Samara. I've been waiting for you," she said in an angelic voice.

"You know who I am?" Samara asked.

"I knew of your arrival from the minute you stepped into this realm. After all, I know everything that happens in my kingdom—as well as what you seek to destroy." A red glint was visible in her eyes.

Rook remained out of earshot, kicking stones with his tattered boots, stealing glances at Samara. This did not go unnoticed by the queen.

"I see you have met my son, Rook."

The queen looked from Samara to Rook, a smile coming to her mouth.

"There's nothing wrong with forgetting your duty for a couple of days. Stay with me in my castle and get acquainted with my son, if you like."

For the next week, Samara felt like she finally had a family. She walked the grounds with the queen, speaking to her like a mother, and spent long afternoons with Rook in the clearing.

One night, Samara began thinking of her past and decided to take a walk around the castle. Once outside the outer walls, Zanzabar appeared, his face hostile.

"You weren't supposed to tie yourself down to any mortals. As the Winter Goddess, your intention isn't to indulge in infantile emotions like love. What's worse is that you have been deceived this entire time by the queen. She isn't who she says she is. She is Tatiana. She is your enemy, and she must be defeated in order for the wood to continue with the cycles and bring peace."

"What do you mean bring peace? How long have you known about Tatiana?"

"She cursed your mother seventeen years ago. Your mother is frozen somewhere in the earth, and the only way to pull her from it is for you to overthrow Tatiana!"

"My mother isn't dead?"

"No, all that time you felt alone, you really weren't because I was looking after you. For the first time, you will be able to choose your own path, but it will also mean a sacrifice. Are you ready?"

"No!" Samara screamed. "I can't kill Rook's mother! I love him. He will never forgive me. He would never understand!" It was a horrible sacrifice. The queen was the reason she was without a mother all those years. But she was also the closest thing Samara had ever had to a mother. She finally felt loved like a daughter.

"So, you finally uncovered who I really am, have you?" said Tatiana, coming down the castle's steps, startling Zanzabar and Samara. Zanzabar raised his staff, but Tatiana was too quick for him. She restrained him in a giant bubble, her eyes filled with hatred and amusement. "What were you trying to do, Zanzabar? Kill me?" Her shrill laughter echoed over the castle grounds. "You know perfectly well who needs to kill me." Her cold eyes fell on Samara. "But she won't do it. I know she won't. Rook will never want to look at her again. And she'll go back to being the miserable girl she always has been. Do you really think that killing me will make you happy?"

"Don't listen to her, Samara!" screamed Zanzabar, his face distorted with pain.

"Samara! What's happening?" cried Rook's panicked voice. "Mother, what are you doing with that man? You're hurting him!"

"She's not your mother, Rook!" shrieked Samara. "I have to tell you something. From the moment I saw you, I knew that I loved you. But I am the Winter Goddess, and this is my destiny. I will never be fully happy if I don't do this. Please forgive me." Tears fell from Samara's eyes.

She directed her staff at Tatiana. A bright bolt flew from the staff and hit Tatiana with incredible force. Tatiana's eyes widened in surprise and fear as Samara's spell hit her. The bubble encircling Zanzabar disappeared, and Tatiana's body went limp on the ground.

Michelle Bautista
THE HERO IN ME

I believe anyone can be a hero. I thought heroes were Spider-Man, Superman, and Batman, but I realized this is not true. A hero does not have to have fantastic powers. A hero does not need to have superhuman strength, flexibility, or invisibility. Heroes must be confident and have the courage to overcome their flaws. Being a hero means reaching for one's dreams and overcoming one's fears.

I have been a hero my entire life. I was born in Los Angeles, but my parents decided to move to Tijuana, where my father was born. He had a good job there, and he was buying a house. My mom loved the idea, and we left. When I was five years old, we moved again, and I went to school in San Diego. My mother wanted me to learn English and get a good education. I learned English and songs that I loved to sing; I still remember my favorite: "Yellow corn, yellow corn, what do you see / I see the yellow corn looking at me."

With no explanation, my mother decided to send me back to Tijuana when I was in the first grade. I did not understand. It was really scary. All the kids looked at me for speaking English. In school, I quickly learned to speak Spanish. I met new people and made a friend. Tijuana became a comfortable place to live: I had my own room, my dog, and my father's grandmother. I was really happy there, but when I turned nine my parents decided to move back to Los Angeles.

It was shocking. I did not know any English anymore. I did not make friends right away. I was scared and hopeless, and I thought people were talking behind my back.

But in the fifth grade, I learned how to speak and write in English. This experience was the hardest of all, but I made it through the humiliation and sadness. I had the courage to overcome my fear.

In the ninth grade, I felt I couldn't trust myself. I was lost. I had the worst friends. They always wanted to ditch, and that was just not me. I was the sheep, following others. In the tenth grade, I quit being friends with them. I started to hang out with others, but it was really hard. I felt like I did not belong. Things changed in eleventh grade. I learned to trust my instincts and not have pity for anyone, not even for myself. I learned not to follow anybody but me. I learned to live in reality instead of a world filled with dishonesty, lies, and ignorance.

Writing the hero's journey has changed my life: the way I think, the way I act, and the way I don't let other people use me. I learned that people judge you without even knowing you. There were times in my life when I just did not want to be around my family or my friends. I have some family members who think that I am not clever, that I can't write or think. It makes me miserable, but I don't pity myself. I make things happen. I signed up for Great Books and Creative Writing, and I wrote a story that everyone thought I couldn't write, even though it was difficult and I had to write about experiences that I've never had. When my family found out that I wrote a story, they couldn't accept the fact that I am clever and that I don't care what others think of me.

With effort and courage, the hero's journey changed my life forever. I'm proud of myself; at seventeen years old, I wrote a short story published in a book. It is like a dream come true.

Maria Diaz
METAMORPHOSIS

One can be a true hero, but one needs to find the hero within oneself first. I have met amazing people throughout my life, made fantastic friends, and met extraordinary teachers who taught me very much. I have learned from them, and that has built up my character. I know heroes are all around me—people like my friends, teachers, firefighters, lifeguards, and the most important ones, my parents. They've worked hard to raise my brother, sister, and me. They have placed a roof over our heads, put food on the table, and provided everything we needed. I know how hard they struggle when their alarm goes off at two or four in the morning. I know how tough and tiring it is at work, and I see their agony every day in their sad expressions. I try my best to help them but can't do much. The only thing I can give to my true heroes is appreciation. I believe heroes like them are always there, even where one least expects them to be.

It all began back in middle school in the sixth grade, when I was involved with the wrong people. That was my call to adventure. I guess I didn't have friends before, and I began hanging around with people who were bad influences, convincing me to ditch classes and causing my grades to go down. I had no idea why I was doing those things at the time, but I know why now. It was fear, fear of being alone and having no friends to talk to or laugh with. I hated being lonely at school. The only place I wanted to be alone was my home. It was a safe place where I could be myself. At school, I was someone different. I was more of a maid: I followed orders to satisfy my so-called friends, except I wasn't doing the right thing. Yet I did it all just to have someone to talk to: to have "friends."

Luckily, being a maid did not last long after my parents discovered my report cards and received phone calls from school about the days I missed classes. I can still picture my mother's face, furious as she looked at me, and my father lowering his head with disappointment. My mother has a very bad temper, so she refused to deal with me. She asked my father to talk to me instead. My father also has a bad temper, but he is able to control it. As my father spoke to me, I began to realize my mistakes. I was surprised I wasn't spanked. He said there was no need to hit me to make me understand. He knew I realized my mistakes. He had, and still has, faith in me; both my parents do. I was their only hope. I didn't want to end up like my older brother or sister, who both ended up on the wrong road. They believed I could be better. They knew I didn't belong with that crowd because that wasn't the way they raised me. I started to look toward my future and dreamed about going to college.

Ever since that moment, I've changed. You could say my days weren't as gloomy, and the sun shined on me. It wasn't too late to make changes because it was only the first semester of sixth grade. But I knew I had lots of work to do. In the long run, I brought my grades up from F's to C's, and then to B's and A's. I impressed myself with the things I did to achieve my goal. Even one of my sixth-grade teachers, whom I later had for eighth grade, was amazed by the phenomenal work I did during those last two years of middle school. My parents were astonished, but they weren't the only ones who were surprised: my brother and sister were, too. Somehow it embarrassed them that their baby sister was accomplishing what they failed to achieve. That is what my mother wanted me to do, to demonstrate that if I could do it, so could they. In that instant they learned a lesson. I told them it wasn't too late for them either, but they had to want to accomplish their goals. I reached my ultimate boon just by realizing and accepting my mistakes. I became more self-aware. I was finally beginning to be myself. I remained a little fearful, but I was coming out of my cocoon little by little.

High school was the best. It has been a home for me, especially in Humanitas. I was ignorant before, but I have become conscious, mature, and confident. I am wiser, yet I still have lots to learn. I make mistakes all the time, and I hate them because sometimes I end up hurting people. Deep within my heart I don't mean to hurt anyone, but I still fail to forgive myself for mistakes I commit. I have to remind myself that not everyone is perfect and that no one wants to make blunders. One has to first admit the mistake, then learn from it. Every journey I take, I learn something new, and it prepares me for the real world. Now I can say I am out of my cocoon and have turned into a butterfly.

Maria Diaz
THE SYMBOL OF THE SNAKE

Prologue:

One dim freezing night, Emperor Ozomatli's wife died after giving birth to their first child. The emperor lost his wife but had the son he wished for. Days later, Ozomatli gave his son the gift that every emperor of their blood possessed, and tattooed a snake on his child's left palm, marking him as the next emperor. The symbol was handed down from his great-grandfather to his grandfather to his father, to Ozomatli, and now to his first child.

After Ozomatli gave his child that royal gift, he made plans for a small ceremony to present his child and give him his name. But Ozomatli was murdered that same day by his envious, selfish, and evil cousin, Ocelot, who then became the evil tyrant of the Aztecs. The child never received his name. He was hidden in the dungeon for a day while Ocelot thought of a plan. He did not want the people of the empire to find out the child was still alive. He wanted them to believe the child had died at childbirth. Ocelot ordered one of his secret servants to send the child away and kill him.

The servant took the child out of Tenochtitlan. He took him to an old man who was a hunter and a fisherman because he didn't have the courage to kill him. Instead, he ordered the old man to kill him because it was the emperor's command, and left. However, the old man decided not to kill the child, but instead raise him as his grandchild. He named the child Coatl after the symbol on his palm.

I walk out of the house's front door and feel the bright glittery sun gleaming on my face. The fresh, clean breeze softly caresses my skin and gives me chills. The wind blows crimson and ginger leaves from the trees, and the birds leave their old nests to make new ones as havens for the winter. I see the coast and its blue water glinting beautifully from the sun's reflection. Wow, she is remarkable and deserves to be admired.

Early every morning, I watch my neighbor walk out of his door to go out and fish, while I prepare my hunting bag. I see his nervous face hoping to catch fish for all his people and the empire. I pity him and all the men out at the shore. It takes patience, hope, and chance to capture at least a few fish. For us hunters, it takes an active role. Our bodies need to be strong, and our vision, clear. We need to be quick in order to catch deer.

I started hunting at age twelve. My grandfather trained me when I was eight. He was also a hunter and a fisherman. My grandpa also trained my best friend Cuetzpallin, and together we grew up like brothers.

I was always taught that our elders need to be respected. They are our role models, and they must be the ones to teach us because they are full of experience and are sacred to us Aztecs. But now, I see no respect for our elders. Even old men need to hunt and fish these days.

Our traditions are not the same since Ocelot became emperor. I was just a baby when he ascended the throne. My grandfather met the previous emperor, Ozomatli, at a young age. They were close friends. My grandfather even went to the ceremony when Ozomatli became emperor. My grandfather said he was a great friend and an excellent emperor until the day he was murdered. No one knows who did it. All I know is that his cousin Ocelot then became emperor, and now everything is different.

The poor have few rights. Ocelot sends his warriors to spy on us and to make sure we are doing our work. Many men, women, and children out there get whipped. It is tough, but no one complains: we all do the work because it is a necessity. I wish I could help, but what can I do? I'm only a hunter. I hate when my grandfather gets whipped and I'm not around. He's old. He cannot do much work anymore. I try my best every day to help him and do my job, but sometimes it is impossible.

As I stretch my muscles, my grandfather comes to the door, calling after me. "Wait, my boy! You forgot your knife!" he yells.

"Thank you, Pa. I knew I was forgetting something," I say, laughing.

"Well, make sure you do not forget again."

"I won't; I promise. Goodbye, Grandfather. I'll return this evening. Oh! And try not to do too much work today. I'll help you when I come back," I say, waving my hand.

"I'm sure it's your lucky day!" he says, excitedly.

"We'll see, Pa. Goodbye."

"Hmm...good luck, Son," he says, hesitating.

As I take faster steps toward the forest, I hear stomping feet and laughter coming from behind. I know it's the rest of the hunters, laughing and shouting, "Wait for us!" I glance at them and begin to run so that they have to chase after me. I always make them do that; it's fun. Except today feels different; it looks different and smells different too. Autumn has arrived. There isn't much to hunt for. All the animals are getting ready for winter.

We walk deeper into the forest while looking around carefully.

"Hey Coatl, do you see it?" asks Cuetzpallin, my best friend.

I look ahead and see a deer eating the leftover grass. Sensing my presence, it turns to face me. It stays still.

"Go get him; he's all yours," he whispers. I slowly take out my bow and shoot, but I miss it. It starts to run away when I realize I can't let it go. Grabbing on to my bow and my bag, I chase after it. I run further into the silence of the forest. It gives me chills. As I look for the deer, the sun begins to set. The sky turns dark, and the silver-white moon glows in the beautiful deep blue sky. Suddenly, I lose sight of the deer. I turn everywhere trying to find it, and then I hear its footsteps. I turn nervously and see it run through the bulbous bushes. My zombie eyes stare into the dryness of the bushes, and my mind wonders what is in there. I amble through the frizzy round bushes to discover a beautiful, empty land in a shape of a snake. The naked trees and the precious multi-hued flowers that only grow during the fall make this place sad and beautiful at the same time. I know it is the cycle of life: everything needs to die, and life starts again. This is one of those places where one can be in peace.

I feel the cool night wind hitting my face as I step on the parched, crunchy fallen leaves. I hear the birds moving in their nests trying to get warm, and as I continue walking forward, I observe the bushes masking an orange sunset.

Thud!

I trip on a tree root and fall to the ground when I notice a snake right in front of me, staring into my eyes. I stand still, but it's ready to attack. It bites my left hand. I look around quickly, grab a rock, and smash its head. It squirms until it lies motionless. I immediately get up and kick the dead snake away from me. I look down at my bitten hand and squeeze out the venom. I stare deeply into my palm and notice something: this land is in the shape of a snake, and I have a symbol of a snake on my palm. I glance at the land and then my palm. What a coincidence!

I've always wondered if the symbol on my palm was something. When I was little I thought it was a birthmark and felt special because of it, but as I grew, I detected the ink under my skin. I asked my grandfather who tattooed my palm and when, and he said the gods asked him to when I was a baby. I believed him because my grandfather is very spiritual and very connected to the gods. I began to believe that my symbol had some significance.

Gliding into the land, I spot large puffy bushes covering the peak of a stone. My curiosity tempts me as I shift toward the bushes. I part them and stroll through, noticing it isn't stone but a small golden pyramid about ten feet tall, covered with blurry symbols. As I stand before the pyramid, I begin to wipe the dust off the hot golden surface with my fingers. The sun's rays hit the exposed surface and sparkle beautifully, mirroring the sun itself. The engraved silver hieroglyphs twinkle like stars.

One symbol stands out to me. A snake. It is traced by beautiful, rich rainbow rocks. I stare at my palm, and then at the pyramid, and I notice that the symbol on the pyramid appears to be the same as the one on my palm. I look to the bottom of the pyramid and read the epitaph.

This pyramid is in memory of and a sign of respect for the royal snake emperors, with the snake symbol on their left palms.

It has Emperor Ozomatli's name, his father who was emperor before him, his grandfather, and his great-grandfather too, but the strangest thing is that they all have the symbol of the snake on their left palm, just like I do. I begin to wonder about the night my grandfather had a private conversation with Cuetzpallin's father. I was behind the kitchen door when they began talking about me. I remember my grandfather telling Cuetzpallin's father that he couldn't hide the truth from me anymore.

I do not know what's going on. I am so confused.

As I reach home and run through the door, I see my grandfather kneeling on a red mat in front of our altar, praying to the gods and the four directions. Smoke is all over the room. The smell of sage makes me cough. As I stand there staring and waiting for him, he finishes his last prayer and turns to face me. I am so confused and anxious that my grandfather notices. I tell him what happened. He stares into my eyes and says nothing. He seems to know something. Then he comes closer.

"You said you found the symbol on your palm on the pyramid?" he asks calmly.

I wonder if he knows what I am talking about. Then, as my thoughts begin to run like crazy, my grandfather begins to talk again.

"My son, you must go back. You must go."

"Why? I don't understand."

He says nothing else, but turns away.

"What in the world is going on with you? You seem to know something. You even look nervous, and you never get nervous!" I exclaim.

"NOTHING! I know nothing about this."

I am in shock. There would be no need for him to yell unless he knew something. As I stare at him with surprise, he turns to face me again.

"Look my boy, I'm very sorry, but you must go back."

"Why? Tell me: why must I go back?"

"I can't! I can't tell you. It's for your own good. I care

for you."

"Oh, so it's for my own good! Why can't you tell me? I mean, if you really care about me, you will tell me."

"No! I didn't want you to find out because I was afraid you would get hurt, but you have the right to know, and now you are old enough to understand. I can't tell you, though. You must learn how to find the answer for yourself, my boy."

I can't think about anything else except discovering it on my own. Tomorrow will be a new day. Tomorrow I will learn what my grandfather is hiding from me.

Walking through the bare forest, I begin to wonder why my grandfather told me to go back to the pyramid. Why wouldn't he tell me? Could it be that he knows something about the pyramid? The clear blue sky, the cool wind, the smell of fresh wood, and the touch of the sun's rays on my back all relax me. I walk deeper into the forest, whose ground is covered with brown crunching leaves.

Thud!

I hit the ground and lie there, motionless. My body begins to hurt. I can't move, and close my eyes for a few minutes. When I open my eyes, I can see I fell into a deep deer trap—my own deer trap. I didn't notice it because of all the leaves on the ground. I cannot think of a way to get out, so I yell to see if anyone will hear my call for help.

"Help! Can anyone hear me? Help!" I yell for help all through the afternoon, after the sunset, and through the night.

The night winds are so cold that my teeth begin to chatter. My nose is freezing, and my lips are dry. Although I am stuck in a hole, I can see the glow of the white moon and the precious stars. I start to count the stars and make figures with them since I have nothing else to do. I hear noises and think it is an animal, but it is probably just the wind blowing on the leaves.

I wish to be warm right now, and then I wish for someone to come rescue me tomorrow. I wonder what my grandfather is doing. I wonder if Cuetzpallin is sleeping. I begin to shiver more. I can't feel my hands, my feet. I close my eyes and fall asleep.

I can sense the morning as the sun comes out. I do not open my eyes until the sun's rays hit my head. I stand and feel the air, now much warmer. I hear the lovely birds sing as they fly, and the warm wind whistle above me. If I listen, I might be able to hear deer strolling around. It is a perfect time to call for help because everyone is out working.

"Help! Can somebody please help me?" I cry out loudly.

I begin to pray to the gods for someone to rescue me. Nothing happens.

"HELP! HELP! Someone, please..." I cry again.

At that moment I hear footsteps. I hear a man's voice. "Who's calling for help? Yell again so I can find you."

The man is one of Ocelot's warriors, the ones who spy on us. He grabs onto my hand tightly and pulls me up. As he takes me out, he stares at my left palm and looks at me strangely.

"There, you're finally out. How long have you been stuck in this trap?" he asks.

As I explain what happened, he stares at my palm once again, and then at my eyes.

"How did you get that?"

"The symbol on my palm?"

"Yes, where and how did you get it?"

"I've had it since I was an infant."

"Well, you are not allowed to have that, and I'm going to have to take you into prison."

I run before he tries to tie me up, and he chases after me. I can hear him call for the others. I sprint as fast as I can and leave him behind, but the others are coming toward me. One warrior takes out a sword to frighten me. I quickly reach for my ax and fight him back. He swings his sword, and I block it with my ax. At the third hit my ax breaks. I run away from him, but they're surrounding me, so I begin to dance around them to find my way out. I stop between two warriors; I hit one and kick the other. The third one jumps on my back, and I flip him over onto the ground.

Despite my efforts, they are all very close, and there is nowhere else to run. They all jump on me. I feel one warrior
holding on to my legs while another ties my hands with a
rusty metal chain. They leave me on the ground, and they
all begin to laugh. After a couple of minutes, they start to
whip my back. I feel the first cut. I can't do anything but
close my eyes.

The night is young, and it's a full moon. The clouds shift,
and the stars shine brightly. I am trapped and tied up with
metal chains. The warriors all walk around next to me to
make sure I don't escape. I feel the whiplashes on my back
as I walk.

The fresh wind hits my face. I can see the palace from
this distance. I don't want to step near the palace of Ocelot.
He treats my people unfairly. Someone should make him
pay. The men laugh as they whip me again. I am tired from
the torture and can't continue to walk up the steps. *Whapa!*
I get whipped again and again, and fall to the ground. My
eyes feel heavy and begin to close, and suddenly I see nothing but black.

I wake up and notice I am in a room with weapons on a
table. My arms and legs are tied to a pole. I cannot stand
anymore. I hear my stomach cry for food. My mouth is dry
and rough as wood. Everything is a blur, and my body feels
weak. When I put my head down to rest, I hear a woman's
evil laugh. I feel her presence as she comes closer. I smell
flowery perfume and look up to meet her. She is covered
in gold and fancy jewelry. She must be that beast's wife.
She is covered in sin, just like Ocelot. As I glare at her, she
begins to mock me.

She sits in front of me and says, "I know who you are,
Coatl. Do you know why you have that symbol on your
palm? Hmm? Ozomatli was your father. Ocelot murdered
him. You were supposed to be dead, but apparently you are
not. That old man didn't do his job. Well...you are an attractive man. Or, should I say, hunter," she says, laughing.

"What? How do you know this?"

"Let's just say I have my ways of finding out, honey."

She stands closer to me, and I grab her long hair with my

teeth. "Tell me, how do you know these things?"

"You know, you're hurting me."

I pull her hair harder.

"Ouch. I like rough men."

"Stop being funny."

"Okay then. You know who Coyotl is? He was supposed to kill you, but he didn't have the guts. He told me all about what happened after you were born."

I let her go, and she begins to walk around me. She laughs again. She asks if I am hungry or thirsty, but I refuse to answer. She snaps at her servants, ordering them to bring her what she wants. The servants quickly attend to her, and she begins to eat in front of me.

"You snake, you treat my people like animals."

She begins to laugh.

I look up at her. "Shut up!" I cry. "Why are you here?"

"I'm here because I can help you become emperor. I can kill Ocelot for you, but what's in it for me?"

"Nothing! Nothing is in it for you. I don't need you. If I want to kill him, I'll do it myself. I don't need help. Now leave! Get out of here!"

She throws the food in front of me and walks out angrily.

As the morning comes, I can barely see the sun rising through the small window. My weak and gaunt body lies on the ground as if I am dead. My wounds hurt as I slowly move. I feel the dry blood on my skin. My lips are dry like paper. I have been in this dark room, with one window, for about four days without food and water. Not only does my body feel weak, but I am starting to lose my mental strength. I have no idea why they want to keep me here. They should have just killed me the day I was captured.

I heard two guards talk about Ocelot last night. They said he was on his way back to Tenochtitlan. I think he was out with another tribe, one of our allies, Cholula. I wonder if he is here now. I want to tear his face into pieces.

The door opens. It is hard to lift my head, which is heavy because of all the pain, so I can only glance up for a few moments at a time. My vision is unclear. I see a blurry man in the doorway. As he gets closer, I see he wears a royal crown, with the finest feathers, covered with sprinkles of gold and gorgeous stones. He wears a jaguar cape and golden sandals. It is Ocelot, the one who killed my father, the beast who treats my people like slaves. He walks toward me, and our eyes meet. I grimace with anger, and he spits on me. His disgusting saliva runs down my cheek, but I do not show fear, and his venom does not hurt me. He lets out an evil laugh, and I feel a knot of wrath in my throat. I close my fists tightly.

I stand up and look him in the eye, showing no fear, only disgust. He looks down at my palm and gives me an evil look.

"Where did you get it?"

I remain silent. I refuse to answer him.

Whapa! The guard whips my back.

"Answer me! How did you get it?"

"I thought you knew. Your evil wife knows it all. Let her tell you."

He looks at me with disgust and turns around to call his servant.

"Coyotl, bring Itztli to me. I need to ask her a few questions."

Coyotl bows to him and runs to look for Itztli. That name is perfect for her. She is a knife that stabs through your back.

Itztli walks in, taking a look at me. Ocelot looks at her and gently touches her chin.

"Itztli, do you know this young man? Do you know why he carries that symbol on his palm?"

She responds nervously, "No, I do not know."

"Now, my dear, I know you are lying. Tell me what you know."

"The day before you arrived, I asked Coyotl who this young man was, and he looked nervous. I offered him gold, and he revealed a secret about Ozomatli's child. He didn't kill him, and now that he's seen the symbol on this man's palm, Coyotl is afraid this might be the child."

Ocelot's eyes widen. He stares at me and calls Coyotl in.

"Coyotl, we need to talk." They both walk out the door. Itztli and the guards follow, shutting the door behind them. Now I am all alone. I feel so tired. My body is beaten up. I put my head down to pray to the gods.

Suddenly, a sweet voice from behind the door says, "Stand up; do not feel weak. Think strong." The door opens slowly, and a beautiful woman walks in. She smiles and pours crystal clear water into my lips, and I drink. "Now you have to promise not to give up." She takes a last look at me and smiles before closing the door. Her words have filled me with power. My body remains weak, but my spirit and my mind are strong again. Now I have the strength and courage to confront Ocelot and everyone else. I will not give up.

The guards return, and I wait until they get close to me. One unties me so that they can transfer me into another room, and I know this is the time. I hit, punch, and kick him. When the other jumps on my back, I hit him with my head and smash him back against the wall. I run out the door to find that beast Ocelot. He must be around here. I run into his royal room and see the royal crown on a pillow. I destroy all his jewelry. I see my hunting bag with my weapons in it, and I put the crown in there. I run out when I hear someone cry, "Master, he's gone!"

As I run outside the palace, I see Cuetzpallin. He is here with the rest of the hunters. They all have come well-prepared, as if to hunt animals.

"Coatl?" Cuetzpallin yells, surprised to see me alive.

"Cuetzpallin? What are you doing here?"

"I came to look for you. We are here to help. Coatl, there is something I need to tell you. Your grandfather is with the gods. These warriors destroyed our home, and they took your grandfather. All of us hunters followed them, and we saw them whipping him. They wanted him to tell them some secret he knew. We tried to save him, but he died from the torture before we could do anything."

My body stiffens. I can't say a word, but a teardrop falls down my cheek. I feel a knot in my throat, and my heart feels the flames. Cuetzpallin hugs me as I cry. At least Grandfather is resting now.

"My grandfather knew. He was hiding the truth from me all this time."

Soon, we have all spread out. My fellow hunters are fighting the palace warriors, and I am looking for Ocelot. It is raining hard now. The sky is angry. I can't think of anything to do but run to the top of the ceremonial pyramid. When I see Ocelot at the bottom of the pyramid, he sneers and starts to walk slowly to the top.

He finally reaches the last step. He is holding onto a sword, but my old hunting knife in my left hand and a stolen sword in my right are ready to chop off his head. Then Ocelot slips. He tumbles down the pyramid, all the way down to the ground. Blood comes out of mouth. He lies there motionless. He is dead.

Cuetzpallin comes running up the pyramid. "Coatl, you must go. You must go to your empire. You're the emperor now. It belongs to you. It always did."

"I killed him," I say, shocked.

"No, you didn't. He fell on his own, and that's what evil people like him get. That devil destroyed almost everything. Come on, Coatl, your people are waiting for you, and there is a disaster here. We are all waiting for your orders, my emperor."

I feel proud and thankful, but I am so confused. I can't do this. I just can't. Let someone else do it. Someone who is royalty, who is responsible, who knows how.

"I'm just not ready. I have no idea what to do. How do I rule? I was never raised to be an emperor," I say.

"But you have the heart. You can do it. We will all help you."

As we walk down the stairs of the pyramid, the rain stops. The clouds and the gloomy sky fade away as the sun comes out and begins to shine. Cuetzpallin urges me to hurry.

I begin to feel butterflies in my stomach. All of a sudden, out of the forest I hear a tender, familiar whisper: "You did it, my son."

Goose bumps rise on my skin. It isn't scary—the voice touches my heart. Even though I have never met my father, he is in my heart. Though my grandfather is not my real grandfather, I'm never going to forget about him. He raised me. He brought happiness and love into my life. He taught me everything I needed to know, and I will always be thankful. Always.

"Come on, Coatl, you're going to be late to your festival."

I'm going to be late to *my* festival?

Cuetzpallin begins to laugh, and I laugh with him. We start talking about our childhood, and I suddenly stop laughing. Cuetzpallin looks into my eyes. I begin to look around; the crowd is watching me. Cuetzpallin kneels in front of me, takes the crown out of my dusty hunting bag, and says, "Here is your crown, my emperor."

The crowd begins to cheer. I have no idea what to do next. I begin to walk toward the palace, trying to avoid the looks from the crowd. I look at the floor, but I hear that tender voice again say to me, "Lift your head up, Son; you should be proud." The voice once again touches my heart, and I am not afraid anymore. I feel ready. I know my grandfather and my father are here with me.

I walk up a couple of steps, enough so that my people can see me. "My people, this is an honor to me and you, but not just us. I know my father is proud of me, and he is by my side. My grandfather is here, too. He is proud of me; he was the man who raised me when I was lost. Now I am back. This is my destiny. I was meant to be found. The gods know I belong here, where my father used to be. This moment is not just mine, but ours. Let's celebrate!"

The crowd begins to cheer louder and louder. I know they went through a nightmare with Ocelot, but they have been saved. I have been saved. "One more thing: the rules that Ocelot established are changing immediately. From now on, my people from the coast are always welcome to the palace. Everyone is."

I can see Cuetzpallin's smile from far away. The music begins, and people start to dance. Watching everyone laugh, smile, sing, and dance makes me very happy. A man behind me says, "You did it; you are our hero, my emperor." When I turn around, he smiles, shakes my hand, and walks off. I look up to the sky and smile. "Thank you."

Gloria Rosales
STARS OF HOPE

Each glistening star above me
Hovers like a balloon
Represents a dream of mine
That I can never reach

The more stars that are visible
The more my dreams become unreachable

As each dream grows dimmer
I only want to reach them more

Maribel Juarez
THE GAUCHE ACCIDENT

The afternoon is warm; the yellowish sky remains hot yet shows signs of cheer. My mom is still not home from work, and I am hungry, so I go to the kitchen to see what is in the refrigerator. Bread and peanut butter—gosh, isn't there anything good to eat in this house? I make a sandwich then take a shower, filling the bathroom with hot steam. I hear my mom's jalopy pull up in our driveway, and then my mom shouting, "Honey, I'm home!"

"It's about time," I reply with attitude.

"Well, sorry, there was traffic. Hungry?"

"Not anymore, I had to eat a sandwich."

As I am changing, my mom comes into my room and sees that I am getting ready to go out.

"Where are you going, young lady?"

"To a party with Joyce. Her mom is taking us."

"I don't think so. You aren't going anywhere!"

"Why? I am not going to stay here all bored. It's Saturday; you know that, right?"

"I don't care if it's Saturday or not. I said you are not going!" She slams my bedroom door shut.

I don't care what my mom says. I am not staying home. When Joyce arrives, I run out the door, and my mom screams, "When your dad calls, I'm going to tell him that you left without permission!" I ignore her and leave. After all, all I get from my dad is money and a postcard two times a year. I want to live my life without limits.

When I get home at four in the morning, my mom is in deep sleep. I go to my room and knock out instantly.

The next morning, I wake up with an immense thirst. I go to the kitchen and gulp down a glass of orange juice. I call my mom to see what there is for breakfast.

"Mom! I'm hungry! Mom!"

There is only silence. I start throwing papers and kicking the walls; I am irritated that every time I want my mom to be here, she isn't. How does she expect me to be a child who feels loved and important to her parents if no one is here when I need something? I wish I had a family to share my life with.

Outside after school on Monday, the cold air penetrates my heart. The dark sky is full of clouds, ready to drizzle. What a day to wear my favorite pink Coach shoes. I think about calling Joyce, but I decide not to. She is most likely busy taking care of her brothers and sisters since she is the oldest. She may be my best friend, but I wouldn't want to give her more work.

It's starting to get dark. I have to go home; my mom must be worried. I walk toward the bus stop and feel a wintry sense through my spine. I start to shiver. Leaning on the wall and getting lost in my own thoughts, I gaze at chirping birds taking care of their young affectionately. How I would have loved to have my father with me, to chirp at me like these birds do at their little ones. One day he just left, leaving me with only my mother, and no brothers or sisters to play with. It's just me and my mother, trying to work together so we can be both be happy. But it's not that easy.

Finally, the bus arrives. I walk up the steps and slip my dollar and quarter in. I walk to the back of the bus, sit next to the window, and watch the cars go by. As I'm staring at the freeway, there is a light that brightens on my side. I turn, but I just hear a big collision, and everything goes blank.

I open my eyes, blinking at the intensity of the light. I realize I'm in the hospital. Feeling very sore, I try to sit up straight but can't. The nurse comes in with my mom; she is sobbing, and I ask her why is she crying.

"What happened?" I mumble.

"When you were on the bus, a car was being chased by the police. It lost control and hit the bus that you were riding.

"Mom, I don't remember anything. I don't feel my legs."

"It's okay, honey, you don't have to move anything right now."

"Yes, but I don't feel my legs. I can't even sit."

The nurse and my mom look at each other. I am confused. They sit next to me and tell me that I have to be strong. They tell me my legs are paralyzed.

"What?"

"Try to keep calm, and try not to get angry. It's going to be all right; don't worry," my mom says.

I just stare at my legs. It must be a dream I'm living. This can't be happening.

Three months after my accident, my mom enrolls me at the Advantage Resource Group to get some therapy. As I arrive, I feel sick to my stomach. I don't want to be here. While my mom signs me in, I observe what the others are doing. Everyone seems content, but I just feel more depressed.

"Hey there, are you lost?" asks a young boy in a wheelchair, wearing a big smile on his face.

"Um, no, I'm just waiting for my mom."

"Oh, I see, you're a mommy's girl," he says with a big laugh.

"For your information, I am not a mommy's girl, so get out of my face. Get lost!" I shout.

People around me turn and look; I am so embarrassed. My mom asks why was I shouting. She sees the guy next to me and tells me to introduce him to her.

"I don't know him. He just came by to make fun of me."

"No, I didn't," he says. "Sorry for what I said."

"Just get lost."

"Well, let me introduce myself first. I'm Jaden."

"Okay, Jaden, now you may leave."

When we come back the next day, the supervisor gathers everyone into the meeting room and announces that there is a new member joining them. He points to me and asks me to tell them about myself. I feel my face turn red, but I manage to let go of my fear and gain the confidence to talk about myself. I talk about my accident and the way I feel, and at the end everyone claps. Tears roll down my cheeks. It feels like I just let out my greatest fear.

As I start spending more time at the center, I develop a colossal interest in art. It is the only way to get distracted and forget about my legs. My friends help, too. Throughout my rehabilitation, Joyce has been there for me. Ever since my accident, she has been like my sister whom I can confide in and tell my fears and hopes. The time we spend together is like being in heaven: I forget about my worries and look toward the future. And Jaden, who was a wise guy when I first came to the center, is now the guy whose big smile always brightens my day.

As time goes by, my art gets better and better. I start a mural project, and the themes are courage and comfort. It takes me a whole day to think about the colors I am going to use and how I am going to establish the themes through the mural. With time, I am able to create a startling piece of art. After I finish my mural, I am exultant. It is the first project where I did something on my own. I realize that anything is possible after a tragedy.

OVERBOARD!

Jesus Enriquez
RUN FROM IT

Saturday morning, 5:09 a.m., *buzz, buzz, buzz!* The alarm clock breaks the peaceful silence of a good night's rest. Sleepy, Jimmy Phaeton awakes, only to slam the snooze button with his clenched right fist. He falls victim to his much-needed sleep once more. *Buzz, buzz, buzz!* Getting up, he gives in to the call of his alarm. Trying to distinguish reality from fantasy, he looks around his room. "What a mess...I'll just clean it later." At that moment, a familiar aroma wafts by Jimmy. His eyes widen as his nose leads him to the source. He walks into the kitchen with his nose held high and stomach empty, in need of fuel. Cooking at the stove is Maria, Jimmy's stepmother. Turning to him, she smiles. "Good morning, sunshine."

"Good morning, Mom," replies Jimmy, now sitting at the table and waiting for food. Walking over to him, Maria is holding a plate of food and a glass of juice. "I made your favorite: eggs with a hint of black pepper, bacon, toast, and freshly-squeezed orange juice."

Jimmy attacks the food without hesitation and, with an over-stuffed mouth, replies, "Thanks, Mom."

Maria makes herself a plate and joins him. "Are you nervous?"

"Yeah, just a little, but I'm sure anyone would get nervous for an Olympic qualifying match."

"Jimmy...whether you go to Beijing or not, I'm still going to be proud of you."

He looks down toward his plate and closes his eyes. "I have to go, Mom. Don't want to be late."

Ready to face his big day, he walks to the staircase. To

his surprise the door is stuck; its hydraulic piston is broken. Jimmy rams the door open and paces himself down the stairs, skipping every other step. He enters the parking lot and stops in front of his Mitsubishi Lancer. After stepping into the car, he puts the key into the ignition, bringing his baby to life. It purrs as Jimmy happily revs the engine. His nostrils flare with each long breath, savoring the smell of new leather. "Metal Meltdown" by Judas Priest plays on the car stereo.

Something's calling, in the night

With his left hand on the steering wheel and his right hand on the gearshift, he drives off. "I can't believe it. I'm going to Beijing. Today the city, and then the world."

Electric madness roars in sight

Los Angeles is like the heart of an old man; its arteries are congested with poor circulation. It's hard to be in LA without facing the traffic.

Heat is rising, blazing fast

This is why Jimmy decides to take surface streets to Staples Center.

Hot and evil, feel the blast

He makes a right on Whittier Boulevard from Lorena Street. The stoplight on Soto turns green, letting Jimmy pass. He smiles and accelerates.

It's coming at ya

There is a BMW on the road, and the driver is drunk. He can't tell the difference between green and red. He is delusional from tunnel vision.

Here comes the metal meltdown

"Oh, no—" Jimmy sees the BMW coming toward him, fifteen feet away. He slams his foot on the brakes. Imagining the worst, he closes his eyes and grips the steering wheel tightly.

The BMW buries itself in the Lancer, and its engine

block rips into the cabin, crushing the drunk driver. Jimmy is hugged by the airbags and loses consciousness.

Suddenly, Jimmy finds himself standing in a stadium, filled with people screaming and chanting his name: "Phaeton! Phaeton! Phaeton!"
"I did it...I won...I won!" he screams.

"Jimmy, Jimmy...Doctor! I think he's waking up!"
Jimmy opens his eyes in pain, and tears run down his cheeks. It's not the injuries that hurt most. It's the pain caused by the destruction of a dream, the pain of trying to move your body only to realize that you can't feel any part of your legs.
Maria is stressed and shocked, but she is relieved to see Jimmy awaken. "It's okay, baby, you're all right now. I'm here for you." Her voice is weak and shrill from days of crying. "It's okay."

Later, after being checked by the doctors, Jimmy's feeding tube and oxygen mask are removed.
"What happened to me?"
"You were in a car accident. Maria has been sitting next to you as much as possible since then," replies a nurse.
"Where is she? I want to see her!"
"All right, just one moment."
Little did Jimmy know that visiting hours were over. It is now Sunday, and the hospital has a no-visiting-hours policy on Sunday. Maria won't be able to visit until Monday.

Monday morning, Maria walks into the room with the shadow of guilt hanging over her. "Jimmy, hey Jimmy," she gently whispers into his ear.
Jimmy awakens with a blank look on his face. He stares into her eyes. "I want to go home. I hate this place."
"You have to stay here until you recover, and then you can come ho—"
"No! I want to go home today!" screams Jimmy.
"Okay, I'll tell the doctor." She leaves the room.

The patient next to Jimmy gets up from her bed. She is a seven-year-old cancer patient who has been undergoing chemotherapy since she was three. She walks to Jimmy and introduces herself. "I'm Sarah. Are you going home? Because you've been here forever. Since my birthday— that's how long you've been here. You're always sleeping, though. Why do you sleep so much? Is your name Sleepy?"

"I'm going home, Sarah. I don't even remember sleeping, but yes, my name is Sleepy," he answers.

"Well, I got to go to the bathroom. Bye, Sleepy." She leaves.

Two minutes go by before Maria walks in with a nurse; they have a wheelchair. Jimmy refuses help and struggles to get in. "Let's go home," he says.

In the car, Maria begins to explain. "The doctor said your arm will heal soon, and your ribs are okay now."

"When will I walk again?"

"I'm not sure about that, Jim."

"How long was I in the hospital, Mom?" asks Jimmy, surprised.

"You were there almost a month and a week. You were in a coma. You broke a couple of ribs, you broke your arm, and you damaged your legs."

Awkward silence fills the car on the way home. Jimmy knows, though; he knows that he will no longer walk because he feels nothing in his legs.

The elevator doors open. Jimmy is anxious to be at home. Hurt and angry, he retreats into his room and logs on to MySpace. He deletes everything from his page, then deletes his account. MySpace is a place for friends; if you have no friends, why have a MySpace account? He spends countless hours on the computer, and he comes across something interesting.

He rolls into the living room to talk to Maria. "Hey, how does stem cell surgery sound to you?"

"It sounds illegal and expensive."

"What about Amsterdam? Everything in Amsterdam is legal. And I can probably walk again."

"How will we pay for it?"

"What about that fifty-thousand-dollar settlement we got?"

"We don't know anyone over there."

"Well, there is this surgeon guy I found online."

"I have to think about it, Jimmy. That's a complicated decision."

"Okay. We'll both sleep on it. Good night, Mom."

"Good night."

Wednesday morning, 8:13 a.m. Jimmy is watching TV in the living room, and in comes Maria.

"If we go, how will you finish school?"

"You can homeschool me."

"If this trip doesn't help you, you have to accept the fact that you won't be able to walk anymore. Okay?"

"Okay, when can we leave?" Jimmy answers, happy and thrilled.

"After you hear from that surgeon."

Jimmy goes to his computer immediately and sends Dr. Ike an email.

> *Dear Doctor,*
>
> *My name is Jimmy Phaeton. I was in a terrible car accident, and I am seeking anything that can make me walk again. I understand you are a stem cell surgeon. I am interested in your work because it might be my only shot at walking again.*
>
> *Please reply,*
>
> *Jimmy*

Two minutes later, he receives a reply.

> *Dear Jimmy,*
>
> *I'm sorry for your accident, but I'm sure I can help. Whenever you are in Amsterdam, just call this number: 020 323 0492*

"Mom, we're going to Amsterdam!"

Maria hugs him. "Hope this works, Jim."

✧✧✧

After getting off the plane, Jimmy calls Dr. Ike. He is surprised to hear that the doctor is outside the terminal waiting for them.

He is a bald man with a thick upside-down mustache. There is a young girl with him.

"Hello, I am Dr. Ike, and this is my assistant Amy Kissinger."

"Hi Doctor, I'm Jimmy, and this is my mom Maria."

"Come, we'll go to my office and then find a hotel for you."

"Sounds good, doctor."

While Maria fills out paperwork for the surgery in Dr. Ike's office, Jimmy stays outside with Amy.

"I'm from England," she explains.

"Oh cool, I'm from America," Jimmy says.

"Oh, that's why you talk that way." Amy giggles. "I don't have many friends here because I'm on vacation, so I decided to get this job for fun."

"We can hang out if you want."

"That sounds nice."

"What about later today?" Jimmy asks.

"Sure, let's go. Just tell your mom."

He goes into the office and tells Maria that Amy is going to show him around and help cheer him up. The two of them eventually end up at an old café called De Shmugen. They sit at a table and start to talk.

"So tell me about yourself, Amy."

"Well, I'm an only child, and my dad was a drunk who left my mom. Then my mom went crazy after my dad left, and I became a foster child. What about you, Jimmy?"

"That's weird; I'm kind of in the same situation. I'm also an only child. My biological mom died in a car accident after finding out my dad was gone with his other family. So we're pretty much alike."

Several hours later, Amy tells Jimmy, "I have to tell you something. I feel really close to you, but that's not all I need to say. I'm leaving for the UK. I have to be there in two days."

"Why are you leaving so early?"

"My grandmother is terribly sick. She can't walk. I have to go and get her medicine."

"Do you want to go back to your place and pack?"

"Yeah, that would really help."

That night, at the hotel, Maria tells Jimmy, "The operation is tomorrow, Jim." Awkward silence fills the room. Jimmy can't help but think about Amy leaving.

He is unable to sleep. The next morning, he waits for his mother to wake up. They take a taxi to the hospital, silent the whole way. Amy is there waiting for them.

"I hope the operation is a success, Jimmy. If you're ever in London, look for me at this address." She hands Jimmy a piece of paper. "Bye, Jimmy." She leans toward him and kisses his cheek.

"Amy, I want you to know that you're not like anyone else; you make me feel different. When I'm better, I'll find you. Bye, Amy."

"Bye, Maria. Bye, Jimmy."

Jimmy changes into a medical robe before the doctors take him into the operating room.

Dr. Ike tells him, "Okay, take a deep breath, and just give in to the sleep, okay."

Jimmy falls into a heavy and vacant sleep.

Saturday morning, 5:09 a.m., *buzz, buzz, buzz!* The alarm clock breaks the peaceful silence of a good night's rest. Sleepy, Jimmy Phaeton awakens, only to slam the snooze button with his clenched right fist. He falls victim to his much-needed sleep once more. *Buzz, buzz, buzz!* Getting up, he gives in to the call of his alarm. Trying to distinguish reality from fantasy, he looks around his room.

He stands, stretching his arms and legs. His eyes widen, and his jaw drops.

"Mom...Mom!" He walks into the kitchen, where the smell of his favorite food tickles his nose. "Mom, the operation worked!"

"Jimmy, what operation?" asks Maria.

"Dr. Ike's operation, in Amsterdam!"

"Did you have a bad dream, Jim? Oh, I get it. You're just nervous about qualifying for Beijing."

None of it—the accident, Amy, the operation—ever really happened. Jimmy never could distinguish reality from fantasy.

Eddie Flores
THE MEANING OF LIFE

What you mean to me
Is what Pablo Picasso meant to art.
And what he bled out is his heart.

Running to stay ahead of the clock hands
To sense that time is up
And to sense what is right
But not doing what is expected.

And many speak out from their soul
Even though it takes a toll.
Many people bleed their heart out.

But that's why they are remembered
And wise men say a lot of things.
Didn't the sun once revolve around the Earth?
Didn't we once place our trust in priests?
Now the beliefs are long forgotten
Rotten, like fallen apples.

Nataly Chavez
MOLAA

I walk around and around.

Looking through green glass
Brown newspaper clippings announcing organized crime
and MASSACRE!

We glance and walk.
Only a second of pity and only two minutes of sympathy.

Volcanoes shooting a cloud of flowers to oblivion.
Two mandarin men saying "I think we're being followed"
and sure enough
a massive head behind them.

Big Brother is that you?

A couple lies in love in the middle of a nightmare.
Piles of blue faceless bodies sprawled against a white
wall.

I walk around and around.

Lorena Karen Arriaga
THE PUSH

When adventure interrupts your path,
lets this lifetime experience become
only a slight breeze that brushes through your plain skin:
unconsciously life will begin to fade away

All of this will only haunt you
like a ball and chain,
will become your shadow:
don't hesitate and just take the dare

Jocelyn Marchan
ESSENCE

The moon dazzles behind the ominous black clouds as a man ambles home from his nightly stroll. Suddenly he feels a cold blade on the right side of his neck. He grasps the assailant's arm and twists, causing a shriek. He snatches the blade and spins around, coming face-to-face with olive green eyes, brown hair, and pale white skin. It is a face he knows.

"Did I scare you, Dad?" she laughs.

His face hardens. "What is wrong with you, Andromeda? Did you lose your mind? You gave me a heart attack."

"Relax; I was only joking."

"Do that again, and you'll regret the day you were born."

"You've got to learn to let things go."

Andromeda opens the gate to their apartment building and heads into the elevator. On the third floor, they exit. Hearing their annoying phone ringing, Andromeda opens the door and rushes to answer it. She hears Thomas, the head of Interpol, ask, "Is Darien Welish there?"

"Yeah, hold on. Dad, it's for you."

Darien's face looks serious. He talks for only a minute.

"What is it, Dad? What did Thomas want?"

"We have to go to Winchester."

"Not another mission, Dad! I'm sick of it. Ever since you made me your apprentice, I've felt like a ping-pong ball going from mission to mission. What is it this time?"

"Winchester police caught a serial killer, and we have to escort him to Newgate prison."

She pauses. "Okay then, let's get this over with."

✧✧✧

Dark clouds black out the sky, and thunder roars in the distance. Waiting outside for her father, Andromeda curses as it begins to rain. A black Audi TT pulls over in front of her.

"Get in," Darien says.

She gets into the car and turns on the stereo. Rock music blasts inside the car, and her father gives her a look. She turns it off.

"How far is Winchester?"

"Two hours away."

"In that case, I'll take a nap." She rests her head on the window, and the next thing she knows, it's dark. The only thing visible is a red dragon flying above the wooden bridge she is standing on. Fire comes from the dragon's mouth, and sweat pours down her face as she runs to the end of the bridge. A black figure stops her. She screams and runs in the opposite direction. There, a light stops her. It turns into a woman so bright that she can barely make out her green eyes, wavy brown hair, and long white dress. She realizes who it is. This is the woman Andromeda wishes still lived.

"Mom." Andromeda embraces her and breaks into tears.

"Andromeda, there's nothing to fear. I'm here with you and I love you."

Andromeda sobs, holding her tighter. "Don't leave me, please. I beg you. You don't understand how miserable my life has been. Sometimes I feel empty to the core, like my essence and hope have withered away. Outside I'm cold and calm, but on the inside I'm a mess."

Pressing her lips on Andromeda's forehead, she wipes away her daughter's tears. "Don't cry. I'm here and always have been." Andromeda tries to stop, but her tears continue to cascade over her cheeks. "I want you to know something." Andromeda listens. "I gave my life so you could live."

Before she can say anything more, Andromeda feels a tug, then hears her father's voice. "Andromeda, wake up." She opens her eyes. "We're here."

Darien opens the police station's green door for Andromeda. She finds herself in a small white room. Darien holds out his badge to the first police officer they meet.

"You must be from Interpol," he says. "My name is Matthew Vanzant."

"Name's Darien Welish. This is Andromeda," he says. "What's the name of our little pal there?" Darien points at the tall white man with short red hair pacing in a cell at the back of the room. The man kicks the wall and howls.

"His name is Christian Demond." At the mention of his name, Christian flashes his wild dark blue eyes at them, locking onto Andromeda. She hears her heart beating in her ears.

Suddenly, brown fur sprouts from Christian's skin, and fangs gleam from his mouth. The werewolf's sharp claws breach the bars. Vanzant opens fire, but the bullets cannot penetrate his brown fur. Christian lunges toward him. A snap echoes, and Vanzant's head falls at an unnatural angle. Officers open fire, and Andromeda throws herself on the floor. Darien pulls out his gun, but Christian slams him into the wall and runs out of the building.

Terror seizes Andromeda as she crosses over to Darien lying on the floor of the police station. Blood drips from a small cut on the side of his head. She shakes him. He doesn't budge, but his badge falls from his pocket. She quickly tucks it away. She presses her fingers into his wrist and feels his veins throb. "He's alive." Then her thoughts shift. *What am I doing? I have to get out of here; this is my chance to escape.*

From the corner of her eye she spots the gun Darien dropped when he tried to shoot Christian. She grabs it and heads for the door just as Darien's eyes open. "Andromeda?" He stands, and she takes off into the night.

The streetlights illuminate the pavement in the dark night. Andromeda spots Christian sniffing the air. His ears prick, and she begins shooting. Enraged, he pounces, his sharp claws reaching for her. But before he reaches his target, a black werewolf emerges from behind a building and attacks Christian.

Andromeda presses her body against a nearby wall, watching. "Am I still dreaming? This is a nightmare..." She hesitates, then starts shooting at both of them. The black werewolf turns and glares at her, allowing Christian to shove him off and dart away.

In a blink of an eye, the other werewolf shifts into human form and heads toward Andromeda, his broad shoulders moving up and down as he breathes. He grabs her tightly by the shoulders, and his dark black eyes blaze out from his sunburned face.

"Why did you do that?" he asks. "I had him, but you started shooting!"

"What is going on?" she demands.

"None of your business." He walks away.

Andromeda charges after him.

"I'm making it my business."

"You're a stubborn little thing, aren't you?" He snarls over his right shoulder and turns around to face her. "What's it to you?"

"Two reasons: first, I want to help, and second, I'm sick of my safe mundane life."

His eyes are fixed on her.

She stares at the pavement and mutters, "By the way, thanksforsavingmylife."

"All right. You can help me. But if you get killed, I wash my hands of you." He looks at her and starts laughing. Andromeda feels her anger boiling, and her face turns red. He laughs even harder. Andromeda punches him on the arm. He rubs it. "Did you know your face is as red as a tomato?"

"Why are you laughing?"

"Well...um...I don't think you can handle it. I just imagined you running your head off and crashing into everything that comes your way."

Her eyes narrow. "Try me."

"Fine." Black fur sprouts from his skin, and claws as sharp as daggers appear from his fingertips. He's at least ten feet tall. She stumbles back, screaming. He growls, exposing sharp white teeth.

"Andromeda! Andromeda!"

She turns to see Darien calling her name. Desperate, she looks at the werewolf. He picks her up and bolts away.

"Put me down! Put me down!" she cries.

He drops her and chuckles. "You said, 'Try me.' I was only trying you."

"Oh, shut up. Aren't we supposed to be looking for Christian?"

"He might be crazy, but he isn't stupid. He knows I'm after him," he explains. "He's probably hiding. He knows if he stays out of sight it'll be impossible to try and track his scent down with all the people out during daylight."

"Wait a minute." She stops. "If you're after Christian, why haven't you stopped him yet?"

"Because someone always interfered. Before you, the police used tranquilizers to capture him in his human form because they knew what he was."

"How did they know he was a werewolf? And why didn't we know at Interpol?"

"Because he transformed during the day and night in front of people!" He shakes his head at the thought. "And some of those who saw him knew him. And I guess the police wanted to keep it a secret so you'd take him."

"So you guys don't transform under the moon."

"No. Our mood triggers our transformation. Kind of like a human with a bad temper who starts throwing punches. So make sure not to tick us off, especially loony Christian. He doesn't try to control himself like the rest of us; we try to blend in with people and live a normal life."

He starts walking. She follows as he talks.

"This morning, I finally had managed to track him down when the cops emerged from behind some trees and started shooting tranquilizers. I barely managed to escape. Luckily, they didn't see who I was."

"We have to think about a way to get to Christian," she says.

He turns and looks at her.

"Before that, I need to ask you a few questions so I know where we stand. Aren't you supposed to be in school?"

"Actually, I'm seventeen. I'm my dad's apprentice. I graduated from high school two months ago."

"But you're just a kid." Disbelief crosses his face. "Your father must be crazy to let you work at Interpol."

"He forced me to be his apprentice because he thinks his enemies want to kill me to make him suffer." She sees his face sadden. "At least that's what he tells me. One of his enemies killed my mother...I don't want to talk about it."

"That's crazy. Doesn't he realize that endangers you instead of protecting you?"

Frustration crosses her face. "He's just overprotective, that's all—"

"He thinks he can protect you from every bad thing in life, but he's wrong. Life's a series of obstacles: there are good and bad things, and the only way you can live is by experiencing them."

"You're not my father."

"You're right. I'm not. I was just trying to make a point. Anyway, it's daytime."

"What? Does the sun affect your werewolf side?" she asks mockingly.

"No, I'm just hungry, sleepy, and tired."

"So, where to?"

"We're here," he says, pointing at a light brown house.

Andromeda stares at the four large windows—two alongside the white door and two above—then hears a car honk. She realizes she is standing in the middle of the street, holding up traffic. Her cheeks flush and look like they are on fire. He grabs her arm and pulls her to the sidewalk, then knocks on the white door.

A woman with white blond hair answers. "Justin," she says, "did you get Christian?"

Andromeda looks at him. *His name is Justin?*

"What is she doing here?" the woman asks.

"She's going to help us," Justin says. "Andromeda, this is Gillian."

"You're involving a human in this mess. What's wrong with you?"

He pushes them both inside and turns to Andromeda, smiling. "Please wait by the stairs while I explain to Gill what's going on."

"Yeah, sure thing." Andromeda smiles back, unsure of why she is doing so.

She's surprised by the interior of the house. It's not the wreck she would have expected from a werewolf. Instead of toppled furniture, cracked walls, and broken windows, it is well furnished, with yellow walls that brighten everything. As she walks to the stairway, she notices a glass door leading to a garden outside, with flowers of all colors and an oak tree with a table under it. She sits on the stairs and watches Gill and Justin in the kitchen. Five minutes pass. Then ten. Every now and then, their voices rise, but she can't make out the words: they speak in a different language.

As she starts to nod off, she hears footsteps. Justin stands over her and says, "That went well."

Gill walks up to them and stares at Andromeda. "You look just like your mother, you know, only taller. What are you, five foot five? You have a little of Darien in you—"

Andromeda stands. "You knew my mother?"

"I used to work for Interpol years ago. I knew your father, but I only met your mother a few times. I didn't see you last night."

"Of course you didn't; you left right after you saw Darien," Justin snaps. "One moment I was talking to you, the next you were gone. I thought Christian had snatched you or something."

Andromeda asks, "Why did you leave?"

"Darien used to be my best friend," Gill says. "He was like my brother. I knew Christian would break free, and when he did, he would kill someone. I didn't want it to be your father. So I left."

"You used to work at Interpol? You knew my father? What is going on?" Andromeda demands.

"We're part of a secret werewolf society that protects humanity." Gill taps her finger on the glass door. "You both have huge bags under your eyes. Why don't you rest? There's much to do later."

Gill leads them upstairs. Justin slams the door to his room. Gill takes Andromeda to a room of her own, where rays of sunshine beam through the window.

"Do you want something to eat?"

"No thanks. I just want to sleep."

Gill nods and steps out of the room. Andromeda makes herself comfortable under the quilt and drifts off to sleep.

The sun is still bright out when Andromeda wakes to a raking sound. She puts on her shoes and runs downstairs, where she sees Gill raking leaves outside.

Andromeda opens the door. "Do you need any help?"

"Yeah, help me put the leaves in the trash bag." Gill points to the trash bag on the table, and together they begin to stuff it with leaves. Gill pulls a white withered rose from a bush and throws it in.

"That was one of my favorites. White roses. I'm sure others will grow. It's like a cycle. Things die and are born again."

Gill sits on the table beneath the oak tree and gestures Andromeda over.

"Tell me the real reason you decided to help us."

"I was tired of following orders. I wanted to be free," says Andromeda. "I used Christian as an excuse to run away from my dad," she adds.

"You need to be yourself and not what others expect you to be. That's the problem in this world. People just care about what others say or think about them."

Andromeda knows she's right. "Why are you two the only werewolves after Christian?"

"Because nobody knows Christian as well as we do. He used to be a good friend until he went mad over his son's death. Mike was his world." Gill pauses. "It was a dark night. A little girl crossed the street without realizing that a truck was coming her way. Her father told her to run, but she just screamed. Mike heard her screaming and transformed into a werewolf, running and snatching her away before the truck could hit her."

Gill's eyes well up with tears, and her voice breaks. "Before the little girl could see what he was, Mike changed back to his human form. But then the girl's father, the one who tried to warn her to run, came up and shot Mike.

"The loss of Mike filled Christian with great agony. He

vowed to avenge Mike by killing every human being on this earth."

Andromeda was silent, unsure what to say. She wondered if Christian felt the same agony she did after her mother's death, that great hole in her gut that seems to get bigger as the years pass, the same absence of life and hope. Agony clouds her face. Gill's forehead creases with worry.

"What's troubling you?" Gill asks.

Andromeda knows Gill is a stranger, and yet she feels this bond between them, like that of a mother and daughter. She clears her mind and speaks. "I was four years old when my mother died. She was reading to me in the living room. Then we heard loud noises outside, then the smell of gasoline. She tried to open the door, but it wouldn't budge. She tried and tried. I was so scared. I hugged her legs.

"The room was consumed by the flames. She tried breaking a window, but the flames kept spreading. She covered me with her body. Black smoke was everywhere, in my eyes and lungs. I thought we were goners.

"Then water drizzled over us. Sirens. My dad broke in and carried me outside. Someone put my mother on a stretcher. She had third-degree burns and didn't make it to the hospital."

Crying, Andromeda puts her head down on the table. Gill gently rests her hand on Andromeda's shoulder. She turns and sees Justin; she didn't know he was there, listening. He walks over and sits next to them both.

Gill takes Andromeda's chin into her hand. "It's time for you to move forward in life. Dwelling in the past will only hurt you. Your mother might not be alive, but her spirit is. That is something death can never take away. Your mother gave her life for you. So you could live. Now live."

Andromeda recalls the dream she had last night and envisions her mother saying the same thing.

Justin's stomach rumbles, and everyone laughs. He walks straight to the kitchen to make himself a ham sandwich, and Andromeda and Gill join him. When they all have their sandwiches, Gill leads them into the living room and turns on the TV. A werewolf movie is on, and the werewolf on TV is attacking and eating a human. Andromeda freaks out and stares at Justin. "Do you ever do that?" she asks, pointing at the TV.

Justin laughs. "We may be werewolves, but we're not human-eating dogs."

Suddenly, a news alert interrupts the movie. A reporter stands in front of a cathedral. "Horror strikes the streets of Winchester," he says. The screen shows Christian, in werewolf form, chasing a little girl. Everyone is running wild.

"I thought he'd be smart and stay hidden," Justin says.

Gill turns to them both. "Let's go."

"Wait." Justin grabs her arm. "That's less than a mile away. It's as if he's baiting us."

"He probably wants to get rid of you two," Andromeda points out.

Gill sighs. "We might as well end this now."

At the cathedral, they find Christian. He tightly holds the girl and howls. White fur shoots from Gill's skin, and her jagged teeth gleam. She rushes off and confronts Christian.

Justin grabs Andromeda's hand. "Run! And don't turn back."

She studies his face and furrows her brow. "I'm part of this now. I'm staying." Justin's mouth grows tight in anger. He seems like he's about to argue, but Andromeda punches him in his stomach. "Go help Gill."

Justin nods. Black fur sprouts from his skin. He reveals his sharp claws and joins Gill, the two of them circling Christian. The little girl faints. Gill distracts Christian long enough for Justin to grab the girl, and he quickly hands her to Andromeda.

As he's returning to the fight, Christian slams Gill against the side of the cathedral. She slides down, and he lunges at Justin, pinning him. Gill wraps her claws around Christian's neck, but then Christian's claws dive into her side. She falls. Christian reaches for Justin's throat, but Andromeda throws rocks at Christian's head. He looks up, and she runs, trips, and falls.

Panic washes over her when she sees Christian peering down at her. Realizing she cannot hurt him, she screams the first thing that comes to mind: "Do you think Mike is proud of you?"

He shifts into his human form and howls, tears running down his face. Justin tackles Christian and quickly finishes him.

Justin transforms and lifts Andromeda from the ground. "Where's Gill?" She spots Gill, human and lying in a pool of blood. Andromeda runs to her and kneels in front of her. Gill smiles and closes her eyes, and Andromeda's heart beats itself to pieces. Justin comes over and picks up Gill's body. "The cops are coming. I'll meet you at the house."

Andromeda nods. A werewolf once more, Justin bolts away.

Alone, she wipes the tears that pour down her face. Five police cruisers stop in front of her, and Darien steps out of one. He marches toward her, passing Christian's body and the unconscious girl.

"Did you do this?" he asks.

Andromeda realizes that if she says no, Christian's death will be investigated, and that could lead her father to Justin. "Yes."

"I'm so proud of you," he says. "I thought you were kidnapped by those beasts."

Andromeda starts walking down the block. "I need to do something."

"I'll come with you," he says.

She doesn't turn back. "No. Take care of this mess. Take the girl to the hospital."

She runs all the way to the light brown house and rushes through the door.

"Over here!" Justin shouts from the garden. He has already dug a grave beside the barren rose bushes.

Fresh tears run down her face. "I hate this world. It's evil. It's taken everyone I love."

"You're wrong," Justin tells her. "There's still good in this world. Your mother and Gill sacrificed their lives to save the lives of others. Think about it. Your mother loved you so much that she was willing to give her life for you.

Gill gave her life to save innocent people and to protect our society. I know it's difficult to lose someone you love, but their spirits live."

His words sink deep into her mind. She remembers the dream and Gill's advice. Understanding flickers in her eyes. She smiles.

"You're right."

Lorena Karen Arriaga
HERO OR NOT

Sacrifice and independence
Revealing that hero
The call is your only prayer
To see equality
Hereafter you will have the choice
Hero or not

Mirian Martinez
KIDNAPPED

As I leave the police station, I decide to visit my mother. Driving down Sunset Boulevard, I see a woman selling flowers on the street, and I decide to buy my mother a bouquet. It has been a long month since I've seen my mother and little brother, Matt. I park my black Mustang in the driveway. Soon Matt is running toward me, and he screams, "Mike!" He smiles and gives me a big hug. Mother's in the kitchen.

"Sweetie, how are you? I've missed you so much," she says.

"I've missed you, too. Mmm, it smells delicious. What are you cooking?"

"Your favorite: chicken with mashed potatoes."

I give her the flowers, and she puts them in a vase. I take off my coat and loosen my tie.

"That suit makes you look old, and you already have gray hairs. That's odd for a twenty-nine year old," she says.

"Yeah, I know, Mom, but it's better than the uniform," I reply, laughing.

We finish eating the delicious chicken with mashed potatoes, and while Mom washes the dishes I wander around the house as if I were a guest. It has been such a long time since I actually felt at home. As I walk down the hallway toward my mother's room, the first thing that catches my attention is a picture of my father wearing his police uniform. He sure looked like a hero—my hero. As I stand before it I feel someone behind me: my mother. I turn around with tears in my eyes and ask, "Why did he have to go? I miss him so much." Mother quietly puts her arms around me and softly says, "We all do, Son, but just remember that he's protecting you from wherever he is, and he loves you with all his heart." Smiling, I kiss her forehead.

Soon it's time for me to go, and as I get in my car, I say, "Bye. I'll come tomorrow, and we can all go for dinner. How does that sound?"

"Excellent, sweetie! Take care, and thank you so much for coming."

I arrive home around eight and turn the lights on. I look at myself in the living room mirror. My brown eyes look swollen; that's how tired I am. My mother is right: I do look older. I pull the refrigerator door open and pour myself a glass of nice, cold water. All I want to do is change clothes, watch TV, and sleep after a long day at work.

Ding, rings the doorbell. That's odd; no one visits at this hour. I open the door, and a little girl scout is standing outside. She's wearing a green dress with long socks. Her dress has only a couple of badges; she looks adorable. "How can I help you?" I ask. She timidly shows me a box of cookies and says, "Would you like to buy some cookies? They're for my school." I end up buying three boxes. As I close the door, I hear a thundering sound but pay no attention to it.

I sit down for my Monday routine and watch *Monday Night Raw*; the match is Edge and Randy Orton taking on The Miz and John Morrison. I'm too caught up in the match, with Edge about to get the pin, and I open the box of cookies without looking. The Miz kicks out angrily, and I scream, "What? Come on, referee!" I put a chocolate chip cookie in my mouth and feel something odd on the tip of my tongue. It's a note that says, "Because of you, I spent the worst days of my life behind bars. Wait for my call."

I can't understand what is going on. I wait for the call, but nothing happens. I try to think it through but can't come to a conclusion. Then my cell phone rings. The caller ID says *Private*. "Hello?" I answer. I hear a strong, deep male voice say, "Listen up. I'm only going to say this once." I stand motionless as I listen closely. "Your mother and little brother have been kidnapped. Soon the two people you love most will die if you don't do as I say." Then all I hear is a beep.

I wait a couple of minutes for another call, but I soon become impatient. I pick up the phone and call my mother. No one answers. As soon as I put the phone down, I hear a loud thunder strike, and rain starts pouring down. The apartment lights flicker, and I can hear the wind blow furiously.

Grabbing my keys, I rush out of the apartment. I step on the accelerator and drive as fast as I can to my mother's house. As soon as I step in, I see the vase of flowers on the floor. The phone is disconnected; the chairs, pushed over. A portrait of my father is broken in half. I run out of the house and drive toward the station.

When I arrive I see a large crowd. Paramedics are all around, and the flashing lights of the ambulance hit my eyes. I walk toward the crowd, worried at what I might find, and as soon as I get there I see a little girl dressed exactly like the one who was outside my apartment a couple of hours ago. She is lying on the cement limp: finished off without compassion. I cannot believe this is happening. Someone is after me, and that someone is not playing around. I see my colleague Mary nearby.

I remember how we met at the supermarket. I was in a hurry, and apparently she was, too. We bumped into each other; the impact was so intense that her purse flew off her arm. It turned out that we were attending the same high school. Since that day I've had a secret crush on her. I rush to her.

"Mary, I'm so glad to see you! Can...can I talk to you? It's really important."

"Oh, hey, can you believe this? What kind of sick-minded animal would do something like this to a poor, innocent child?"

"It has something to do with what I want to talk to you about. Can you come to my office?"

"Yeah, sure." We walk toward the station and into my office.

"Mike, are you okay?"

"Listen Mary, I...I trust you, and I really need your help. My family has been kidnapped, and a couple of hours ago that little girl was standing outside my apartment selling me cookies."

She sits there without saying a word.

"Did you hear what I said?"

"How did this happen?"

I tell her the story. I tell her about the little girl, the box of cookies, the note, the phone call, and my mother's house. She can't believe it.

"Have you received another call?"

"No, not yet."

"When was the last time you received one?"

"Two hours ago."

"Do you happen to have any enemies, or people who dislike you?"

"I can't think of any."

"You mentioned a note. What did it say?" I read it to her, and soon as I stop she says, "I don't know if it's the right thing to do, but I'll help you with whatever I can."

Relieved, I hug her. We search my office, looking at files, but we don't find anything. I gather all the papers that might be important or give me a clue.

Suddenly Mary says, "Why don't we ask for help? I mean, we're in a police station, for Christ's sake."

"I know, Mary. But I don't want anyone else to get involved. This is my personal case, and I'm going to solve it." Mary just looks at me without saying a word. I grab all the files in my office, and we walk out. We both agree to meet at my apartment tomorrow morning. She needs to rest, and I need to work on my case.

I get to my apartment, put all the papers on the kitchen table, turn my laptop on, and read the letter once again. I keep repeating that same line over and over: "Because of you, I spent the worst days of my life behind bars." Next to the telephone I see a picture of my mother and little brother. I think way back to when we used to spend so much time together. I remember how I used to play soccer with my brother, how he laughed when he scored a goal. I remember my mother, how she spent most of her time in her favorite room in the house cooking her delicious foods. The smell was always unbelievable in that kitchen. Suddenly I stop. "What are you doing? They're not dead!" I feel like I'm not the same person I was a couple of hours ago, as if someone had taken something away from me and I had to take it back.

I spend long, sleepless hours looking at old documents, going over all the cases I've solved: my life's work. I rest my head in the chair, and as soon as I do I fall asleep.

As I begin to dream, my life passes in front of my eyes in a matter of seconds. Everything stops, and I see my father and me at the park. I can see his wide smile in front of me, his eyes shining with the sun's light. I remember how we used to have this special connection. He was more than just my father; he was my friend. He would tell me how his job was amazing, how he enjoyed fighting for justice. But he also said that it wasn't an easy task. He didn't want me to become a cop; he didn't want me to be in danger.

Now I'm at a funeral. The room is small and dark. I see my mother, and my brother is crying into his hands. I walk toward a coffin in the center of the room and see my father's body lying there helplessly. I feel my world tearing apart, tears running down my face. I look at my father's white face and make a promise to be the man of the house from that point on. I am going to take care of my mother and little brother. I am never going to let anything bad happen to them.

Suddenly I wake up, keeping that promise in mind. This dream gives me the strength to find my family. I am not going to break that promise; that's for sure.

It is four in the morning when I wake up. I grab my laptop and look at my saved files. I see all the cases that I've solved and all the people I've put in jail. But all of those criminals are still behind bars. None of them could have kidnapped my family. I go through each file, looking closely at each one, and a certain name catches my attention. The file reads: "Frank Goldberg Andrews. African American descent, born in Los Angeles California in 1981, son of Talia and Shawn Goldberg. Parents were successful investors in Coca-Cola. Talia and Shawn passed away in a car accident when Frank was thirteen. After his parents died, he was left with his uncle Jason Andrews, a drug addict, apparently the only family member he had left. Frank was abused by Jason when he was fourteen. Convicted of abusing and killing his sixteen-year-old cousin. Sentenced to life on July 15, 2002. Escaped on January 1, 2009. Still a fugitive."

"Why didn't anyone tell me about this?" I furiously ask myself. I call Mary immediately.

"Hello?"

"Mary, I need to see you right away."

"I'm on my way."

She arrives at my apartment ten minutes later. I show her Frank's file. As she reads through it, I tell her how I met him a couple of years ago after he committed his terrible crime. He was a fugitive, and it was my job to find him. It took me months to get the job done, but I finally found him hiding in an old warehouse in Santa Monica.

I was just doing my job. He had to pay for his crime, and he sure did. I'm sure he's the one who has my family. I'm not going to rest until I find him. Unexpectedly, the phone rings. I stand there motionless and panic. Mary's look gives me the strength to answer.

"Hello?"

"Hello, Mikey, do you miss your family yet?"

"What do you want from me? Let's settle this like men, Frank."

"Ha-ha-ha-ha! So you found out who I am, huh? It's a shame. I was having a good time."

"It's me you want. Let them go!"

His tone of voice quickly changes. "Okay, I'll give you a chance. Listen carefully: I want you to come alone to that abandoned warehouse in Santa Monica. I'm pretty sure you remember where it is. Be there at ten thirty. If I see someone with you, your mother dies." He hangs up. I tell Mary and explain that I have to go by myself.

"No. I have to go with you. I'm not letting you do this alone."

"Mary, if I don't show up alone, my mother dies. Please." It's nine o'clock now. As I gather up my belongings, I look at Mary. "Thank you for everything you've done," I say. I lean in to kiss her soft lips, but something holds me back. I kiss her cheek and leave.

Driving down the Santa Monica Freeway, I keep thinking about my family, about how soon I'm going to be able to see them safe and sound. But I also think of what my reaction will be when I see Frank. Will I contain myself, or will I do something I'll regret? I notice that my hands have turned sweaty, so I wipe them on my pants and keep driving. All of a sudden the memory of my father pops into my head, and I promise him once again that I will find my family no matter what it takes. I understand now more than ever that he was right: being a cop is not an easy job.

It is now ten minutes to ten, and I don't know what to do. All I want is to see my family. I decide to walk into the warehouse. As soon as I'm about to step in, my cell phone rings. It says *Private*.

"Hello?"

"Stop right there. Don't take another step, or she dies."

"Okay. You got me. Relax. Don't do anything to her."

"Listen carefully. In five minutes two of my men are going out to get you. This better not be a trap, or else."

I hang up the phone and put it in my pocket. I wait there patiently and nervously. I feel like someone's behind me, but when I turn there's no one there. I turn to walk toward my car, and suddenly I feel a gigantic hand covering my face. There is a horrible smell, and soon I faint.

A splash of cold water hits my face. I wake up not knowing where I am or what has happened. I notice that I am surrounded by huge men. Now I remember. One of them must have put me to sleep. I hear a voice coming close: "Well, well, well, who do we have here...Michael Jones."

"Where are they?" I ask, weakly.

"We'll get to that. Now bring him over," he says to one of the men.

One of them grabs my hands tightly, but as soon as I get the chance I elbow him right in the ribs. I run toward Frank as fast as I can, but instantly all the men are running behind me. One catches up to me and wrestles me to the ground. Frank screams furiously, "Tie him up!"

I hear someone crying. It's my mother. I try to get up and run to her, but those thugs did an excellent job tying me. My mother's face is thin and pale; her arms are covered in bruises. Seeing her in this condition is breaking my heart, but I keep my head straight. I run out of patience and shout, "Let her go! It's me you want!"

A man walks in and whispers into Frank's ear. "Bring her in," Frank says. I can see two people approaching: one of the thugs and a young woman. She screams and resists; he is pulling her by the hair. As they come closer and closer, I see that the woman is Mary. I move around in the chair I am tied to and fall to the side. Mary slaps the man holding her and runs toward me. She touches her lips to mine and says, "I love you. We're going to get through this." I stare into her eyes and smile. The man grabs her by the hair again. I feel helpless; I can't help my family or Mary.

As I witness my mother and the love of my life being tied up, I hear a voice behind me. It's Matt, hiding behind some huge cardboard boxes. He escaped somehow. I whisper and tell him to stay there. I shout, "Frank, where's my brother Matt? I need to see him." Coldly, he tells one of his men to bring Matt over. In a few minutes the man comes back and reports.

"Boss...the kid's gone!"

"You idiot, how is this possible?" Frank orders all his men to look for Matt. As all his men leave, he walks slowly toward my mother. I can tell something is about to happen, and I pray to God that it's not what I'm thinking. With great force he pulls her toward him and lays her on a table. All the while my mother screams and resists. I can hear that she's in pain, but I don't know what to do. I can hear Mary yelling and sobbing, "Leave her alone, you animal!" Then I remember about Matt. This is my opportunity to get free.

I look at the cardboard boxes and whisper, "Matt, are you there...Matt?"

"Yes, I...I'm...I'm here," he replies, crying.

"Listen, Matt, I really need you to come toward me, really carefully and quietly."

Matt comes running toward me and accidentally pushes a box over, but luckily Frank doesn't hear. Matt finally reaches me.

"Okay, Matt, now listen to me. Forget all that's happening right now. I promise this nightmare will be over soon, but first I need you to untie me. Think you can do that?"

"It's too tight. I can't do this. It's too tight."

"Okay, look at me. Inside my sock I have a knife. Grab

it and carefully cut the ropes." He cuts the ropes off, and I tell him to go back behind the boxes and hide. "Close your eyes and cover your ears. This will end soon, I promise," I tell him. I remain seated and pretend that I'm still tied up. Mary looks at me. She knows what I have in mind. I nod, and as soon as she sees me she screams, "Leave her alone! Take me instead, you sicko." He furiously pushes my mother aside and walks toward Mary. He shoves her to the ground.

Mary does not stop. She keeps shouting, telling him what a coward he is. "What kind of a pig would do such things to his own cousin? You sick son of a—how dare I compare you to a poor animal? You're worse than that—you're a monster! Yeah, that's what you are, a disgusting monster."

In rage, he pulls Mary right off her feet and throws her back to the ground. He stands over her and yells, "Never talk to me that way ever again! You hear me? Huh? You hear me?"

His psychopathic look stuns me. All I can think is that this is the time to help my mother. I know that Mary can handle Frank for a couple of seconds. I run toward my mother and try to untie her, but I struggle.

Frank turns and catches me in the act. He pushes Mary down one last time and then runs toward me. I finally cut the rope holding my mother, but I hear a gunshot and feel a burning sensation. He got me...right in the arm. I scream to my mother, "Run...take Matt and Mary with you!" I struggle to my feet, but as soon as I'm up Frank kicks me and I collapse. My head spins. All I can hear is Frank screaming to his men, "Where were you? Go after them! Get them! Now!"

I hear gunshots, and I pray to God that nothing bad has happened to my family. There are no signs of my mother and brother, but I can still see Mary lying there on the cement floor. Frank stands me up and says, "You piece of garbage. You should've listened to your father. Becoming a cop was the worst mistake of your life. Now you're gonna end up the same way he did: dead, useless, inside a casket." He punches me in the guts, and in a way I feel relieved, almost like I deserve what's happening to me.

I remember my father, how the entire family used to

spend so much time together, how I hated when he had to go back to work. I remember that promise: I was going to take care of my family, no matter what. I've let my father down. I'm about ready to give up, when I see a face in the distance: my father's. I hear him loud and clear: "Mike, don't give up. You can still keep that promise." He smiles at me, and I smile back.

Frank hits me again, bringing me back to reality. He keeps talking trash about my father, and I become tired. I try to fight back, but I'm too weak. Then I hear a voice say, "Leave him alone." It's my mother with a gun shaking in her hand. Frank's men are lying on the ground behind her. I see the fear in her eyes, but I also see how strong she really is. All this time, Frank is trying to convince her to put the gun down, but she won't do it.

He pulls a gun out of his pants. As I see it, I scream to my mother, "Watch out!" I get up as fast as I can, but it feels like an eternity. Frank fires the gun. I tackle him to the ground, but it's too late. I look in my mother's direction and see Mary on the floor. She looks just like the little girl outside the station. He got her. Anger is running through my veins. I get on top of Frank and punch him with all my might. He reaches for the gun, but I beat him to it. I grab the gun and say, "Rot in hell, you fiend!" I take care of him and stand up, staring down at what I've done. My mother comes and stands next to me. I can't help but cry as I look over at the love of my life, gone forever.

Jessica Zamary Marroquin
FALL OF THE TOWER

My phone rings and disrupts me from my sleep. I answer
and hear Talon's voice telling me to quickly get dressed and
pick him up. He hangs up, and I look at the time: 1:00 a.m.
What can he possibly want at this time? I slip my jacket
on, open the curtain, and smell the rain, which must have
started while I was asleep. I close my eyes and take a deep
breath. The cold comforts me. I grab my keys and head to
my car.

The rain makes it hard to see the streets, but I arrive
safely in front of Talon's house. Bright blue lightning illuminates the sky, and I see Talon walking toward my car.
He gets in and I confront him.

"What is going on? Why did you wake me up?"

"We need to get to the Black Tower, fast!"

Startled by the harshness in his voice, I don't even argue.
I speed to our destination. Once there, I follow Talon to his
office. He closes the door.

He still hasn't answered me, so I ask again. Ignoring me,
he goes to his computer. He shows me an image of a young
girl. Confused, I ask him, "What are we looking at?"

He responds, "A misled target. We have been tracking
the wrong girl."

"What?"

"The Tower has been after this young girl for many
years, yet we haven't found her. You want to know why?
Because she isn't the girl we thought she was."

Talon hits a button, and a new image pops onto the
screen: a photograph of me.

I panic. I start inspecting his office, looking for a way to escape if anything bad should happen. I wonder if he's going to shoot me.

Talon's face is unreadable. *Will he turn me in? Me, who has always been there for him? The girl he has always protected?* I take a step away from the desk, positioning my body closer to the gun on the cabinet. Talon notices and looks surprised; he hesitates.

His phone rings. I freeze, my face impassive. Never taking his eyes off me, he answers. I am sure it's the Committee from the Black Tower. I think about going for the gun, but I can't move. I strain my ears, hoping I will hear what the other person is saying, but I can't.

"Yes, I understand. Yes, I will take care of it."

He closes his phone. I take a step closer toward the gun and grab it before he does. Talon takes a step toward me, and I point it at him. I'm terrified. The faces of all the people I have killed flash before my eyes.

Talon walks toward me slowly, his face unsure. I am sure he is thinking that I am going to shoot him, but I wouldn't do that, would I?

As he walks closer to me, my heart jumps. Suddenly, he stops. I realize that the gun is still on safety. *I don't want to hurt Talon, just as he wouldn't want to hurt me. We've been close since the day I started working at the Black Tower. He's like a brother to me. He has always protected me, and he will keep protecting me.*

I'm numb. The room becomes incredibly bright at first, but then everything goes black, and I feel like I am falling. When my vision returns, I am in a dark office, darker than any other in the Black Tower. I feel strange and know that I am not truly awake. It's as if I've entered a dream. There are three people in my vision: Talon, myself, and one of the Committee's assassins, Kevin. Looking around, I get the chills. I can see my breath in the air, but no one seems to see me. Kevin turns to my vision self and speaks.

"You have failed, Kenley," he says.

"Why?"

"Do you not remember? You had a simple task, to kill Alhrick, and you didn't."

I try to make sense of what he is telling me. Slowly, it comes back. I remember Talon handing me a yellow envelope that contained information and a picture of my target: Alhrick. *I chased a man through the halls of the Tower. He was running toward a big glass window. I knew he was going to jump off. But why? Would he rather kill himself than be killed? Either way he would die. I could not fail. A job is not complete unless you, yourself, kill the target. I pulled my white Walther P99 out of its holster and fired several times. I knew he was dead, but the momentum of his panicked escape caused his body to crash through the window. A fifteen-floor fall. I watch his body hit the ground and will remember that image for the rest of my life.*

I hear myself reply that Alhrick is dead. Kevin laughs. "What a fool you are. The man that you killed was not Alhrick, but merely an impersonator. How can you, one of our most successful assassins, be blind to what is in front of you? Either you were ignorant and did not wish to see it, or you were distracted and didn't do your job."

Disturbed, I remember hesitating as I chased that man. I had a feeling it was not him, yet I wanted to believe it was, because otherwise I was murdering a stranger.

I feel my body regain consciousness. I am moving, but not. *Where am I? How did I get here?* I have a severe headache, and everything is a blur. I hear Talon's voice say, "So you finally woke up? I thought I had lost you there for a moment." I try to focus on his face. He gives me some sort of oval capsule, and from the way it smells and feels, I realize it is a pill. I wonder if it will kill me. *Then again, it could make this headache go away and clear my sight...* I decide to take the pill. "It takes a while for it to kick in," says Talon. I close my eyes for what seems to be only a few minutes but wake up half an hour later. I feel much better and realize that Talon's intentions were good.

As the car speeds through the dark streets, I slide from one seat to another.

"Why are we in such a rush; where are we going?"

"We have a new target."

"Who?"

"The man that you didn't kill. We need to take care of

him before he takes care of you."

"Why now and not before?"

He doesn't answer. Just as I put my seat belt on, a midnight blue car comes from behind and cuts us off, causing Talon to swerve. *Stupid car, how can he be in a bigger rush than us? What kind of a fool would cut off a car going this fast?* I hear loud honks from cars on the upcoming cross street. Suddenly, the same blue car speeds toward us. "Watch it!" I hear myself scream. But the car is going too fast for even Talon to outrun it.

My body is once again numb. The seat belt rips as the force from the crash pushes my body toward the door. My head hits the window. The car stops. I hold my head to stop it from spinning, hoping my vision will return. I look for Talon. The door is open. I lean over the driver's seat to see if he is there, but before I get far enough to see, two men dressed in black wearing white plastic masks grab me. I know I can easily take them both, but their grip is loose, and I sense they do not want to hurt me. I control my breathing and my heart rate. *I need to stay calm so that the men kidnapping me can see I am not scared of them.*

The men grab me and carry me out of the car. As we leave, I lean back to look for Talon. His head leans on the steering wheel. Scared he might have gone unconscious, I try to escape from the men's grip, but they have tied my hands and feet together. They throw me gently into the midnight blue car next to another man in a mask.

In the car, the minutes pass by. The man next to me removes his mask. It is Alhrick. I glare at him, but I sense that he doesn't want to hurt me. He is watching me with a soft and sincere look in his eyes. A chill runs through me. I flinch and he turns away. No one speaks. *What do you say to a target you let live?* I think about Talon. I wonder if he is okay.

The car comes to a sudden stop, and I look out the window. I see a long driveway leading to the front of a large house in the middle of the forest. It's a three-story house with a large pool. *Why take a hostage to such a luxurious home?*

I eye ways to escape as they lead me into the house. But suddenly, I see Talon sitting in the living room. I blink. *Was he really unconscious in the car? Why wouldn't he try to help me if he had been awake? What is he doing here? Have they taken him hostage too?*

I am pushed into a chair and glare at Talon. He hands me a cup of tea.

"Why didn't you tell me?" I ask.

"Because then it wouldn't have been real," he replies.

"Then *what* wouldn't have been real?"

"The kidnapping."

I just stare at him. He sighs.

"The Committee is after you, so I had to pretend I was going to kill you so they wouldn't come after me. I couldn't kill you. I've known you for so long. I even knew who you were before we met."

"How is that possible?" I ask, still upset.

Talon hesitates. "Well, I know your father."

"Don't you mean *knew* my father? He's dead."

"No, he isn't." Talon sighs again. "Alhrick and I didn't want this day to come."

"What does Alhrick have to do with any of this?"

"Well..." Talon begins.

Alhrick jumps in. "Kenley, I am your father."

I drop my tea. I calmly turn toward this man.

"How can you be my father? He died years ago."

"That is just a lie that the Committee told you. I didn't want you to grow up knowing that your father was a double agent on the run. You wouldn't have been able to live a normal life. You would have always been on the lookout, convinced that they would soon be after you too."

I stand up quickly. They are still looking at me but do not move an inch when I walk into the hallway. Once outside, I let the news sink in. Maybe Alhrick really was my father. *He is a target I let go for an unknown reason, which just doesn't happen with me. He seems to know Talon very well. I trust that Talon would not lie to me. How can I find out if he is telling the truth? I can always pretend that I believe he is my father and wait to see what happens.*

✧✧✧

Staring out the window, I watch the baby birds fly away from their nest, and come to realize that now I am in hiding, just like my father. I will be unknown to everyone in the world I once lived in and loved, a world that took me in and protected me. The people in that world taught me how to perfect the gift I had. That world made me who I am. *How will I be able to let go? I feel unfulfilled. I was to become part of the Committee. But if Talon and Alhrick are telling the truth—that the Black Tower knows who my father really is and wants me dead now—I have no choice but to hide, for now. Something I have never done.* Yet I couldn't stop thinking about going back to the Tower.

I don't want to hide from them. Why should I listen to a man I just met? A man who claims to be my father, yet throughout my life has been hiding from me?

What about Talon? I thought I knew and trusted him. Yet he kept such a big secret from me for so long. Didn't he ever think that maybe I would have liked to meet my father? I had apparently lived with him until I was seven years old, but I didn't remember him. Could he not have told me that Alhrick was my father as soon as they assigned me the mission to kill him? Why now? Why would he wait and tell me now? How do I even know that the Committee wants me dead? They took me in as a child; they know more about me than my own father. They know I believe he was murdered. They know me as I am now, not the person Alhrick and Talon tell me I am. I know I have to find out who to trust for myself. I have to go back to the Black Tower to see if the Committee is truly after me or if Talon and Alhrick merely want to use me as some form of revenge.

I stay for too long at the house, waiting for answers that never come. I decide to get them myself by going back to the Tower in disguise. The Tower seems darker than before; the white numbers on the walls bring panic to my mind. A man stops me at the elevator. My body shakes, but I quickly control it. He is unable to tell that I am afraid. He is an attractive, tall, well-built man with light brown hair and sapphire eyes. He asks if I know where the Committee's office is located. I relax. I want to know why he is heading there, so I tell him I will show him where it is. The Committee never speaks to any agent directly, let alone a stranger. So why would this man I've never seen before be called in to meet the Committee? They only talk directly to each other or senior assassins. This man is neither.

In the elevator, he comments on my eyes. I forgot that I was wearing fake contacts. I pretend to blush and ask him why he is going to see the Committee. He answers, "To track down someone very important. A woman who used to be a top assassin here." I stiffen. Alhrick and Talon were telling the truth. I must hide now or take matters into my own hands. I will find a way to bring down the Black Tower. But how?

The elevator dings as soon as it stops. The man moves to the side. "Ladies first." I smile and show him to the Committee doors. He asks for my name. I hesitate for a second before I say, "Ken."

"That's a unique name, my first time hearing it," he says.

I feel a chill down my spine.

"My name is Darien; try to remember it. Hope I see you again soon."

I nod, sure we will see each other again, but perhaps not in the way he expects. He starts to open the doors but turns one last time to smile at me, and his sapphire eyes have turned silver. I gasp. Immediately after the doors close, heat starts to flow through my body, and I place my ear against the door. I hear my name and panic. I run toward the elevator. Once in the lobby, I sprint toward the doors. A man looks at me suspiciously, but I give him a deadly look and keep running. Once outside, I hear my name, but I don't stop. I get to my car and glance back. It's the man from the lobby, and he's shouting at me.

Talon is sitting in the passenger seat of my car. I stifle a surprised yell as I speed out of the parking lot.

"We were not lying to you."

"What are you doing here?"

"I merely came to check on you. Now do you see that we

weren't lying? Do you trust us now?"

"Yes, I guess I do."

Back at the house, I try to get some sleep, but I can't. I don't want to hide forever. Every night I have dreams of being in a dark room, surrounded by agents and flying bullets. When I try to shoot back, I realize my gun is empty. Then I fall into darkness and I see Darien. We are in some sort of park. I have seen it so many times that now I know every detail; I know all of its dark and bright places, its hills, and all of its trees. I stare into Darien's eyes, which switch from sapphire to silver. I wonder what he is.

Awake, I make myself tea so that I can relax, but it doesn't work. Without knowing why, I grab my keys, get in my car, and start driving. Soon, unaware of how I got there, I am in the same park from my dreams. *How can this be? I have never been here before.*

I step out of the car, shocked. I start walking to the empty concrete spot in my dream. Darien appears out of nowhere with two men who also have silver eyes. Intimidated by their tall, muscular bodies I start to slowly walk backward; they have not seen me yet. I try to be silent, but I step on a tree branch. Their heads quickly turn, unnaturally fast. Before I am able to move my foot off the branch, our eyes meet. I start to run as fast as I can, but they are much faster. I panic, and suddenly I am moving quickly and smoothly through the air. I feel as if I am flying, but it seems as if I am merely jumping large distances at an incredible pace. I come to a stop in the forest. I look for the silver-eyed men, but there is nothing but trees. The trees are swaying like a strong wind is moving them. The whistling air through the leaves sounds as if someone is running. Turning back quickly as I hear a leaf crackle, Darien is standing behind me.

I panic. He reaches for me; my vision blurs, and I start to feel faint again. The branches move as if a sudden breeze hit them. I close my eyes and sense being lifted up like a leaf in the breeze. Once I feel like I am no longer moving, I open my eyes. I am in my room. I look down at my shoe and see that I have a branch stuck in it. *How did I get here? I know I was in the forest… What happened to Darien?*

I panic again, and suddenly I'm transported back to the forest for a moment before I am once again in my room. *Teleportation?* I'm afraid. I close my eyes; a strong breeze gushes right through me, freezing my body. *Am I asleep? This feels so real…* Suddenly, I feel rain, and I'm back in the park. Instinctively, I run toward my car. I get a bad vibe as I approach. Yet I get in, and nothing seems to be wrong, so I start the car and drive lifelessly through the streets until I find myself circling the Black Tower.

The parking lot is almost empty, except for Talon's car, parked with the headlights on. *Why are the headlights still on? What is he doing here?* I step out of my car and walk discreetly toward his. I try the door and it opens easily; he has not even locked it. I get inside and start thinking. *Should I turn off his light? Maybe I should go inside and look for him.* As time passes by, I become more impatient.

Suddenly, I see Talon quickly returning from the Black Tower. He sees me in the car and looks surprised, but he gets in quickly, doesn't speak, and speeds off. I look through the rearview mirror and see three black cars following us. I look toward Talon as he swerves and tries to lose our followers. He says, "The Committee wasn't happy to find out that I was double-crossing them."

"How did they find out?" I asked.

"Someone working at the Tower saw me get in the car with you," he responded. My mind quickly went back to the man from the lobby so long ago.

I become angry and know what I must do. Using my new gift of teleportation, I close my eyes and think about the Tower. I focus on its black walls, and the sound of the car's engine is helpful. Once the sound of the engine dies away, I know I have materialized in the Black Tower. I open my eyes. Everyone is staring at me, but I hardly notice. My mission is clear: I must free myself from everyone trying to control me. I want to be free.

No one dares to come near me. As I walk confidently through the crowd, the image of Darien walking into the Committee's office comes to mind. I walk toward the elevator, with everyone's eyes following me, and make my way up to the Committee's office. The once-dark office is now silent and bright. As I walk in, the Committee members freeze. They all have weapons: machine guns, sniper rifles, and pistols. They have every type of gun available, and they reach for them. It's like my dream, but this time I'm prepared. My years of training and the discovery of my new gift help me take them all out, one by one. I leave without a scratch. As I exit the Tower, everyone in the lobby remains silent. The Committee is no more.

Years pass. I finally have peace. Since that day in the Black Tower, no one has dared to come after me. I live alone, away from Talon and Alhrick, but I still keep in touch with them and keep an eye on the Tower. Occasionally, I stop by the Black Tower and check on things. Everyone knows who I am, but no one acknowledges me. There is no one trying to take complete control anymore, and everyone is civil. I have one last thing to do. I have not been able to find the man who gave Talon up—until today. When I walk into the old Committee's office, there he is, staring at me with a smirk on his face. He is standing next to Darien and his two silver-eyed partners. Without a word, I take care of the smirking man. I see Darien and his partners watching me. Staring into Darien's eyes, I place my gun on the table and make my way to the elevator, leaving the Black Tower with everyone's eyes still on me.

Michelle Bautista
TO THE LIMIT

I look out the window of my room. Daisies are blooming. I smell the pine trees and breathe their scent in and out of my lungs. It brings up a lot of memories from my childhood. Music was and is my inspiration. I love to sing on stage and perform in front of people. As a child, I would dress up like Selena, wearing high heels with a microphone in my hand. My dad's music, especially, is my inspiration. He listens to U2 and the Goo Goo Dolls. We always sing "Beautiful Day" together. When he first heard me sing, he insisted that I always practice. Since that day, I've gone to after-school lessons for my vocals.

My father has always been there for me when I needed him the most. One time, when I was in the third grade, I was going to sing at a school play. I was really scared. My father told me not to be scared and to imagine that I was the only one in the room. I listened to his advice, and everyone liked my performance. My dad's face always has a handsome smile. When he smiles, you feel happy. My father is everything in the whole wide world to me. I think he is perfect.

My mother is beautiful. She is the type of mother who does not need night creams or makeup to look younger. She is five feet six inches tall, and has short brown hair and brown eyes. When she smiles I can see her dimples. She loves to wear suits, or skirts below her knees with button-down dress blouses, and of course her black high heels. But she is a cold person who does not show her feelings to me, the person she loves. She doesn't go to my performances, and I cannot tell her what I feel. I don't want to beg her to come see me in my musicals. She's always in a meeting, and when she does come, she is too late to see me perform. My mother doesn't care, though: she doesn't like me performing. She wants me to become a doctor or a lawyer. She thinks that being a vocalist is not a career because you don't need an education. I do want to be a vocalist, even though I'm only seventeen, and I'm really excited to start that career, but I have to finish high school first.

On Monday morning I get up and dress. I put on a pink shirt and dark jeans and go downstairs to the kitchen to have breakfast. Entering the kitchen, I see my father eating.

"Good morning, Daddy," I say, kissing him on the cheek.

"Hi, honey. Come and eat with me. Your mom is too busy."

"Where is she?"

"Talking on the phone, as usual."

After I sit down, I start to eat pancakes, scrambled eggs, and bacon, with a glass of orange juice on the side. After finishing, I get my backpack and head out the front door to go to school.

"Goodbye Daddy. See you in the afternoon?"

"Okay honey, have a good day at school; be careful."

Man, one more day at school. I enter the gates of Culver High School and head to my first period math class. I don't want to go, but second semester finals are coming. I need to pass the class, or else I don't graduate. There, I see my friend Richelle. She's in my band, and she helps me practice my vocals. Sitting next to her is my dream guy, George Ames. I have known him since I was in the fourth grade. He is tall and light-skinned, and has green eyes and a perfect smile. He doesn't know me. I don't exist to him. I don't belong to his world. He is popular, and all the pretty girls are after him. I don't have the guts to talk to him, even though I want to. The funny thing is that I know more about him than he knows about me. It's so ridiculous.

The bell rings. As I'm heading to my second period class, I realize I left my cell phone at my desk. I rush back and see

George holding it.

"Hey, you forgot your cell phone."

"Yeah, I know." He hands me my phone, and I say, "Thank you."

"You're welcome."

I wonder how he knew that it was mine.

The rest of the day goes by fast. Next thing I know, I'm in my sixth period class, and my day at school is finally over. *I actually talked to George for two minutes, and he held my cell phone,* I told myself. *How cool is that?* I wait for the bus, but it never comes, so I call my dad to pick me up.

As I sit in my room looking at a *J-14* magazine, I see celebrities like Rihanna, Beyonce, Alicia Keys, and Amanda Perez. I finish looking at my magazine and wonder how it feels to be a celebrity. I see my reflection in the window, while outside there's the clear blue sky and shining sun. There is a bird chirping in its nest, waiting for its mother to feed it, but she never comes. *We have so much in common.* The phone suddenly rings.

"Hello?" I answer.

"Hi, is this Marlette Keith?"

"Yes, that's me."

"I'm John Sims, a producer at Nick's Records, and you have been selected to audition for a music school scholarship."

My heart starts to beat really fast. *Could this be happening to me? No—it's just a prank call.*

"Sorry, but you must have the wrong number," I say.

"No, please don't hang up! We are serious. We've been hearing about your band—that you're a good singer."

"Really? Okay, I'll go. Can I please have the address?" I walk through the living room, trying to find something to write on. I look down at the table in the middle of my living room and see my notebook.

"It's going to be on Thursday at eight o'clock at 7354 Culver Boulevard."

I hurry and write the address carefully. I end the call and run to tell my father the news. He is glad and gives me a huge hug that almost takes my breath away.

"Honey, I will be there, I promise. I wouldn't miss it for

a U2 concert."

"Thank you, Daddy," I say, laughing. "Should I tell Mom?"

"No, let's keep it to ourselves. She is going to get mad."

I head to my room and pick up my guitar with the colorful heart around it. I start to play, blissful and inspired.

The day of the competition finally arrives. The sun is brighter than ever. I wait for my father, but he never arrives. I get a bad feeling, as if something happened. A crow outside stares at me through the window and gives me the chills. My hands start to sweat, and then the phone suddenly rings, vibrating on the table in the living room. I jump to answer it.

"Daddy, where are you?"

"Sorry, this is Dr. Thompson calling from Saint Daniel's Hospital. May I speak with someone regarding Joseph Keith?"

"What? Is there something wrong with my father?"

"Your father had an accident."

The hospital doors slide open. Ambulances arrive with bloody bodies and a young lady in labor. I can't focus. I am thinking about my father and what happened to him. Nurses go back and forth helping the ill patients. I sit in the waiting room, waiting for an answer. A man comes toward me and introduces himself as Dr. Thompson. He has a long face.

"Dr. Thompson, what is wrong with my father? Please tell me!"

"I'm so sorry, but your father has just passed away."

I'm stunned. For a few seconds I can't breathe. Tears drip from my eyes. Thousands and thousands of tears fall, and I can't stop crying. I think of how I am going to miss him so much. How I am going to survive?

My mother comes in and sees me crying.

"What happened? Is everything all right?"

"My daddy passed away."

She looks at me, and her mouth opens wide. Only one tear falls from her eye. She tries to hold in her pain, but out of nowhere she collapses. I try to help her up, but she pushes me away.

I need to tell my father goodbye for the last time. I head to the room where he is lying in bed, dead. The room looks full of tubes, and that makes me scared. When I enter, I see a girl holding my father's hand. She looks about twenty years old and has hazel-colored eyes, long light brown hair, and a mole on her left cheek. She is wearing a pink spaghetti-strap shirt and dark jeans with rhinestones on the back pockets. I head toward her.

"Why are you holding my father's hand?" I ask angrily.

"Sorry, but this is my father. Can I please have some a moment by myself?"

"What? Your father? No, he's my father. I'm an only child."

"He is my father too. My name is Debby Keith. I have my birth certificate if you want to look at it."

"Let me see it."

Debby Keith, born on October 3, 1988. *This can't be.*

"You must be Marlette. My father told me about you. He didn't want to tell you because it would hurt you a lot.

I stopped and stared at my father's dead body. *Why did he lie to me? He could have told me the truth. I can't believe this! Now I have a half sister.*

For a moment I look at her. Then I run and hug her, and she hugs me back. A tear falls on my shoulder.

The door opens. It's Dr. Thompson.

"Sorry, Marlette and Debby, I'm going to take your father now."

Tears fall from my eyes. "No, don't go!" I scream. "I'm going to miss you."

Debby holds me up. "Marlette, everything is going to be all right."

After my father's funeral, Debby and I take the bus together. I don't want to ride with my mom. I feel like I'm falling apart. Debby tells me the story. Her mother had a one-night stand with my father. She got pregnant with Debby. The relationship did not go well, but Debby loved our father. I stop at my house. Before Debby goes on to hers, she tells me she is going to call me.

On Friday morning the phone rings. I get up, stomping my feet and slamming my bedroom door. *Man, who is calling so early?*

"Good morning," I answer.

"Hey, good morning. Sorry for waking you up, but I have a surprise for you."

"Hi Debby. What is it?

"You need to e-mail some of your songs tomorrow to my boss. He's in charge of Nick's Records."

"What? You must be kidding."

"No, I talked to him, and he wants to meet you and see you perform. I told him what happened to our father and why you didn't make it to the audition."

"I'll be there all right."

Hanging up the phone, I mourn for my father. I remember his smile when he would see me perform. I enter his library. He had paintings by Van Gogh and Rivera, and Dodgers bobbleheads. He also had a picture of me performing for the first time. I can still smell his cologne in here, and it makes me feel as though he is still alive.

I think of what I'm going to tell my mother. I know she's going to be furious, so I decide to keep it a secret. I go back into my room and look for my demo CDs, but there is no sign of them. They're gone. I am shocked. I run down the stairs to the living room.

"Where did you hide my CDs?" I ask my mother.

"Honey, I threw them away. I thought they were old CDs. Besides, I want you to become a doctor, not to follow that dumb vocalist career!"

"What? Mom, those records mean everything to me, especially since my dad died. How could you?" I run to my room, crying. This is the end of my dream. After all the effort I put into those CDs, they're gone. All that's left are my lyrics.

I spend the day in my room. It is raining outside. Trees wave back and forth, and kids get wet stomping in puddles. The sky is as gloomy as I am. I think back to what my mother did, and I go to my secret place. There is a door in the back of my closet, behind my clothes, that leads to my secret place where I can be alone with my memories. It is decorated with pink and purple wallpaper, and on the wall there are pictures of my dad and me at the beach, Disneyland, and my favorite place, a karaoke spot called Johnnie's. I also have a picture of my best friend Nettie. She moved to San Francisco when we were in the fifth grade. I never saw her again. I remember how she loved singing with me. She would tell me that I was going to be a pop star one day. I never believed her. I never thought I was that good.

I see my father's old picture album. It has yellow pages that rip very easily and a picture of Winnie-the-Pooh on the cover. I open it, and I see my father's picture. He is smiling next to me. I look at the picture over and over again, and start to cry. Time goes by really fast.

I decide to call Debby and ask her to come over to my house as fast as she can. I wait for her, and I am scared to tell her that my mother threw away my demos. I hear a knock on the door; it's Debby, wearing a smile on her face. I immediately tell her everything, detail by detail. How Mom and I argued about what I want. How my mother slammed the door to my room. How she threw away my CDs.

"I can't believe this. How could you let your mom throw away your records?"

"I know it's my fault, but now that my father is dead I don't really care anymore." My lips turn down and quiver, and my eyes get watery. "I don't want to be a singer anymore."

Debby shakes me. "Are you out of your mind?" She hugs me.

I whisper to her, "Thank you for believing in me."

Later we go to the record studio where Debby works for the auditions. There are a lot of teenagers like me waiting. Debby introduces me to the producer, and I tell him what happened to my CDs. He asks me to sing, and I sing just like my father told me to. I stand up straight and sing with all my strength.

After I finish, the producer says, "Wow, you're good; where did you learn to sing like that?"

"Thank you, my father helped me with my vocals."

The producer then tells me that he did not like how I sang the last words, though. He says I still need more practice and have to sing more clearly.

Suddenly, a girl enters. She is tall and has long hair. She struts in front of me like a model and her hair waves back and forth. *I'd better get out of here.* She is Nicole Sims. I met her in kindergarten, when she would steal my crayons. Now she pushes me in the hallway when I'm by myself. I know she's here for a reason. I have to be strong; I know I am better than her.

A week later, I get a letter from Nick's Records. I am selected as one of the finalists! I hear Nicole got selected, too. I smile, though, as if my father is alive again. I jump up and down while reading the letter. I cannot believe it. I made it. I'm going to audition. I couldn't have done it without Debby's help, so I call her right away. I hear her yelling and screaming. She tells me that she will pick me up at my house right away.

I hang up and go to my secret place. I see my father's picture, kiss it, and say thank you. I know I am going to become a famous singer. The first thing I have to do is beat Nicole, and I know I have to practice a lot. I pick a pastel lime green dress from my closet. It has gold flowers on the side of the waist. I don't tell my mother about going to the audition. I want her to be proud of me and to love me like my father always did, though I don't know if that's ever going to happen. She'll get mad at me and destroy my chances of winning. I leave without putting the dress on. Instead, I put on a plain shirt and dark blue jeans. I tell her that I am going to be at Debby's house for dinner. She ignores me and walks away.

When I get to Nick's Records, there are a lot of people there waiting for the auditions to start. I see Nicole getting ready on stage. When she starts to sing, she sounds like Alicia Keys. I am next. Up on stage, holding the microphone in my sweaty hand, I freeze. My legs are stiff, and

I cannot concentrate. I suddenly remember that I have to beat Nicole. I start to sing. I feel a teardrop falling down my cheek. I sing a song that my father dedicated to me when I was a little girl.

You're the spirit of Christmas
My star on the tree
You're the Easter Bunny
To Mommy and me
You're sugar; you're spice
You're everything nice
And you're Daddy's little girl

When I finish, everyone applauds. I'm happy; I know my father is looking down on me. At the end of my performance, I walk off the stage and see George. *What is he doing here? Oh my God, how embarrassing.* He smiles; I smile back.

He comes toward me and says, "You're Marlette, right?"

"I'm—yes, it's me," I say, mixing up words.

"I never knew you sang so beautifully."

"Thank you." My stomach is full of butterflies.

"You're welcome. Hey, do you want to go get something to eat?"

Oh my God. "I don't really know. I don't really talk to you at school."

"I know, but I always wanted to talk to you."

"Well, in that case, I'll go," I say, smiling and laughing at the same time.

We stop at Steaks, Steaks, and More Steaks. I'm really nervous. We get to the table, and George pushes my chair in for me. The waiter comes and asks us what we would like to order. George orders a hamburger special with a chocolate shake on the side. I look at him and laugh. He must have a huge appetite. I order the same thing, except I choose a vanilla shake.

"So, what's your favorite music?" he asks.

"I like hip-hop, eighties, nineties, oldies, and R&B. What kind of music do you like?"

"I like to listen to the same music as you. What a coincidence," he says, laughing.

"I know, huh? I never though you'd like the same stuff. Can I ask you a question?" I ask.

"Sure."

"Why do you want to get to know me?"

"I always wanted to talk to you. I was really scared. I'm a shy person. I always thought you were the perfect girl for me."

My heart starts to beat fast. I look at him and see his face turn red, like he wants to get out of here.

"Thanks. I always wanted to talk to you too, but I'm timid," I reply.

"It's okay. We don't have to be shy anymore."

We head home. On the way, he tells me about his life and how going to college won't be easy for him. I tell him I want to become a famous pop singer. He says that I will make it, that I have the talent.

He drops me off at my house. I know that I have to tell my mother the news even if she is going to get mad at me. I see my mother, who turns and smiles. I smile too. I am surprised, but I'm glad that my mother is happy.

"Hi, Mom, how are you today?" I ask.

"Good, honey. Why?"

"I have to tell you something very important. I made it to the finals."

Her face turns red.

"How could you do that? I don't want you to become a singer!" she yells.

"What you think does not concern me." I run to my room and slam the door.

I can do anything. I can be a singer. I don't have to hide stuff from my mother anymore. I now have the strength to tell her how I feel; I am glad that I know she's mad at me. I have to do this for myself. My life is changing. I have a half sister who is helping me accomplish my dreams. It's like my dad is taking care of me from heaven. I know there are surprises to come. My mother wants me to become a doctor and make a lot of money, but that is not what I want.

I decide to go to my secret place. I want to organize it. I want to change everything because there's a new me. I take down the pictures that I posted up on the wall. As I take down the picture of me and my father at a concert, a letter falls down. It's a letter from my dad. I can't believe it. I'm shocked, and I wonder how he knew about this place. I read the letter patiently.

> *My Dear Marlette,*
>
> *I never told you this, but there is stuff you need to know. I wrote this letter because I knew I would not be able to tell you in person. You might wonder how I put the letter here. I found out about your secret place when you were in the seventh grade.*
>
> *You are a wonderful vocalist, and you have a lot of confidence. You are a brave person; you can be who you want to be. Don't let anybody put you down. I know your mother loves you deep inside; just give her time. She has a lot of reasons for hating the singing career.*
>
> *And one more thing: I love you with all my heart.*
>
> *Sincerely,*
>
> *Your father, Joseph Keith*

As I finish reading the letter, a thousand tears start to fall. I can barely breathe. I cry like a baby. I know that I can become a good singer.

Weeks pass, and I become curious about my mother's past. I need her to tell me the truth. I hear her coming inside the house, and I run downstairs.

"Mom, I need to ask you something."

"What is it? Please hurry; I'm waiting for a call."

"Why do you hate the fact that I want to become a vocalist?"

"I don't want to talk about this," she says, walking away.

"Mom, wait. Just tell me, please." I run after her.

"Joseph Keith is not your biological father; your father died a long time ago."

I keep going around in circles before taking a seat in the living room. Joseph Keith is not my dad. This can't be happening. Oh my God, Debby is not my half sister; she is my stepsister. I run to my room. I don't want to see my mother. My heart starts to feel weak; it's falling apart. They both lied to me all these years. I thought my father was perfect, but he and my mother were both liars. I don't understand.

I hear a knock on my door.

"I don't want to talk to you. Leave me alone!" I yell.

"Honey, let me in. I can explain."

I let her in. Her eyes and nose look red, and she is holding an album.

"Why did you lie to me? What does all of this have to do with my career?"

"Your biological father's name is Kevin Jones. He was a rock star. He died before you were born. I don't want you to become like that."

"Mom, you know me better than that."

"I know, honey, but I'm scared something will happen to you. I don't want to lose you like I lost your father."

I run toward her and hug her. My mom and I cry so much. I tell her about Debby, and she tells me she knows. They have to meet each other. Then, my mom shows me the album. I see my biological dad. He is tall with brown hair and has hazel eyes. I look at my mother.

"Mom, I want you to be proud of me and of what I've accomplished throughout the years. I need your support and love," I say, crying.

"Honey, I love you with all my heart. I want you to be successful."

She leans toward me and gives me a huge hug for the first time in years. My world changes; I feel like me again. She tells me that she will go to the finals with me, like my father would have.

The day of the finals is here. I'm excited, and my legs want to jump up and down. My mother comes to my room and kisses me on the forehead. She tells me that Debby is going to be waiting for me at Arena Stage.

"Everything is going to be all right."

"Thanks, Mommy."

At Arena Stage, I see a lot of people gathering to see the performance. I panic for a few seconds, but I see my mother and Debby sitting in the front seats. They smile at me. When I'm on stage, I dedicate the song to my father.

> *When I think of you*
> *The sun shines*
> *The sky is blue*
>
> *You were everything*
> *My inspiration, my hope*
>
> *Why did you have to lie?*
> *Why did you have to go?*
>
> *I'll miss you, but I'll be strong in my life*
> *I'll miss you, but you'll still stay in my heart*
> *I'll miss you*

Everyone applauds when I finish. Nicole is next, and everyone likes her performance, too. I'm anxious; I want to win.

The votes come in. They call Nicole for third place. They call this girl I don't know for second place. Marlette for first place. I won! I run toward the stage, and I accept my prize, the scholarship. When I leave the stage, I see George.

"Hey, I love the song you composed for your dad," he says, hugging me.

"Thank you."

"I want to ask you something."

"What's up?"

"I really like you; would...would you like to be my girlfriend?"

I throw my arms around his neck. Close to his lips, I say yes as he leans toward me and gives me a kiss.

I thought my life was a disaster with no hopes or dreams. I found out a lot of truth. I have my perfect boyfriend. I have a stepsister whom I love a lot. And my mother and I trust each other now.

Jocelyn Mariscal
EVERYWHERE I LOOK

Heroes are everywhere and can be found inside everyone. Not only police authorities, firefighters, or doctors can be heroes. Anyone can be, from children to mothers to workers; it's just that sometimes they don't know it. Being a hero depends on whether one chooses to accept challenges and not be a bystander. Heroes must break away from the pack and take action, either voluntary or forced. They help others and then go through a change, learning more about themselves and the world around them. And the most powerful weapon heroes have is self-reliance: without it, they're just followers. As Ralph Waldo Emerson said, "Trust thyself: every heart vibrates to that iron string."

Heroes are needed in life to act as role models. Even though heroes in literature, movies, and mythology—such as Hercules, Superman, Hester Prynne, Luke Skywalker, and Wonder Woman—are exaggerated, they are there for people to look up to. They show that the world isn't all bad and that there are those who care. These heroes inspire people to be heroes themselves, which means that heroes are not only found in fiction and myths, but also in our everyday lives.

My parents are heroes to me. They have gone through many obstacles in the pursuit of happiness and a better life. Through my parents, I learned the true meaning of sacrifice. They have given up many things for their children and their siblings. When they were growing up, both of my parents had to drop out of school and work so they could help support their families and pay for the education of my uncles and aunts. As the oldest child in his family, my father was under even more pressure to work since my grandfather died when my dad was a little boy. My mother was the second-oldest child, and she had to give up her education as well because her family couldn't afford it. They worked and never stopped, always putting their families first.

Even now, with my siblings and me, they put us first and worry about themselves afterward. For example, when we go shopping for clothes, we children get to pick our clothes first, and if there's enough money left, then my parents buy something for themselves. Dreams were broken and life never went as they planned, but my parents kept moving forward, doing their best along the way. My mother never got the chance to become what she wanted to be, a teacher. Yet in a way she has become my teacher. When I was young, I never saw my parents as heroes, but as my dictators with the ruling *chancla*; yet, as I grew older, I learned why they imposed rules and why they were the way they were. From "Get your face away from the TV; you're too close," to "Do the dishes; do your homework," or "Get those things out of your ears! Are you listening to me? You're going to go deaf," and, of course, all the *nos* given, my parents are always trying to prevent my siblings and me from committing the same mistakes they did. They are trying to do things for our own good, and they're trying to teach us to be strong. This makes them admirable and inspiring.

Before I took this class, I was clueless about the stages of the hero's journey. I never noticed before how in stories and belief systems many things are similar, and how people are more similar than different. Everywhere I look, I see the hero's journey—it is impossible not to recognize it now. Everyone goes through the stages of the hero's journey in life, and it always happens more than once. Every day is an adventure waiting to happen. It's just that sometimes people don't even notice their own journey. Usually that happens because the specific journey is a small one, and the person is so busy that he or she doesn't see it. For example, a day at school is itself a hero's journey. A student can be the hero, a teacher or bully can be the villain, and the boon is what the student learned that day.

There's a hero in everybody, even in the most unlikely

person. I can be a hero myself. Leaving home to go to college will be the beginning of one huge adventure, my hero's journey with smaller adventures within it. As a hero, I will have to deal with many trials by myself, but I will always find support along the way. My parents have taught me what they have learned from their own experiences in their own hero's journeys, and I plan on using that wisdom to make it through.

Lisbeth Aguilar
CRYSTAL VANISHED

The sky is as black as the devil's soul when I arrive home from the criminal justice department. The furious wind blows the trees from side to side, making my black skirt dance. My muscles aching, I run toward my house. Where are my keys? I think to myself, shuffling through my black leather purse. I finally find them hidden in with my make-up. I open the door and sneak in really slowly, as if I am a thief.

As I stumble past my porch I realize how tired I am. This is the second straight day that I've been working on this case, and I feel like the work I've done is leading me nowhere. My eyes are irritated, so I close them and open them again, blinking repeatedly. I take a glance at my watch and see that I'm late again. I jog into my daughter's room, open the door, and watch my little princess sleeping. Her clothes are all over the room; following the path to her bed—ouch!—I trip over a basketball. I reach my daughter's bed and kiss her soft forehead. Crystal slowly opens her hazel eyes, and I see her sweet gaze. "Mommy, I miss you," she says, making me feel as if I haven't done my job as a mother to spend time with her.

"I'm sorry, my darling, but I've had a lot of work. Now go to sleep," I say. "Remember that you're taking your English test tomorrow."

She leans toward me, and I feel her soft and small lips give me a kiss. I tuck her into bed.

"Good night, my princess, don't let the bugs come and bite you." I blow her a kiss. Before leaving her room I take a last glance at Crystal; her curly hair is spread all over the pillow. After I walk outside I stand next to the door, holding the oval knob, and Kathy, the seven-year-old girl who was kidnapped, comes into my thoughts. This is the case that has been haunting me for the past forty-eight hours. I can't even imagine what her mother is going through: pain, depression, anger. But I promise I'll find that guy, I think, closing my fist as if I'm going to punch someone. No matter how long it takes, I will find him. I can't believe that there are still people like him in this world. I can't even imagine myself going through this experience. Just having the thought makes my heart go one hundred beats per second.

It is midnight, the house is dark and quiet, and I finally have the opportunity to work on Kathy's case. As I walk toward my office, I grab a cup of coffee in the kitchen. Ever since high school, coffee has been my best friend. Walking through the hall, I hear my husband John snoring. I laugh. As I step into my office, I realize how lonely I am. The cold air embraces my body, giving me goose bumps. I open my black suitcase, full of papers covered with my writing. I've always had the habit of putting my thoughts and notes on paper; I never know if something will help me solve a case. I start going over my notes, analyzing every single detail and gathering information little by little, as if I'm working on a puzzle. I'm never going to find this guy, I think. But, no, no, no! I can't quit; I have to do this for Kathy and her mother. Suddenly my cell phone rings: ...*ring, ring, ring.* I jump out of the chair wondering who would be calling at this hour.

"Hello?" I answer nervously.

"Hello, Violet. Did I wake you up?" the voice says.

"Oh, hey Stacy, I was just working on something, but what happened?"

"I'm sorry to call you at this time, but I was just going to remind you that tomorrow Kathy's parents are coming."

"Oh my God, that's right. I almost forgot about that. I totally forgot."

"That's fine. I'm just reminding you."

"Well, thanks for the reminder. I'll see you at nine thirty."

"Okay, see you there."

"I'll see you then. Good night." I yawn.

Ever since I started working as a detective, Stacy has always been there for me. It's been ten years of good friendship. She is a clever woman who is always advising me. One time she helped me overcome some of the most depressing days of my life. My ex-boyfriend Henry James was obsessed with me. I remember those days when he would call me all the time, asking too many questions:

Who are you with?

What are you doing?

What time are you getting home?

He treated me as if we were married already, or as if he owned me. Who did he think he was? Stacy noticed the type of guy he was and told me, "Violet, you should think about telling him you need some time away. Don't make a big mistake that you'll regret." There were times after I finished working that I would walk outside, and he would be waiting for me, leaning against the wall. Henry was like my shadow; he would follow me everywhere. His angry voice made me feel as if he controlled me. If he called, I would hang up on him, but he would keep on insisting.

Finally, one day I decided to confront him. His face got red and he became aggressive, not wanting to accept that our relationship was over, yelling, "Why are you doing this?" If it weren't for Stacy I don't know what would have happened to me. That afternoon that jerk tried to hit me, but thanks to Stacy everything ended there. Bam! I open my eyes, and I'm face down on the stack of papers on my desk. I finally decide to go to sleep. Inside our room, John is fast asleep. I whisper to him, "John, babe, move over." I give him a kiss. "Babe, move over."

He doesn't move.

I push him and he rolls over, falling off the bed. I giggle. John wakes up with an annoyed look on his face.

"What did you do that for?" he asks.

I laugh again. "Babe, I asked you to move over," I say, still giggling. "I'm sorry. I guess I really pushed you hard."

"Oh, babe, it's all right," John says with a smile. "It was an accident. Let's go to sleep." He extends his arms and I rush to hug him. His warm arms embrace me, and I stop shivering. We lie down, and John leans over toward my ear.

"Violet, I love you."

"I love you, too, John."

He kisses my forehead. As soon as I close my eyes I fall asleep. All of a sudden I'm dragged into a nightmare. It's really cloudy. I call my daughter: "Crystal!" I walk outside to my porch where the only signs I see of Crystal are her toys on the ground. I hear no response from Crystal. The wind is so strong that I can hear it, and it blows my hair around. Then I walk toward the gate, but before opening the door, I feel a hand on my shoulder. The nightmare stops abruptly, and I hear the window slam shut. "Crystal, Crystal!" I continue to exclaim until I notice that John's hand is on my shoulder.

"Babe, what happened, what's wrong?" John asks. I was practically panting. He hugs me tighter.

"Nothing, babe," I reply. "It was just a nightmare."

He asks one more time: "Are you sure you're okay?"

"Yeah, I'm all right. It was just a nightmare, a nightmare." My heart feels as if it's going to pop out of my chest.

Beep. Beep. The alarm sounds on Tuesday morning. I wake up nervous, thinking that I'm late for my appointment. I look at my watch and see that it's six thirty. I take a deep breath and hear the birds chirping outside the window. The sun is brighter than usual.

"Good morning, darling," John says.

"Morning, babe."

"Were you able to sleep after all?"

"It took me a while, but I did."

I go to Crystal's room to wake her up.

As I open the refrigerator, the cold air embraces my face. I grab some eggs and low-fat milk. Crystal comes running in, her curls bouncing up and down. John gives us both a goodbye kiss and leaves for the firehouse. Before stepping out of the house, he calls out one more time: "Bye babe, bye Crys."

We both reply back, "Bye!" As we sit together, Crystal

looks at me. "Mom, are you gonna pick me up?"

"I'm sorry, honey, but I have an interview today."

Angrily, she replies, "Why did I ask if I knew the answer already? I guess I'll have to walk home."

I grab my suitcase. Stepping out of the house, the sun's rays burn my arms. We move quickly toward my black Nissan Altima. Inside the car, the smell of rosemary-and-roses air freshener fills the air. As I drive through Malibu, I watch the overcrowded highway. Fifteen minutes later, we arrive at school, and I park along the sidewalk. Before leaving, Crystal gives me a kiss, opens the door, and steps out of the car.

"Bye, Mommy."

"Bye, Crystal. Be good in school."

I watch my princess fade away in the rear-view mirror. Then I drive away, singing along with my favorite song "Nobody," not caring how ridiculous I may sound.

I arrive at work. *Tap, tap, tap*—my high heels make my presence known. Walking down the hall, I see Mr. and Mrs. Peterson sitting down in my office. As soon as I walk in, they stand up. Mrs. Peterson has a slender figure, her bangs covering her black eyes; but one can tell that Kathy fills her every thought. Her face looks worried and confused. Mr. Peterson looks impatient. He taps his fingers on the desk, and the dark circles under his brown eyes contrast with his light skin. After introducing themselves they sit down simultaneously, and I began the investigation by asking questions:

How was your relationship with Kathy?

When was the last time you saw her?

Did you have any problems with her?

Did you notice anything suspicious about her?

Asking these questions makes me realize that my relationship with Crystal is not good. As the investigation goes on, I tell them my worst fear is Crystal being missing. I thank them and let them know that I will call as soon as I have any updates. After the long interview, I take a look at my watch, noticing that Crystal's school ends in ten minutes. So let's see, I think, if she comes out at 2:20 p.m., she should be home by 2:40 p.m. As I'm sitting down at my desk working on Kathy's case, I grab my cell phone and decide to call Crystal at home. *Ring, ring, ring.* Come on, honey, answer, I think. But she doesn't. I leave her a voice mail. "Crystal, honey, I was just calling you to make sure everything is fine. Please call me back as soon as you hear this message. Remember that I love you. Bye."

As I wait for Crystal's call, all of sudden I recall the dream I had. Having a bad feeling, I make another phone call, but there is no answer again. Now I feel more nervous than ever; my body is shaking, and my heart starts to beat faster. At 2:50 p.m. I call home, but still no one answers. A chill runs down my spine. I fling my paperwork into my briefcase, slam it shut, and run out of the office. Though I'm quickly driving home, the other cars seem to stand still. When I get home, the door is open, the windows are broken, and I start to call out Crystal's name. I take some steps forward—"Oh my God!"—the couches are turned upside down, the lamp is in pieces, and my clothes are all over the place. The portraits I had in the living room are on the floor. I run all over the house and go inside the bathroom; on the mirror, it says the following in my red lipstick:

I love you Violet and Crystal too

The house phone rings, and I run to answer, thinking that it might be her.

"Hello?"

I hear heavy breathing. "Violet, I love you."

"Hello, who is this?"

"You don't recognize me? After all the time we spent together?"

I stand in panic trying to figure out who it is.

"Henry? Henry, it's you?"

"Ha ha ha! I knew you wouldn't..."

"Henry, did you—"

"Did I do what?"

"Henry, did you do this? Where is she? I want my daughter back!"

"You want our daughter back?"

"Henry, what do you want? I'll do anything. Please don't do anything to her. I beg you."

As I'm talking, I hear Crystal's voice screaming in the background: "Mom! Mommy!"

"Henry, let me talk to her."

"I'm warning you. You better watch out. Don't open your big mouth..." He pauses.

"Henry, I'm going to find you; I promise I will."

He laughs out loud and hangs up. I feel like a bullet has hit my heart. I immediately dial 911.

"911, what is your emergency?" a woman answers. I report everything, but as I talk to her it feels as if I'm losing my daughter more and more. The woman tries to calm me down by saying that the police are on their way. But my only concern is Crystal, and I feel that time is running out. Tears run down my cheeks as I make calls to John and Stacy. Minutes later, I hear the sirens. The police come running inside, and I run toward them.

"My daughter has been kidnapped. I know who did it!" I yell. "I know who did this!"

"Who?" they ask.

"Henry James!" I yell my lungs out.

"Henry James," a policeman repeats. "We have been looking for him for the past few days. He escaped from jail; he's a very dangerous man."

When John arrives, we are interviewed by a police officer who asks us to go to the police station. Just walking inside makes me feel angry, reminding me of Henry. He should be here, not me. I keep asking myself why he is doing this. Why? If he said he loved me, then he would never hurt me. They were all a bunch of lies. He is a liar. How could I believe him? How? After filing the report, the police started the search process, telling us to leave everything in their hands.

As we're leaving, Stacy comes running inside. "Violet, are you okay?" she says. "Now listen to me. I contacted our boss, and Mr. Dennis already said he would help. I promise we will find him. Don't worry, Violet, I'm here to help, no matter what. We are going to find her. Violet, I know that you're going through a tough time, but stay strong, and don't give up."

✧✧✧

After trying to sleep at home, I have nowhere to go but back to work. When I arrive, my boss calls me over.

"Ms. Bryant, can you please come to my office."

I wonder why he wants to see me, and as I enter his office, I shiver.

"Yes, sir, you wanted to see me."

"Ms. Bryant, yesterday at ten o'clock, I was trying to contact you to let you know that Kathy's body was found. Isn't that your case?"

"Yes, sir, it is, but something really terrible happened: my daughter was kidnapped. Why not Stacy?"

"I needed you. She was on the Colfer case." He looks straight into my eyes. "Now I heard what happened to your daughter, and from the bottom of my heart, I'm sorry. But you do not have the right to decide what case you want to work on. You were supposed to be there at the scene. You know how it works: you have to work on your job, no matter what. I understand that it is your daughter who got kidnapped, but you cannot work on that case. I'm sorry to say this, but I believe you need a break. I think it would be good for you to relax and leave everything in the police's hands."

"But—"

"No, that's my final decision. I know that you're a hard-working detective and that we need you, but I have to do this. It's for your own good."

I stare in disbelief. It feels as if my heart is breaking into pieces. I stay still like a stone, shocked to hear the news. Before stepping out of his office he says one more thing: "May I please have your badge?"

He takes my badge away, and I hand over my files, too. My career meant a lot to me. I loved my job. First my daughter, and now I lose my job. Oh God, please help me; give me the strength to fight. I feel weaker than ever. As I exit the office, Stacy comes over to ask me what happened, and I tell her that the boss decided to suspend me. She gets angry, but she tells me that it doesn't matter if I'm suspended: she's still going to help me. I thank her and leave the building, but before leaving I take one last look and recall all my work there over the years.

My eyes are numb; the tears run down during the entire drive home. Once I'm there, I walk toward Crystal's room. I turn on the light, but there is no Crystal. Her bed is well organized, with her pillow surrounded by her Elmo collection—just how she left them. As I sit there, I remember when I used to tuck my princess into bed. Those were the sweetest moments of my life, looking at her curls spread all over the pillow as I waited for her to fall asleep. Going through her clothes, I find her diary, an old notebook with a picture of her favorite basketball player, Kobe Bryant. I open it to the last page. In her neat cursive writing, it says, "Ever since my mother started working there, we haven't spent much time together."

As I keep on reading, I read that her favorite moments were when we went to the park as a family. I realize that she might be there. I grab my keys. When I get there I see children playing, and I look around. And then I see Crystal, with her curly hair, on the slide. I walk toward her and hug her tightly. She starts crying, "Mommy!"

A woman comes over. "Excuse me, ma'am," she says, "leave my daughter alone, or I will call the police."

Then I realize that it is another girl. "I'm sorry, ma'am," I say. "I'm sorry."

I walk away, crying. No, no, no! *Ring, ring!* It's Stacy calling my cell. I answer, but as she is about to give me more information, someone calls on the other line. I answer it.

"Hello?"

No one answers.

"Hello?"

"Violet, my love."

"Henry—"

"Violet, if you want to see your daughter alive, meet me at 248½ Garfield Boulevard in thirty minutes. Don't be late."

He hangs up on me for the second time. I click back over to Stacy, and we decide that we are going to meet each other there.

Out in front of the abandoned factory, I grab my gun and hide it under my waistband. It has quickly turned to a dark and cold night. My body shaking, I step out of my car. I decide to go inside by myself, knowing Stacy will follow if something happens.

That idiot left the door open. I look inside, and there she is; there's Crystal, my princess. She is lying down on the floor. Feeling some relief, I take a deep breath. Henry is talking on the phone with someone, laughing out loud: "Ha ha!" When he turns around, his fierce look makes me uncomfortable. Then he comes toward me.

"So, Violet. I'm glad you came."

"Let me see my daughter." As I see him getting closer, I yell, "You better back off!"

"No. Not until you say you love me."

I grab my gun and hold it behind my back. I try to look at my daughter, but she is too far away from me. When he gets close enough, I shoot once, and he hits the floor in pain. His leg is bleeding. Stacy comes running inside, yelling, "Violet! Are you all right?" She points the gun at Henry, telling him, "Do not move. If you dare move..."

Noticing that she is taking care of Henry, I run toward Crystal, but it's too late. Her little body is motionless; her pale face, still, with her curls spread all over the dirty-looking mat. Watching her in that position, I feel like killing myself. A child can't be replaced. I hear John calling for me, but I stand still and silent like a statue. Then everything goes blank.

⬥⬥⬥

I open my eyes slowly. Everything seems blurry. Then I see John standing by my side, and he is crying. My body hurts from not being able to move. I realize that I'm at the hospital.

"John, where is Crystal?"

"Darling...the coroner came for our princess."

"Oh my God, John—"

I break into tears and John hugs me. He wipes the tears from his eyes.

I wear a black dress to my daughter's funeral. It is a gloomy day for John and me, watching our only daughter inside a coffin. I cry throughout the whole ceremony. She will never come out of her room calling for me again.

One day my cell phone rings. I'm unsure whether to answer or not: part of me is terrified.

"Hello, Violet?" It's my boss.

"Yes, Mr. Dennis, speaking."

"Violet, I'm sorry for suspending you. It was a mistake. I know how much your career means to you. Would you like to return to the department?"

I'm shocked, but I reject his proposal. "I'm sorry, Mr. Dennis. I appreciate it, but I'm sorry, I can't."

"But, Ms. Bryant, you're a great detective: we need you. You can't just quit your job."

It's been nine months since Crystal passed away. I have to accept that my princess is no longer by my side and is never going to come back. But I know I will always have her in my thoughts.

"Thank you, Mr. Dennis. Goodbye."

I hang up, and I think about my life.

Jocelyn Marchan
BREAKING THE SENTENCE

Why imprison yourself in the past when you have a
    future?
Why dwell in the memories of long ago
That should be learned from and buried in the distant
    graveyard
What do you gain?
But a sentence of eternal suffering
Why let those painful memories shape who you are
When you can move forward in life?

Lisbeth Aguilar
SEEK ONESELF

Do we consider ourselves to be heroes? Life is like living the hero's journey, where one goes through good and bad times, happy and sad times; experiencing such obstacles makes one a stronger individual. Like Ralph Waldo Emerson, the founder of transcendentalism, stated, "Nothing is at last sacred but the integrity of your own mind." Before taking this class I never really thought that I could be a hero myself. To me a hero was the soldier who gave up his life for our country, or a doctor who saves people's lives. But now I realize that we are our own heroes—because everyone is a hero.

In my perspective, a hero is a person who doesn't give up. A hero has to be like a strong and confident boxer who takes punches and falls down to the floor, but keeps fighting. A hero has to fight harder to overcome obstacles. One has to pursue one's dream by putting one's mind and heart toward accomplishing it.

I never thought that I would come this far. Every day I wake up at six in the morning to get ready for school. Each day I spend eight hours in school studying. My goal is to go to college and become a detective. Both my parents believe in me. They believe that I'm a clever girl who can do anything. My aunts and uncles, on the other hand, believe that my sister Jessica and I will commit the same mistake as many teenage girls: getting pregnant or running away. I will prove them wrong. It doesn't matter if I go through many obstacles along the way; I believe in myself. I know that I can do it no matter what. I have been accepted to college, and I have proved to myself, my parents, and my brothers that anything is possible.

Writing a story based on the hero's journey was a good experience, but a difficult task. Throughout this course I have learned many things. For example, I realized that an author has to put a lot of time and effort into his or her job. There are many types of heroes: a hero can be a teacher, a friend, a counselor, or anyone who helps us in everyday life. And without heroes, our stories would be uninteresting.

Gloria Rosales
NIGHT DREAMS HIGH

"But understand, Michael, I want Genesis to grow up as a normal girl."

"I know, I understand, but you cannot hide this from her. This is a part of who she is," Michael responds.

She sighs. "I know, but not yet. I'll wait until the time is right, when she's old enough to fully comprehend."

"All right. I know you'll make the right decision on when to tell Genesis," he reassures her. "It will take a while for her to get used to it, but if she's anything like Dad, I know she'll be fine."

Standing in front of my locker, I enter the combination, but yet again, it doesn't budge. I grab the handle and shake it like crazy, then punch it. "Damn you, locker!" I let out a sigh. I wish I could have stayed home in bed, but no, I'm forced to come to school. There really isn't anything special here, just chipped paint on the walls and brown, rusted-shut lockers, lined up like soldiers ready for battle.

After that's finally over with, I leave school through those gates of hell. My cell phone reads 5:56 p.m. I can't believe I stayed after school so late; I'm just going to get home and knock out. Yawning, I take a shortcut through an alley. I feel a cold chill run up my spine, giving me goose bumps. Even after I zip my black sweater up to my neck, it seems to be colder. Before I get a chance to place my hands in my pockets, something pushes me back against a damp wall. Two piercing red eyes stare at me, and I'm immobilized. I gulp, and before I know it I feel sharp fangs pierce my skin, like two thick needles. Clenching my eyes tightly I let out a scream that echoes through the alley.

My entire body goes limp; whatever bit me is nowhere in sight. I look for my cell, but as I do, I feel as if someone has been spinning me around like crazy. With each step I take, this feeling grows worse. My throat closes up, my throat goes dry, and it's hard to breathe. What's going on here? Stumbling out of the alley, I place a hand against the icy cold wall, trying to regain my balance. I take a deep breath to get more oxygen into my lungs, but a sharp pain stabs through me. I can smell something in the air...is it going to rain? My eyes are glued to the wall, which now seems freshly painted, with paint running down the wall. Then there is another smell. Blood? Where are these smells coming from? I flip open my cell and dial as fast as I can, but before I hit the call button my vision turns blurry. I lose my balance and fall down to the ground, where my head makes contact with the hard concrete floor.

She checks the caller ID; it's Genesis. *Genesis never calls; this is a first*, she thinks.

"Hello, Genesis," she says, smiling.

There is no response.

"Genesis?"

Still nothing. Her heart begins to race.

"Genesis!"

This isn't like her. She drops the phone, runs outside, and rushes into the car. *What could have happened to her?* The thunderous clouds above roar, and the lightning cracks like a whip. *Where can you be, Genesis?* She drives past the old bookstore around the corner from the school. When she passes the alley, she makes out a blurry figure lying on the ground. "Genesis!"

She runs out of the car and crouches down to Genesis's body, hugging her. She removes the dark blue hair from her daughter's eyes and examines her face. She sees no bruises or bleeding, but then her eyes lock onto the girl's neck. *Oh no...not this...why now?* She picks up Genesis, puts her in the car, and drives her home. *Genesis...how can I tell you now?*

Once she enters the house, she sets Genesis down on the couch, heads upstairs, and gets her belongings ready.

"Please, Genesis, wake up...please," I hear my mother's voice. Soon my eyes open and I look around. I see my mother holding a handful of tissues. Her eyes are red. Why is she crying? I sit up and feel pain jolt through my body.

"Sweetie, you're awake!" She pulls me toward her.

"What happened?"

"I don't have much time to explain, sweetie. Your cab is almost here."

Cab? What for?

"Genesis dear...you're no longer a normal human. You're a vampire."

I stay silent, then laugh. "Good one, Mom," I say, wiping away tears of laughter.

"I'm being serious. You have to leave tonight. I have your things already packed," she continues, while standing and holding my luggage.

"Mom, seriously, I would believe you if you were kicking me out, but to say I'm a vampire, that's just dumb."

"I have no other choice, Genesis...please, just know that I love you," she says, while tears well up in her eyes.

"How can I be a vampire? They don't even exist... right?"

She shakes her head. "They do, sweetie. There's a special school called Night Dreams High, where all new vampires are sent. You have to go."

"What? Wait, no! I don't want to leave. I like it here. My friends are here, and you're here!" My head spins after I finish.

"I wish you could stay, sweetie, but you're going to find out that...you haven't always been human...but half-vampire. Don't strain yourself. You're still weak from the marking," she says in a motherly tone while caressing my cheek.

No, what? This makes no sense. Can this all be true? Ah!

It would make things easier if I didn't have this splitting headache! "Mom, I—" I struggle to speak, and I'm feeling faint—

Where am I? What happened? My eyes flutter open slowly. I take a deep breath, but then a gagging sensation comes up. There is this overwhelming smell of pine scent mixed with cigar butts. I peer up and see a glass barrier separating me from the front of the cab. I place my hand over my nose and mouth to block out the horrible smell. I shuffle my legs around and feel my foot hit something; I glance down and spot a bag.

The cab suddenly brakes and sends my body forward, and my head hits the glass. "Ow!" I yell while massaging my head. My ears catch the sound of the doors unlocking, and the door swings open on its own. It's silent. This uneasy feeling starts to rise up inside of me.

Bark! There on the edge of the seat is a small dog that looks like a wolf. He has gray fur all over, with lightning streaks of darker gray. "Huh? What the?" I say, as I jump out from the cab. The dog steps closer and wags his tail. A sudden wave of pain runs through my body; I drop my bag and feel the pain rush up toward my neck. My breath comes out in short pants. I feel so light-headed. What's going on? The pup barks again, but this time it rings in my ear, making this feeling worse. I stumble forward again and try to make out the image of the pup, but my sight just keeps getting less clear. Is this what becoming a vampire feels like? Oh...God...

And then, I burst off in a sprint. I feel the cool air hit my skin, sending chills throughout my body. Soon my ears can distinguish between the sounds of the countless twigs and leaves crunching under my feet. I shut my eyes and inhale even deeper than before. The smell of wet dirt hits my nose along with the smell of humidity in the air. I turn around when I hear a sudden rustle, but my feet fumble, and next thing I know I trip and my body hits the ground. As I sit up and lean against a tree trunk, I hear that bark again. There is the pup right next to me. Then there is that smell again…blood. I feel a warm droplet on my arm; I lift it up and notice a cut. I stare at the small droplet of blood slowly sliding down; the smell becomes even stronger, and it's making my throat drier. The pup continues to bark. It's as if he wants me to follow him. What other choice do I have?

I follow for a few minutes until we come to a set of doors. I wonder what's behind them. I hope the pup has some answer, but he just wags his tail and runs off. "Great." I take a step forward. Then the door opens, and out walks a girl no older than me with blond hair and blue eyes. She glares at me in disgust. God, what's her problem? I send her a fiercer look right back. She sneers and walks off without a word.

As soon as the door closes, I turn my gaze and notice lettering that reads, "Welcome to Night Dreams High." This is the school that Mom was talking about! I didn't think it was real—I guess she was right. I turn the knob and walk inside. The room is dark with painted blue walls and windows hidden behind nice purple curtains.

"You must be Miss Miller; your mother called ahead and told of your arrival," a woman informed me. She seemed to be in her mid-twenties and had dark brown hair up in a messy bun.

"Oh…yeah," I respond, still lost.

She laughs. "You seem a little lost. Well, here you go: this is a list of your classes. You're an official student here. Your locker is just down the hall to the left. I'm sure you won't have trouble finding it. Oh, and before I forget, we have arranged a tour so you won't feel so lost," she says with this terrific smile that just makes me smile back.

"Thank you."

Stepping out of the office I stare at my schedule. My classes are printed in bold letters. What kind of classes are these? Bloodlust 101? That's just plain dumb. And what's Vampire Sociology? I've never heard of that, but at least it sounds interesting. Letting out a heavy sigh, I walk down the empty hall. Okay, so where do I go from here? Turning a corner, I bump into a tall, pale guy. He has autumn-colored hair, cut in layers, part of which covers his left burgundy eye. I can't help but gawk: his features are flawless.

"Yeah, so my name's Kyle, and I guess I'm gonna be your tour guide for today," he responds, while scratching the back of his head. I nod up at him, and like that, he turns and starts walking. I follow. Okay, gotta get this straight: he's a vampire...but he sure doesn't act like one. I mean, wouldn't he be carrying around a bottle of blood or something to quench his thirst? He seems like any other guy.

He finishes the tour maybe twenty minutes later. "All right, so you got any questions?" he asks while turning back to face me.

"No," I respond.

"All right. Cool. Nice meeting you, Genesis. I guess I'll see you around." He takes a sharp turn and walks off.

Standing in the middle of the hall, I sigh and start walking again, hoping I don't get lost as I turn right around a corner. So far the only student I've seen is Kyle, and he seems like any other student. Making another turn, not knowing which way I am going, I come to a dead end with a huge gothic window. Stepping closer, I look at my reflection. My eyes are an emerald green, and my skin now is as pale as the moon. Before it was just a plain pale, but now it's as if my skin glistens. My skin has never looked like this. Opening my mouth, I stare at my sharp fangs. Then, I look up, and my eyes lock onto the moon. It is full and looks simply amazing, glowing like a night-light. Leaning against the cool wall, I continue to gaze. I know I have to face it—this is my new life, I can't just turn back. I can only move forward and hope for the best.

Right. So today is my first day of school. While making my way to my locker, I now see some students lounging around. All of them have slim figures with pale, glowing skin and shimmering eyes. What catches my eye are the strange symbols on their necks. Some students gaze at me as I walk by. I feel their eyes pierce me like jagged knives. Some of them even sneer at me, giving me glimpses of their sharp fangs. The glares of these students make me slow down, then stop completely. I stand there and take a moment of silence to gather my thoughts, then take a giant step and turn a sharp corner. My heart is beating like crazy—like drums. Shaking off this feeling, I continue down the hall and come to my locker, number 5107.

All right. Hopefully I won't have the same bad luck as my old one. After dialing the combination, I hold the handle and pull it. It opens on the first try! Peering inside, my eyes grow wide: all of the books I need are neatly piled in order of my schedule. Wow, this sure beats my old high school; they are way more organized here. I grab Introduction to Vampire Sociology and trace my finger over the embossed letters. I think I'm going to like this class. Examining the book more closely, I notice it is made out of leather and seems a couple of hundred years old. The writing inside is still legible, though. Closing my locker, I commence my way to class but realize I will have to go by the group of students that hissed at me earlier. I can't let down my guard; I know I'm going to have a hard year here, but I hold my head high as I walk past.

I am in front of the classroom door when a very girlie voice says, "Excuse me." Before I even have a chance to move out of the way, a hand presses down on my right shoulder. Shutting my eyes I wait for the impact, but nothing happens. I look up and come face to face with Kyle, my tour guide.

"Hey, Genesis," he says with a soft smile.

"Uhh, hey," I say while looking down. Kyle caught me? Was he even standing there? I feel my face flush from the embarrassment, but I quickly regain my composure.

"I see you ran into Daisy."

"Yeah, I guess I did. Who is she?" I glance into the room. Inside, there are only a few students huddled together, chatting away like parrots. In the corner there's a curly-haired blond with blue eyes.

"That's Daisy. She's a junior. All you need to know is that she thinks the whole world revolves around her," Kyle says while massaging the back of his neck.

"Right," I reply, looking back at him.

"Don't worry about it. You'll do fine," he says with another of his warm smiles before walking into the classroom. I wait, take a deep breath, and step into class.

"Welcome, class, to Introduction to Vampire Sociology. I will be your teacher, Ms. Kendra," the female figure announces while she steps from behind her desk. She seems about five feet six and has slick, dark, black hair that goes all the way to her butt. I look straight into her eyes; she seems to be the type who takes guff from no one. I can tell by the structure of her jawline and how she looks at each student. "For your very first assignment, I want you to partner up with another student. You have five seconds," she says with a smirk. All of a sudden, I hear a rumble and feel the room shake as all the students stand and run to partner up. Why does this have to happen on the first day?

"Well, it seems that there are only two students left. Daisy, partner up with—" Ms. Kendra says while looking at me, waiting for the answer.

"Genesis."

"Well, Genesis, you will be partnered with Daisy," she says with a smile that masks an evil sneer. My gaze turns to the right where Daisy is sitting. She is just fixing her nails, not paying attention to a thing. I am stuck with Miss Congeniality.

"Now then, you must spend at least one hour a day with your partner for two weeks, getting to know how becoming a vampire has changed not only their appearance but also themselves. For the rest of the hour, you will be discussing with your partner how they have changed since they have arrived here," Ms. Kendra says as she walks around the desks.

"So, *you're* my partner," Daisy says.

"Yeah, I am," I reply. She rolls her eyes and continues to attend to her nails, which must be more interesting than talking to me. Of all the people in this school, I'm stuck with her! This is just great; this is the type of person I try to avoid.

Halfway through the class, Ms. Kendra announces that we're gathering for an assembly. "Class, get into line and follow me." She walks out the door, and the other students shuffle out of the class.

"Kyle, what's this assembly being held for?" I ask as we walk through the door.

"Well, I guess you can call it an assembly, but it's more of a meeting. You'll get to meet the headmaster," he replies, walking ahead.

Headmaster? I wonder about this for a while, then snap out of my thoughts. I look around and notice that Kyle, and the rest of my class, are gone. There's no sign of anyone. Great, now for spacing out on my first day I'm left behind and lost. Feeling a light tug at the bottom of my jeans, I look down and notice the small pup from before. Crouching down, I pet him gently. "Hey there, little guy," I say with a smile. He happily wags his tail and licks my hand. "This is the second time I've run into you. Are you following me?" He just continues wagging his tail, then takes one more glance at me and runs off. "Hey, wait!" I say, chasing after him. Now I know that every time I run into this pup I will have a good workout.

Bam! I hit the ground with a loud thud.

"Ow," I say while rubbing my butt. Looking up, I see a tall guy with short, dark blue hair and familiar jade eyes.

"I'm sorry," he says softly.

"No, no, it's fine. I wasn't looking where I was going," I reply quickly.

"Here," he says, holding out his hand.

I take it, and next thing I know I'm up on my feet.

"My name's Michael Miller. I'm the headmaster," he says with a very soft and sincere smile.

"Hi, I'm Genesis Mi—whoa, wait, headmaster?" He chuckles; I must have amused him.

"Yes, why are you so surprised?"

"But you look like a senior. I never expected a head-master to be so young," I say, then realize what I have just blurted out. Covering my mouth, my face turns beet red.

"Ha, it's okay. You did say your name is Genesis...Genesis Miller, if I am correct?"

"Um, yeah...how'd you know my last name? I never finished saying it."

He chuckles and replies, "I'm your older brother."

"Say what?" My mouth drops open.

"Here, come with me," he says.

He leads me to his office. "Please take a seat," he says, gesturing to a chair in front of his desk.

I keep my gaze down on the carpeting until I sit down. Walking behind me, he goes to his seat across from mine.

"Like I said earlier, Genesis, I am your brother," he says with yet another one of his smiles.

"You're lying." I keep looking down at my lap.

"Please, Genesis, just hear me out," he says, rising to his feet.

"No, give up already," I say, crossing my arms.

"You have to believe me. I am your brother," he pleads.

"You expect me to believe you when I know nothing about you, and yet you claim to be my brother. For all I know, you could be a senior trying to pull a joke on me just because I'm new here."

"I wouldn't hurt you; you're my little sister. I would die to protect you," he says, taking my shoulder in a firm grip.

"Let me go! You're hurting me!" I struggle to get free from his grasp.

"I'm sorry," he says. His grip loosens, but before I have a chance to make a run for the door, I am pulled from the chair into an embrace. Time seems to slow down, and a small smile creeps across my face. By the way he embraces me, I know that I can trust him.

"If you don't believe me, then believe our father," he says while pulling away. Walking back to his desk, he unlocks a drawer with a key, then opens it. He takes out an old yellow envelope. Extending it toward me, I take the letter and gaze at it.

"That is the last thing our father wrote...he wrote it to you," Michael says, interrupting my thoughts. I nod, take a deep breath, and open the old letter. It reads:

Dear Genesis,

> *I know this may come to a shock to you but I, Alexander Miller, your father, want you to know that you are a vampire, or at least a half-vampire. All I want for you is happiness. When you read this letter I will no longer be with you, but please know that I would give anything in the world to see you grow up. When I heard that your mother was pregnant I could not hold in the joy—but dismay came when your mother's friends found out about us. Let's just say you don't want to hear what they*

planned to do to me, what your mother had warned me about. All I really want is for you, Genesis Miller, to run Night Dreams High. Please fulfill this wish for me.

Your father,

Alexander Miller

I feel hot tears running down my cheeks. This means Father gave his life for Mom. I look up, and my eyes meet Michael's. He then presents me with an old book. I take it in my hands and open it slowly. On the very first page there is a black-and-white picture of a young man with long hair. I flip to the next page and skim. I learn that Dad was the one who founded Night Dreams High. He was responsible for bringing peace to the human and vampire worlds back then. But things went awry just a few years ago, and the feud between the vampires and humans started again. Dad must want me to step up and stop this.

"I understand. I won't let Father down."

He approaches me and wipes away my tears. "I know you will make him proud."

Raising my head high, I smile at my brother again.

"Before anything else, Genesis, I want to show you something," Michael says. He walks out to the hall. "This way." I step out after him and follow him until we are outside. It is raining; no, it is pouring. My clothes are quickly drenched. I smile, though; rain always calms me down, no matter what.

"Look down at your reflection," he says. I look into the pools of water. Raising my hand I gently trace my neck with my finger. The bite mark has changed. In its place are two solid crescent moons, surrounded by fine, thin swirls that look like grape vines.

"You're the first vamp to have two crescent moons, you know that?" Michael teases.

"Really?"

He nods.

I look back down at my reflection and stare at the mark. If only they weren't visible, the humans wouldn't fear me. I close my eyes and inhale. When my eyes open, the mark has vanished! I know I can do this; if I can make this mark disappear, speaking with the humans should be a piece of cake. I won't let you down, Father. Taking over Night Dreams High is the first step; next is changing the thoughts of humans.

"Come on, Genesis. You've learned a lot over the last few weeks. It won't be that bad," Michael says. Gee, I'm glad he thinks things are easy here. I follow Michael like a lost puppy in the rain until we come to a classroom. I've started with the basics, and now I have to be a teacher's assistant. I don't even like to talk—why me?

"Ah, Headmaster Miller, welcome, please come in," says a male voice.

"Morning, Mr. Clarkson. I came here to tell you that you now have a TA. I know it's hard the first weeks of teaching, but Genesis here will help you out," Michael announces. He pushes his hand into my back, forcing me into the classroom. All eyes fall on me.

"I have to leave you two. I have some work to attend to. I'll check up on you later." Before I get a chance to say something, Michael's gone.

"It's a pleasure to meet you, Genesis. You must feel pretty out of place since you're new here, but that only makes us more alike. I'm new here as well," Clarkson says. "I have to run out and grab some books. Can you stay here and look after the class? Thank you!" He exits the room. Gee, thanks, leave me with an entire class.

Once the door closes, the entire class explodes; students move their desks around into groups. Some place their feet on top of the desks; it looks like a mall, with everyone just lounging around. What am I supposed to do?

"Well lookie here, it's Miss Soon-to-be-Headmistress," comes the sneering voice I recognize as Daisy's. "Looks like this is all she will ever be, a good-for-nothing teacher's assistant." I groan. What am I supposed to do? If I talk back, she'll just keep ranting. Maybe, if I keep my mouth shut, she'll get bored and leave me alone. "Aw, the poor baby vamp can't even stand up for herself. What a shame." She laughs, and the entire class joins in. This feels like when my mom decided to move me to another school since I wasn't social enough. All the kids picked on me, calling me a freak just because I was new there, saying I was a reject at my old school and that things would be the same there, too. Who am I trying to kid? Myself? As I hear Daisy's echoing laughter, I don't dare look up. I'm always going to be an outcast, no matter where I go. The salty tears that are welled up in my eyes start to plop down to the ground.

"Daisy, this is your final warning. Must you always interrupt the class?" Michael's voice echoes.

"She has been getting more and more disruptive, Headmaster. I do think she needs a few hours of detention," Mr. Clarkson adds as he walks in.

"That is what I'll do. Come on, Genesis," Michael continues. He places a hand on my shoulder and leads me out of the classroom. Out of the corner of my eye I see Daisy looking at me; if looks could kill, I would have been long dead.

"I know it must be extremely hard for you to adapt, Genesis, but trust me on this: not all students are bad. They just tend to follow Daisy since her parents are wealthy. All the kids want to get on her good side."

Michael was right before. I never realized that I could make so many friends; I just had to learn to be a little more social. I have to thank Kyle's friends for that: they're just too funny and easy to get along with. And from there, I began to socialize with everyone else. Everyone now treats me with respect, and we still hang out, but only when I'm not busy.

For a few months, being a counselor was annoying, but now being Michael's assistant is even more of a pain. He makes me stroll all over the school and drowns me in paperwork: sign this, approve that, send this to there, ugh! There are always people walking in and out of my office. I think I've met everyone now because my office seems to be open 24/7. Staying up practically until sunrise, I know I have definitely gotten a lot more organized.

And Daisy—even though I've had many problems with her throughout the months, I find myself handling them very well now.

"Please believe me, Headmistress; I didn't do it," Daisy says, as tears well up in her blue eyes.

"Calm down, Daisy. I will give you one last chance, but if you fail me, you will have to suffer expulsion," I say.

"Thank you, thank you!" she says as she wipes away her tears, and I smile at her. She darts out of the office as Michael walks in.

"So, you gave her a second chance?" He cocks an eyebrow and smiles.

"Yes, I mean, I admit we didn't get off to a grand start, but I still have to be fair with all the students," I say, sitting down. "Besides, her grades have improved. I know she wants to change."

"Yes, that's true. Today you have the meeting with the humans, right? I've been meaning to ask: how did you get them to meet with you?"

"Look!" I reveal my neck, where my mark is not visible. It took more than that. If only Michael knew how long it took me to arrange this meeting, how many phone calls I had to make, and how they always had me wait for who knows how many hours on the line—it practically killed me, but I did it.

"Wow, where's your mark?" he says out loud.

"I'll tell you later. I don't want to be late," I say, rising to my feet and leaving.

Okay. This is all that really matters; I can't let them intimidate me. Walking down the halls in silence, I come to the giant doors. I push one open, and I see a long table in the middle. Sitting there are the mayor and the principal of the local high school. As soon as I step in, I feel their glares, but I do not give them the satisfaction of lowering my head. I sit down.

"First, let me thank you for coming here. I know it is very hard for you, but rest assured that I have talked with the teachers and deans of the school, and they are making sure that all the students are kept in the auditorium. Rest assured: you are safe."

They simply nod. I can hear their hearts beat; they are far from calm.

"Very well, let's get started," I declare. "Please understand that the students here are here for a reason. They are being taught how to control their bloodlust, to respect human life, and so forth. They are much like humans. You can't expect to keep them here forever."

"Well, what would happen if one of them were to attack another human? These vampires don't have self-control," the mayor huffs.

"That is a lie right there." I rise to my feet, turn my head sideways, and reveal my mark. "You have been waiting here for some time now, and I could have easily pounced on you."

"You're one of them, too!" the mayor says, his eyes growing wider.

"I prefer to be called by my name, not 'one of them.' I'm just like any one of you. The only difference is this," I say while pointing to my now-visible mark.

The rest of the meeting went so much more smoothly after that.

"Thank you, Ms. Miller," the mayor says with a smile.

"No, thank you for taking time and coming here to this meeting," I reply.

As soon as they are all gone, I leap into the air. "YES!"

Michael walks in. "Someone sure seems happy," he says.

"Of course I'm happy. Can't you see, Michael? This is all a new beginning. Now we vamps won't be easily judged!" There's absolutely nothing that can ruin this day. I start to skip out of the meeting room.

"You got a call from the hospital...Mother wants you to go back home."

Mom's in the hospital? What! I don't want to leave...I just can't...I'm not ready...not yet.

"Genesis?"

"Huh?" I look at him, dazed.

"Mom needs you...go." He places his hand on my shoulder to reassure me.

"Thanks, Michael," I say, dashing off. Mom, please be okay; that's all that matters.

I continue sprinting down the halls and through the huge gates of the school. I just hope I don't get lost on my way back home. Up ahead I notice a fiery blaze. Torches? "Keep these creatures locked up!" I thought these issues would be settled; instead, an angry mob is coming and blocking the only road leading to town. There is no way around them. A woman steps forward; she looks around my mother's age. I examine her more closely. Oh my God, that's Ms. Rae, our neighbor.

"Look, there's one! Kill it!" Ms. Rae throws her torch at me. I leap back, but the flames disperse and encircle me. She continues to scream. "There! We have her now! Shoot her!" I jump back through the fires, and as soon as my feet hit the ground, I roll and hide behind a tree. The mob's feet become louder; they're getting closer. I peek from behind the tree; there are three bulgy men, all armed with shotguns, and Ms. Rae is standing in front, leading them all. If I make it out of here alive, she is off our Christmas list.

"Keep your eyes peeled. Those pesky vampires are sneaky," she says. I look at the mob, and all of them looking around, trying to catch a glimpse of me. I close my eyes and take some deep breaths, and all of a sudden I hear some light footsteps. I open my eyes and see the small pup running in my direction. If they see him, they might shoot him! I wave my hands, signaling for him to go away. But no, our eyes lock, and in an instant the pup is standing in front of the mob, growling.

"Look, it's a dog!" "What's a dog doing out here?" "It doesn't seem too friendly." The pup just crouches down more and growls more loudly. That's it; just distract them a while longer. I stay low to the ground and start moving around the trees, making sure not to make noise. I'm almost home free.

"It's just a mutt. It's not like anyone will miss it!" shouts Ms. Rae. After a loud blast, I look back and see the pup fall to the ground. *No!* He was just helping me! I break into a sprint, and all I can see are the blurred images of trees and bushes that I run past. "No! She's getting away! After her!" says Ms. Rae. The mob makes its way in my direction, so I run even faster until I see the dim lights of town. My legs begin to burn, and I'm out of breath. The brisk air hits my face and arms, makes them feel like icicles. But still, behind me their feet sound like a stampede of bulls. Won't these people give up? "Get her before she takes an innocent life!" Oh, God, they're the ones trying to kill me.

I look up and notice that I have run up to my old school. I look down at my watch, and it reads 7:10 a.m. Maybe I can blend in. I push myself through the mob of teens standing outside and run into the halls. Leaning against the lockers, I try to catch my breath.

"Genesis, is that you?" asks a familiar voice.

"Amy?" I manage to say.

"Oh my God, it is you!" she squeals before pulling me into a hug. That is just the type of girl Amy is: no matter how long it may have been, a few days or a few hours, she would always be glad to see you.

"It's good to see you too, Amy," I say, pulling away.

"Dude, is it true?" she whispers.

I cock an eyebrow at her. "Is what true?"

"Is it true, that...you're a vampire?" she asks.

"Yes, it's true," I respond.

"That is so"—I am waiting to hear *weird*—"awesome!"

Did she just say *awesome*?

"Wait until Conor and Jack hear. I'm friends with a vampire!"

I clasp my hand over her mouth. "Shh, not so loud, I don't want another mob chasing me," I tell her while removing my hand.

"Oh, so that's why there's a mob outside," she says, pointing out the window.

"Just great," I say, leaning against the wall and sliding down.

"Well, how do they know you're a vampire? You look pretty normal to me." She sits down next to me, and I turn my neck and reveal my mark. "Oh my God, that looks so pretty," she says, sparkles in her eyes.

"Yeah, I guess so. I might as well make the best of being here. I need your help: go out and spread the word that there's a meeting in the auditorium, okay?" I say while getting up.

"Sure, no problem, Genesis, but what do we do about the teachers?"

"Trust me. The teachers around here will be relieved to get rid of their students. That's how they've always been anyways."

"All right, got it." She salutes me like a soldier would and sprints off.

I come to the auditorium doors, peer inside, and go in. Nothing has changed. I walk up the stairs leading to the stage, knowing this is my last chance: if I can't change the minds of the students here, then I know I can't change the minds of their parents. I don't want to think about what would happen then. And after this is over, I don't care how impossible it is; I'm gonna go and see you, Mom, even if it kills me. I sit at the edge of the stage and let my feet dangle.

I hear a faint sound coming, growing louder and louder. The auditorium doors open, and a swarm of teens walk in. "Everyone sit down," Amy says while motioning them to sit. How on earth did she get so many people to come? Well, that's just the type of girl Amy is; she's always been the popular girl. I still wonder why a girl like her would hang out with a girl like me. I still feel the same, just the exact opposite of her. She's outgoing, the student body president, while I'm just a regular teen whom nobody ever noticed. But I guess I do know now how it feels to have all eyes on you. I mean, with all the assemblies I have done, stage fright is a part of the past.

"Genesis, there you go!" Amy shouts.

"Thanks. Amy, you don't know how much I owe you for this." I go over to her and give her a hug. But she doesn't hug me back. She always hugs back tightly, like she doesn't want to let go. "Something wrong, Amy?"

"I can't believe that this day came. You actually hugged me first; I'm so happy," she says, choking down the tears.

"You're crying 'cause I hugged you?" I ask while holding in my laughter.

"Yes, I mean you've changed so much. Before you wouldn't even let me come within two feet of you."

"Ha, guess you're right. Okay, I have to get this assembly rolling before that mob finds me," I say, jumping up on the stage. She skips to a seat in the front row next to Conor and Jack. I smile and wave at them, and they all wave back hysterically. I stand there and laugh in front of the entire school.

Feeling a cold shiver run up my spine, I take a deep breath and stand tall. "Hello there, students of Charlottesville High!" I yell while throwing my fist into the air. They all raise their fists into the air in response. "I know you have absolutely no clue as to why you were called here. Let me just say that I'm the reason why. You may not know me, but my name's Genesis, Genesis Miller. I recently transferred from this school. I know you're thinking, 'Why should we care?' Why? Because I know that you've heard rumors of killer vampires. Raise your hand if you've heard such rumors." A good number of the students raise their hands, some slower than others. "Now, how many of you believe that there are such things as killer vampires?" There is the same number of hands as before. "Have any of you actually encountered a vampire?" None of the students except Amy raises a hand.

She stands on top of her seat. "Yeah, I've been face-to-face with a vampire, but you don't see me hurt or any bite mark on me, do you? Vampires aren't all that bad. Just because our parents have talked so badly about them, it doesn't mean that it's true! It's just like when our parents told us about Santa Claus or the Tooth Fairy. Was it true? No, it was all just made up, so how can you know that they're telling the truth now?"

"How can we trust you, Amy? How do we know you're not lying?" a guy asks.

"I can answer that!" I jump down from the stage, and my hair falls over my face. I turn and reveal my neck, my mark visible.

"What, she's one of them?" "What!"

"See, you can't believe everything that your parents say. Vampires aren't all that bad. We're just like you. Just because I have this marking, does this make me any different from you? No, it doesn't. I'm just your regular teen, trying to get through life like anyone else." The teens buzz among themselves.

"Genesis!" my friends' voices echo. Just as I turn, both Conor and Jack push me down and embrace me.

"Hey!" I say, and hit the ground.

"Wow, it's so good to see you," Conor says with a grin.

"We thought you would never come back," Jack continues. Amy walks over too.

"Well, I guess I proved you guys wrong, huh," I laugh, while standing up and dusting myself off. I start running toward the nearest exit. "I have to go see my mom. She's in the hospital, so I have to split."

Pushing open the doors, I see the mob of parents there. It has grown in size. I back away, but I end up tripping and landing on my butt. "There she is! Get her! Save the kids!" I shut my eyes tightly, and pictures come into my head—first my mother, then Michael. These are the people I have let down because I wasn't fast enough to get out of here.

Several moments pass by, and I feel no pain. I open one of my eyes and notice that a bunch of students is standing there, making a wall between me and the mob.

"What are you kids doing?" Ms. Rae screams. "There's a killing machine right behind you. Move!"

"You're wrong." "She's not a monster." "You guys have been lying to us." They believe me. They believe me. I wipe away the tears in my eyes.

"Are you kids crazy? Move!" Ms. Rae yells.

"No, you're the crazy one!" Amy says. I feel hands under my arms pulling me to my feet.

I step through the crowd and glare at Ms. Rae. "You can't continue to judge us vampires."

"Why should we trust you?"

"I'm not asking for your trust, just a chance to prove that we aren't that bad." I look at each and every one of the parents. Things are silent for a minute or two.

"Fine, but if things go wrong, we blame her!" Ms. Rae says, storming off. The students all roar with cheers.

"Genesis, this is great!" Amy says, embracing me.

"Yeah, I know." I smile. "But I have to cut the celebration short. I have to go see my mom."

"Oh, that's right!" She lets go.

"Yeah, sorry. Bye!" I burst into a dash before she even says goodbye. I hear a faint laugh, and I run out. I'm so glad: this is the beginning of something new, of change for the better. I think about telling Mom what happened, while running down the same sidewalk where it all began, where I turned into a vampire, where my life changed.

Zooming past the double doors, I race to the counter, where I see a nurse typing away.

"Nurse, please tell me what room Jane Miller is in!" I manage to say between breaths.

"Are you a relative?" she asks.

"Yes! I'm her daughter—what happened to her?"

"I see. The doctors say that she fell down some stairs, but that's all I really know. She's in room 619. Go down this hall until you reach some stairs. It's the very first room in that hallway," she says, seeming bored.

I stumble as I begin running once again. Mom, please be okay. As soon as I see the door, I stop to catch my breath. Reaching out I turn the knob and open the door slowly. It lets out a low creak. I step in and search the room quickly. There is my mom, lying motionless in bed. I walk over to her quietly and just stand next to the bed. I feel overjoyed to see my mother, but I hate to see her in this state.

I choke down the tears, get on my knees, and place my head next to her hand. Closing my eyes, I let the hot tears slide down. A warm tender touch wipes them away.

"I missed you, sweetie," she whispers.

"I missed you more, Mom."

"How are things at the school?"

"Mom, we'll talk about that later. Tell me how you've been doing." I open my eyes. Smiles creep across both of our faces.

"I want to show you this," she says. She lifts up her arm, and in her grip there is a picture. I reach for it and examine it. It is a guy who looks like the one from the book that Michael gave me, only this picture is in color, and the man's hair is much shorter. "This man is your father, and I know that he is proud of you, Genesis."

OVER THE RAINBOW

Alexandra Jimenez
MY BLEACHED SHIRT

I have this shirt.

Can never be bleached as much as I've tried.

I wear it,
not remembering how stains claimed it.

Some are
light taco stains,
Others are black as tar.

I tend to forget to remember to forget
And every so often, remember why I wanted to forget.

I know I'm not alone
in wearing the shirt.
Even when we try to wash it away,
Those taco stains still remain.

Jessica Zamary Marroquin
WAVES COME AND GO

Waves come and go
wash everything away
leaving nothing behind
but the empty landscape
forgetting what was once there
vanishing without a trace
leaving nothing behind
but the empty landscape
Waves come and go
filled with dark regret
as they come and go
washing all they have witnessed away
Waves come and go
I wish I could be as free as the land
washed by the waves

Maria Maribel Meneses
PROVING THEM WRONG

Do you know anyone who is a hero? I used to think of heroes as doctors who save lives, police officers who risk their lives to make the community safer, or soldiers who give up their lives for their country. Even characters like Spider-Man, Superman, and Batman came to mind. But this class allowed me to realize that ordinary people can be heroes. A hero could be me or you or anyone who overcomes his or her challenges to accomplish something.

I consider myself a hero: I've lived through many difficulties and have endured many obstacles that prevented me from accomplishing my dreams. My own family, particularly my uncle and aunt, thought I wasn't going to graduate from high school. When I was only a freshman, my aunt said that I wasn't going to graduate because I was a girl, and from their point of view, Mexican girls either get pregnant or leave with their boyfriend at age fifteen. My aunt told me that I was going to end up like one of those girls as soon as my Quinceañera passed. So far, I am proving them wrong. I haven't gotten pregnant, and I'm going to graduate from high school. I'm going to show them my diploma so I can be proud of myself and prove to them that not all girls make those same mistakes. Admittedly, I have made a lot of mistakes, but now I'm fixing them and trying to survive this journey.

One reason why I have been getting more courageous is because my mom told me her story of coming to the United States with my brother. She told me that she suffered a lot and that she didn't have money. Since she was one of the first of her family to come to the Untied States, she had no help, and it was difficult for her to feed my brother. Making matters more difficult, my dad was involved with another woman whom he had two children with. My mother did not receive any support from him. It got worse when my sister was born. My mother couldn't afford the baby formula or the diapers for her. She had to pick up cans and cartons from the street. My dad was no help at all. He was abusive, and he spent their money on beer. This revelation made me realize that women shouldn't rely on men.

Now that I see life more clearly than before, I am ready for anything that comes my way; I'm ready to take on any challenge because now I'm more confident in myself. For instance, I never thought I would collaborate on the production of a book. It never occurred to me that I could be creative with a story. I remember telling my teacher Ms. Crosland that I didn't know how to draw, that I wasn't creative at all. She told me that there are many ways to be creative, not only through art, and that sooner or later I was going to find my creative side. When she asked who wanted to be part of the book class, I was worried. I was afraid to sign up and not come up with a story. But why not give it a try, I thought. I told my friends about it, but they said that it wasn't for them, that it was going to be too much writing. That made me doubt myself even more, but it was too late. I had signed up already. I wanted to drop the class, but I decided to take it, and I've learned that if I propose an idea to myself, I will accomplish it. Ms. Crosland's class made me more confident, and now I trust myself more.

Maria Maribel Meneses
WILLIAM AND AMIE'S MYSTERY

For a week William has been seeing a shadow out of his right eye. He goes to his room and lies in bed. He tries to take a nap but can't. It's been a year since his father died, and he can't stop thinking about him. All of a sudden, the shadow appears near the closet. William gets up and closes the window, just to make sure what he is seeing is not coming from outside. His hands start to shake. The shadow begins to form into a human shape. He runs to his mother's room and tells her, "Mom, I just saw a ghost in my room."

"No, William, there's no such thing as ghosts. Stop watching *Ghost Hunters*."

Disappointed, he goes back to his room. The shadow starts to reappear. This time, he quietly observes while the shadow is forming. He grabs a baseball bat, thinking he'll be able to protect himself just in case the ghost does any harm. His face gets pale; he wants to look away but can't.

The shadow transforms into a ghost that stares at him with big blue eyes. It is dressed in dirty clothes, and has dirt and burns all over its body. William's face turns purple. Scared, he takes a step back and bumps into the door. Nervously looking for the knob, he sees the ghost point to the picture of his uncle Jerry and his dad.

"Yesterday I was about to take a nap when suddenly this ghost appeared in my room," William tells his friend Amie.

"What! You're crazy! There's no such thing as ghosts.

You've been watching *Ghost Hunters* again, huh?" Amie giggles.

"That's exactly what my mother said. C'mon, Amie, I've known you for about five years now. Do you think I would lie to you?"

Amie notices that William is serious and pays attention. "Okay," she says, "I believe you. What happened?"

William tells Amie about his uncle's picture.

"I have an idea," says Amie. "You should come over to my house."

Later, in her room, Amie pulls out her sister's Ouija board.

"Is that a game? I don't have time to play games, Amie. I want to find out what happened to the ghost!"

"No, dummy! It's a Ouija board. It will help us contact the spirits. We have to contact the ghost fast and take it back to my sister's room before she notices it's gone. Let's go to the basement so my mom doesn't see us."

They sit facing each other on the basement floor. There are spiderwebs all over the place, paint chips coming off the wall, and roaches hiding from the light. They place their fingers on the planchette. "What do you want to ask, William?"

"I don't know. What should I ask? Is somebody here?" he says nervously.

Nothing happens. The Ouija board doesn't move.

"Hmm, well, let's try again. Is somebody here?" Amie asks, staring at the board.

Frustrated, William stands up. "This is not working!"

"C'mon, let's try one more time and see what happens."

"Okay, one more time, and if it doesn't work, we take the Ouija board back to your sister's room." He sits down and puts his fingers on the planchette. Amie does too.

"Is somebody here?" asks William. The planchette starts to shake. Like a snail, it slowly moves to the right and points to the word *yes*. As soon as they see the planchette move, they back up, turning pale. Slowly, they put their shaking fingers back on the planchette.

"Who's here?" William asks.

A-D-R-I-A-N.

"Adrian," he whispers to himself. Suddenly, the planchette stops. William and Amie stare at each other, and they both get goosebumps. Suddenly, they hear a loud noise coming from a closet. Something wants to get out. It sounds like somebody rattling the door.

They rush to the closet to see what it is. Amie slowly opens the door, and a crow shoots out like a bullet. Amie and William duck down, and the crow flies through the window.

"I better head home. This is getting weird," William says as he stands up.

William rushes home and calls Amie.

"Hello?"

"Hey Amie, I found something. Come over to my house."

When Amie gets there, he shows her two diaries he found at his uncle Jerry's house. One says *Jerry* in nice writing on the cover, and it looks well taken care of. Inside, there are plenty of lines like "I don't know what happens to me. One moment I'm doing something, and then I go unconscious and the world goes blank. I find myself in my car out on the street. I just don't know what's happening to me." The other diary has the name *Adrian* written on it in big letters and is covered in scribbles. One line stands out: "I wish this Jerry would just go away."

The next night William starts to sweat and gets the chills. All of a sudden, he sees a guy walking toward him. He covers himself with the blanket. When he peeks to see who it was, he notices there's something written on his mirror in his mother's black eyeliner: "*You know too much.*"

At the window, William sees the crow.

Maribel Juarez
THE ANCIENT HEROIC OUTLINE?

*Self-reliance is the only road to true freedom. Being
one's own person is its ultimate reward.*
—Patricia Sampson

What is a hero? What are the characteristics of a hero? There
are fictional and non-fictional heroes, war heroes, political
heroes, athletic heroes, legendary heroes, and ordinary heroes. The pattern of the ancient value system is the hero's
journey, but do our modern heroes follow the ancient heroic
outline? The destiny and the quest, the journey home and
the reward? The ancient heroic outline has developed over
time, from Oedipus to Hamlet, and from Hamlet to Holden
Caulfield, a recent ordinary hero.

In Greek mythology, Oedipus is a tragic hero, a successful man whose life ends up in ruins. He makes the mistake
of marrying his mother and killing his father, which leads
to his downfall. He can see nothing until he blinds himself,
thereby breaking free of the human compulsion to understand forces that one should simply obey. Only then does he
recognize his failures. In Shakespeare's *Hamlet*, the prince
of Denmark is another tragic hero who ends up in ruin. He
cannot avenge the murder of his father, and he causes the
deaths of everyone. His choices ultimately determine how
his fate will defeat him.

Another hero in literature is Holden Caulfield from
The Catcher in the Rye. Holden is a young teenager who
isn't aware of what he really wants: he says that adults
are phony, yet wants to act like one. Throughout the novel,

his little sister Phoebe is the only one who seems to connect with him, yet Holden doesn't want to accept this because he wants to abscond into the adult world. Holden is a teenage hero who commits many mistakes but learns from them. Along his hero's journey, he travels alone and becomes more aware about society.

In my perspective, though, a hero is not necessarily someone who confronts fate or explores society. A hero is someone who is aware of himself and is self-reliant, someone who is not a follower but instead always follows his own instincts. A hero is aware of his own talents and skills, and aware of the skills he lacks. A hero doesn't have to be intellectual or have superpowers. By believing in himself and trusting his own instincts, he will be able to achieve his own dreams. A hero has to take risks and go through trials where he will face both adversity and fortuitous experiences, through which he learns and becomes conscious of the world around him. A hero learns to follow his own intuition and not others, because those who follow others won't find felicity, and those who follow their intuition will be composed in their own actions.

Alexandra Jimenez
WHAT ABOUT PAUL?

He woke up, fell out of bed, dragged a comb across his head; Ringo Starr tidied himself up after a hard day's night of recording with the boys—John, Paul, and George—at Abbey Road Studios. It was a cool, brisk Liverpool morning, so Ringo decided to have some tea. He made his way downstairs, had a cup, and looking up, he noticed he was late. He hurriedly looked around to find something to eat before he left and picked up a bag of chocolate truffles.

"Good morning, good morning!" exclaimed a voice, startling Ringo. Lovely Rita, the local meter maid, sat on the island stool glaring at Ringo with glee. Rita was a big Beatles fan who insisted on visiting Ringo during her morning shifts almost eight days a week. Ringo rarely minded. He was amused how she'd wear a cap, looking much older, with her bag across her shoulder, making her look a little like a military man. Rita had recently traveled outside of England. But where exactly, Ringo didn't know. She left right out of college and spent all her money. Seeing no future, paying no rent, all her money was gone with nowhere to go, so she decided to leave her troubles behind.

"You nearly scared the pants off me, love," he started, as he nervously ran a hand through his hair. "How exactly did you get in 'ere, then?" he asked, puzzled.

"Came in through your bathroom window," answered Rita without missing a beat.

"Ah..." he responded before scratching his eyebrow in tired surprise. He continued to eat his Mackintosh Good News chocolates and served himself tea.

"You know..." started Rita, "you keep eating sweets as

much as you do, and you'll rot your teeth clean out after that Savoy Truffle you're about to have."

"Eh," Ringo said, shrugging his shoulders and popping a chocolate into his mouth. "So when did you fly in?" he asked, changing the subject.

"Flew in from Miami Beach BOAC, didn't get to bed last night," she said through a yawn.

"Sounds tragic...so what brings you 'ere then?" he asked before offering her a truffle.

"Wanted to see an ol' friend is all," replied Rita as she took it.

After hours of catching up as old mates do, they talked until two, and then she said, "It's time to bed."

After they parted, Ringo headed upstairs to sleep, and the doorbell rang.

"Hmm. That's odd. Who would visit this late?" Ringo wondered. As he opened the door, he saw Mr. Mustard standing on the porch with the devil in his heart. In an instant, Mr. Mustard threw a pair of drumsticks at him and left. In a state of amusement and confusion, Ringo took the drumsticks inside to give them a closer look. Suddenly, the drumsticks transformed, grew mechanical legs, and chased poor Ringo 'round and around, eerily screaming, "Paul is dead! Turn me on dead man! Paul is dead!!!"

"Help!"

Then, someone emerged from the darkened hallway across the living room. It was Ringo's old friend, Sgt. Pepper. With a blow of his trumpet, the drumsticks collapsed and lay limp on the rug.

"Well—I'm glad that wore out quickly, anyway...what're you doing 'ere?" asked an overwhelmed Ringo. "Better yet, how did you get in 'ere?"

"Yer bathroom window of course."

"I should really start closing that bloody window," Ringo commented to himself. "Well then, while you're 'ere, would you like some tea?"

"No thank you," said the aging sergeant. Sgt. Pepper was an old war veteran who led the revolution during the invasion of Pepperland by the Blue Meanies. His trumpet was his sole weapon. He walked over to the drumsticks and picked them up. "By Neptune's knickerbockers! These were sent by the Blue Meanies!"

"Well, you'd think they'd be upset after the boys and I helped you get rid of them," Ringo replied.

"I have reason to believe that the Blue Meanies took Paul and are planning another invasion."

"Why?"

"According to Dr. Maxwell Edison, the Blue Meanies devised a plan to use Paul and his Höfner bass to find a way to get rid of music."

"Sounds serious."

"Very. I'm going to need you boys' 'elp again, so gather up John and George for a quick briefing." And the night ended with that.

Next morning, there was a thump at the door.

"I'm only sleeping!" Ringo yelled, covering his face from the shining sun. He reluctantly headed downstairs and opened the door to find the taxman, who, without saying a word, dropped a tiny glass onion into his hand. "A day in the life, I tell you, a day in the life," Ringo said, shaking his head to no one in particular. Curious about this gift, he drove to George Harrison's house (an "old brown shoe," according to Lennon) in search of an answer.

"Who is it?" asked a falsetto voice from within.

"The Tooth Fairy," replied Ringo.

John Lennon opened the door and let a distressed Ringo in.

"'Ey there, Rings. What's the matter?"

"It's Paul."

"What about Paul?" George asked from the other room.

"The Blue Meanies got him and his bass."

"Not his bass!" John said sarcastically.

"How will we go on without that bass?" George added unenthusiastically. He walked over to them and motioned them to the living room, where they sat on the floor. George's sitar was beside him, so he picked it up and decided to tune it.

"You look like you've got a case of cold turkey or something, lad!" John said as he shook Ringo by the shoulders.

"First I'm visited by people who come in through me bathroom window, then Mr. Mustard, of all people, throws drumsticks at me!"

"That mean ol' Mr. Mustard," added John.

"At least he didn't throw jelly beans at you," George quipped sullenly.

"And they attacked me, screaming, 'Paul is dead' and 'Turn me on dead man,' until Sgt. Pepper saved me," Ringo said.

"So...if it's war they want, it's war they'll get," John said.

"Oh! And that odd taxman gave me this," Ringo said as he took the glass onion out from his coat pocket. Just as he took it out, it began to glow. Ringo was so surprised that he accidentally dropped it, and it rolled across the floor.

"That's a glass onion, son," John said matter-of-factly.

"A what?"

"Sailors used to use them to carry wine and liquor," John added.

"Good to know," Ringo replied.

As the boys followed the small piece, they found a dark mass on the floor.

"Ever thought 'bout sweeping fer once in yer life, George?"

"It's not dirt, ya git. I'm fixing a hole where the rain comes in; that's all." The glass onion continued to roll until it reached the center of the hole and disappeared. Compelled to explore the hole, the three stepped on the dark spot and were instantly sucked in. A hole where their minds are kept from wandering; where it'll go?

The fall into the hole seemed endless. They fell through what looked like a room of holes until they passed through another hole, and, with a thud, fell unconscious. A couple of minutes later, Ringo awoke when he felt something poking his nose. Rubbing his eyes, he looked around and saw John and George sleeping next to him. Suspicious of them, Ringo shook them awake to get some answers.

"'Ey! You've been messing about with me in my kip?"

"Eh?" grunted John as he awoke. "When I'm in the middle of a dream, I stay in bed and float upstream..."

"No, I mean...you know, with a fishing rod."

"I wouldn't touch it with a plastic one. What are you doing on the floor?"

"I'm tired." Just then something else poked him and

made Ringo jump. He looked like a doctor.

"You look down, lads. Would you like a sip from my special cup?" he asked.

"Sorry, we don't subscribe to any religion," John answered. As Ringo observed his surroundings, he noticed that they were atop a hill near a body of water. John shook George awake. As they looked at the strange man, he paced in circles mumbling to himself, referring to himself as Dr. Robert. "What a fool," said John.

"Do you know a place where we could 'ang?" Ringo asked.

"You didn't want none of Dr. Robert's cup...he won't let you in. You see, he doesn't let in those who disagree, and yet wonder why they wait by his door..."

"What door?" asked George.

"...to Dr. Robert's newspaper taxis that wait by the shore...they wait to take you away..."

"There's more 'ere than meets the eye." Ringo said.

"Ho?" John murmured.

"Not now," whispered George as he nudged John.

"Sorry, duck. We 'aven't got any money," Ringo told the doctor.

"A riddle!" he exclaimed, making the boys jump. "A riddle's all I need!" The boys scooted closer to the deranged doctor for the riddle. "What is within you and without you?"

Without a second thought, George gave his answer: "A rubber soul, mate."

And at that, the fool vanished.

"That poor lad wears no shoe shine," John said as they mounted the taxi by the shore. The taxi started moving on its own, so they lay back staring at the blue sky.

"What do you think the Blue Meanies meant by saying, 'Turn me on dead man'?" asked Ringo to no one in particular.

"Sounds like they've decided all you need isn't love," John answered.

"Why's that?"

"To be, is to know the meaning of within," George commented.

"Yup. Them Blue Meanies love the sky just because it's

blue, it almost makes 'em cry," said John.

"Well...the world's round, the sky turns them on...what if Paul was in a round place?" asked Ringo.

"Tomorrow never knows," John finished, shrugging his shoulders.

On and on, across the universe almost, they floated along upstream until they found the sea of green.

"What's that?" George asked as he spotted something in the horizon.

"Almost looks like Her Majesty's castle," Ringo said, which resulted in a couple of playful punches from the boys. When they reached the shore, they were greeted by a woman. She was tanned and seemed to be having trouble walking along the sand.

"Ze wind carried your voizes to my palace..."

"Look, Lady Madonna, we're 'ere looking fer our bassist, Paul McCartney," said Ringo.

"I'm sorry, boy...I 'aven't donned a lucky fur vaze," replied the woman, slightly confused.

"She's blind and deaf?" whispered George to John.

"Nah...she's just blind on some of that California grass," he replied. Then, extending his hand to hers, he introduced himself: "I'm John Lennon."

"Oh, my...Prudence," said the woman, extending her arm out to no one. John shifted over to shake her hand. Then both Ringo and George introduced themselves as well, and all three were invited into the palace.

"Welcome to my humble abode, Bee-a-tles. I hope you do 'ave time to meet my husband, ze Sun King," Prudence said as she gave them a tour of the palace.

"Bee-tells," corrected John.

"Forget it, John...she won't see nor 'ear you," George said. He turned to Ringo, who seemed to be in a trance since they arrived. "'ey Ringooo!"

"There's something peculiar about dear Prudence," Ringo commented. "Nothing is real and nothing to get hung about."

"Just relax and float downstream; besides, where else are we gonna stay? She's not a girl who misses much," said George.

And so the Beatles, minus Paul, were kept safe in

Prudence's palace—or so they thought. The longer they stayed there, the more enchanted they seemed to be. Except Ringo. He seemed impervious to the castle's spell. Months passed. Then one day Ringo found Paul's Höfner bass in Prudence's bedroom. He rushed to the boys to warn them.

"I've got a feeling that Prudence has something to do with Paul's disappearance—his Höfner bass is in her bedroom stashed in a cabinet made of Norwegian wood!"

"Probably not the only thing," murmured John, which elicited a smirk from George.

"So, dizcovered my intentionz and partnership with ze Blue Meanies, you 'ave," said Prudence as she entered.

"Discovered I did! C'mon boys!" yelled Ringo, trying to get John and George to follow him out. But they wouldn't budge. "John! George!"

"This boy won't leave," said John flatly.

"That boy won't leave...this boy don't leave," added George, just as eerily.

"This boy doesn't care! Snap out of it!" Ringo screamed with little result. They remained as still as the paintings on the wall.

"Ha! Now I've got ze witty one, ze cute one, ze quiet one, and now ze funny-looking Bee-a-tle with ze big neb!" Prudence cackled as she slowly cornered Ringo. As she got closer, her skin began to turn blue. So she's a Blue Meanie, too! Ringo, certain of his demise, looked over to John and George.

"Help! Help me if you can!"

Suddenly, Ringo thought of an idea—he'd sing! The one thing Blue Meanies hated the most! He slowly rose and began to clap his hands on beat. "What would you think if I sang out of tune? Would you stand up and walk out on me?" His voice cracked a little.

> *Lend me your ears, and I'll sing you a song,*
> *And I'll try not to sing out of key.*
> *Oh I get by with a little help from my friends,*
> *I get high with a little help from my friends,*
> *Oh I'm gonna try with a little help from my*
> *friends!*

Prudence began to shriek in pain and agony, while John and George slowly regained consciousness with looks of confusion across their faces.

"It worked!" Ringo exclaimed in delight.

"AHH!!! My earz! My earz!" Prudence screamed as she melted into the floor.

"Those are some lungs there, Ringo," George said as he patted Ringo on the shoulder.

"Blew me away, even," added John. "My mind was going all helter skelter. I thought she seemed real...prudent."

Just then, a loud, thundering noise roared through the palace.

"Who darez disturb me while I sleep ze slumber of kings?" a man's voice bellowed. It was the Sun King. He made his way down the spiral staircase and saw a black puddle where Prudence once stood. He grew furious and was suddenly engulfed in flames.

"Now, look 'ere...and don't get yer knickers in a twist," started John. "We've been traveling so long I hardly know the place. We're just looking for our best mate, Paul."

The Sun King began to laugh. "You fool! I'm ze one who took your friend! Ha! I even manipulated ze Blue Meaniez to help me do it!

"Where's Paul?" George asked.

"Tell me why!" John yelled.

"I hate ze Bee-a-tles!" screamed the Sun King.

"Is that it then?" Ringo shouted.

"It's the Stones who are ze best! Ha!"

"Figures," said John.

Just then, an army of Blue Meanies came marching down, accompanied by the Dreadful Flying Glove. A platform beside the Sun King arose. It was a giant glass dome, and inside it was Paul, fast asleep.

"Hey! Look up there, lads! It's Paul!" Ringo pointed out.

Although he seemed to be asleep, he was standing and wore the same suit the Beatles wore when they performed at Shea Stadium. His Höfner bass lay on his shoulder. The Blue Meanies stopped abruptly.

"And now! With McCartney's bass, I will control ze Blue Meaniez, and so my plan to get rid of ze Bee-a-tles is complete! Play, McCartney! PLAY!"

Paul suddenly awoke. He seemed confused and somewhat dazed. Then, without any self-control, he started playing bass lines. The dome was connected to a blow horn that translated the bass lines into sounds that controlled the Blue Meanies, who were rapidly approaching the Beatles. Paul just kept playing. His fingers calloused and blistered and bled, but he didn't stop playing. The boys ran as fast as they could until their feet were too tired. They hid behind a statue to catch their breath.

"Boys, is it getting hot in here?" Ringo asked.

"Stop bringing things down to your own level. It's immature, son," John said.

Ringo shed his jacket, and out from the pocket fell the glass onion, which rolled then jumped right into Ringo's hand, as if it had a mind of its own.

"What's this?" Ringo said, bewildered. Not really knowing what to do with it, he threw it at the Sun King. The Sun King was still laughing, so when Ringo threw the glass onion, it sailed right into the Sun King's mouth. The Sun King evaporated the instant he swallowed. The Blue Meanies stopped advancing, and holes appeared in front of each Meanie. They recovered from the spell and instinctively jumped through the holes back home. The palace, along with everything else, disappeared. It became a mass of blackbirds that looked like a giant black cloud. All at once, they were back at the beach. They saw Paul lying down ahead, beside the shore, wrapped in silvery gum wrapper.

"Paul!" they screamed, running to his side.

"Paul! Speak to us, lad!" said Ringo.

"Thus die I," Paul whispered.

Though he was incomprehensible at first, the boys slowly realized what he said.

> *Now am I dead,*
> *Now am I fled,*
> *My soul is in the sky:*
> *Tongue lose thy light;*
> *Moon take thy flight,*
> *Now die, die, die, die, die!*

Paul finished by pretending to stab himself. He started laughing, while the others started to pounce on him.

"Ah! Quit being daft, ya twit!" exclaimed John.

"Just pulling your legs, lads," Paul said, giggling.

Suddenly, an overwhelming sleepy feeling came over the Beatles, and they all fell into a golden slumber. Just then, they were awakened by hundreds of blackbirds—the transformed Sun King, hungry for vengeance. The beach suddenly became dark, as if the sun had been obliterated from the sky. They desperately searched for a way out in the dead of night, when strangely and quite extraordinarily, Sgt. Pepper appeared again. And through some crack of light in the darkness, singing a lullaby, he led them through a crack in a door that led them all back homeward.

They found their way back to Paul's flat. As the Beatles hugged and messed with Paul, everybody laughed and came together.

"What would you lads have done without me?" joked Paul.

"Learn how to sing trios," retorted John.

"How do you think we could've gone without you?" George added as he noogied Paul's head.

"Either you or a new bassist," said Ringo.

"You and I have memories longer than the road that stretches out ahead," John reassured Paul, setting a hand on his shoulder.

Paul thanked the lads once again and assured them everything was fine. Then, speaking words of wisdom, like his mother had taught him, he said, "Let it be, boys, let it be."

Steven "O" Andrade
AWAY FROM THE NEEDLE

With tears in her eyes she screamed violently "Just let me
   go!"
I held on to her
With a face so emotionless
I took a deep breath and said
"I can't let you go..."
Rain helped me wipe the tears from her eyes
While she let out heavier cries
I tried to hold on as tight as I could
No use
She was gone...
Ran down the trail of our past
What else could I do?
But mope around wondering
Was it all worth it?
Were the good times worth letting go?
I think so...
Without breaking free from you
I would've never found this...
This new feeling of joy
That beckons me on this clear winter night
Where the trees in the park come to life
And chase me through the cold wind
Run, Run, Run!
They're gonna devour me...
Grass strangles my ankles
Falling backward
Now lying in the middle of the busy city streets
Lights flash...Green, Yellow, Red

Stop...Red, Green
Go...Move out of the way they all scream
Honking their horns of anger
Buildings break free from the concrete
Running toward me
Bright lights chasing highways
"This way" the squirrel says
I follow
As this furry angel leads me
Down the right path
Away from this needle
To reunite
With the one I
Still
Always
Loved

Steven "O" Andrade
THE FALL OF AUTUMN

The Knitting Factory has a full house tonight. This has to be the biggest crowd we have played for this year. My friend Brainz and I had been waiting for a breakthrough, and this was it.

Brainz and I have been friends since middle school, and we were both trying our hardest to become rock stars. You could say we had fallen in love with the idea. I can still remember the day I knew he was my best bud. It was a cold winter night, and I had just been dumped by the hottest chick to ever come my way. She had stolen my heart and run off with it. I'll admit it—I loved her.

When Stacy left, I thought it was the end of the world for me. Just the sound of her name made me shudder with pain. But Brainz showed up out of nowhere with something to take away my pain. According to him, the stuff was going to make me feel better. I took it and instantly forgot about her.

Putting my memories of her behind me, I moved on to a new love. I never felt alone when I had it. It was my medicine for heartache. Spiraling downward, I couldn't stand to be around anyone but Brainz and my new best friend. My meds and Brainz would stick by me no matter what, or so I thought. Once, while under the influence, Brainz and I thought up the idea of creating a two-piece band. With my monotone voice and Brainz's mellow bass playing, we hit the underground scene as a gothic/alternative band with heavy synths and drum machine beats. And now we're headlining for a sold-out audience. I can't let this opportunity pass me by. I still have to perform!

As I drink from the red cup in my hand, a horrible taste, something like battery acid, fills my mouth. I had rum in my cup—is it my cup at all? Minutes later I start feeling dizzy. My vision is distorted. All I can see are blurred images and scratched out faces. I hear a voice calling out to me, but I cannot put the words together into a sentence, and the echoes bounce around in my head.

The room starts spinning, and I feel a hard hit to my face, like a brick has been thrown at me. Blood begins to drip from my left eye. I can't make sense of what is going on. I stumble and realize that it was Brainz's fist that hit my face and that I'm on stage. Why did my best friend hit me? When did we begin performing? How did I get on stage? Without any answers, I have no choice but to fight back. Suddenly I am restrained, and we are escorted out of the club.

We blew it. No more chances. It is all over. It's the end.

Now it's back to the beginning, back home with nothing but the clothes on my back. As I begin the long walk to the subway station, the darkness is my only friend, and the rain is my only shelter. With heavy drops of rain pounding on my head, I realize it's time for a change, time to leave this all behind.

As I sit waiting for the subway to arrive, the walls close in on me. It feels as if I am being suffocated slowly. I notice an old man nearby using the pillars of the subway station to hold himself upright. Maybe he had too much to drink tonight. He is wearing old raggedy clothes, and there is a greenish tint to his somber face. This is probably his home. A glimpse of my future?

Nothing seems right. I am still struggling to put together what happened when I hear echoes of footsteps dragging through the subway station. I pay no attention, thinking it is my mind playing tricks on me. Cold air sends chills down my spine. I hear heavy breathing. It feels like someone is standing behind me.

Suddenly there is an intense pain on my right forearm. Looking down I see the somber-faced man gnawing away. Screaming in agony, I dig deep inside and gather all my strength to toss him off of me. The loud thud of his body hitting the cold concrete floor combines with the screeching sound of the subway train's brakes. Fearing for my life, I run for the first car I see.

I hold my arm and apply pressure to the bleeding wound while the lights in the car flicker on and off. What is going on? The hole in my arm is worse than I thought: the man's bite did so much damage. I slowly make my way to the subway map. Oh, great. I've gotten on the wrong line. Thankfully, it says I'm going in the direction of Kingdom Hospital. I need to get this bite checked out. As I sit and wait to reach my destination, I black out from the pain.

I wake and am startled to see Brainz sitting not far from me. His head is sunk down, and drool is hanging from his mouth. Someone had a hard night. As I reach to wake him up, I have this weird feeling of my stomach turning inside out, growling loudly. I stare at Brainz's pale flesh, and my hunger grows stronger. I am instantly attracted to the smell of the blood running through his veins. I don't know what's coming over me: I'm beginning to see Brainz as a tasty meal. I can't control myself, and I rush toward him. Before I can tackle him, the pounding of my boots wakes him.

"What are you doing, man?"

"I...I really don't know. This weird man bit me at the subway station—"

"Bit you? What the?" he stops, and his eyes pop wide open as he catches sight of the tremendous hole in my arm. "Dude! We gotta get you to the hospital!"

I have not seen the wound since I passed out from the pain. It is turning a sickly green color, just like the homeless man. Who was he? *What* was he? My heart sinks as I realize I've seen movies about this. The man was a zombie. I am becoming one of the undead.

"I'm becoming a zombie, Brainz."

"What do you mean, a zombie?"

"You know, man. You've seen the movies. You've read the books. You know what I mean."

Brainz's face turns even paler as he looks down at the wound. I can't stand to imagine what he's thinking. There's fear in his eyes. In an instant I am alone in the subway car; I can still hear Brainz's footsteps pounding on the concrete floor. First he picks a fight with me at our show, and now he leaves me alone like this. What a friend.

My wound won't stop bleeding. I struggle to my feet and slip on the pool of blood beneath me. I can feel myself going unconscious—again. Birds fly in circles around my head, just like in the cartoons. Slipping into darkness, I hear a squeaky voice.

"What are you doin', home slice? Wake yourself up!"

Lifting my head, I'm startled by what I see and scream. It's Chimpy, my pet squirrel. Why did I scream? One, squirrels don't talk. Two, he died accidentally a month ago when I shared Brainz's gift with him. Why shouldn't a squirrel get to enjoy it, too?

"Chimpy? You're dead! And why are you talking? Why am I talking to a dead squirrel?"

"Hmm, let's see. Well, first of all, you killed me. Don't I deserve a better greeting than 'you're a dead squirrel?'"

"No, get away from me!" I shout, while picking myself up.

"I'm only joking." Chimpy laughs loudly.

"Okay, so if you're not here to haunt me, then what exactly are you here for?"

"I'm here to help you, stupid," he says, winking at me.

"Help me with what? I don't need help."

"Denial, denial, denial. Look, stupid: you have a hole in your arm. It's really gross. I can see through that thing for miles. Your skin is turning paler with each second, and your eyes are black as night. I know what's happening, and I want to help you."

"Um...okay. You got a point there. So you know that I'm turning into a—"

"Zombie. Yup, I know. I know everything, just like I know that you're not wearing any underwear."

"Huh?" I stick my hand down to check. Oh my God, he's right. How did he know that? "That was freaky. Are you like some sort of—"

"Angel? Yeah, I'm your guardian angel, actually!"

Great. I'm turning into a zombie, and God sends me a squirrel. What's the use of a dead squirrel?

Chimpy goes on to explain that the government is behind this whole situation. The president was injecting himself with a smart serum so that he wouldn't mess up when making speeches and decisions. It turns out that the serum causes an infection that left our president dead, and now the country is being run by a robotic replacement. No wonder this world is going to seed.

Chimpy tells me more. Underground research is being run by a doctor named Deck Holly. She is running tests on, get this, homeless people. She thinks of them as the perfect lab rats. To get out of this alive I have to find her secret lab, located in the sewers of Los Angeles. There's a cure, according to Chimpy, and Deck Holly found it. So there's hope that I'll get out of this alive.

With Chimpy by my side, I set out to find this underground laboratory. It isn't difficult to start—all we have to do is find a sewer hole. I look down at my watch and see it's one in the morning, which explains the abandoned streets. While everyone's asleep in their cozy beds, I'm wandering the streets with a squirrel trying to stop my zombification.

"Here's one!" Chimpy exclaims, pointing down.

I look up to see where we are. Hollywood and Vine. Apparently the subway went nowhere. That, or I went back and forth while I was passed out from the pain, and I ended up back here. What a waste of time.

I lift up the sewer hole lid. A black spider runs across my hand. No sting. Oh well—you can't always get what you want. Here I go, into the darkness. I feel a rush of adrenaline as I plunge into the shallow waters of the murky sewer. The smell of rotting flesh fills the air. I can't stand it. I kneel down and vomit nothing but blood. I need to find that laboratory before it's too late. I get up and start to walk away.

"Hey, wait for me!" Chimpy yells.

Dang, I forgot about the squirrel. Forget him. I have no time to go back. He'll find his way. Without looking back, I stumble forward and slip into a different tunnel with deeper water, bright lights, and the sound of growling. What is that? Where's it coming from? I hear gushing waves crash against the walls, and I take cover, lying flat on my stomach. The growling is getting louder. Splish splash. Two webbed feet stand in front of me, red slime oozing down them. I slowly look up to see a mutant creature with the body of a bear and the head of an eagle. What the— I rise to my feet but then freeze in shock. No movement. No breathing. No nothing. The creature stares at me and suddenly lets out a screech. Is this thing challenging me? Or letting me go? I take one step back, but the creature moves a step closer to me.

"Autumn! Get down!"

I turn around to see Brainz with a machine gun in his right hand and a grenade in his left. He launches the grenade and pulls a shotgun from behind his back. Deafening explosions and bright lights fill the sewer tunnel. Brainz is acting like a superhero in a slow motion action sequence. The creature doesn't even budge; the grenade and bullets just make it angry. The creature suddenly pulls back, and all I can do is watch as the creature lifts Brainz up and takes one look at me.

"Run, Autumn, RUN!" he shouts.

"I'm sorry, Brainz…" I say tearily, and then I jet down the murky sewer tunnel without looking back. The sound of cracking and ripping echoes around me, creating a vivid image in my mind of what has happened. My true friend Brainz is dead because of me. I crawl into a different sewer tunnel, pause for a moment, and break down and cry.

"What's wrong, homes?" asks a familiar voice.

"I don't feel like talking right now, Chimpy, so just leave me alone!"

"So your best friend's dead. Life goes on, Things happen for a reason. Now get up; you're running outta time! You know that Brainz would have wanted you to survive this." Chimpy is angry.

The stupid talking squirrel is right. Brainz gave his life to spare mine. I wouldn't want to be a lost cause—I need to survive. I run, and run, and run. I know I'm weak, but I dig down deep and find the strength.

"There it is." Chimpy's eyes widen.

Standing in front of a metal door, I look at Chimpy, and he nods his head. We are finally here. Now, we confront the monster behind the madness: Deck Holly.

"My work here is finished, home slice," says Chimpy, with a sigh of relief.

"What do you mean? You gotta go in there with me."

"No I don't, ese. My work here is *finished*." And with a little wink, he's gone. I hope he did the right thing in letting me confront Deck Holly on my own.

The laboratory isn't heavily guarded. I push a big red button, and the doors slide open. I see bright lights and experiments in water tanks as I walk inside. I feel a hand on my shoulder.

"Help you with something?"

I turn straight into a handgun pointed at my mid-section. I close my eyes, bracing myself for the end.

"You're infected."

Where have I heard this voice before? It's so familiar. I open my eyes and am shocked at whom I see standing in front of me.

"Stacy?"

"No, sir. Deck Holly."

"Stacy—I know it's you. You think I wouldn't recognize you?"

She looks into my eyes and lowers her gun.

"Autumn?" She moves my hair out of my eyes. "Is that you?"

Tears start falling as she rushes to give me a hug. I haven't felt warmth like this in some time, and to be honest, it feels good.

"So you're Deck Holly, huh?"

"Yeah. I had to change my name to stay safe. Some people want me dead for what I do."

"I never thought...well, let's chat after I know I'm gonna survive this nightmare. Can you help me before it's too late?"

"Yes," she replies with a smile. She runs to a cabinet and comes back carrying a purple vial containing a neon liquid. After everything I've been through, that liquid is the difference between survival and living death. I can't help but rush toward it. My eyes fill with tears from all the excitement. It's all about to be over.

There's a small blast, and smoke fills the air as I remove the cap from the vial. Jumping back, I trip over a metal platform. My hands are thrown back, and time slows down as the vial spins in mid-air. There's nothing I can do but watch yet another tragedy unfold.

Smash! The sound of glass hitting the metal floor makes my hair stand on end. I crawl to the liquid and break down. Stacy is standing by my side, and I turn to look up at her.

She rests her hand on my shoulder to comfort me, but there is no use. I can't help but cry.

"I've lost you, I've lost my best friend, and now I'm gonna lose my life."

"You didn't lose me...you never did. It was all in your head, Autumn. You just made the decision to erase me from your life. Through it all I was there. I never left your side."

"You know, you could've told me this before I got bit by a zombie!"

We laugh, and it feels like old times, when we could talk about anything and wouldn't care what anyone said. Those moments—when she was mine—will be engraved in my memory for the rest of my life.

I think back to the moment in the sewers when she returned unexpectedly. I was in deep trouble, and she was there for me. After the death of my dear friend Brainz, she was there. I guess it was all in my head after all. I was too worked up about the rock star life, the life that I chose to kick her out of. I should've realized all this before turning into a zombie. I should've realized all this when I was pouring liquor down my throat and putting junk into my body. There was nothing good about the life I lived. The only good thing was her. Damn it. It's way too late to realize I was ruining our relationship.

Now it's time. My flesh is going green. It's over. I lost.

"Autumn! Wake up!" Someone sounds like an angel.

I open my eyes to a white room with blank walls. "Where am I?"

"You're in the hospital, Autumn."

"Stacy?" I'm amazed to see her by my side.

"Yes! Who did you think it was, dork?"

"Well, to tell you the truth, I thought you were an angel. Come to think of it, you are an angel."

"Aw, how sweet. See, that's why I never left your side. You make me smile even if I'm feeling bad, and you're always there for me no matter what. You're thoughtful and sweet, and you'd never hurt me. Even if I hurt you, you'd never hurt me back." Stacy has a huge smile on her face.

"Hold on a sec; just why am I in here?"

"Well…" projects a familiar deep voice from behind Stacy.

"Brainz, is that you? I thought you were dead!"

"No, Autumn, I can assure you I'm very alive," he replies, chuckling.

"No, no, no, you don't understand! I got bit by a zombie! Stacy, you were the reason why the zombie bit me. Brainz, you popped out like Rambo with a machine gun, and then you were killed by some creature that looked like a bear chicken thingy! And my annoying dead pet squirrel was guiding me the whole time—"

"Calm down, Autumn. It was probably just the effects of the drug," Stacy says, looking down at the floor.

"What? I don't remember taking anything. I just remember being outta my mind at our show. Hold on—how'd the show go?"

Brains shakes his head. "Not good, Autumn. Not good at all. You somehow managed to make it up on stage all messed up, but you were teetering around. I tried to catch you, and for no reason you punched me."

"I did?"

"Yes, and we were banned from the Knitting Factory."

"Great. Now how are we gonna get noticed? The Knitting Factory was supposed to be our big break!"

"Yeah, well, I guess some things just don't go the way you want 'em to."

"Okay, so please explain just how the heck I got in here."

"Well," says Stacy, "someone put something in your drink. We don't know who did it yet, but the police are investigating."

"What a drag. Brainz, you got a little something to take the edge off, man?"

"No! No more, Autumn!" Stacy screams at the top of her lungs. "Can't you get it through your head? You almost died, and now you wanna go back to what almost killed you? God, you're hardheaded. I don't even know why I still love you."

"Hold on. Repeat that?" I ask, puzzled.

"You're hardheaded!"

"No, that other thing, the last thing you said."

"I still love you."

"You do?"

She hesitates. "Yes, Autumn. I do."

I swear I feel like the Grinch on the day that Christmas came without presents. My heart grew three times its size.

"So then I need nothing more to cure my pain. All I ever wanted was for you to love me."

"Well I do, Autumn. So much. Too much," she replies, laughing.

"Oh God. No more mushy gushy mushiness!" Brainz covers his ears and jets out the door.

Stacy and I laugh at Brainz.

"Well, you should really get your rest. I'll visit you tomorrow."

Her lips touch mine. Finally, I have a reason to get away from the depressing life I was living.

"So, you really do love me, right?"

"Always."

The door closes behind her, and she's gone. It feels great to be loved again.

When I turn to my side to try and fall asleep, I notice my arm is heavily bandaged. The bandages are wrapped where I was bitten by the zombie during my bad trip. I sit up quickly and unwrap the bloodied bandages. I can't believe my eyes. There's a big gaping hole in my arm. I close my eyes and hope that when I open them again the hole will be gone. Before I can do this, I hear a familiar squeaky voice.

"I'm back!"

"Chimpy?!"

Gabriela Tiscareño
NEVER AGAIN

Reflecting upon my life I realize that the heroes weren't always the obvious ones. I'd say that they were actually very unlikely. I found them in classrooms, in meetings, or on the streets. They are heroes because they influenced my attitude, which led to great opportunities, and opened my mind to broader thoughts that helped me make better decisions. They have set examples for who I should be. Until now, I have always disregarded them and have failed to acknowledge them as contributors to the person I am.

Back when I was in preschool, I was a very selfish, proud, and inconsiderate child. I was the kid who had to be right and had to be the boss of my friends. I liked to determine what we'd play, and I liked to establish the fact that I held the authority. I was the kid who had to be the Pink Ranger, and I was the kid who bit the teacher when I was falsely accused of saying a profane word. I was never hesitant to retaliate against classmates who committed foul acts against me. I am nowhere near that child I once was, and I believe that it was all thanks to Brandi.

I met my best friend Brandi in kindergarten on the first day of school. Our friendship was born from the words, "Oh! We have the same backpack! We should be friends!" As it turned out, we had more in common than backpacks. We both shared a love for fiction, and we always entertained ourselves with the latest updates to our false lives. We remained best friends throughout that year and all of first grade. It was perhaps the most memorable friendship I've had. She was very optimistic and amiable, and had the most positive personality I had ever met. She would assume the role of mediator and attempt to settle disputes between classmates by making them shake hands and hug. (I dreaded the times when she approached me to make me apologize to other classmates, especially when I believed I wasn't at fault.) She incorporated a rule requiring us to befriend the "new girls" and to introduce them to classmates until they found a best friend. At the end of the school year, she told me that she was going to attend a different school the following year, and I became really upset. Luckily, we met again in the fourth grade. Once again, we became inseparable, and she continued to influence the person I was becoming.

Seeing her fall into a sudden depression was surprising. She began speaking indifferently about death. She spoke of disappearing. I failed to help her or understand her. She insisted on being alone and never quite reached out to me for help, but when she realized that she needed my friendship, I chose to ignore her and not forgive her. Now I think back and realize her devastation. Now that I have finally learned what had caused her so much grief, it saddens me. She spent the last weeks that we saw each other attempting to get me to forgive her. She would send letters and bracelets, all of which I tossed into my desk with a shrug, not looking in her direction. It was not until she sent me a letter that offered her complete apology and expressed how much my friendship meant to her, that I decided to finally forgive her. Unfortunately, she left, once again, for another school. She disappeared from my life, and I never had the chance to tell her how much her friendship had meant to me.

She influenced the person I was in the beginning of elementary school. She taught me to befriend others, to respect others, to be courteous and considerate and generous. She embodied all those qualities, and yet I couldn't forgive her for dismissing them when she was going through her personal troubles. She was a hero to me, and I tried to be hers, but I couldn't save her. I think she has ultimately influenced me to help everyone I call a friend because I don't want to ever fail again. Now I can be a hero in other people's lives, and I can only hope that she has gone back to her old self, has learned to smile again, and has continued to have a positive impact on other people's lives.

I believe good heroes can make other people heroes. No one can change by themselves. They need help from someone. To find the hero within yourself you need a little insight from someone else. You need someone who will help you realize your flaws, sort of like constructive criticism. I am a new person. I will never be that child I was years ago. I will never let a friend down, never again. Heroes are all born from some motive—fear or desire. I fear disappointing a friend. I desire to save someone. I wish I had saved her.

Jocelyn Marchan
DAUNTLESS

I believe that fear and courage drive humanity to what it
    is
If one had the courage to know himself like the leader of a
    pack of wolves
If one had the courage to pursue goals like a wolf hunts a
    rabbit
If one had the courage to leave that pack
One would grow as a human being
For that is the purpose of life

OVER AND OUT.

AFTERWORD

Arlette Crosland

This journey began with a phone call from my friend Jane Patterson, director of Humanitas, who asked me if I would be interested in producing a book with my students. My first thought was "How on earth would I ever do that?" My second thought was "I'd be crazy not to." This journey with my students and the fine folks at 826LA has only furthered my belief that, given opportunity and support, students of all abilities will rise to the level of expectations.

Without the support of 826LA, many of these young writers would never have believed themselves capable of writing this book. Without the support of each other, they may not have been able to produce the poems, essays, and stories that touch upon the truth that drives their heroes through each journey. Without the support of the Urban Education Partnership and Humanitas, we would never have been able to create our small learning community, offering our students an alternative curriculum and this amazing opportunity.

If we want students to fly, we must believe that they can and value their creative skills. To divert support from art programs is to forsake and dismiss qualities that have made our country so unique: those of self-expression and innovation. At a time when curricula are mandated and school budgets are forcing the elimination of electives, especially those in the arts, it is important to remember that learning should not always be measured by test scores alone. The experience of this journey, along with the works written, is what these students will remember. In the years to come, they will reflect back on the many volunteers who spent their afternoons with us and our visits from Father Greg Boyle.

Our education system is at a turning point, and we are in danger of losing the battle. If any of part of this book evoked an emotional response, I urge you to volunteer your time at a local school or nonprofit and be a hero to the children of our country. It just might make the difference in all of our lives.

Eddie Flores, Nataly Chavez, and Jesus Enriquez
FOR STACK

The first time we met you
It felt like we'd known you for years
We'll never forget what you have done

All that we have is you.

We will always remember your loud
Chattering voice
Like a crazy uncle who raises everyone's spirits

Strong as a lion's roar
And we are all your cubs
Secure, like a kangaroo in its mother's pouch

We have our mothers
But you will always be our daddy
It's all a big happy family

We unite despite our separate worlds.

Thank you for being
STACK

ABOUT THE AUTHORS

Lisbeth Aguilar is a seventeen-year-old girl from East Los Angeles who loves Kobe Bryant. She loves to play basketball, even though she's not really good at it. She enjoys watching *CSI: Miami* and would like to be a homicide detective.

Steve-O's birth name is *Steven Andrade.* He lives in a space world in his mind. He is often described as a weird/hyper dude who can't sit still. He is addicted to anything that contains sugar and can't live without Monster Energy. He hardly lets stress get to him; it kills.

Lorena Karen Arriaga loves purple, flat soda, and suspense movies and books. She likes touching fluffy animals. She loves grapes, but hates raisins. She questions everything. She trips at least three times a day in dance class. She gets the chills when she sees someone get cut, but she wants to study forensics.

Michelle Bautista loves to bake cupcakes, cakes, and brownies. She loves Betty Boop. (If you don't know who she is, you should find out; Michelle thinks you'll like her.) She loves when people laugh at her silly jokes. You can make Michelle like you by bringing her string cheese.

Rafael Cruz is strong and silent in the classroom, but gentle with a pen.

Maria Diaz loves to make people smile and laugh. She loves to see people happy.

Susana Flores is from Torrance and used to live near Cabrillo Beach; now she lives in Boyle Heights. She remembers writing an amazing story about World War II and her tenth-grade English teacher loving it. She believes that her teacher signed her up for this class because of that story, and the weirdest thing happened. She created a character named Richard Blitzkrieg and began to write about World War II. She finds everything about that period so interesting.

Maribel Juarez comes from a Mexican background, but she does not eat chilis. She loves dairy, though, and sweets. She loves playing with cars with her nephew. Her favorite instrument is the accordion.

Most people don't know *Jessica Zamary Marroquin's* middle name or how to pronounce it. She loves sports and used to love math. She enjoys reading and writing when she chooses the book and topic. She was born in South Central, but grew up in East LA and wants to live in Russia.

Mirian Martinez is trying to get people to call her Greenie. Why? Because she loves green, duh! She's seventeen years old and is very shy; she hates speaking in front of people. She loves WWE (and shame on you, she says, if you don't know what that is). She's a good listener, and that's probably why she wants to major in psychology.

Maria G. Mena was born and raised in Los Angeles. She loves to eat ramen and shrimp tempura along with Thai iced tea and boba. She adores small dog breeds and exotic animals. Her dream is to become a well-known veterinarian, and maybe even a pastry chef.

She was raised with the name *Maribel Meneses*, but her birth certificate says *Maria*. She was a girl who used to ditch a lot in tenth grade. Then she realized she was making a big mistake, so she made up all her classes and ended up being a part of this book project, which gave her confidence.

Jeanette Perez is always energetic and tries to cheer people up with her stomach-poking game. She loves anime, reading, and undertaking challenges both on the track and in the classroom. If you're looking for competition, you've found your girl.

Gloria Rosales is a proud Chicana. Going through this experience has really changed her. Not only has this experience shown her a new perspective on writing, but it has also opened up more possibilities.

ACKNOWLEDGMENTS

Sheep Can't Fly is 826LA's most ambitious publishing project to date; it is approximately 100,000 words, the length of a good-sized novel. These efforts are never easy, and without the help of scores of people, *Sheep Can't Fly* would not have grown, in such a short time, from inchoate thoughts in the minds of a few to this collection of writing from twenty-three authors.

The most important contributors to this book are the authors themselves, the students at Garfield High School. For nearly four months, through final exams and college application mayhem, they wrote and wrote and wrote, demonstrating a tenacity that would make many writers jealous. (Just ask some of 826LA's volunteers.) And though their work spans several genres, it always returns formally and thematically to Joseph Campbell's hero's journey; just as importantly, it always speaks to the truth of their lives in East LA, their sorrows and struggles, joys and triumphs. Thank you all. Know that our small tribute here pales in comparison to what you have given us through your writing.

There are many at Garfield who deserve our thanks, who welcomed 826LA and helped make this book possible. We would like to thank Mario Carrasco, Lisa Cheby, Charles Andrew Davis, Deana Duran, Andrea Martinez Gonzalez, David Rodriguez, Claudia Rojas, Yolanda Roura, Michael Sarabia, and Principal Michael Summe for their support of the authors and this project. Special thanks go to Kevin Stack, GEAR UP adviser at Garfield, for his masterful work with the students and their poetry, and tireless, daily commitment. Most of all, we must not forget Arlette Crosland, the English teacher of this book's young authors. She created the two elective classes that allowed them to focus on this book, and she has been their steady guide through most of their high school years. She was the one who realized the inspirational effect the monomyth could have, and her enthusiasm and ambition were the wind at our backs that helped us complete the journey.

826LA's most valuable resource is its volunteers, and dozens of them lent their support, helping the students shape their words and reach their potential. Jessica Burkhart, Michelle LaPlante, Diana McCrimmon, Lucas Peterson, and Peter Wendel were the first 826LA volunteers to meet with the students, encouraging them one morning at 826LA West to build on those first foundations of their stories.

Scotty Crowe, Allison Doyle, Reaux Flagg, Shannon Flaherty, Michael Hagler, Talya Klein, Michelle LaPlante, Kathleen Mackay, Susan Mathison, Jessie Nagel, Craig Phillips, Joanna Sese, J. Ryan Stradal, and Alissa Walker all sat with the students, week after week, in their classroom at Garfield. They led mini-workshop sessions and helped guide the students' pieces from draft to draft.

Of the above in-school tutors, Allison Doyle, Reaux Flagg, Michelle LaPlante, Joanna Sese, and Alissa Walker went a step beyond and helped edit the students' final drafts to prepare them for publication. Rebecca Dameron, Beth Goodhue, Liz Miller, Amy Orringer, Alejandra Riguero, and Edward Truong also helped edit. Melissa Crowley and Diana McCrimmon, in particular, were the most tireless of editors: they helped edit pieces for content and copyedited the majority of the book.

We must recognize two tutors once more for their outstanding contributions. Michelle LaPlante's assistance in planning mini-lessons was invaluable, and her care and thoroughness in helping to revise and edit student work was second to none. And in her dedication to the project and students, especially the editorial board, Reaux Flagg was without peer.

The Garfield student editorial board deserves special recognition for not refusing their call to adventure. They not only wrote poems, essays, and stories like their fellow classmates, but they also stayed for hours after school (and even a few times during vacation) and spent much of their own time writing extra material and helping shape this book. Nataly Chavez, Jesus Enriquez, Eddie Flores, Alex Jimenez, Gaby Maldonado, Jocelyn Marchan, Jocelyn Mariscal, Ana Perez, and Gabby Tiscareño: thank you for your passion, vision, insight, and leadership. You carried this project on your back at times, and it has been our privilege to work with you.

Thanks to the Urban Education Partnership for its continued support of 826LA and Humanitas at Garfield, and thanks especially to Jane Patterson for introducing us to yet another outstanding educator in Arlette Crosland. We are also grateful to the 826LA Board of Directors for its guidance, especially Mac Barnett, Nínive Calegari, Jodie Evans, and Sally Willcox. Special thanks go to Chris Young and Westcan Printing Group for helping us meet our deadlines, and to Jessica Burkhart and Amy Martin for their masterful and elegant design work. And we are indebted to Father Greg Boyle, who may very well have the most stressful job in LA; thank you, Father Greg, for taking the time to inspire us and share with us a little something about heroes.

And last, but certainly not least, we must acknowledge The Goldhirsh Foundation, whose grant funded the production of this book. Thank you for your support, your trust, and your generosity; without you, we would never have dreamed of flying.

—Joel Arquillos, Bonnie Chau, Christina Galante, Danny Hom, and Julius Diaz Panoriñgan 826LA

826LA IS...

STAFF

Joel Arquillos, Executive Director
Julius Diaz Panoriñgan, Director of Education
Danny Hom, Programs Coordinator
Bonnie Chau, Programs Coordinator
Christina Galante, Retail and Events Manager

BOARD OF DIRECTORS

Miguel Arteta
Mac Barnett
Joshuah Bearman
Nínive Calegari
Dave Eggers
Jodie Evans

John T. Gilbertson
Naomi Foner
Keith Knight
Melissa Mathison
Salvador Plascencia
Sally Willcox

ADVISORY BOARD

Judd Apatow
Fiona Apple
Steve Barr
Stefan G. Bucher
Mark Flanagan
Mitchell Frank
Karen Fried

Nicole Holofcener
Spike Jonze
Catherine Keener
Al Madrigal
Will Reiser
Brad Simpson
Sarah Vowell

ABOUT 826LA

826LA is a nonprofit organization dedicated to supporting students ages 6 to 18 with their creative and expository writing skills, and to helping teachers inspire their students to write. We believe that strong writing skills are fundamental to future success, and, with this in mind, we provide challenging and enjoyable programs—all of them free—that ultimately strengthen each student's power to express ideas effectively, creatively, confidently, and in his or her individual voice.

DROP-IN TUTORING

Our method is simple: our tutors provide students with one-on-one help. It is our understanding that, with concentrated help from knowledgeable tutor-mentors, students can make great leaps in English skills and comprehension within hours.

WORKSHOPS

We offer writing workshops taught by professional artists and our talented volunteers. From comic books to screenplays, bookmaking to radio, our wide variety of workshops is perfect for passionate young writers.

IN-SCHOOL PROJECTS

Our extensive volunteer base allows us to partner with many schools in Los Angeles. We send volunteers out to support teachers in their classrooms by providing one-on-one tutoring on assignments ranging from fractured fairy tales to college essays.

FIELD TRIPS

We want to help Los Angeles teachers get their students excited about writing while helping students to better express their ideas, so we welcome classes for field trips during the school day. Our most popular field trip is Storytelling & Bookmaking; the entire class works with our tutors to create a story with illustrations, which is made into a book for each student to take home.

For more information, please visit 826LA.org or email info@826LA.org.